ANDREW M. GREELEY

"A fascinating novelist...with a rare, possibly un-matched, point of view."

—*Los Angeles Times*

"Greeley writes with passion and narrative force."

—*Chicago Sun Times*

"He's a true Irish-American storyteller.... Greeley deals with relationships in a realistic manner, tasteful manner. Only a puritan would object."

—*Beckley Register-Herald* (Beckley, WV)

"A genius for plumbing people's convictions . . . that and his rich literary imagination make him truly exceptional."

—*Cleveland Press*

"Andrew Greeley always writes a gripping novel!"

—*Chattanooga Times* (Chattanooga, TN)

Angel Light

An Old-Fashioned Love Story

Andrew M. Greeley

TOR®

A Tom Doherty Associates Book
New York

This is a work of fiction. All the characters and events portrayed in this book are either products of the author's imagination or are used fictitiously.

ANGEL LIGHT

Copyright © 1995 by Andrew Greeley Enterprises, Ltd.

Cover art by Jeffrey Terreson

A Tor Book
Published by Tom Doherty Associates, Inc.
175 Fifth Avenue
New York, NY 10010

www.tor.com

Tor® is a registered trademark of Tom Doherty Associates, Inc.

ISBN-13: 978-0-765-35597-3
ISBN-10: 0-765-35597-3
Library of Congress Catalog Card Number: 95-23450

First Edition: December 1995
First Mass Market Edition: December 1996
Second Mass Market Edition: December 2006

Printed in the United States of America

0 9 8 7 6 5 4 3 2 1

In memory of Jack Durkin, *cum angelis in caelo*

This story is based on the book of Tobias (or *Tobit*) in the Old Testament. To my dismay, most people are unaware of the existence of that splendid romance.

You don't have to read it to understand this modern version of the same story. But you're missing something wonderful if you don't read *Tobias* sometime in your life.

I don't know whether there are actual beings in creation like Rae and her crowd. Experts on the Holy Scripture tell us that the "Malek Yahweh," the messengers of Yahweh, are metaphors, stories, of God's personal and individual love for each of us. However, it seems to me very likely that other rational beings do exist in creation, precisely for the reasons advanced by Rae in this story: Since the Other is patently exuberant in Her styles of creation, it seems most unlike Him to have produced only one rational species. Thus I hope there are beings somewhat like the beings in this book. As I said apropos of her mother, Gaby, in my previous book, *Angel Fire*, I'll be disappointed if there is not, somewhere in the Other's creations, a being like Rae.

The basic theology of love that supports this book is quintessentially orthodox. The fantasies about how angels look and act are merely efforts of my imagination to suggest that they are beings of massive knowledge and mighty love—as well as of shrewd ingenuity and enormous charm.

Air Aran now flies not from Galway Airport but from an airport out in Connemara only six minutes by plane from Innismor. There is no pool at the golf club, but my friends in that city insist that there ought to be. I have moved the Galway Races up a month for reasons of the story. I should also note that, unlike the Guards in this story, the Guards in real life were fully prepared for terrorism at the Races and searched everything.

1

"I do not want ten million dollars, I do not want to visit Ireland, I do not want to end a Tobin family feud, and above all I do not want to court my eighth cousin, once removed."

To emphasize this last point I threw on the coffee table the photograph of Sara Anne Elizabeth Tobin. She seemed in the snapshot to be an attractive young woman, possibly even beautiful in the Irish fashion——dark black hair, penetrating blue eyes, pale skin, a radiant smile, all giving her finely carved face an appearance of merriment which promised to be constant in her life. Sara Anne Elizabeth Tobin, minus the sweatshirt and jeans that were a uniform for her kind and in the appropriate peasant garb (with red petticoats), might well be a character in a play by William Butler Yeats or John M. Synge, an attendant to Kathleen ni Houlihan in the former or a rival to Pegeen Mike in the latter.

Yeah, I know about Irish literature. It doesn't follow that I should want to visit the place.

"She looks like a darling girl," my mother said mildly after a loud sigh, "just the sort that would settle you down."

That was just the problem. Sara Tobin's lovely oval face ended in a chin that indicated fierce determination, and her eyes for all their dark beauty hinted that she would tolerate no opposition from someone as foolish as a man. I knew her kind well—mothers, sisters, classmates, dates—all determined to settle me down and make something out of me.

For my own good, naturally.

Sara Tobin would take it as her mission in life, in conspiracy with my mother and sisters, to woo me from my computers and my experimental programs and into a respectable profession—law, medicine, commodity trading, maybe even into the academy like my father. Teach accounting and be a dean like he is, not all that much money when you have four children (three daughters and a son) but very respectable just the same, and look at all you can earn by consulting with business firms.

"Respectability," my priest says, "is something for which the Irish will always seek, no matter how many generations they have been in America. If they gave up the search, they would deprive their woman kind of their perennial cry, 'What will people say?' "

It would be all right to teach computer science (at the college level, of course) and to earn a Ph.D. as a condition for that. Just so long as I wasn't a visionary hiding in the attic, pondering the mysteries of the Internet, and planning to be the Bill Gates of the *fin de siècle*. That wasn't respectable.

No future in it.

Nor was it respectable to refuse an offer of ten million dollars. A point my father was eager to make.

He cleared his throat as he always did, the business school dean with weak eyes preparing to deliver wisdom. *Ex cathedra* as they say at the Vatican.

"I, ah, would not want to suggest, Toby, that you should court this young woman merely for the, er, ten million dollars. I admit that your great-uncle's will is a little strange. Why it should be necessary for you to make peace with our distant relatives in a feud of which we have never heard and marry your distant cousin escapes me completely. Yet I would think that the challenge would be a romantic adventure that would appeal to a young man. It's a lot of money to turn down flat."

"I'm too young to marry."

"You're twenty-five," my sister Maureen, age twenty-eight and already the mother of two children, insisted.

"Too young."

"You'll never be old enough," my sister Megan, age sixteen and obnoxiously bright, said with an affectionate chuckle. "But that's what makes you attractive to women!"

Megan was the only woman who seemed to like me as I am.

"She looks like she might be pretty good in bed," my sister Nicole, twenty-seven and engaged, observed. "That's what you want, isn't it, Toby? A woman to sleep with. That's what all men your age want. Too bad Great-Uncle Gerry insists that you marry the girl."

Nicole was absolutely correct. A man my age cannot escape obscene fantasies as his hormones push him towards sexual union. I had indeed evaluated the lovely Sara as a possible partner. One couldn't tell about such matters from a picture. But one could see in the picture the chin and the eyes. Not worth it.

"No," I said. "No way."

"Long speech for you," Megan informed me.

So it had been since we had been summoned to the old-fashioned law office (complete with a rolltop desk) in East Bend, South Dakota, where one Joshua McAdam, an elderly lawyer in a string tie, had read Great-Uncle Gerry's will. He had bequeathed to one G. Patrick Tobin Jr. ten million dollars (after taxes) if I (a) bore a letter to Galway, Ireland, to his distant cousin Ronan that would end the Tobin family feud and (b) married Ronan's daughter Sara. I was forbidden to discuss the bequest with her until after the marriage.

"Why me?" I protested.

"It is a bit unusual." The lawyer chuckled. "Your great-uncle was a very successful rancher and businessman, as you can tell, but he had some strange ideas."

We did not know he existed. Indeed he was not, strictly speaking, a great-uncle at all, but rather some kind of shirttail cousin.

"How wonderful," my mother said.

"An exciting challenge, Toby," my father said. "We didn't even name you after him. Apparently he thought so."

"Toby with a wife." Maureen giggled.

"She'll never marry you," Megan challenged me. "Why should a woman that beautiful settle for a creep like you, especially since you can't tell her about the will or you lose everything?"

She winked when she spoke, making fun of the family party line about me with which she disagreed.

"Gorgeous boobs, Toby." Nicole considered the snapshot carefully. "Might be worth the effort."

"No."

"What was the feud about?" my father asked.

"The late Gerard Tobin did not say. I'm not even sure he knew. It seems to have persisted since 1807. Incidentally, Mr. Tobin Senior, he has bequeathed to you title to whatever rights the family may have to Tobin's Mountain in Ireland."

"I'm afraid," my father said primly, "that there is not much value in an Irish mountain."

"Maybe it's one of those under which there is a lot of gold," I said, trying to distract attention from Sara Tobin.

"Please, Toby." My father sighed loudly. "Would you try to be serious for a moment? There are no mountains of gold in Ireland."

Actually there were. Or at least there was a serious claim that there was a lot of gold under the sacred mountain of Crough Patrick and other mountains in the area. But I knew better than to try to argue when my parents insisted that I be serious—no matter what the facts of the matter were.

"You really wouldn't have much to lose, Toby Junior," my mother pointed out. "It's not like you'd have to take time off work or anything."

In the view of my family, I was unemployed. That I made more as an occasional programmer and consultant than my dad did as a dean was irrelevant.

"We went to Ireland on our honeymoon," Maureen said proudly.

"I'm authorized as the executor of the late Mr. Gerard Tobin's estate to advance you the money for one round-trip coach fare to Ireland. Unfortunately there won't be any funds for room and board. You will have one month from this date to win the hand of Ms. Tobin."

"One month!"

"That makes it a real challenge, Toby!" My father

smiled happily, like it was his challenge, and like it hadn't taken him four years to work up enough nerve to propose to my mother.

"I'm not going to Ireland. I don't like to travel."

The University of Notre Dame, which I did *not* attend, seventy-five miles away from the city limits of Chicago on Interstate 90, was, in my considered judgment, too far to travel.

I must say a word about my family since they play an important if indirect role in my quest for the Galway Grail (which could be a name for an NBA team when it expands to Ireland). They are all good people and they worry about me because I don't follow their plans for me.

My mother, a not unattractive, plump and silver-haired woman in her middle fifties, is the daughter of dirt-poor Irish immigrants who came to America in the 1930s. She graduated from high school but did not attend college. She has never quite recovered from the poverty of her youth; she feels that when she married a professor, she married up; and therefore (in her logic) she believes that it is her solemn obligation to achieve respectability for all her children. She also breeds (skillfully and successfully) Irish wolfhounds, which I admit does not fit the pattern.

I think my father loves her, though he does so with the passion appropriate for a business school dean—which means that he is never demonstrative. Some of the women I have dated—if what I do can be called that— tell me enthusiastically that Dad looks like Captain Jean Luc Picard of the starship *Enterprise*. Bald, it would seem, is now beautiful. In fact, my father has somewhat more hair and a somewhat less lean face.

On the rearing of his children he deferred to his wife completely. Hence the two oldest, both daughters, have been molded in their mother's image and likeness. Presentable enough blondes (with the lean and hungry look of dedicated joggers and consumers of "natural food"), they live in a fantasy world in which they must not only be paragons of respectability (as they rigidly define it) but also must sit in judgment on the respectability of everyone else in the world, from the people who live next door to Hillary Rodham Clinton. They are so busy at this task that they have little time even to read the daily papers.

Maureen's husband and Nicole's fiancé, like their women, work in "financial services," which is a thoroughly respectable occupation, though the men are both hollow and will never rise above lower middle-level positions. Jogging is for all four of them an activity that, like eating "natural foods," has acquired the aura not only of respectability but of moral excellence. They have little regard for my dedication to basketball and Chicago (sixteen-inch) softball because such amusements are "competitive."

No one pays much attention to tall, rangy, black-haired Megan, who plays basketball and serves as class president (elected without opposition) at St. Ignatius College Prep, where she has a 4.0 average and plays the guitar. She writes music, using a computer program I designed, but no one else in the family knows that.

As the first and only son in the family, great things were expected of me—success, respectability, public acclaim (the public being St. Hilary's parish on the north side of Chicago and the parish environs). When I chose in grammar school to go down my own path, the family made a project out of me, a project that eventually deteriorated into beating up (figuratively) on Toby at every possible opportunity. It mattered not what I did. If I chose to go north, then the only proper course would have been to go south. If on the other hand I changed and went south, they criticized me for not having the courage of my convictions and sticking with north. Heads they won, tails Toby lost. So what else is new?

My name says it all. My father is Gerard Patrick Tobin, as he is called by the *Wall Street Journal* when it quotes him on business ethics. (His positions are always highly ethical, as is his own personal moral code.) But he has been Toby all his life to those close to him. I am a Junior, but my mother has always insisted that I am G. Patrick Tobin Jr. or, more informally, Toby Junior. She says my name sounds like that of a tycoon, apparently because in her days as a stenographer she worked for a bank vice president (not a senior vice president) named R. Burke McGee III. So I have been "Gerard" in school, "Toby Junior" at home and "Toby" to my friends, never "Pat," a name of which I would have been very proud.

"Toby Junior" has given way to "Toby" some of the time when the tone of Mom's voice reveals that it is me to whom she is addressing a complaint.

Mostly I tune them out. Their morally high-toned complaints are the Muzak of my life. I should have moved out of the family house long ago, but I was too busy with other matters to find the time.

"I hear Irish women are pretty easy these days," Nicole said sarcastically. "Maybe you can get her to sleep with you. That would be typical of you, wouldn't it?"

"They'll wear you down, Toby," Megan chimed in. "Face it, you can't stand up to the whole family when we gang up on you."

"Yes I can."

"No, you *can't*."

As usual, the little brat was right.

❧2❧

>**Internet.**

I was logging on through the computer "gate" at the university to the worldwide network of computers that is supposed to be the first step towards the much-hyped "Information Highway." Anyone who has tried to struggle with the Internet knows that in fact it is an information cow path. As in everything else in the current world of computers, our software has not kept up with our hardware. That's where I would make my fortune. I would design user-friendly (and I mean totally friendly) software for the Information Highway. My users wouldn't have to worry about such things as TCP/IP, SLIP/PPP, WAIS, WWW, Gophers, Veronica, etc., etc. They'll merely tell the NET what they're looking for and it will respond to them.

Long wait. Then the usual log-on gibberish which impressed second-rate hackers but which disgusted me because it was just one more touch of elitist crap designed to make ordinary folks feel that they were computer-illiterate, folks who I hoped would someday be my clients.

>

At last. Now I would activate my preliminary design for mastering the Net—and the first step to mastering the Information Highway, should it ever exist.

>DABEST

I'm a nerd and a hacker. As one of my dates (my most recent failure) said, "Toby, you're a nerd. You don't look like a nerd. Sometimes you don't act like a nerd. But you're a nerd just the same."

I had been explaining to her that the Information Highway, about which Vice President Gore had been talking so much, wouldn't work unless there were absolutely user-friendly interfaces. "Don't believe all the stuff you read about Internet. It's about as user-friendly as a cyclotron."

Then she asked what a cyclotron was and I tried to explain, knowing that the relationship had no future. In the middle of my first sentence, she informed me that I was a nerd.

Probably she was right. But I wished she had given me a chance to explain about DABEST, the first step in rendering Internet and the Information Highway user-friendly—Data Access and Better Entry System Technology.

Area of interest?

I paused, shook my head in dismay at how easily my family had worn me down.

>Travel Agencies
List criteria
1>Ireland
2>Young man who has not been there
3>Never traveled before
4>Does not like travel
5>Absentminded on occasion and needs
watching.

As I told everyone who would listen to me, you had to be honest with DABEST if you wanted good results.
    6>

I hesitated before responding to that prompt.
    6>Must court young woman
    7>Enter
    Criteria finished. Searching.

The system rummaged around for several minutes. While DABEST speeds up access, it still is held to the upper limits of the Net. Its main contribution is its friendliness to the user. It does all the work of navigating the Net for you so long as you give it adequate criteria.
    Yes?
    >I am G. Patrick "Toby" Tobin. Junior. I want to travel to Ireland.
    So?
    >You're a travel agency, aren't you?
    In a manner of speaking.

DABEST sometimes produces odd results. I have not tried to argue that I have eliminated all the bugs from the system.
    I am very busy, G. Patrick "Toby" Tobin. Please do not bother me again.

> **END**
> >**Hey, come back!**
> *Yes?*

Now, I should have realized then that there was something strange going on. Very strange. Neither the Net nor DABEST should be responsive to a command like:

> **Hey, come back!**

I may have shivered slightly, but I guess I paid no attention.

> *I said yes, G. Patrick "Toby" Tobin. Are you asleep?*
> >**No. You responded to a nonexistent command.**
> *I don't have all day to discuss your primitive program with you. What do you want?*
> >**I said I wanted to go to Ireland. Are you any good at arranging trips?**
> *We are very experienced. The best.*
> >**Good. Will you arrange a trip for me to Galway?**
> *Maybe. Why?*
> >**That's none of your business.**
> *It is if I make it my business.*
> >**You're violating Net etiquette.**
> *So? I'm waiting. Hurry up or I'll flame you out.*
> >**I have to court a young woman.**
> *Ah. And?*
> >**And if she marries me, I'll inherit ten million dollars.**
> *What will you do with the money? Don't argue again about it being none of my business or I'll terminate the program.*

This was not only one very pushy travel agent. It was a person who had absolutely no regard for the rules of the Net. I'd have to warn others about him.

>**I'll give some of it away.**
How much?
>**Half. Do you want to know to whom?**
No. THAT is none of my business. You're generous. The rest?
>**I'll use two million to organize my software company and put the rest in a mix of tax-exempt municipals and commodities.**
At this time I would concentrate on the commodities.
>**OK. Will you arrange the trip for me?**
I must talk to my boss. End.
>**Hey!**
What now?
>**How do I get back to you?**
I'll get back to you. End.
>**Wait a minute.**

This time the travel agent did not respond.

Ever since I took a course in metaphysics in college, I wasn't sure that the Net actually existed. How can electronic links between networks of computer systems be real? I use it because I find it reasonable to assume that it's real, but sometimes I'm not sure that even my assumption is real.

Even less real, I often think, are the various "rooms" on the Net, electronic places where people with common interests interact one with another. Where are these "places"? I'm not sure. They're probably just fictions.

Many of the rooms are for serious purposes—learning more about how to deal with the intractabilities of the Net, for example. Some of them, however, are for fun and games, like the room in which a number of us work out complicated medieval conflicts according to the principles of game theory. I'm kind of good at this improbable nonsense, so I go into the room when I need relaxation. And adventure. And romance.

Without having to travel away from our neighborhood of Peterson Woods on the North Side of Chicago.

Today was clearly a day for taking temporary refuge in the distant past. Before I turned to the room where we waged our prolonged medieval war and in which the tide was beginning to turn in my favor, I pondered this very strange conversation. I was not at all sure I wanted to trust this weird travel agent with my life.

Not at all.

In the room my side routed the foes by resourceful if somewhat reckless strategy and the Princess Melanie began to hint that she did not find me unattractive. As always I wondered if she really was a "she." You could never tell on the Net, and the rules said you couldn't ask.

In my dreams I made wanton love with my imaginary Melanie; recently she looked, some of the time anyway, like the photo of Sara Anne Tobin.

The next morning I made coffee in my attic office, next to my bedroom, and removed a glass of fresh orange juice from the fridge and the raisin bran from my cabinet. I'm a hacker, not a health nut.

Then I did my exercises in the small gym I had put together at the back of the attic.

(Sometimes, for weeks, my mother insists, we don't know you're in the house. I know what she means, but that complaint is somewhat of an exaggeration. She sees me when I come down the steps for my softball and basketball leagues—two of each, though softball runs only

from April 15 to November 1, and basketball all year
long.)

Then I went into the computer room, the third room
in the attic apartment I had fixed up for myself.

My computer was on. That was strange. I usually turn
it off at the end of the day. Moreover it was already on
the Net, even though I was sure I had logged off.

> *All right.*
> >Who are you?
> *Travel agent, naturally.*
> >Did you turn on my machine?
> *My boss has instructed me to arrange your
> trip. It will be necessary for you to get a
> passport. Dirksen Federal building. Today.*
> >What about tickets?
> *We will take care of it.*
> >What is your name?
> *Irrelevant.*
> >Of what gender are you?
> *You're breaking your own rules.*
> >You can break them.
> *That's different. End.*

I stared at the screen in disbelief. What the hell.

> *Well?*
> >Well, what?
> *You always try to prevent end.*
> >How can I get in touch with you?
> *Unnecessary. I will contact you. Carry com-
> puter at all times.*
> >But
> *Very well. In DOS give the command GO RAFE.
> That will find me.*
> >But the Net?
> *Primitive. End. This time I really mean it.*

The screen went blank. I must have turned the system off.

Rafe? I had been sure that the travel agent was a woman. The mix of impatience and amused playfulness suggested a woman. Well, it really didn't matter. Maybe Sara Tobin and the Princess Melanie had stirred up too many hormones in my bloodstream.

I bounced down the stairs to tell my mother I was going downtown to arrange for a passport.

"Don't get lost," she said anxiously.

It was a reasonable warning. I get lost easily.

"I won't. I'm taking the bus to the el."

We live in an old two-story home (with a large attic) on the North Side at Hollywood and Virginia across the street from Legion Park on the banks of the North Branch of the Chicago River. Our home is in St. Hilary's parish, a wonderful place, though my priest is the rector of the cathedral, and of course, I go to Mass at Old St. Patrick's, where all yuppies go to Mass.

I went back to the room and after some hunting found my black White Sox jacket. On the desk in my office was my new Compaq Contura Aero 4/25, 3.3-pound sub-notebook computer.

Funny thing. I had planned to buy one to take with me on consulting jobs, but I couldn't remember ordering it. Still I must have because there it was.

I took the Lincoln Avenue bus to the Ravenswood el— the shortest and most quaint of the Chicago rapid transit routes. It wends its way down back alleys and by people's bedroom windows like it is never quite sure how to get to the loop. On the jerky, meandering ride, I pondered, as I usually do when nothing else is on my mind, the maddening problems of the Net. Like the Ravenswood el it had come into being mostly by chance and didn't make much sense. Someday it might just fall apart. We'd have to begin all over again, which would not be such a bad event.

I made it downtown all right but didn't realize until it was almost too late that the train, having finally found the Merchandise Mart, had sailed triumphantly into the Loop and was about to leave again. I jumped off at State and Lake station by the Chicago Theater. With the Net still preoccupying me, I must have turned north instead of south and crossed the Chicago River without noticing it. Finally I recognized Holy Name Cathedral and then the new Loyola tower behind it. I knew the place because I had attended Loyola for four years—degree in English literature. I picked up the computer stuff on the side.

The new tower was kind of nice. My priest, who is among other things the rector of the cathedral, had told me that the Jesuit provincial had informed him of the construction of the building. "Mind you, G. Patrick, the good Ridley Becker did not ask my permission because that would have been inappropriate, but he was at pains to let me know unofficially." He sighed. "As if I didn't know long since about the project. Still it was a respectful courtesy."

He paused. "Tomorrow I fully expect that the cow will jump over the moon."

Anyway, I turned at the cathedral onto Chicago Avenue, walked by the new Tower, and arrived in due course at Michigan Avenue. I consulted the scrap of paper on which I had written the address of the Everett McKinley Dirksen Federal Building. It was on *South* Lasalle, and I was on North Michigan. That meant I should turn left and walk north, didn't it?

Or did it?

I stopped an attractive young woman in shorts and T-shirt. "Pardon me, ma'am, can you tell me which way is south?"

She smiled, as such folk often do until they find that broad shoulders, curly brown hair, and a genial grin hide an absentminded, easily befuddled nerd.

"You're kidding."

"No, ma'am."

"You're from out of town or something?"

"No, ma'am. But I'm easily confused."

She considered me for a moment, wondering, I suspect, whether I was engaged in a particularly dumb come-on and whether she should respond by offering to walk with me.

"Yeah, you do look kind of confused . . . It's that way, to the right; your right, that is."

"Thank you, ma'am."

I turned right and ambled down Michigan Avenue. It might not have been a bad idea to ask her to lead me to the Federal Building. It would have been an honest request, and she seemed both pretty and friendly.

But hardly likely to know what a cyclotron was or to care about the Net. Or to think I was sane when I told her about the war going in our medieval room—a room that existed only in electronic reality.

If there.

What if her name was Melanie? I wondered.

It was a gorgeous day in early June, and the Magnificent Mile was crowded with lovely young women in thin spring clothes—I personally preferred dresses—which delighted my hungry male fantasy life. There were also many other people, so I enjoyed a fine late morning of people watching, an activity almost as appealing as working on DA-BEST or warring in the room.

To be candid about myself, I can understand my family's concern about me. I am kind of weird, I guess. My refusal at first to even consider the pursuit of my "inheritance," as Megan called it, was just one more piece of evidence that I was the kind of person who belonged in a Trappist monastery where the Father Abbot would take care of me for the rest of my life. We didn't need the money—though we could always use it as a backup for the college education of nieces and nephews. It was the principle of the thing, you see. How can one turn away from a great, romantic adventure? With a vast pot of gold at the end of the rainbow?

Easily, it seemed to me but not to them.

And it was not like I had met the fair Sara and had been rejected or had rejected. "She seems a sweet little girl, Toby. Maybe you'd end up liking each other."

"What's to risk?" my dad added.

"The plane might crash."

I really didn't mean that, but they were never sure when I said something crazy whether I meant it or not. All too often I mean it or half mean it. Sometimes I enjoy exaggerating the nerd image. But mostly I was in fact a nerd, and one who plainly could not be counted on to take care of himself.

Even if I become the Bill Gates of the Third Millennium, and I have every reason to think that I will, I'll still need people to take care of me. But then they'll work for me and I can fire them when I want.

Except I'd never have the nerve to fire anyone.

I finally arrived at the Dirksen Building and, by the simple strategy of checking the directory on the first floor, managed to find out where the passport agency was.

From then on the next hour was all bad.

I waited in a long line to speak to the single uniformed

public servant who stood behind the desk, rather enjoying, it seemed to me, her responsibility to be nasty to everyone. After a half hour or so it was finally my turn.

"I will be traveling to Ireland," I said with my most polite smile, "and I'd like to have a passport."

"Where's your form?" she barked at me.

"Form?"

"Can't you read?" She gestured impatiently towards a sign that read, "Take form and fill out before coming to counter."

"Oh," I said meekly. "I can read, all right, but I guess I didn't see the sign."

"Well, fill this out if you can write." She lifted a sheet from a pile in front of her and threw it at me. "And bring it back. Answer all the questions, and I mean *all* of them."

There were a number of chairs with desk arms attached, like the kind we used in class at St. Ignatius and Loyola, arranged around the room. But they were all occupied, so I tried to fill out the form by writing against the wall with one of the government-issue pens that had been distributed generously enough on the counter. It didn't work very well, and my usual terrible handwriting became even more obscure.

The questions were maddeningly imprecise, it seemed to me. I tried to answer them all to the best of my ability. Then I reread my answers and decided that I hadn't done an adequate and accurate job.

So I went over the form again and crossed out about half of the answers and scribbled what I thought were more adequate responses to the questions of my nation, one and indivisible, under God, with liberty and justice for all.

Having accomplished this task, I joined the line again, not really expecting that I would pass muster.

I didn't.

"Man, you can't write, can you? No way we're going to take this shit. Do it over again. And this time no cross-outs."

It was already one o'clock, and I wondered if I had stumbled into the anteroom of purgatory.

I tried again. This time I followed her orders exactly. I found an empty desk and wrote all my answers with firm confidence and refused to reread the results. Maybe there were no program bugs in this office.

On my third try, she paid me a mild compliment. "Well, it's better than it was . . . Now, where are your proof of birth and your photographs?"

"Proof of birth? I've clearly been born or I wouldn't be here."

"VERY funny. Where were you born?"

"St. Mary of Nazareth Hospital."

"Is that in America?"

"Yes, ma'am. In Chicago even."

"Well, you need proof of that. Birth certificate, baptismal certificate. Something like that. And four passport photos."

"Where can I get them?"

"Any place," she snapped. "Now, these people in line are waiting."

"How long will it take to get the passport?"

"Ten days, two weeks after you fill out the required form and bring in the required documentation . . . NEXT!"

"Is Mr. Kafka here?" I asked as I bumbled away from the counter.

"He doesn't work here anymore."

I went back to the chair and considered matters. Great-Uncle Gerry had put a time limit on my courtship of the fair Sara. Win her in a month—by June 25—or all bets were off and the ten million went to the Internal Revenue Service, which, heaven knows, is an unworthy cause. A little more than three weeks. The baptismal certificate, I could get from St. Hilary's. Passport photos were still a problem. How many did you need anyway?

Maybe it would be better just to let the money go to the IRS.

Yet I was a certified, card-carrying hero, wasn't I? I had on one glorious occasion routed the forces of darkness and saved a fair damsel. And her name wasn't Melanie either. And it wasn't in the room, though you could argue that I was so drunk that I thought that's where I was. Or acted like I was. Or whatever.

If I had routed the forces of darkness at a cash station near Armitage and Halsted, could I not deal efficaciously with the federal bureaucracy?

The answer seemed to be that no, I could not.

"Can I help you, sir?"

A very attractive woman, stunningly attractive, in fact, had appeared next to me. She wore the same uniform as did the witch of Endor behind the counter and was perhaps five years older than I was and seemed to have a wedding ring, though, for some reason, it was hard to tell whether there was actually a ring on the appropriate finger. Her body was rich and glorious, the kind of mix of full breasts and hips with slender waist against which I imagined myself leaning in my most delightfully obscene fantasies. Her hair was curly and brown, her eyes gentle and brown, and her smile warm and maternal.

I adored her at once.

"I seemed to have messed this up." I handed her both my forms.

"Let's see what we can do about them." She took my

applications and walked towards the counter.

I admired her withers as she walked away from me. Lusted after them actually. But lusted respectfully. Very respectfully. I had the distinct impression that she wanted me to admire her but to admire her appropriately.

Whatever "appropriately" means in the ongoing and probably perpetual misunderstandings between men and women.

Yeah, I had been a hero, all right, though as I say, not a sober one. It had been the might that John Paxon had sunk the tray in the last seconds of the game when the Bulls had won their third championship. I had watched the game in a bar on Armitage Street, a respectable bar, I would add, and had consumed two drinks too many, which for me is four. Sometime later, after midnight, I subsequently learned, I stumbled forth from the bar after telling some delightfully amused "brothers" that black men can't shoot trays. I even offered to engage in a three-point shooting match with them, an offer that afforded them more amusement.

Actually I probably would have beaten them, but I couldn't remember their names the next morning.

I stumbled down the street; even now I don't know in which direction but in all probability away from the el instead of towards it. After a while I noticed that, citywide celebration or not, I was alone on the street, which probably but not certainly was still Armitage.

Then in the darkness of a summer night I saw three people huddled around a cash station. One seemed to be a woman, the other two were men. It seemed like one of them was holding a gun to her head.

It had happened before. You stop a woman at the entrance of her apartment, force her to take you to an obscure cash station, and withdraw whatever her limit is.

Then you kill her (because maybe she recognizes you or can recognize you again) and use her money to buy drugs.

I told myself that in my advanced state of disarray I was imagining this scenario.

But some part of me did not listen. I found myself rushing across the street at full speed and crashing into the guy with the gun, my head into his stomach actually. I guess I must have broken his arm when I twisted the gun out of his hand because he let out a wild scream of pain. I used the butt of the gun on the other guy, who was coming at me with a knife. He went down pretty quickly when I hit him over the head.

"Don't kill him," a hoarse womanly voice gasped next to me.

"Good idea," I agreed as I tapped the other guy on the head with his own revolver and thus put an end to his screams, which were annoying me. "You call the police. I'll keep an eye on these guys."

She hugged me and ran.

Well, it turned out that there were no romantic payoffs from my drunken bravery. She was well and truly engaged to a guy I had gone to high school with. ("I never thought you had it in you, Toby.") Nonetheless, the mayor of Chicago, a certain Richard M. Daley, praised me at a press conference the next day as "one of Chicago's real heroes."

Off camera, I told him that I was drunk when I had done it, four drinks. With his vast laugh he replied, "Toby, maybe we ought to give you four drinks every night and make you wander the dark streets of the North Side."

My family, characteristically, was not pleased with me. They were not opposed to my being a hero, but had I not risked my own life? Would it not have been better to summon the Chicago Police Department? Why had I not been more circumspect in my heroism, gone for help, perhaps?

"The least you could have done," Megan commented, "was find a gorgeous woman who was not engaged."

"I wouldn't worry, Dad," she continued. "He says he was drunk, and Toby is almost never drunk. He's too short a hitter."

"We'll have to watch him if the Bulls win next year."

That was before the media idiots drove Michael out of basketball.

Now I limit myself to one beer.

But Megan insisted that I would have gone riding to the rescue if I were stone sober.

"I think everything's all right now." The brown-haired Juno—no, better, Diana—handed me a blue book that seemed to be a passport. "Have a nice trip."

I walked out of the Dirksen Building in a daze. Inside the passport was a baptismal certificate from St. Hilary and two extra passport pictures, relatively flattering, I thought. Another picture was affixed to the passport itself. In the pictures I was wearing my White Sox jacket. Good guys wear black. Even if they are turncoat Cub fans, North Side yuppie scum, as the Comiskey crowds would have it.

Had I gone back to St. Hilary's and obtained the certificate? Had I found one of the many camera shops around the Dirksen Building and asked for and received passport pictures? Had I become so preoccupied with the latest planned improvement for DABEST that I had forgotten completely what I had done?

I had done such things before, had I not?

Yes, I had.

I looked at my watch. Two-thirty. There was enough time for these ventures if I had thought of them.

Had I thought of them? I would ask Father Hanafin, whose name was affixed to the baptismal certificate, that night.

No, on second thought, I would not. It was supposed to take from ten days to two weeks to receive a passport. I looked at my watch again. It was the same day that I had ventured forth from our family's modest home in search of the first lance I needed to pursue the fair Sara. No way I could actually have a passport. Even if the mayor of Chicago had called me Toby once, I did not have that kind of clout.

Yet I had the passport. It was dated today. Good for ten years.

I shivered despite the hot spring day. This was turning into a bad dream, real bad.

I walked over to Michigan Avenue, found an empty bench in Grant Park, opened my Aero 4/25, and turned it on.

Color screen. I remember distinctly that I had decided against a color screen. The extra five hundred dollars were not worth it for an occasionally used subnotebook.

Go Rae, I typed at the DOS prompt.

Then I realized that I was truly an idiot. You could not access the Net without a modem and a line—not unless you had a complicated and expensive radio link, which I did not have because I did not believe that they worked yet.

Yeah?
>**What the hell is going on?**
You forgot a letter. It's R A F E.
>**Sorry. But I repeat: What the hell is going on?**

*Toby, please don't use bad language on the
Net.*
>Why is this working without a modem?
*The Net is primitive but a lot less primitive
than you think.*
>What happened over at the Dirksen Building?
*We'll take care of this stuff, Toby. Just don't
ask questions.*
>Are you a demon or something?
Hardly.
>An Angel?
Don't be absurd.
>What are you then?
*An old and established travel firm with a good
reputation and lots of clout. Just leave every-
thing to us.*
>Who was that woman?
What woman?
>The good-looking one with the brown hair.
Oh, that woman? Actually her hair is chestnut.
>Who was she?
You found her attractive, didn't you?
>Very.
Good. She works for us. End.

I walked back to Madison and Wabash and got on the
el, not at all sure that I liked what was happening.

During the time I had reflected on my so-called heroism on Paxon night, after the lovely Diana had taken my
applications, the world had seemed hazy, not very hazy
but just a touch of mist that permeated everything.

What, to repeat myself, was going on?

There was, however, no mist after I got off the Lincoln
bus and walked up to our house on the corner of Virginia
and Hollywood. I began to relax.

Until our two dogs, Fiona and Patrick, went wild when

I came into the yard. They always greet me like I've been away on a long trip. But there was something different in this greeting, something almost ecstatic.

"Is she in heat?" I asked my mother, who was in her "office" poring over her records.

"No, Toby. If you lived with us instead of up in that attic, you'd know she was pregnant."

"What's the matter with them?"

"Just glad to see you at last."

"More than that. Like maybe they had a whiff of the bog."

"Don't be silly, Toby. They're just happy you notice them."

I notice them all the time. They smelled something they liked a lot.

I showed my mother the passport, and she marveled at the photo. "Toby Junior, dear, it's the best picture you've ever taken!"

It was always counted as one of my many annoying habits that I never took a good picture.

"Oh, by the way, a very lovely young woman from your travel agency brought your tickets this afternoon. My, they're very efficient."

"They sure are," I said with little enthusiasm.

I opened the tickets as soon as I had reached the safety of my office.

Chicago-Manchester-Dublin.

Reasonable enough.

"First class!" I shouted, and turned on my system.

>**Go Rafe**
What now?
>**I can't afford to fly first class!**
Sure you can. Don't be a cheapskate, Toby Tobin, Junior.

>I won't fly first class.
Yes, you will. The tickets are already paid for.
>Whom do I pay?
No one.
>What do you mean no one?
It's on the house.
>Whose house?
Our house, whose else?
>How much do I have to pay you for this whole trip?
Complimentary. Reservations at the Shelbourne in Dublin and the Great Southern in Galway are with the tickets.
>What are you?
I've already answered that question. Like I told you, I'm busy.
>You said you were not an angel.
Correct.
>An archangel?
Absolutely not.
>A Throne or a Principality or a Power or a Domination?
Don't be absurd. There never have been nine choirs, not exactly anyway. You shouldn't pay any attention to Denis the Areopagite.
>Pseudo Areopagite. Are you a Cherub?
Cuddly little brat? No way.
>You're a Seraph?
You missed one of the nine choirs.
>You ARE a Seraph.
High-class angel. Very high-class.
>You lied.
Not at all. We can't lie. But we don't have to tell the whole truth all the time.
>You stand before the face of God.
Metaphor. Nice one, though.
>Which one are you?

I've already told you my name.
>You're the Archangel Raphael!
You really are swift, Toby Tobin Junior. Seraph
Raphael, actually Patron Saint of travelers.
And of medical personnel. Read the book of To-
bit or Tobias if you want more information
about our work. I told you we were an old
firm with a considerable record of success.
>What the hell is going on!
You keep asking that. It should be clear. We're
taking over your account and going to Ireland
with you.
>I want out of this deal.
Too late, Toby Tobin Junior, much too late. We
never lose an account.
End.

3

A huge black shape hovered over me, like the vampire in the film *Bram Stoker's Dracula*. Inside its blackness a fire was burning. With invisible hands it dragged me towards the sulfurous flames. I sliced at it with my sword, but the blade cut through air. On the bed beneath me a naked Sara Anne was screaming in terror. The sword fell from my hands. I felt the heat singeing my face. Damn it, Rafe, I seemed to be shouting, you're supposed to help me now. No Rafe. I grabbed at the demon's throat. It was solid muscle. I wouldn't let go. It tried to brush me off with a jet of flame. I hung on and began to squeeze. Rich Daley appeared nearby and shouted something about four drinks. Asmodeus was coughing nosily, each spasm enveloping me in flame. Rich disappeared. Megan replaced him. The demon's hands found my throat. We were choking each other. He was a lot stronger than I was . . .

*   *   *

I rolled off my bed coughing desperately and feverishly hot.

Had it all been a dream?

Then why was I clutching my hands together like I was trying to choke someone?

Asmodeus!

I turned on the lamp next to my bed. No demon, no vampire, no monster.

I dashed into my computer room, turned on my pentium, and typed the command.

>Go Rae.
It's Rafe. What now?
>What was that dream all about?
We don't monitor dreams. We can read minds.
>Asmodeus!
You read the book of Tobit.
>And Asmodeus came to my dream to kill me.
You're being hysterical, Toby.
>He looked like the vampire in *Bram Stoker's Dracula.*
English novelist.
>Irish, damn it.
I stand corrected. Now, go back to bed and get a good night's sleep.
>In the dream you ran out on me.
Seraphs don't run out on people. You read the book of Tobit. You know that.
>Is Asmodeus really waiting for me?
Among others.
>Is this going to be dangerous?
For you or for Sara?
>For both of us. Me especially.
Moderately so. Faint heart never won fair lady, Toby Junior.
>I want out.

Too late. Now, go back to sleep.
>*It was a terrible dream.*
I am not your mother or your wife. Your
dreams are not my job. End.
>*Hey!*

The screen went blank. The computer turned itself off. Damn Seraph.

It took me a long time to go back to sleep. I didn't want to get in a wrestling match with a demon. Then I tried to recall what the naked Sara Anne looked like. But I couldn't remember.

The next afternoon I was sitting in front of my pentium system waiting for DABEST to hunt down information about the book of Tobit, putting off packing for my departure to Manchester and Dublin. The tickets left no doubt that today was the day. Rafe and friends were not wasting any time.

Maybe if I didn't finish packing. I wouldn't have to leave today. That way I'd never run into this Asmodeus character.

The book of Tobit is a love story with some nice touches, like when Sara's father prepares the tomb for young Tobit because he is sure that he's already dead like all of Sara's previous suitors. Edna, her mother, sends a maid to peek into the bedroom door to find out if the groom is already dead. She sees them both sleeping, peacefully and contentedly, though the Bible doesn't use those adverbs. But what else would young lovers be like on their wedding night?

That's exactly what my father and mother would have done. I permitted myself some pleasant fantasies about a naked Sara Tobin in my arms and then quickly dismissed them. There were lots of differences—my father's sight had been saved by laser surgery, so he didn't need any magic potions to heal his blindness. He had never been a courtier at anyone's court nor buried any dead bodies. We had dogs around our house, but surely there were no massive and playful Irish wolfhounds in Tobias's place. I would not take a wolfhound with me to Ireland. Ronan Tobin owed us no money. It was most unlikely that Sara had already lost seven husbands. Surely she was not haunted by a demon named Asmodeus.

Was she?

Anyway, I had Raphael on my side, didn't I?

Raphael meant "God heals," I had learned, and Asmodeus (from the Persian *aeshma daeva*) meant "demon of wrath" or "destroyer." Like the Bulls versus the Knicks. I was the Bulls, naturally. He was the Knicks, of course, a team of the world's dirtiest basketball players.

Raphael was undefeated, wasn't he? An angelic Michael Jordan, right?

DABEST performs its searches in a highly personalized fashion. It knows my age, education, income, gender, interests, level of intelligence, language, and such demographic matters. But there was a lot of stuff in the libraries that are on line about the book of Tobit. Even with all the information and criteria it had, DABEST had located thirty-five articles. It asked for more criteria.

Best to tell it the truth.

>**More about two lovers.**

It rummaged around some more and printed out a very short note.

> **The book is certainly a love story, a quest tale like that in many other ancient cultures. The author has grafted on it many lessons for Jewish life such as loyalty, respect for parents, and concern for the dead, but these mor-**

alistic additions do not notably weaken the
love story with its profound and powerful and
modern, almost feminist, concern for respect
of women. It is not the smoke that Raphael
blows in the eyes of the demon that saves the
young lovers, but the integrity of their love
and the young man's sensitivity and respect
for his bride. Raphael was probably a good
spirit who figured in many Israelite folk tales
because then, as now, readers like a touch of
the occult. However, in the Hebrew Scriptures
the Malek Jahweh, the Angel of the Lord, is
not distinct from the Lord Himself but merely
represents God's concern for each individual
person. Hence the existence of a being named
Raphael is a fictional artifact. The angel may
safely be considered merely a useful addition
to the tale, but not the cause of its happy
ending.

Yeah? But then who was playing games with me on the
Net? Was DABEST a target for industrial espionage?

I worried about that for a few moments and then told
DABEST to provide me with articles on angels, avoiding
all superstition, piety, mystical speculations, and devo-
tional nonsense. It still came up with over a thousand
references.

Toby Tobin Junior, what are you doing?
>You know damn well what I'm doing.
*Trying to find out whether I'm a fictional arti-
fact.*
You're not supposed to eavesdrop on the net.
*How do you think you found me? We eaves-
drop all the time. The Net helps us to stay in
touch with our responsibilities. That's what
it's for.*

>You're manipulating something that we hu-
mans created.
*Don't go self-righteous on me. The Net was our
idea. Your species hasn't made much of it yet.
Anyway, if you want to know about angels,
why not ask me?*
>You'll answer my questions truthfully?
*I TOLD YOU WE DON'T LIE. CAN'T. I won't even be
evasive when you ask about us.*
>You really are an angel, uh, Seraph?
*We are those beings who are responsible for
the events that your species normally attrib-
utes to angels. My position in our species is
roughly equivalent to that of a Seraph in the
nine choirs of Pseduo Dionysius. Satisfied?*
>Are you from this cosmos?
Not entirely.
>Are you pure spirits?
*Negative. We are created beings like you. Our
evolutionary process began earlier and has
proceeded further. We are better suited for
intense thought and love than you are. Hence
our bodies are what one of your fathers of the
Church called ethereal, bodies indeed but
highly sophisticated bodies of the sort that
you cannot see, which is just as well for you.*
>Too ugly?
*Rather the opposite. Even by your standards.
No scales or horns or long tails or anything of
that sort.*
>You die?
*We live very long lives, but not long enough.
We face the same ultimate anxiety as you do.*
>So you have reproduction?
*Brilliant, Toby Tobin Junior! How else would our
species survive.*
>So?

You're wondering whether we have sexual differentiation?
>Well, kind of wondering. It seems to be an interesting way of doing it. Complications, of course.
You mean do we screw? A characteristic human concern, I must say. Of course we do. Do we enjoy it? What do you think? How long? Oh, weeks on end. Envious?
>So you fly around running errands for God?
Actually we spend most of our time singing and dancing and telling stories and arguing and making love. We are really very lazy creatures. Terribly vain too.
>Really?
Really.
>Do you drink?
You are Irish, aren't you? No, but singing and dancing has something of the same effect on us.
>Where do you live?
In our place, and I'm afraid I couldn't explain that to you. It's a long way from here.
>Are you married?
Do I have a companion? Yes indeed, and progeny too. Two progeny.
>Do you miss them?
Miss them?

There was a momentary pause.

Oh, I see what you mean. Toby Tobin Junior, we cannot live without love. We are not like the Other who is simply and totally love, but we are something like Her, a pale reflection if I may say so. We must be loved so there is a response to our own love. I don't mean what you would call sex, though that is important too. We must be loved, and therefore we must be close to those we love. My lover is never far from me. Cannot be. Distance as you would measure distance is not a problem. Making travel arrangements for you will not interfere. Nice of you to be concerned, however.

I was beginning to like this travel agent.

>Do you fight?

Of course. Fighting enhances love. My companion complains that I am particularly contentious, but that is an expression of love.

>Death?

Another long pause.

We mourn like you do and we hope like you do and we find another companion eventually. My mother lost her companion when they were both very young. There are accidents in our, ah, world too.

So angels have sad memories too.

>You are God's messengers?

The Other does not need messengers, Toby. But it delights the Other that our insatiable quest for knowledge and love leads us to help in the work that needs to be done. You might consider us busybodies, but fortunately the Other finds us amusing. So we take care of many things—under the constraint of rules that I am not free to discuss. There are what I would call interstices or gaps in creation which the Other permits, some of which we can correct. I love my progeny, Toby. But we are all progeny of the Other, and our love is weak by comparison.

I didn't quite get that. But I'm not exactly a theologian.

>So you work a lot of miracles?

Absolutely not. Perhaps the Other does miracles. If You produce creation, You can make

Your own rules. Our powers, however, are purely natural. They seem extraordinary to you because you are not like us. But they're not miraculous or supernatural. Sometimes we fail. Often we fail. We tried to prevent these terrible things that are happening again in the Balkans. We seem to be doing better in Northern Ireland now, but you can never count on the Irish to be reasonable. We have been failing there for centuries. There are no guarantees.

A warning shot?

>No guarantees that I will win the fair Sara Anne?

Absolutely not. A guarantee, however, that she would be worth winning. Much more so than that silly Princess Melanie you are pursuing in your silly games. And oh, yes, there are two things we can't do: We can't read minds and we don't know the future. We're pretty good guessers, however.

>So what am I thinking about now?

I would guess that you are thinking about the body of the fair Sara Anne, as you call her. How could it be otherwise given your hormone system? As one who has somewhat more information on the matter than you do, I would say that your fantasies are too mild.

Wow!

>Do you think we're inferior?

Long pause. Bad question?

You do not understand us at all, Toby, if you think that. Our species are different, that's all. If you only knew how much we love your kind and want to help you, you wouldn't think of that question or worry about it. Sometimes we

*become a little impatient, of course. Only the
Other does not have that fault.*
>Sounds like you do a lot more than sing and
dance and argue and tell stories and make
love.
*Let the record show, Toby Tobin Junior, that I
laughed at that.*
>You're kind of an extra terrestrial? Sort of
an alien from another planet?
*I can tell by the look on your face that you're
trying to bait me. I'm not from another planet
and I'm not an alien. We were here first. Long
before you were. SF creatures are not like us
at all.*
>You folks are certainly getting enough atten-
tion these days. Books about you on the best-
seller lists, TV programs, angel clubs, you've
become celebrities.

Nothing on the screen.

*Color me angry, Toby. We hate that stuff. It
reduces us to cute little creatures that run
around doing whatever humans want us to do.
It is not our job to protect your kind from its
folly. We become involved with your kind
when we want to and only because we want
to or the Other asks us. This current tripe
about us is degrading. By our standards we are
giants of knowledge and love and, we ought to
be imagined as such. It is not our role in the
cosmos to pull stupid humans out of the way
of oncoming buses or trucks because they're
too dumb to take care of themselves.*
>I understand.
Good!
>OK. Now I have some questions about this
book of Tobit I read last night, like you told me
to.

**This has been an interesting conversation and
you are a nice young man who might just possibly be worthy of the fair Sara Anne. Maybe.
But I am needed elsewhere at the moment.
And you're leaving for Manchester and Dublin
tonight. So why don't you see to your preparations and we can talk about that at O'Hara.**
>O'Hare.

They made mistakes too.
Of course. End.

The system went down.

My head was spinning. Had Rafe gone off to make love
to his companion? What was she like? How did he know
the expression on my face? Was he in the room with me
all the time? What did he mean that my obscene fantasies
about Sara were too mild? And that I might be worthy of
her, maybe?

It was a different view of angels than I had found in
the Net. But none of it was inconsistent with what I had
been taught in theology courses in college about God.
Was I loved by a whole host of beings like Raphael? Why
me? Did I really want that attention and affection? Did I
have any choice?

Sara, Sara, Sara.

I think they love you more than they love me.

And Rafe guaranteed that you were worth winning.
More so than the Princess Melanie. She doesn't really exist. Only an electronic fantasy. You really do exist. Don't
hang yourself like the Sara in the story thought of doing.

I shoved back from the chair and went into my bedroom to pack, a task that I dreaded. My mother and sisters had offered their help with intimations that a poor

dumb male like me, especially like me, could not be expected to do it right.

I replied that, right or wrong, I'd do it myself.

A carry-on roller bag rested on my bed with the ticket envelope and my passport on top of it—also an American Airlines Admiral's Club card to which I was surely not entitled. Next to it was my Compaq Aero. On a hanger outside the door of my closet was a new suit—blue blazer, charcoal gray slacks—a white shirt, and a tie with the Irish Tricolor and the Stars and Stripes crossed on it. Gray socks and green Jockey shorts waited on my dresser, and a brand-new pair of loafers rested neatly at the side of my bed.

I glanced at the clock. Two o'clock. The plane left at six. My family was to accompany me en masse to the airport. The airline wanted me at four. The family decreed that we had to leave home at three because of construction on the Kennedy. Plenty of time for a shower.

I wondered in the shower whether Rafe and his buddies were watching me. He certainly had information on Sara that suggested he had seen her in the nude. Voyeurs.

Lucky voyeurs.

All right, I liked him. But that didn't mean I wanted to get mixed up with him and his crowd.

No way. I did not want to go to Ireland. I did not want to pursue Sara Anne Elizabeth Tobin, no matter how gorgeous she was.

So I would not do so, right?

I emerged from the shower and grabbed a towel, absolutely convinced that I was going to fire my travel agents.

Instead I docilely donned my new clothes—even the shirt was tailor-made—tied my politically incorrect Irish tie, and glanced in the mirror. Presentable enough six-footer, if you don't mind nerds.

I noticed a wallet on the dresser, which surely had not been there before. I picked it up. American dollars, British pounds, Irish punts, mint-new. I didn't bother to count them. Doubtless Rafe and his friends had more where that came from.

Also brand-new credit cards. And a photo.

I took the photo out of its slot, knowing full well who it was. They—whoever they were—had retouched and blown up Sara's face. Gorgeous. For just a moment it seemed that the sweatshirt had vanished and I was staring at two wondrous breasts. I blinked. She was properly clad again.

The bastards cheated.

Then I looked at her eyes. They no longer seemed cold and calculating. Rather they seemed very vulnerable.

The bastards got you coming and going, desire and tenderness. Damn them.

I picked up the subnotebook and walked down the steps to where my family waited. I did not expect a "beat-up-on-Toby" scene. However, I never expect them. Fiona and Patrick jumped and barked and dashed around.

As if, I thought, they knew it was the last time they'd see me alive.

❧4❧

*It wasn't your fault, G. Patrick "Toby" Tobin
Junior, not your fault at all.*
>Don't call me Toby. I hate it.
All right. Will Pat do?
>Fine. I would have missed the flight if it
wasn't for you.
*I told you we were the best travel agency in
the world.*

When I came downstairs with my roller bag in hand
and my computer bag over my shoulder, the whole family
(including my brother-in-law and my future brother-in-
law) were waiting for me.

"Do you have your tickets, Toby?" my father demanded.

"Sure."

"Let me see them."

"You're not traveling with just that little bag?" my mom asked.

"Let's see how you packed it," Maureen said, grabbing at the bag.

"Toby, these are first-class tickets!"

"I got an upgrade."

"How much did it cost?"

"Nothing."

The womenfolk were pawing through the bag, which had been packed, I discovered for the first time, with incredible—one might almost say supernatural—efficiency. With all new clothes, of course. An account of the Raphaelite Travel Agency had to look sharp. Right?

"Toby, you packed this bag just like a man would."

"Actually not."

"Since when (my father) did you join the Admiral's Club? This note says you should check in there."

"It goes with first-class tickets."

"You should have packed more shirts."

"I can buy them if I need them."

"There's an Admiral's Club card here."

"My travel agent got it for me."

"I don't think it's a very good idea, Toby. The IRS won't admit it as a business expense."

"Dad, look at the mess Toby made when he packed!"

It was a mess, all right. The women in my family had picked over everything and in effect had unpacked the bag.

My father put the tickets on the coffee table and came to look at the bag.

"Toby, are you ever going to learn to apply yourself to your work?"

I had been asked that question since third grade when

my teacher had reported to them that I was bright but given to daydreaming.

"I think this sport coat is ugly," Nicole announced. "Where did you get it, Toby? Carson's?"

I had no idea where I got it.

"Lord and Taylor," Megan giggled, as she checked the label.

"You can't afford that kind of money," my mother insisted.

Actually I could. Even without Rafe's deep pockets.

"You definitely should not take it with you," Nicole said, tossing the coat on the floor. "I don't care how much it cost. It looks awful."

"Probably doesn't fit either." Megan continued to giggle.

It would, of course, fit perfectly. Just like my suit.

Then they started on the suit.

"Did some illegal Mexican immigrant make that suit for you, Toby?"

"You really ought to wear something more conservative, Toby Junior, dear."

The pin-stripe suit in the roller bag, now jumbled into a tight ball by my sisters' efforts to unpack my bag, was conservative enough. But I knew better than to argue.

"You're not a yuppie, Toby. You don't look right in a navy blue blazer. Where did you get it?"

"You should try to impress the young woman, dear."

"Maybe the fair Sara Anne will think Toby looks cute as a yuppie."

(Megan, of course, the little imp.)

"You need more shirts and socks and underwear, dear. Laundry in those Irish hotels is expensive."

"Toby, if you would only apply yourself, you'd show more foresight."

In fact, all my traveling clothes were elegant and expensive and revealed much better taste than I possessed.

"Sara Anne has her work cut out for her to straighten you out, Toby."

"Toby, why do you have all these Irish punts? The exchange rate is terrible here. You would have saved a lot of money if you did the exchange in a bank in Ireland."

My father had been probing my wallet, the one with the tickets and the passport.

How did I know where Rafe got the money? Or at what exchange rate?

"My travel agent took care of it for me."

"They must be making a big profit off of you . . . Who are they?"

"Pre-Raphaelite tours."

If Rafe was lurking in the room and watching the melee, he might get a kick out of that response.

"Never heard of them." Dad shook his head sadly as he put the wallet back on the coffee table. "You would have been much better off if you had chosen an established and responsible agency."

"They've been in business for a long time."

"Really, Toby Junior, dear, I don't know what we're going to do about you."

A mother's ultimate cry of despair.

"I guess you're going to let me repack my clothes so we can leave for the airport."

I picked up the discarded gray sport coat and tried to fold it neatly before putting it back into the roller bag.

Like avenging Valkyries my sisters shoved me out of the way and swarmed over the bag. "No man knows how to pack," Maureen proclaimed.

They stuffed my clothes in recklessly and then tried to zip the bag shut. They couldn't move the zippers more than a third of the way around.

"Toby, dear, you should have packed a bigger bag."

"I don't know who's going to look after you, son, while you're in Ireland."

You'd be surprised.

I put the bag on the floor and sat on top of it. I managed just barely to tug the zippers the rest of the way around.

"You do have the envelope from Uncle Gerry, don't you, Toby?" my father demanded.

"Certainly."

"I didn't see it."

"It's there."

I hadn't seen it either, but my travel agent wouldn't make mistakes like that.

My father sighed loudly. "We'd better check through it again. It wouldn't do you much good to travel all the way to Ireland and not have the papers."

"There's always FedEx. We should leave for the airport."

"Not till we're sure about the letter to Ronan Tobin."

The Valkyries swarmed again. They yanked open the zippers and dug into my now twisted and wrinkled clothes and poked around in search of the thick manila envelope.

"It's not here!" Nicole announced triumphantly.

"Toby forgot it!"

"Dear, what are we going to do with you?"

"Son, will you ever learn a sense of responsibility?"

"Here it is." Megan waved the envelope triumphantly. "In the compartment for papers and documents, just where it should be."

Hooray for the Seraph team!

My father opened the larger envelope to make sure that the smaller envelope (with the letter to Ronan) and the legal documents were inside.

"It all seems to be here," he said, putting the envelope on top of my wallet and tickets.

"Now let's repack my bag and drive to O'Hare. It's already three-thirty."

"Don't worry about that. The Kennedy crowds up only after four."

"There's construction!"

"We'll miss most of it."

So we went through the ritual of shoving clothes back into the bag and tugging at the zippers. This time they couldn't even start the zipping process. I stood on the bag while the ingenious Megan pushed and pulled and yanked and jerked at the zippers and finally closed the bag.

"Nice going, Meg."

She wiped imaginary sweat off her brow. "Neat thing, your roller bag. It can resist almost any trauma."

"You're not taking that computer thing with you, Toby?" Nicole said in horror. "You're supposed to be courting a girl, not playing with that silly toy."

"Woman."

"What?"

"Sara Anne is a woman, not a girl."

Another giggle from Megan.

"Do you really need it, dear? What if she doesn't like computers?"

"That will be her misfortune. I don't propose taking it to bed with us!"

Omnes: "Toby!"

I hoped Rafe wasn't offended.

"Now can we please leave for the airport?"

My older sisters and their men took their departure, the former proclaiming repeatedly that Ms. Sara Tobin was going to have a difficult challenge if she tried to "set-tle Toby down." Only my parents and Megan were ac-companying me to O'Hare.

If the witch tried to settle me down, that would be END. Log-off. General System Failure.

If we had left our home on Virginia Avenue at three, we would have indeed arrived at O'Hare long before four despite the endless repairs on the Kennedy Expressway. Moreover there was not nearly enough time to take a cab back home to pick up what I'd left behind.

As it was, I finally escaped from the house at three thirty-five. Even then we would have arrived at the airport on time if my father had taken Devon (accent on the second syllable, please) to Manheim Road as I suggested. However, he insisted that the Kennedy would be smooth sailing west of California Avenue. That we were late was not his fault because of his mistake about the expressway but my fault for not being prepared to leave on time.

"You do have your tickets, Toby?" Megan asked, as we finally broke out of the traffic jam at the Eden's junction.

"Of course." I tapped the inside, left-hand pocket of my jacket.

The tickets weren't there. They were back on the coffee table with my passport, my wallet, and the documents for Ronan Tobin.

Where my father had put them.

Over to you, Rafe. No way am I going back to that madhouse now. Maybe there'll be time to take a cab back home. My parents were going to join the others for din-ner. They'd never know that I had sneaked back in and grabbed the tickets.

And the money.

And the documents.

And my hotel reservations.

And my Admiral's Club card.

Finally we arrived at O'Hare, an ongoing surrealistic nightmare of a place, an SF fantasy, an anteroom of purgatory, a monument to the madness of the jet age.

Yet it was the biggest and the best in the world. Naturally. It was Chicago. Richard M. Daley, mayor.

"We'll park the car and come with you, Toby. Make sure you get on the right plane."

"No need. I check in at the Admiral's Club; that's what the travel agent said to do. They'll tell me where the plane is."

"And lead you to it?" Megan was still giggling.

"I'm a first-class passenger, after all."

We both giggled.

"Besides, we're already late, and by the time we park the car, I might miss the plane."

"We'll drop you off and then park the car."

"You'll never find me in that mess. Besides, I have to go to the Admiral's Club to check in."

Reluctantly my parents agreed to consign me to the designs of Providence. I kissed my mom, shook hands with my dad, hugged the grinning Meg, and got out of the car—three lanes away from the curb and under the watchful eyes of two Chicago cops who were talking to each other and ignoring the traffic.

I looked at my watch. Not a chance to return home now. I'd bluff my way into the Admiral's Club and see if they could help me out.

The security guards hassled me about my computer bag. The mists seemed to drift in and surround the checkpoint. Each time the mists appeared I hardly noticed them. Only on reflection afterwards did I remember them.

What was it like in the mists? Even now it's hard to say.

Something like a door opening into another place or another reality. Maybe I should say a "port" because that's appropriate SF vocabulary. Time seemed to slow down or even stop for a few moments. How can time slow down for a few seconds when seconds are time? I don't know. I'm just trying to describe what it was like. As my trip—quest if you will—went on, I realized that the mists meant "Seraph at work! Stay out of the way!"

The guards made me turn on my Aero to prove that it was a computer and not a bomb. Then they insisted I open the roller bag because of a "cylindrical shape" inside it—the extra Duracell battery which was at the bottom of the bag, so far down that my prying siblings had not found it.

I opened the bag. Traveling, a friend had told me, puts you at the mercy of bureaucrats and security guards with negative IQ. It was pointless to argue with them.

The battery was on the top of a neatly packed bag of freshly pressed clothes.

"What's this for?" The security guard shook the battery at me.

"It's a Duracell battery, ma'am."

"Never saw one like it before."

I demonstrated how the battery could replace its identical twin inside the Aero. She seemed skeptical but waved me on. Security guards, I would learn, never admit that you may not be a bomb-toting terrorist after all, even if, as in my case, you don't fit any of their terrorist profiles.

After I had replaced the computer in its bag and zipped up yet once more the roller bag, I touched the pocket of my jacket. Yep, everything was back in place. Come to think of it, the manila envelope was right beneath the Duracell battery.

Not bad, Rafe. Not bad at all.

I managed to find the Admiral's Club on only the third try and dug the membership card out of my wallet to show to the woman at the desk.

"I'm going to Ireland," I told her, pulling out my tickets.

"Wonderful." She smiled. "You check in on the third floor. Take the elevator to your right."

I stumbled over to the elevator, pulling my faithful roller bag behind me, and remembered that I had put down my computer bag to get at my tickets. I hurried back to the counter and there it was, safe and sound.

Was that good fortune or Rafe again? As the trip continued I would stop asking that question.

"Can't leave that behind," the admissions woman said, smiling again, "can we?"

On the third floor I tried to check in at the domestic counter and was directed across the way to the international counter, where I presented my ticket and passport to the young woman in charge with a minimum of fuss—once I had found the passport.

"You must do a lot of traveling, Mr. Tobin."

"Not really."

"You're too modest. Not many people have Platinum Advantage cards. That's fifty thousand miles a year."

"That's not *really* a lot of travel."

She smiled again. "Boarding at five-fifteen, but we'll come and get you just before flight time, say a quarter to six."

"Thank you." I smiled at her like an experienced traveler—whatever that was.

Not when you're a Seraph who moves almost as fast as the speed of thought—and presumably from one universe to another.

I resolved that I would ask no questions about whence

the money, the clothes, the tickets, the hotel reservations, or anything else came. Who was I to try to understand the ways of Seraphs, right?

I collapsed into a chair near a window and looked out at the lines of slim, slightly sinister aluminum monsters which were lined up for departures to such far and mysterious places as Milan, Frankfurt, Düsseldorf, London, Manchester, Los Angeles, and Milwaukee. If God had meant us to fly, She would have provided us with wings and feathers.

Someone had put a large, very large, glass of Bailey's on the rocks next to me. I sighed and picked it up. Then I noticed that my Aero was out of the bag and open, and Rafe was absolving me from blame. Holding the Bailey's cautiously in one hand, I joined the dialogue.

Naturally we were not plugged into a modem.

They mean well, Pat, and they love you. And you love them, especially that impish little tyke. But they eat you alive. They can't help themselves. They've been doing it all your life.

I would be Pat for the rest of the trip. I not only hated "Toby," I hated even more "Toby Junior."

>Too many older sisters. Now, tell me about the first Toby and your trip with him.
It was not a whole lot of fun, Pat. He was a nice young man but not very swift. I had to push him into that wedding chamber, a fact that the author of the book chose not to mention. And the poor child cowering in fear that he might die, especially because she loved the young idiot.
>Not very swift like me?
A lot less swift, actually. The girl was cute, however, and very brave, considering all the

*things that had happened to her. Also smart
enough for the two of them.*
>Is my Sara thinking of suicide?
*She is not YOUR Sara yet, Pat, and may never
be. I am not going to tell you anything about
her. You'll have to find out for yourself.*
>You already told me she was worth the ef-
fort.
That will be self-evident.
>Is she smart enough for the two of us?
It does not follow that she will have to be.

A seraphic compliment?

>Will my story be just like theirs?
*Nothing is predestined, Patrick Tobin. Admit-
tedly the story in the book of Tobin, oops,
book of Tobit provides an interesting model for
your coming adventures. That's one of the reasons that we decided to get involved after
your primitive but ingenious program found
me on the Net. We don't believe in coinci-
dences. But we don't know why either of you
are so important to the Other, much less can
we anticipate what fool mistakes either or
both of you might make. So no, I don't know
the end of the story.*
>So it's only a model?
*You're going to Galway rather than Ecbatana,
and her father's name is Ronan, not Raguel.
The model nonetheless may have a certain in-
trinsic power of its own. We shall have to see
about that. Drink some more of your Bailey's.
It will calm your nerves.*
>There isn't any Asmodeus, is there?
*You've already asked that, and I declined to
answer.*
>Your real name is Raphael?

A momentary pause.

I have many names among my own kind, some

*of them perhaps a little erotic. Let us say that
Raphael is the name your people have as-
signed to the agent who does the things I do.
It will suffice.*
>It means God Heals.
I know what my name means, Patrick Tobin.
>And you won all the other contests with the
Destroyer?
*My string is a good deal longer than that of
your hapless Chicago Bulls without Michael. So
that's what you're worried about? If it comes
to it, Patrick, I can still blow smoke in his
eyes.*
>Are there really demons?
*Demonic forces and energies, surely. Look at
Bosnia or Rwanda, for example. Or even Ireland. Or Europe when the two military powers
were ruled by sociopaths, Hitler and Stalin. We
have yet to encounter in our wanderings any
demonic personalities.*
>Are we the only other rational creatures in
the universe?
*Not always so rational. But, Patrick, that's a
foolish question for one of your intelligence to
be asking. On the face of it, the Other has certain propensities to exuberance. Even on the
ocean floor, as one of your tiresome poets put
it. You certainly don't think this exuberance
would be constrained when it came to rational
creatures, do you?*
>I guess not. Will we establish contact with
them?
*Not for a long time, if ever. Most of them are
not as far advanced in their evolutionary process as you are, so you need not fear them.*
>And you said that none of the "aliens" is as
powerful as your kind are?

Actually I laughed, Patrick Tobin, at that question. We do not exclude the possibility that in some cosmos we have yet to explore we will find creatures like ourselves. But we rather doubt it. And as I said, we do not have fins and scales and antennae and such apparatus. Now, drink your Bailey's and get ready for the flight.
>*You did say you were rather vain.*
Terribly so. End.
>*No, wait. One more question.*
Well?
>*Will Sara Anne like me?*
You are exasperating, Patrick Tobin. I cannot predict how the young woman will react. She'd be a little fool if she didn't. End.

The screen went dead and turned itself off.

"I notice you have one of those new Compaqs," the man at the next table said (my age and dressed in yuppie clothes like me, though I wasn't wearing the button-down shirt). "Do you like it?"

Computer users have an ethical code of their own. You can ask anyone you see using a unit what they think about it.

"Best yet, smaller, faster, cheaper."

"I thought you were on the Net."

"Yeah."

"Without a modem?"

"Some new gimmicks."

"Your own?"

"More or less."

"You could make millions with something like that."

"You got the general idea."

"Well, good luck to you; I gotta run."

"Thanks."

Had he seen the conversation? Probably not. Rafe and his crowd undoubtedly took appropriate security precautions.

I drained the Bailey's and put the glass down. What was it at the end of the dialogue with Rafe that had intrigued me?

Oh, yes. The fair Sara Anne would be a little fool if she didn't like me. Well, that was a boost to my morale, especially coming from one of those who stood before the face of God, however metaphorically.

I discovered that the glass of Bailey's had been replenished. Was Rafe trying to get me drunk? What the hell, why fight it? My restless imagination drifted to the fair Sara Anne and turned erotic, but gently and tenderly erotic.

"Mr. Tobin, we'll board you now."

A tall, very attractive blond woman appeared next to me. Seraph?

"My name is Donna." She smiled. "If you just come with me."

"Yes, ma'am."

"We're leaving on time tonight from Gate K-sixteen. I'm afraid it's a bit of a walk."

"No problem."

"I'm sure not, for an Advantage Platinum flyer like you."

"Right." If only my heart were beating a little less rapidly.

"No, Mr. Tobin. This way."

I had turned towards the exit, embarrassing myself and perhaps the Seraphs too.

"Sorry."

"You've been to Ireland before?"

"First time."

"I bet you're looking forward to it."

"Sure am."

And to a young woman who would be written off as a "little fool" if she did not like me.

I felt pretty good about that. Cocky, almost.

Foolish on the basis of the events of the next few hours.

Fools rush in, they say, where Seraphs fear to tread.

❦5❦

𝒟espite 𝓡afe, the trip across was a night-mare. I ate too much, I drank too much, I turned off the dull film, I tried to sleep and failed. Then the flight became bumpy. "Moderate turbulence," the captain, who had promised not to disturb our sleep, informed us in the darkness. "Nothing serious. I've talked to planes ahead of us and they say that we can expect it all the way to the coast of Ireland. We're at thirty-five thousand feet and I've asked about other altitudes, but we would have to go down to eighteen thousand to find a smooth ride, and I'm afraid we don't have enough fuel to make it to Manchester if we did that. So let's hope it improves a bit. In the meantime I'd ask you all to tighten your seat belts and remain in your seats."

Oh, great!

Then I began to twist and turn nervously, not quite understanding why because I was not afraid of flying, not as such anyway, and I knew that the odds of a crash were less than the odds of my being hit by a car on Virginia Avenue.

Then I realized I was sick, desperately sick, so sick that instead of being afraid I was going to die, I was afraid that I might not die. So this is what motion sickness is like, I told myself as I reached for the vomit bag.

One doesn't get sick in jets, I had been assured by my family. Well, this one did, though the eating and the drinking might have contributed to my problem.

After three or four efforts, all of my food had been returned to the environment. I was exhausted and still vomiting. How many more hours to Manchester?

Where was that damn Seraph when I needed him?

Was there a priest on board who would administer the last rites?

I thought about my ancestors who had come to America in steerage on cholera-and smallpox-infested ships, some of them seasick for the entire voyage. I tried to feel sorry for them, but alas, all I was capable of was feeling sorry for me.

Then the mists drifted down the darkened aisle of the first-class section of the plane (a rattling monster called an MD-11) and enveloped me. I couldn't quite see her, but I knew the woman with the chestnut hair and the twinkling brown eyes was beside me, this time wearing an American Airlines flight attendant's uniform. The two vomit bags disappeared from my hands and she seemed to sit in the unoccupied seat next to me. Briefly maternal arms enveloped me and my head rested on maternal breasts. Lovely maternal breasts.

What took you so long? I think I murmured as I fell into a peaceful sleep.

Later I was awakened by another cabin attendant who

pressed a glass of orange juice into my hand. Early morning light streamed in through the cabin windows.

"Ireland is just below us, Mr. Tobin. We'll be landing in Manchester in twenty minutes."

I had escaped from hell. Gingerly I tasted the orange juice. It stayed down. I was weak and confused and terribly tired. But I was still alive. For which I thank God, the Other, that is, and all the Seraphs, especially the woman with the chestnut hair.

Lancelot du Lac going forth in quest of the Holy Grail and the magic princess did not get motion sick on his great warhorse, did he?

I had been cast in the wrong film.

I tried to reorganize myself. Were the passport and the ticket to Dublin and my reservations for the Shelbourne Hotel (a suite, naturally) in the right pocket?

They were.

And my English pounds and Irish punts in the proper place?

They were.

And my Aero and its equipment in their proper bag?

They were.

What else?

Nothing else. I was beginning to get the hang of this intercontinental travel business.

"Did you fill out your landing card, sir?"

"Landing card?"

"Are you a citizen of the United Kingdom or any other European Union country?"

"Uh, no."

"Then you have to fill out this card."

All I needed was a pen. I must have lost mine when I was sick.

I pushed the button. She came back with a practiced

smile on her face. "Need a pen, sir?"

"Yes, thank you. I'm not staying in England, ma'am. Do I still need to fill this out?"

"All transit passengers who are not of United Kingdom or European Union citizenship must fill out landing cards, sir."

Maureen had warned me that the British immigration inspectors could be pretty nasty, so I resolved I would be polite and respectful. No point getting into a fight, especially when one felt rotten and resentful.

The Brits wanted to know my passport number, so I delved into my pocket and found the passport. I copied the numbers on the card and put the landing card and the passport back in the inside, left-hand pocket. Right?

Right.

The three-motored monster banged into the runway as though it were greatly relieved to have made it across the Atlantic through "moderate" turbulence. Outside in the clear early morning light, England looked pretty much like the United States, though the Manchester International Airport was no match for O'Hare, but then nothing was.

As soon as the bell chimed, announcing that it was all right to stand up, everyone in the plane leaped to their feet and began to pull carry-on luggage out of the overhead bins. Since my roller bag fit under the seat in front of me, I figured I should be in no hurry.

Mistake. I was almost decapitated by the man in the seat behind me who dragged an enormous canvas contraption out of the bin and down on my shoulder. He didn't even apologize.

Brit, probably.

Then a woman threw a large handbag into my face as I tried to stand up, and another elbowed me as I struggled out of my seat and grabed my computer case. It was like playing the New York Knicks, survival of the fittest.

At the door of the plane I felt a poke on my shoulder and spun around, ready and eager to slug whichever Knick had fouled me.

"I think you must have dropped your passport, sir."

It was the cabin attendant—the regular one, not the young woman with the chestnut hair—with my passport and landing card.

I guess the Seraph bunch could not be expected to do everything.

"Thank you very much, ma'am." I smiled my most genial smile. "It was a very nice flight."

"It's always nice," she said, smiling back, "to have an Advantage Platinum member on board."

Even one who gets sick in "moderate" turbulence. But perhaps she didn't even know I was sick.

In the terminal I became completely disoriented. I was alive and well, more or less, I told myself. But my brain and my body were not operating quite the way they should. I had crossed the ocean for the first time in my life, though I was not quite sure why or where I was or why I was here or where I was going or how I might get there.

I'm going to Ireland, I told myself. I am in Manchester Airport. I must find a plane to Dublin. Aer Lingus flight 661. Why Ireland? Because I was on a quest for the pot of gold at the end of the leprechaun's rainbow.

And the fair Sara Anne, who was perhaps a little fool and possibly suicidal.

Not a very good idea. If I had applied myself more, I'd not be here.

I stumbled along with the crowd, tried to exit through a door that was marked "no exit," was reproved by a stern-faced bobby who directed me to the Immigration Control, and then shuffled off in the direction of his imperial finger.

I decided that I didn't like England. I didn't want to stay here. They had no right to delay Lancelot du Lac on his quest.

Guinevere, I remembered, was no better than she had to be. Was the fair Sara Anne promiscuous too?

I shivered as I entered into the Immigration Control hall, a vast barnlike structure with three lines of humans, one moving very rapidly, on more slowly, and one at a snail's pace. The last was pretty clearly for nonwhite travelers from what used to be the Empire. So I joined the fast-moving line through which people were being waved at a rapid rate.

"Passport, sir," said the bored middle-aged woman behind the desk.

"Oh, yes." I searched for my passport and then searched again. It was not in my left-hand inner jacket pocket where it belonged.

"No passport, sir?"

"Just a minute . . . Ah, here it is."

In my right-hand trouser pocket.

"I'm sorry, sir." She sighed. "This line is only for citizens of the United Kingdom and the European Union. You'll be wanting the next line over."

"Huh?"

She smiled. "The long flight does confuse us, doesn't it? You're an American citizen, are you not?"

"Uh, yes, ma'am."

"Then you'll be requiring the next line, thank you very much, sir."

She looked up at the next person—a young woman my

age who frowned at me impatiently and waved a red passport.

Mine was blue.

So I floundered across the hall and back to the end of a very long line for citizens of the American Republic and other assorted foreign types. Except I was an American, wasn't I? Not a foreigner. I was missing something.

It was a long wait. I must have been asleep on my feet.

"That station is open, sir," a firm womanly voice with what I took to be a cockney accent informed me.

"Thank you."

I looked up at her. Dark skin. West Indies probably. With a radiant smile.

The man at the desk was about my father's age and looked seedy and resentful. I gave him my passport and boarding card.

"I'm a little battered, sir," I said with a grin. "I've had a long trip."

He did not look at me but instead scrawled on the card in a blatant and imperialistic effort to suggest that my handwriting wasn't clear enough.

"How long will you be in England, sir?" he asked sharply.

"I'm flying to Dublin in another hour. Transit passenger."

"What will you be doing in Ireland?"

He had no right to ask that question. But I was determined to be polite.

"Visiting relatives."

"Where?"

"Galway."

"Today?"

"No, I'll stay in Dublin for a day."

"Where?"

"Uh, the Shelbourne."

"In Galway?"

"The Great Southern."

"Um. Where were you born?"

"In America, sir."

"Where?"

"Chicago."

"Um, first time abroad, is it?"

"Yes, sir."

"Can I see your ticket?"

I figured I might as well go along. I gave him the ticket.

"I see." He stared suspiciously at my ticket. "EI 661, is it?"

"Yes, sir."

He opened a book about twice the size of a Chicago phone directory and searched through it, comparing numbers with the one on my passport.

I began to suspect that I was being hassled, not through ignorance and incompetence as at the security checkpoint at O'Hare but out of deliberate malice.

He closed the big book and closed my passport. Then he looked around and signaled with a nod of his head to a woman cop who was waiting at the door of the immigration hall. She walked over briskly.

"One of their lot?" she asked.

"Could be."

"One of what?"

"If you'll just come with me for a moment, sir. Just a routine check."

She took my passport and plane ticket from the immigration inspector.

She was young and blond and pretty in her white blouse and blue skirt and copper's hat. But her blue eyes had the same sociopathic emptiness as did the eyes of the

New York Knicks. I was in trouble. I couldn't believe it. I had done nothing wrong. I was being arrested. I'd miss my plane to Dublin. What would happen then? How would I ever get out of this miserable country?

I went along quietly enough, a picture of injured innocence.

"That's all your luggage, sir?"

"Yes."

"We'll have to check to make sure there is no other luggage when all passengers have cleared immigrations and customs just to make sure."

"To make sure of what?"

"Just step in here for a minute, sir, if you please. It is merely a routine check."

The words were polite, the tone was an order.

She ushered me into a small, windowless room that smelled of cigarette smoke. Two uniformed constables, one of them dark-skinned and perhaps Indian or Pakistani, leaned against the wall. Neither of them said a word during my ordeal. The man in charge was short, bald, red-faced, and smoking. A John Bull caricature. I disliked him at once.

"Immigration sent this one along, sir," the woman constable informed him, handing over my passport and tickets. "Thinks he might be one of their lot."

"As well he might." He ignored the passport and the ticket and glared at me. "Transit passenger, is it now?"

"Yes, sir."

"So, Paddy, on your way home to Ireland, are you?"

"No. Sir. My name is Mr. Tobin and I've never been in Ireland. My home is Chicago."

"Get this into your frigging dense Irish head, Paddy, I'll call you what I frigging well please. Understand?"

"No, sir. I do not."

"Typical of one of their lot, isn't he, sir?" the woman observed.

"This all his luggage?"

"So *he* says."

"Well, let's have a look at it, Paddy."

"Open it yourself."

He had not looked at my passport, so he didn't know my name. "Paddy" was a word of derision.

"Keep a civil tongue in your head," the woman warned me. "Or you'll regret it."

"Sorry, I don't scare easily," I replied.

She opened the computer bag, however.

"Well, what have we here?"

"A Compaq Contura Aero subnotebook computer."

"Yeah?" He sneered. "Turn it on for us, that's a good boy, Paddy."

I didn't want them smashing up the computer. So I turned it on.

"Cute," he said. "What's inside that compartment?"

I'm still not sure whether they really thought I was an IRA terrorist or whether they were just engaged in a routine hassle of someone who looked very Irish.

"A battery."

"Well, let's have a look at it!"

I turned off the Aero and removed the battery from the compartment.

"Doesn't look like a battery to me."

"It is."

"Constable." He gestured at the Indian. "Take this out and run it through the tests."

"What's this compartment?"

"Memory."

"Memory of what?"

"Random-access memory. RAM. Part of the system."

"Well, what are you waiting for? Let's have a look at it."

I opened the memory compartment, pried out the four megabytes of RAM very gently, and showed it to him.

On the side that they were merely hassling me was the fact that he didn't damage the computer.

"So what do you do for a living, Paddy?" he demanded, glancing at my passport.

"I respectfully request, sir, that you address me as Mr. Tobin . . . I'm a computer consultant and programmer."

I reached for the scattered parts of my computer to put them back together again.

"Don't touch those things," the woman snapped. "Those could be evidence for one of Her Majesty's prosecutors."

I decided that it was best not to touch them. I didn't want them to damage any of the delicate parts.

"So you play with computers for a living," the man grunted at me. "Made any bombs lately?"

"I wouldn't know how to make bombs."

"Oh, you wouldn't, would you? Well, let's have a look at your other bag."

"Open it and search it yourselves."

"Carolyn, take care of it." He nodded to the woman.

As a Valkyrie attacking my bag she made my sisters look restrained. She threw my clothes all over the floor and then began to feel each one of them as though she were sure there were drugs or explosives contained in every garment.

"You do drugs, Paddy?"

"Again I respectfully request that you call me by my proper name . . . and I certainly do not use narcotics."

The Indian constable came back with my Duracell and shook his head negatively.

"Here's another one of them." The woman held up the other battery triumphantly.

The two outsized batteries had made trouble for me on both sides of the Atlantic. Maybe I should have bought a Hewlett-Packard 420, which ran on regular flashlight batteries.

"Test this one too," the chief ordered.

The Indian shrugged and departed again.

"What have we here!" The woman held up the manila envelope.

"Personal legal documents. I respectfully request that you do not open them."

"Stop trying to make a record against us, Paddy, that's a good lad. We'll deny this ever happened . . . Well, open it, Carolyn! What are you waiting for?"

She opened the larger envelope and spilled the contents on the desk. He picked up each document separately and read it, though I'm sure the legal jargon was beyond him.

"All very impressive, Paddy. Very impressive. Now, what have we here?"

He waved the envelope with the personal message for Ronan Tobin at me.

"A personal legal document for Mr. Ronan Tobin in Galway city. Again I respectfully request that you honor the personal and confidential nature of the document."

I was acting pretty tough, especially given my confused condition and my conviction that this was all a bad dream. What was happening to me?

Grinning up at me, he slit the envelope with a pocket knife and shook it out. A letter and a check tumbled on his desk.

"Well, will you look at this now, Paddy. This is a lot of money for you to be carrying around, isn't it? Money for buying guns to kill British soldiers, is it?"

"I have no notion of the contents of the envelope."

The woman constable's eyes widened as she looked over his shoulder. "Shit! That's a lot of money. We'll certainly hold that for evidence."

"And I think we'll hold Paddy here too. Public Order Act."

"I want to see an American consular official," I said. "I know my rights."

"This isn't America, Paddy. Here you have no rights. And we can hold you for a week without letting you see anyone. You didn't know about that, did you?"

"I know all about British justice, Johnny. I saw *In the Name of the Father*."

"Maybe we can keep you in jail for twenty years too," the woman snapped. "Put him in the van, sir?"

"Yeah, why don't you do just that? Shackle him and let him roast in there for a while and then have one of these louts take him off to headquarters."

This is not happening, I told myself, this is totally not happening. No one in Ireland is expecting me. When my family doesn't hear from me, they'll think it's Toby being irresponsible again. I'll disappear into the British Gulag.

The woman officer grinned at me and drew a set of handcuffs out of her purse.

"Put your hands behind your back, Paddy."

Before she could cuff me, the door of the tiny room swung open and a woman in a fancy uniform with all kinds of silver buttons stormed in.

"All right now," she said in a tone that I thought must be British schoolmarm, "what's going on here?"

Johnny Bull stood up, reluctantly. He was even fatter and shorter than I had expected him to be. "We're holding this man on suspicion of terrorism."

"On what grounds?" she demanded. "And for the love of heaven, Frank, put out that stinking cigarette."

"Yes, ma'am."

He extinguished the cigarette.

"And, Carolyn, put those shackles away. You'll use them only when I tell you to use them. We have not forgotten the last episode with your lot."

This woman was obviously in charge. She was also just as obviously my friend with the chestnut hair, looking a little older this time with strains of silver in her hair, but quite attractive in her uniform. Only then did I notice that the mists were filling up the room.

"Well, Frank, I'm waiting."

"Look at this." He handed her the check.

"So," she said, "a large draft in American dollars made out to a certain Ronan Tobin." She glanced at my passport, as if she didn't know what my name was. Indeed as if she had not produced the passport for me in a somewhat different incarnation.

"A relative, Mr. Tobin?"

"Distant cousin."

"Do you have anything on this Ronan Tobin, Frank?"

"No, ma'am."

"And you didn't look him up? Did you find anything in his clothes, Carolyn? No hashish of the sort you found before?"

"No, ma'am . . . he just looks like a wrong-un."

"Looks Irish, you mean, like both your parents did. What's this material?"

"He says they're parts for his computer."

"Patently that's the case—a Compaq Contura Aero 4/25, unless I am mistaken, Mr. Tobin."

"Yes, ma'am." I tried not to grin.

"Anything else, Frank?"

"There's this letter." He gestured towards Uncle Gerry's letter to Ronan Tobin.

"A personal legal document and you opened it?"

"We suspected him of terrorism."

"Does he look like any of our profiles on IRA terrorists?"

Neither of them replied.

"Come on now, does he?"

"No, ma'am."

"Or any known terrorist?"

"Like one of them, that Lavin fellow, ma'am," the young woman, now close to tears, murmured.

"Come on now, Carolyn. You should know better than that. Joe Lavin is at least half a foot shorter."

"We didn't want to take any chances," Frank said concretely. "You can't tell what those killers will try next."

"So you will hold every harmless Irish American idiot who comes along?"

Hey, wait a minute!

"We have a responsibility," he said stubbornly.

"And we are a nation of law," she replied. "Why must people like you try to convince Americans that we are no better than the Nazis or the Communists? . . . Let me see, Aer Lingus 661, is it?" She glanced at her watch. "We'll have to get you on board that plane, Mr. Tobin."

She picked up the phone on Frank's desk and punched in a number. "Aer Lingus? Commander Warde here of the Special Branch. We have one of your passengers here, a certain G. Patrick Tobin. Regrettable mistake. He's on your 661. We'll bring him over to the gate on a van. Can you hold for five minutes extra? Oh, jolly good, thank you."

"You can pack your bag," Carolyn said to me, sniffling.

"Pack it yourself. You unpacked it."

Commander Warde, as she was presently calling herself, glanced at me, her eyes glinting. "Perhaps not so harmless after all. Here, Mr. Tobin, is it all right if I pack the bag for you?"

Even without my permission, she began to toss my clothes back in. The mists became palpably dense. My clothes fell into perfect positions, just as they had been a hundred years ago when I was leaving Chicago. Second time Rafe or one of his crowd repacked for me. I was pretty sure by now, since I knew how their kind worked, that the envelope with the letter to Ronan Tobin had been resealed.

"Be my guest," I said, going along with the act.

"Constable Mohammed, would you be so kind as to convey our guest to the Aer Lingus Dublin gate."

"Of course, ma'am," he said in what I took to be a flawless Oxford accent. "Immediately."

Commander Warde stamped something on my passport.

"Here's your documents, Mr. Tobin." She smiled. "I think you'll find them all in order. Have a nice time in Ireland, and don't judge Britain by what happened today, I beg you."

Hell, I knew the lines by now.

"I'll judge it by you, Commander Warde."

She actually blushed. "Thank you very much, Mr. Tobin."

In a moment or two I was in the van that waited at the bottom of the stairs on the other side of the dank office. I sat next to Constable Mohammed as he drove rapidly and skillfully across the airport apron to a second terminal and up to a gate where a much smaller plane (than my MD-11 trimotor monster) waited.

"Seven-thirty-seven," Constable Mohammed informed

me. "Rather more crowded than the plane on which you arrived."

"That's all right."

A flight attendant in a green uniform waited at the stairs leading up to the plane. "Welcome to Aer Lingus, Mr. Tobin," she said with a gorgeous smile as I jumped out of the car.

"You were right, sir," Constable Mohammed said as he handed me my two bags, both of which I would have left in the van.

"Oh?"

"Commander Warde is the real England, sir."

The right words came to my lips. "So are you, Constable Mohammed, so are you."

He grinned and saluted. On to the Kyber Pass, Gunga Din.

Someone had arranged so that I had a whole row of seats to myself and hence enough room under the seats in front of me for my roller bag and computer case.

I pulled the Aero out of its case as soon as we were airborne.

>**Go Rafe!**

Not all that bad, Patrick Tobin Junior, not all that bad at all for someone who had a terrible initiation to intercontinental travel. Sorry about that; we have only marginal control over the weather and over British cops as far as that goes.

>**Asmodeus at work?**

Oh, hardly that. Don't worry too much about how we worked it out, though it was a nice bit of improvisation, if I do say so myself.

>**There really is a Commander Warde?**

Oh yes, and that's who your friends thought

*they saw. You, of course, realized that it was
our lovely agent, with some slight changes.
Your friends will be appropriately punished, of
course. Both of those police persons will soon
be walking beats in very unattractive places.
We don't like people interfering with our accounts.*
>But how
*Don't worry about it, Toby, ah, Patrick. You re-
ally don't want to know, and even if you did
know, you'd get a headache trying to figure it
out. On the whole we are pleased with your
behavior. You might be an adequate quester
after all. Pack it yourself, indeed.
Now have a nice Irish breakfast and I'll talk to
you in Dublin.*
End.

The cabin attendant presented me with a cup of tea
that was so strong that I'm sure the spoon bent when I
put it in. She seemed surprised that I wanted neither milk
nor sugar.

"Black as midnight on a moonlit night."

"You don't look like an FBI agent." She laughed.
Twin Peaks. Nice pickup of a fast ground ball.

I ate the nice Irish breakfast and managed to get seconds on the scones. Then I glanced out of the window.
We were over land again, a land that, beneath rapidly
moving low clouds, was incredibly, almost unbearably,
green.

The island home of my forebears.

With my unsuspecting cousins waiting for me.

Including the fair Sara Anne.

And the Seraphs had decided that on the whole I might not be all that bad as Lancelot du Lac. It was, however, still a long, long way to Tipperary, not to mention Galway city.

 𝓘 strode out of the jetway at Dublin Airport like I was indeed Lancelot. Or maybe Galahad. My heart was pure, was it not? More or less? The angel people, the Seraph persons, were useful allies, but I could handle Asmodeus myself, with an occasional minor assist from them.

Madness? Surely, but no one had warned me of the mood swings that follow a long, overnight plane flight and the disruption of the body's time clocks. So I did not realize that when I reached "downtown" (as I thought of it) Dublin, I would want to abandon my quest and return home on the first available plane.

At the bottom of one of the escalators I met a young woman with the most beautiful blue eyes in all the world. She was standing behind the escalator, almost hiding behind it, and her beautiful blue eyes were filled with tears. Ordinarily I avoid such young women because I do not know how to respond to their tears, but this fine Irish morning I was Lancelot or perhaps his Irish counterpart, Art MacConn.

"You have the most beautiful blue eyes in all the world," I told her. "So why are they filled with tears?"

"Me ma and me da are lost," she told me between sniffles.

"What's your name?"

"Ciara."

"Ah, Ciara, is it? Do you have another name?"

"Anne."

"Ah, Ciara Anne, is it? And another name?"

She shook her head and turned away from me, clutching her dolly as if finding her lost parents depended on not letting the dolly go.

Ciara Anne, you see, was no more than two.

"My name is Pat. Shall we go find your parents?"

She nodded vigorously. I swung her into the air and put her on my left shoulder.

"OK, Ciara Anne?"

She giggled and waved her dolly.

So we walked down a corridor and up a flight of stairs and into the Dublin immigration hall. There didn't seem to be much difficulty getting into Ireland. One displayed one's passport with a wave of a hand and walked by the checkpoint.

A woman, in her early forties perhaps, with a quick smile and a charming voice, spotted Ciara as soon as we entered the hall.

"What a fine young woman!" she cooed. "Aren't you the lucky one to have such a beautiful daughter?"

"Her name is Ciara Anne and I'm Pat Tobin and I'm only her temporary mount. Her parents seem to have lost themselves, which is what parents tend to do sometimes.

Would you ever tell them on the PA that it is time for them to be unlost? And doesn't herself here have the prettiest blue eyes in all the world?"

I knew how they talked in this country from reading Roddy Doyle.

"Ah, doesn't she now? Well, Ciara Anne, shall we see if we can find your parents?"

"They're lost," Ciara Anne replied, now happy because all the attention was being lavished on her.

"We have here in the arrivals hall a young woman named Ciara Anne who has the prettiest blue eyes in all the world," the woman spoke into a phone, and her voice boomed throughout Dublin International. "Her parents are lost, but if they come here, she is ready to collect them."

All in the hall turned their heads to see Ciara, still atop my shoulder. Most of them crowded over to admire her. The Irish, I decided, are kid freaks. Maybe it was the best place in the world to be a kid.

"Sure, child, they'll be along in a minute or two," an elderly woman reassured her.

"Parents never stay lost for long," a young man added with a reassuring grin. "Not parents of little girls. Parents of little boys are another matter."

"Aren't those the most gorgeous eyes!"

"And a smile to go with!"

"I wish she were mine!"

Ciara, of course, loved it. Then she screamed, "Mummy!"

A young couple, younger even then me, were pushing through the crowd of Ciara's admirers. I shifted the young person off my shoulder and handed her to her mother, who looked like what Ciara would be in maybe eighteen years.

"Mummy!"

"Ah, my poor sweet little monkey child," Mummy murmured, as she held Ciara Anne tightly. "We'll never get lost on you again."

The two kids, that's all they were, were dressed in old but presentable clothes. Not much money but a lot of self-respect.

"Pat Tobin." I extended my hand to Ciara's father. "I found her looking for you behind an escalator."

"Sean Whelan," he said with a smile and a loud sigh of relief. "Thanks for taking care of her until she found us. We're going to the States. She seems to want to stay in Ireland, poor tyke. She loves to explore. I set her down for a minute to help Brigid with our bags and I looked around and she was gone. We were looking for her on the departure side. I wonder how she got over here."

"Searching for lost parents."

The audience, undiminished in size and interest, laughed enthusiastically.

They were moving to Chicago, where both her parents had jobs waiting for them. I wrote out my phone number and told them to call and leave a message on my voice mail when they had an address and a phone and I'd be back to them.

"If you don't, I'll hunt behind every escalator in Chicago till I find Ciara again."

They laughed, thanked me, and hurried away to catch their flight.

Poor Ireland, I thought as I walked through the Green exit at customs; she loses her bravest and her best every generation because there are no jobs for them here. And lucky America to have a steady supply of such wonderful people. Country folk probably with a college education and lots of ambition. They'll do well and Ciara will grow up a Yank.

There were worse fates, God knows.

I was very proud of myself. Pat Tobin, as I was now to be known, proving that he was a bona fide quester and that he could take care not only of himself but also of beautiful young women too.

So long as they are no older than three at the most—and are flying away in the opposite direction.

However, I didn't need any Seraphic help.

When I climbed out of my cab at the Shelbourne, my mood had changed completely. Clouds had swept in from the west and brought with them a mixture of fog and drizzle. The approach to the city from the airport was gloomy and depressing. Why wasn't I on the plane with Sean and Ciara and the young mother whose name I had not caught? What was I doing in this place that reminded me of nothing if not Gary, Indiana? Or maybe Whiting. Or East Chicago.

"Ah, Mr. Tobin, is it, sir? Welcome to Ireland. Don't we have the finest suite in the hotel set aside for you, Mr. Tobin?"

They really did talk in questions.

"It wouldn't be the bridal suite, now would it?"

"Ah, sir, wouldn't it now? Would you be having a bride for it before your stay in Ireland is over?"

"Ah, that would be telling now, wouldn't it?"

I must watch myself or I would return to America talking as oddly as these people did. Why couldn't they use declarative sentences like civilized people? But no, they had to keep alive their damn archaic culture.

I was shown to the suite by an assistant manager who was pathetically eager for my approval.

"Isn't it nice now, Mr. Tobin? Two rooms, newly refurbished and overlooking the Green?"

I looked out the window. In the time it had taken me to check in and ride up the elevator, Dublin had changed its face completely. Stephen's Green was radiant in sunlight, its flower gardens stunningly lovely.

"Would those be the Wicklow Hills in the distance?"

"Ah, no, sir, aren't those the Dublin Mountains?"

"Great," I said with as much enthusiasm as I could muster. "Splendid suite."

What did I know about hotel suites?

I collapsed on the bed, comfortable enough, and tried to remember what it was I must do before I slept.

Of course. ET must call home. I began to dial the phone next to the bed. Someone knocked at the door.

"Who is it?"

"Housekeeping, Mr. Tobin."

"Come in." I continued to dial.

"Would you be calling America now?"

"I would."

"You know that it's five o'clock in the morning there? Saturday morning."

The woman spoke with a thick brogue. Cork?

How could it be Saturday morning? I had left O'Hare on Friday night, and whole ages of human experience had happened since then. I hung up the phone.

"Thanks for reminding me."

"Is everything all right, Mr. Tobin?"

I became aware of mists in the room. I tried to focus on the housekeeper. It was herself, the woman with the chestnut hair, now looking fifteen years younger than she had in London and very pretty indeed in her starched black dress with white collar and apron. She had acquired a brogue. Good mimics, Rafe had said.

"Just fine."

What did she want now? I wasn't in trouble, was I?

"If I might make a suggestion, Mr. Tobin, wouldn't it better for you to take the tour that is scheduled in fifteen minutes instead of sleeping now?"

"No."

Even angel agents were falling into this damn Irish habit of indirection.

"Isn't the best thing for jet lag sunlight at the noonday hours? And then sleep at the regular Dublin time for sleep?"

"No."

She smiled at me, patiently, sympathetically, kindly.

"Yes it is."

The mists became very thick.

Ah, now, no indirection here. Jacob had wrestled with an angel, but not one as firmly determined as this one was. What was her name anyway? I wanted to ask, but somehow the words wouldn't form on my lips.

"If you say so."

"Haven't I just said so? And wouldn't you want to be eating this bite of lunch before you leave on the tour?"

A tray appeared on the table in the middle of the room, smoked salmon, cold roast beef, tomatoes, and a salad. Maybe she had brought it with her, but who could tell and what did it matter?

"No dessert?"

"Isn't there a sherry trifle? Next to the pot of tea?"

"I guess there is."

"Won't there be a time during the tour when you can phone home?"

"ET must phone home."

She laughed and disappeared. Went out the door, I suppose. In the mists it was a little hard to tell.

I demolished the lunch and wanted more. But nothing

more appeared. I was to be strictly rationed so that I would not eat too much. That's not good for you after an intercontinental flight.

Damn pushy angels.

But the lunch and the return of sunshine swung my mood again. The tour was fun. My guide (personal guide, no group tours for Seraphic Travel) was a young woman maybe ten years older than me with a wedding ring on her finger, a wonderful smile, lots of charm, and apparently limitless knowledge about Dublin. She was, I decided, not an angel but a human.

What a relief!

(I should add a note here about the use of certain English participles and nouns in this story. The Irish language, which I am told is rich in poetry, lacks any truly obscene words. Thus when the Irish, a word-obsessed people, discovered Anglo-Saxon words that were obscene and scatological, they took to them with unrestrained glee. As my priest says, they mean no harm by it. It's a game with them, as is most of the rest of life. Nonetheless, I shall translate the most popular of them as "frig" in this book so as not to offend readers with delicate sensibilities. I should also add that the Irish use the word, indeed all obscene, scatological, and blasphemous words, far more often than I have recorded them. Again they mean no harm by it. For the full richness of this linguistic style, a reader should read the superb novels of Roddy Doyle—and be prepared to watch an increase in socially unacceptable words in his/her own daily conversation.)

We visited the Martello tower at Sandycove; walked Sandymount strand, where James Joyce was prepared to walk into eternity—though the actual locale had been converted into a factory site—St. Patrick's Cathedral (Protestant); Christ Church (also Protestant); Trinity College (once Protestant but now de facto in the hands of the papists) and its famous book of Kells; Donneybrook (Irish yuppies); Glasnevin Cemetery (the grave of Gerard Manley Hopkins as well as the tomb where Leopold Bloom went on that immortal day); and Howth head at the northern end of Dublin Bay where Dean Swift had ridden on the strand (beach) with one of his girlfriends, poor dear man. We even managed to squeeze in the caves at Dalkey (viewed from above) made famous by Flan O'Brien.

"We don't get many requests for this spot, Paddy," my guide (Nessa by name) told me. "Flan O'Brien isn't as famous as your man."

She meant James Joyce. If you concentrated on it, you could figure out without too much difficulty who was the reference when a Mick said, "your man."

"If I ever write a doctoral dissertation, it will be on him."

She was duly impressed, which was the general idea, I fear.

We consumed tea and scones at Bewley's on Grafton Street—our schedule allowed only fifteen minutes—and then found on Clarendon Street, next to the Carmelite church, a public phone that would accept one of the Irish phone credit cards I had somehow acquired. So ET phoned home. Four o'clock Dublin time; that meant ten o'clock A.M. Chicago time.

Everyone told me how inconsiderate I was for waiting till ten. I should have called at least an hour earlier. Mom had been so worried about me.

Doubtless she had. But there would have been some other complaint if I had called earlier. Perhaps I would have been reminded that it was Saturday morning and Americans liked to sleep late on Saturday.

No one seemed interested in my trip (no sympathy for my motion sickness because that was all "psychological" and hence my own fault) or in what I was doing in Dublin.

I told them that I'd call in a couple of days after I met Ronan and the fair Sara Anne. I was warned that the latter was probably seeking an American husband who would free her from Irish poverty.

"They are real connivers, Toby Junior, dear. Believe me, I know all about them."

I did not protest this change of the party line. It never did any good to complain about such changes because I would be told that if I had listened carefully, I would know that what they *really* said was . . .

The tour ended at eight o'clock. I was to leave for Galway the next morning at noon. I ate a fine dinner in the Shelbourne's dining room (river trout) and drank most of a bottle of the best white wine they had. Why not? The Seraphs were picking up the tab, were they not? Why should I ask questions?

Despite the fact that at nine-thirty the sun was still shining brightly (like in a Bergman film about summer), I fell instantly into a sound sleep, helped maybe by the wine.

I was awakened by noise in the corridor and morning sunlight peaking around the thick window shades and drapes. I looked at the clock. Eight o'clock A.M. My train didn't leave till noon. I rolled over to sleep for another hour, but someone knocked at the door.

Herself with breakfast, I bet. Never a moment's peace when you fall into the hands of the angels.

I grabbed for a terry cloth robe and opened the door.

"Good morning, Mr. Tobin. Isn't this the breakfast you ordered?"

Scrambled eggs, rashers (what we would call Canadian

bacon), fruit juice, cereal with strawberries, sweet rolls, brown bread, and tea.

" 'Tis." I sighed.

"Then wouldn't you like to take a nice walk around the Green and maybe back to Bewley's and then across the river to O'Connell Street? Won't it clear your head now?

"Will it?"

"It will."

A copy of the *Irish Times* came with breakfast. "UFF Bomb in Dublin!" the headline screamed. "One Man Shot Dead!"

The Ulster Freedom Fighters, a Protestant equivalent of the Irish Republican Army, had planted a bomb outside the Widow Scanlan's Pub in Pearse Street in central Dublin. Two men had tried to gain entry to a Republican (IRA sympathizers) "ballad session." When two other men barred their entry, the first two opened fire, killing one and wounding the other, and then fled in a car with a Northern registration. The Gardai had discovered a bag at the entrance of the pub with eighteen pounds of commercial explosives. Apparently the detonator had not worked properly. If the bomb had exploded, most of the four hundred people in the pub would have been killed or wounded.

My hands trembling, I put aside the paper. What was I doing in a city where such terror could happen? Thank God no one had been killed. But this was not my city and not my war.

What if this headline made the American papers? My family would be convinced that I was in the pub.

I reached for the phone and then realized it was just after midnight in Chicago—a city where more than nine hundred people, many of them children, had been killed last year. I was safer in Dublin than in Chicago. Indeed I would have been safer in Belfast than in Chicago.

Fat chance of persuading the family of that truth.

And it wasn't my war.

The racing season started in Galway next week. A major cultural and social event, my guidebooks had told me. If I were the UFF, I'd set off some bombs out there.

So why was I going to Galway?

I tried to banish the horror from my mind and turned to breakfast.

I destroyed the latter altogether, as they would say around here, enjoyed a long shower, put on a sport shirt, jeans, and the sport coat my family didn't like ("lovely coat, Mr. Tobin," the concierge told me when I asked directions to the nearest Catholic church), and ventured forth on my prescribed walk.

The weather had changed again. More drizzle and mists—real mists, not Seraphic subterfuge. I returned to my rooms to collect a travel raincoat that I had spotted in my roller bag.

I removed the raincoat from its hanger and returned to the street, filled with people on their way to Sunday Mass. I felt terrible, groggy, disoriented, sullen, depressed. What the hell was I doing in this rain-drenched, word-intoxicated country? On a quest? Don't be ridiculous, Toby. You're a hacker, not a quester. The fair Sara Anne won't be interested in you, and you won't mind that because she will turn out to be ugly and mean-spirited. The trip has been a disaster. You fouled up the encounter with the Manchester police. You were rude to the security guards at O'Hare. You were nasty to your family. All right, you got applause for finding Ciara's parents when they were lost. But they would have turned up anyway.

You're out of your element and over your head.

The UFF will not go after you because you're not worth anything to them or to anyone else. Go home and be the hacker that you're supposed to be.

I walked along the north side of the Green, thinking about DABEST and ways to improve it before going on the market. I would release a shareware version first because that was the ethical thing to do, and then offer a more sophisticated version commercially. I'd need money to do the latter. But I could probably get a bank loan. I wouldn't need ten million dollars.

Uncle Gerry was crazy.

A new twist to the Boolean search procedures occurred to me. I pulled my notebook out of my jacket pocket and, heedless of the surge of people down the street, began to jot down a diagram.

At the top of Grafton Street, across from the so-called Traitors Arch (which honored the Irish who had fought on the side of England in the Boer War), I decided that I'd cross over to the Green and admire the floral arrangements again.

I looked to the right. No traffic.

So without looking to the left, I stumbled into the street. Somewhere a woman screamed. I glanced to my left and saw that a double-deck Dublin bus was less than half a foot away from me and coming fast.

Traffic runs the wrong way here, I told myself as I felt a violent push. Then my head hit something. After that there was only blackness.

7

Far away there is a light at the end of the tunnel. *I am dead. Or dying. Or in purgatory. I am spinning through dark space, a black hole perhaps, toward that light. Is God waiting for me? I tried my best, I really did.*

No, it's not God. Not yet anyway. It's a room, a lighted room. I crash through the outside wall of the room. I feel nothing. I am by myself in the room. Devoid of willpower, I drift around the room, studying it. It is a woman's room, though I am not sure how I know that. Unlike my sisters' rooms at home, it is as neat as a convent cubiculum . . . though I've never been in one of the latter. Three posters on the wall, U2, the Pope, and Michael Jordan. A guitar leans against the wall, and a small Irish harp. Bookshelves are lined neatly with college textbooks. An expensive CD system on the bottom shelf with a stack of disks—mostly classical polyphony and Irish language music.

I shouldn't be in this room. What if the resident returns? I try to leave, but I cannot do so. I'm trapped here. I drift into the *bathroom, also pin-neat, and look into a mirror. There is no reflection. I feel for the wall. My hand rests against it, but I do not touch it. I am out of my own body, a spirit wandering through space and time. I will be released from my fate only on All Hallows' Eve. That's a long time away, I'm not sure how long. Will all my purgatory be spent in this room?*

I continue to float. I must know it is a woman's room because of the beige and gray colors of the bedspread, curtains, and drapes. And the matching throw rugs on the burnished hardwood floor. Perhaps I smell a faint and enticing scent in the room, though I'm not sure I can smell anything. There are no other signs of gender or age or character. I look in the closet. Dresses, slacks, blouses, jeans, sweatshirts, neatly arrayed on hangers. Stylish but not terribly expensive. Woman, all right, probably young woman. Fastidious. With good taste.

I should get out of here before she comes back. With all the power of my will I strive to escape, but it is as if I am chained in a prison cell. What will she think when she returns and finds me?

Yet I want to meet her.

Next to her desk is a computer. Compaq 486 DX65. Lots of power. HP desk jet printer. Expensive system for a student, though I'm not absolutely sure she's a student. I try to turn on the computer but cannot do so. On the desk itself is a stack of paper with music notations written in by hand. She must be a musician of some sort. Perhaps she writes her own songs.

In another closet I find her sports equipment, a basketball, a soccer ball, a wicked-looking stick longer than a hockey stick, expensive golf clubs in a red leather golf bag, a spanking clean green and white soccer uniform, golf shoes, soccer shoes, basketball shoes, also clean, and a prim stack of white sports bras and matching briefs.

I drift out of the closet and realize that I entered it without opening the door and without wanting to do so. This young woman is being revealed to me whether I want to discover her or not.

Angel work?

I don't think so.

What do I know about angels anyway?

Why do I think of them?

Who am I?

In one corner I see a large wood statue of Madonna and child, modern and stylized but astonishingly tender. An unlighted votive candle stands ready to do homage to the Queen of Heaven. Next to Herself, leaning against the wall, is a Raggedy Ann doll, a relic of a childhood that perhaps has only recently been left behind.

Suddenly the door opens and a young woman storms in. I hear the noise and smell the faint scent, now more strongly. Even if touch isn't working, some of my other senses function. Especially my bedazzled eyes.

She is wearing jeans and a red sweatshirt with the word "Galway" on it. She is young and attractive. Extremely attractive. But her face is contorted in pain. She stares right at me, hovering over her bed. She stares through me; perhaps she senses a presence but does not see me. Her pain dissolves into a frown. Then she shrugs and dismisses her puzzlement with a shrug of her well-developed shoulders.

The young woman has stepped out of a modern painting of a woman from classical Irish antiquity. Despite the jeans and the sweatshirt, she is at least a queen and perhaps a goddess, Sionna, or Bionna, or maybe even Bride. She is the most beautiful woman I have ever been close to—a slender, delicately chiseled face, pale cream-colored skin, a flawless complexion innocent of makeup, glossy black hair falling, cleanly and sharply, to her shoulders, deep blue eyes, now dark with agony.

Her body is lithe and willowy rather than voluptuous, the form of a woman athlete rather than a courtesan. She is a little above medium height, her hips have been deftly carved, her legs are slim and long, her waist is slender, her trim breasts are high and sharply defined beneath her sweatshirt, and her movements are quick, graceful, and determined. One would want instantly to take her in one's arms and kiss her. She wouldn't mind, but she wouldn't let the kiss go on too long either. In bed she would be both pliant and demanding, both submissive and athletic, both passionate and brisk.

She radiates an aura of vigorous, enchanting womanliness. She is, I think, a woman of wit and laughter, the kind who will face the terrors of life with an ironic smile and a wisecrack.

How do I know all these truths about her instantly? I don't know how I know, but I know.

Of course, I want her, albeit respectfully and even adoringly. Am I not a young man with the juice of all the hormones running through my bloodstream?

Do I have a bloodstream?

Am I not a young man? I think I am.

But who am I?

That, I don't know.

Alas, my magic woman is torn by suffering. Her beauty is not blighted by her agony. Indeed she becomes even more appealing. But her beauty is less important. Someone must do something about her pain. The scene in which I have been thrust is not one of eros, but of pathos—though eros is there too.

She kicks aside her Air Jordans, pulls off her sweatshirt, sheds her jeans with several skillful tugs, unhooks her bra and throws it on top of the pile of clothes. Then she collapses on her bed, curls up into a fetal knot, and sobs. She is wearing gray underwear, serviceable and sensible. I want to caress her but only to exorcise her pain. Well, mostly to exorcise her pain.

She uncurls herself and, still sobbing, bounces off the bed. She throws the bra and sweatshirt into a basket in the bathroom, hangs up the jeans in her closet, and places the Air Jordans at *the end of a small line of shoes. Then she returns to her fetal knot.*

I admire her breasts and her belly and her rear end as she performs these rituals of a neatness that is more powerful than pain, but I feel no arousal.

I also note the solid muscles in her arms and calves and thighs and belly. No frail maiden, this one. She surely works out. Probably does martial arts too.

Are spirits like me, whoever I am, capable of arousal? Probably not.

Yet her breasts are undeniably gorgeous, young, fresh, full, challenging. I reach out to touch her, but I cannot.

I seem to hover just above her, so close that I see the tiny imperfections on the skin of her back. I am a protector, not a lover. Not yet a lover anyway, and maybe, given my spirit nature, never a lover.

In my role of protector I try to speak to her, to tell her that all will be well, that I will make the hurt go away.

Of course, she cannot hear me.

Then she stops sobbing and sits up on the side of the bed, her head bowed in thought. I am sitting next to her. I try to help her think.

She bounces off the bed and strides into the bathroom. She returns with a glass of water and a bottle of pills. She sits on the side of the bed and puts the glass on the floor. She pours the pills into her hand and considers them thoughtfully.

She is thinking of suicide. My beautiful one, please don't do it. Your life is ahead of you. You have much to live for. Don't cut it short. All the agony will go away. You must live and love and have children and bring joy to all who know you. Don't waste your existence. Don't! Don't!

I bend all the power of my will to communicate my affection and adoration to her, but she cannot hear me. If my pleas are penetrating her soul, they seem to have no effect. She closes her hand around the pills and reaches for the glass. She lifts the glass towards her lips. Then she returns it to the floor and opens her fist so that she can ponder the pills again.

Don't! Don't! Don't!

Choose life, not death, I beg her in the words of a Scripture passage whose source I had long since forgotten.

Then I have an idea. I bend all my weak energies not towards the child's agonized soul but towards the glass of water. I will that it tip over. I put all the powers of my shadowy being into this effort.

Nothing happens.

I try again. I beg it to move. I beg whatever power has brought me to this room and this woman to help me.

The glass does not tip, but it does move, only a little at first, and then when I make a titanic effort, it slides an inch, maybe an inch and a half.

She has clenched her fist again and is reaching for the glass. It's not quite where she left it. She probes for it and then accidentally knocks it over. Water trickles across the light blue throw rug and onto the hardwood floor.

"Shite," she exclaims.

Then, astonishingly, she begins to laugh. She throws the pills on the floor and dashes back to the bathroom. She emerges with a towel and dabs at the circle of water. She is still laughing, presumably at herself.

She retrieves the pills, returns them to the bottle, replaces the cap, and bounces off to the bathroom, the pills in one hand, the wet towel in the other.

I remain on the floor next to her bed, utterly exhausted. Have I saved her life with my Herculean efforts or did she really want to live?

She comes back to her bedroom, a thin robe now over her briefs and her bare breasts, much to my dismay. She is still laughing. She kneels in front of the Madonna.

"I know that I'm a terrible eejit, not worth a pissant thing, nothing but a frigging asshole," she says, giggling. "Just the same, I'm glad you made me knock over that glass."

"Hey," I claim, "I did it, not Herself."

My woman then babbles fervently at the statue in a foreign language.

Gorgeous, she is, but also flaky.

Then she bounces off her knees, picks up the small Irish harp, and returns to the side of her bed. I am happy to note that the front of her robe slips open and I can worship her breasts again.

I sit at her feet, my head resting against her thigh (though I cannot feel her thigh and she cannot feel my head), and listen as she sings songs in a strange language, songs that are both melancholy and joyful.

Was I to stay in her room forever? A voyeur incapable of arousal? There could be worse purgatories, could there not?

I will protect you always, I swear to her, rather foolishly.

The room fades for a moment and then clarifies itself. I sense that soon I will leave her. I am not in hell. I am not in purgatory. I am going to live. I must never forget the pathos and the laughter of this bizarre scene. Yet I know somehow that as soon as I leave her, it will be all erased from my memory, like an unremembered dream.

Maybe some traces of it will remain in my unconscious to be stirred up again someday.

She sighs loudly, springs off the bed, returns the harp to its assigned place, tosses the robe on the bed, and then, fingers on the elastic band of her briefs, stares at me as I am being drawn out of the room. She frowns as she peers in my direction, not quite seeing me, but perhaps sensing that she's not alone.

"Did you tell a frigging angel to take care of me?" she says, presumably to the Madonna. "Sure, wouldn't that be just like you?"

She discards the briefs and for a tiny fraction of a second I am granted a vision of her full womanly beauty before I am dragged unceremoniously down the long, black tunnel. I don't mind. Any more of that vision would destroy me altogether.

I must remember this, I repeat to myself. I must not forget it.

I know that I will forget it.

Later, much later, I am somewhere else in the darkness, consumed now by my own fears and pain. But I am being healed. I am resting comfortably on firm breasts as lovely as those of . . . I can't remember whose. Where have I been? What wonders have I seen?

I don't have a clue.

I nestle against the breasts, maternal indeed, but not totally maternal. Someone is singing a lullaby to me, a song of peace and serenity and affection. I am recovering from whatever is wrong with me. I must relax and permit the healing and do as I am told. Why fight it?

Then the darkness closes in on me again.

⚜8⚜

I opened my eyes slowly and carefully. Was I in heaven?

No, I was in the Shelbourne Hotel. Battered and bruised, I presumed, but still alive. I tried to move my legs and arms.

"Everything is all right, Paddy."

" 'Tis yourself."

" 'Tis."

"Rae."

"You sure are swift, G. Patrick Tobin Junior."

"I figured you were womanly all along." I closed my eyes. "Especially when you wouldn't tell me your gender that first day. Calling you Rae was a slip."

She was no longer dressed in her housekeeper's uniform. Now she was wearing a smart spring frock, pale green with long sleeves and a high neck, white gloves and white shoes. The dress, drawn together tightly at her waist by a broad white belt, clung subtly to her body, leaving no doubt about her various curves. Sunday Mass dress for a proper young matron, chaste enough so that no one could complain and sexy enough so that she would distract all the men in the church.

I knew the type very well since they had been distracting me at St. Hilary's for years.

"Why did you conclude I was womanly?"

"You were, that's all. Too much sympathy and concern to be a man, maybe. Too much maternal care, maybe. Too bossy. Anyway, I just knew."

"At times you may not be all that swift, but you are also a very perceptive and sensitive young man. We cannot, of course, lie about our gender, especially when we appear in analogues like my present one. We assumed that you would figure out that I was Rafe or, as you now know, more appropriately Rae."

She had taken off my clothes before she put me to bed, leaving me, I noted, my shorts. Thanks.

"You deceived the other guy when you played that Azarias bit."

"Not really."

"He knew you were, ah, a bearer of life?"

"Well, after we bathed together, he did."

"What?" I opened both eyes.

"The young fool was prepared to go to meet his bride with the smell of the desert upon him. So I pushed him into a pond and then jumped in after him."

"Scared the hell out of him when he found out what you are?"

She lifted a shoulder dismissively. "He needed instruction on the life-bearers of his species. Needless to say, he did not attempt to put a hand on me. We do not mate with your species, not anymore at any rate."

"Oh . . . but the book doesn't say you were a womanly angel."

"Can you imagine the scandal such a fact would have created in that patriarchal age? It would offend many of your higher Catholic clerics even today."

"Was Tobit like me?"

"He was not a bad youth, actually, but not nearly as perceptive as some of our other clients."

"I can be pretty unreceptive." I closed my eyes again.

"No way, Toby Tobin."

"Paddy."

"Sorry . . . I repeat, no way."

I opened both eyes and considered her. She really was a knockout. Angels, I assumed, were always lovely.

"I understand . . . It would be an unforgettable experience, however."

She seemed to blush. "It will do no good to appeal to my vanity."

"Is that what you really look like?"

"Of course not. What you see is merely an analogue; it's what I would look like if I were a member of your species. If you could see the way I really am, I would blind you at least temporarily and terrify half the population of Dublin."

"So the analogue is not really you?"

"It is me but not totally me."

Made a lot of sense, didn't it?

"So you're not really sitting over there in that easy chair."

"Of course I am. Not all of me is here, however."

"You're impassable?"

"You do remember your catechism, don't you?"

"So you're an illusion?"

"You simply don't get it, do you, Paddy?"

She rose from the chair, walked over to the bed, and placed her hand on my forehead. It was a real hand, gentle, kind, affectionate, healing. She could have left that hand on my forehead for the rest of my life and I wouldn't have minded.

Instead she strode back to the easy chair and thus provided me with an opportunity to admire, once again, her ample and charming hindquarters.

"Judging by the analogue, you must be one of the most beautiful of all the angels," I said as she sat in the chair again and demurely rearranged her skirt and primly crossed her legs. "Gorgeous rear view, too."

That made her squirm. "It will do you no good, I repeat, Paddy Tobin, to attempt to flatter my vanity by implicitly praising my ass, which, of course, you should admire, though discreetly. But thank you for the compliment."

"You kind of broke one of your own rules out there, didn't you? I thought you said that you don't pull people out of the path of cars and buses."

She lifted her right shoulder again, a gesture of dismissal with which I would become familiar.

"You could become a problem with your contentiousness, Paddy. In fact, we make exceptions sometimes."

"You pushed me, didn't you?"

"Certainly. Your clumsiness, excused partially by jet lag, didn't give me time to do much else. Hence you hit the sidewalk before I could catch you and suffered your injuries, from which you are now recovering nicely."

"Did the bus hit you?"

"How could the bus hit me? I told you we have ethereal bodies. We pass through walls, and buses pass through us."

She raised her right shoulder again.

That made me shiver.

"Why didn't you stop me before I stepped in front of the bus?"

She sighed loudly. "As I have tried to tell you before, Paddy Tobin, we know a lot and can do a lot. But we don't know everything and we can't do everything. You might keep that in mind in the future. We can't protect you from everything, especially from your own stupidity. How was I supposed to know you were about to do something foolish?"

"Sorry . . . Well, thanks for saving my life. I appreciate it."

She beamed. "You're welcome, Paddy, but you must be wary of traffic in this country. Look both ways before you step off the curb."

"Yes, Mummy."

We both laughed. Not only a sexy angel but a companionable one. I decided I liked Rae.

"There wasn't any mist."

She frowned impatiently. "There was no time for mists. You were such an eejit that I had to act with all the speed I possessed, which, as you know, is considerable."

She was already talking like she was Irish. But then she had said that they were skillful mimics.

"What do the mists mean?"

"We really must end this catechism shortly and get you off to Galway. The mists mean that we have moved back and forth across a—how should I put it—a plane so as to operate more effectively."

"Another cosmos?"

"But one that is very close, almost next door, so to speak." She stood up, languidly, sensuously. Or so it seemed.

Lucky Tobias, I thought. Even more lucky, her "companion."

"I can't read your mind, Paddy. But I'm not sure I like the expression on your face. I am not to be evaluated sexually every time you look at me. Once is enough, do you understand?"

"Yes, you are," I replied. "Otherwise you wouldn't appear in an analogue which was so attractive."

She laughed and then smiled at me. "I did tell you we were terribly vain, didn't I?"

"I could stop taking showers."

She blushed deeply. So you can embarrass an angel. And banter with one.

"Paddy, you are becoming impossible. Please stop staring at my boobs and get out of bed. We have to send you off to Galway."

Embarrassing an angel was fun. I didn't move from the bed. She held most of the cards, but she was a creature too, and I could win a few points in bantering with her.

"Don't give me that, woman. If I didn't stare at them, you'd be offended. Does your kind—"

"Very well, we will end this part of the conversation which you are enjoying so much."

She walked over to the window of my bedroom and opened a drape a few inches. The slit revealed more mists and rain.

"Among my kind the bearers of life do provide nourishment for the progeny. Our givers of life do admire the means of this nourishment with the obsessive fixations that are not unlike the human male's fetish for the female's breasts. More obsessively perhaps. They will simply not . . . Well, we also pretend to consider this fixation childish but rather enjoy it so long as it is not too obvious. The Other repeats this phenomena in many rational species because She nourishes everyone and perhaps because She has a sense of humor. Does that satisfy your prurient curiosity, Paddy Tobin Junior?"

"And if your, uh, givers of life don't admire you enough, you become highly incensed?"

She leaned against the drapes and considered me with something like amused affection.

"You know, Paddy Tobin, you're rather good at this game, better than I would have expected given your past performance. It is good for you to be away from your family. But I am beginning to have some sympathy for that poor child out in Galway."

"Sara Anne."

"Fair Sara Anne." She lifted a tiny white hat from my dresser, turned to the mirror, and fitted it adroitly to her chestnut curls. All ready for Sunday Mass now. "Do you feel all right?"

"I guess, a little tired maybe."

"No headache?"

"I don't think so. What happened?"

"Concussion. Moderate."

"You fixed me up?"

She turned away from the mirror. "You remember what my name means?"

"Sure. God heals. You're probably some kind of medical doctor in your own species. Thanks. You did a good job."

"Fine. Now, get out of bed and take a shower and off with you to Galway." She turned towards the door.

I picked up a terry cloth robe she had left on a chair next to my head and quickly put it on.

"Rae . . ."

"Yes?" She turned towards me with an impatient frown.

"I'll never forget the peace and happiness of resting

against your wonderful breasts while you healed me. You're a very impressive woman, er, giver of life or whatever."

She leaned against the door, flattered and embarrassed, her face a deep scarlet.

"You are a sweet boy, Toby, uh, Paddy. Thank you . . . AND does it make you happy to know that you can discomfit a Seraph?"

"Sure does."

"You are impossible! . . . By the way, can you remember anything that went on in your brain immediately after your fall? We noted some unusual brain waves."

I thought about it. "Not really. If there was something there, it was like a dream in the middle of night. Vague images maybe, but I can't give them a name."

She nodded. "No big problem. Now, off with you to Galway and to the fair Sara Anne, who may turn out to be a fortunate young woman after all."

She opened the door and prepared to step into whatever other dimension of reality her kind did Sunday worship.

"Can we talk for another minute, Rae?"

I was standing at the window, looking out at the now driving rain, which obscured the monument to Wolfe Tone just across the street on the corner of the Green (the "Wolfehenge," Dubliners called it). A comparison of this ugly city with Gary, Indiana, was unfair to Gary.

"Certainly."

She closed the door and returned to the chair in which she had been sitting when I had awakened.

"Do I have to go to Galway?"

"*Have to?* I thought you wanted to."

"Look, Rae. I'm not cut out for a grail quest, which is what we're up to, aren't we?"

"Something like that." She nodded in agreement.

"I'm a hacker and a nerd and a failure with women. I'm also absentminded, tongue-tied, and clumsy. I'm not Lancelot du Lac or Art MacConn. I'm Don Quixote."

"No, Roxinate. Or Sancho."

"You know what I mean. I'll make a fool out of myself. And I hate this country and its too clever people and all their fancy use and abuse of language. I want to go home where I belong."

"You fear the fair Sara Anne?"

"I guess that's right. There's no point in any of it. The only reason I'm here and alive is that you and your crowd have had to work overtime. Can I get out of it all?"

"Of course you can."

"You said that your firm never loses an account."

"That's certainly true," she said, choosing her words carefully. "You'll always be one of our accounts. But we don't take away anyone's freedom to terminate the quest. Journey. Pilgrimage. Whatever. We may equivocate, cajole, manipulate, improvise, even cheat a little without actually lying. But like the Other—who often seems to us to be the Great Improviser—we do not violate freedom. We are not your family, Paddy. At the end of the day, we leave you free to make your own choices. Completely free, at least as completely free as any creature can be."

"I want to go home."

She stood up. "Your choice, Paddy. I won't try to argue with you. The tickets are here on your coffee table. The train to Galway leaves the Heuston Street station at four o'clock. That leaves you two hours . . . well . . ." She glanced at the exquisite watch on her left wrist. "An hour and a half to make your decision. We can arrange for you to return to Chicago tomorrow morning. By the way, the weather will clear by the time the train reaches the Shannon River."

"You said you didn't know the future."

"We can watch weather fronts, however."

"Oh."

She smiled at me, sadly, affectionately, tenderly.

"Go with God, Paddy. Wherever you go."

She raised her hand in benediction and slipped out the doorway.

A bit of mist. And she was gone.

To another plane of being, no doubt.

9

>Go Rae.

The Net paused for a couple of moments while its various gophers searched for her.

Yes, Paddy.

>I'm on the train to Galway.

I know where you are, Paddy. Lust. Desire. Need. Whatever.

>Do you know why?

Hormones, I presume.

>What if she would actually like me?

Do you think that possible?

>But if she would and I didn't go, I might miss something wonderful.

Someone wonderful.

>Yeah. I'd never forgive myself for the rest of my life.

So you want to find out if there's a remote possibility that she'd find you appealing?

>Not much of a quest motivation, is it?
You'd be surprised how effective it is for grail
searchers. The "what if" argument.
>But what if she doesn't like me?
Then, G. Patrick Tobin Junior, she would have
very poor taste. End.
>Is she as good-looking as you are?
Paddy, will you please stop acting like a horny
teenager? It's her character and personality
that really matter.
>I know that. But . . .
No human woman can possibly be as attractive
as I am in my reality. As for the analogue,
over which you slobbered, however charm-
ingly, earlier this afternoon, it pains me to say
it, but the fair Sara Anne is far more lovely,
and not merely because she is very young.
Now, does that truth give your testosterone
enough of a charge to prevent you from get-
ting off the train in Tullamore?
>I guess so.
And try to remember, if your perpetual state
of tumescence permits, that she is far more
fragile than I am.
>You're fragile, Rae?
You know that I am, Toby, or you wouldn't be
able to flatter me so effectively. All creatures
are fragile. End and this time I really mean it.
>My name is Pat now. Or Paddy over here, I
guess.
All right.

The screen went blank. She'd shut off the Aero.

The train to Galway leaves from Heuston Street Station
and wends its way along the Liffey and the Grand Canal
as it pokes tentatively towards the Shannon River and the

West of Ireland—Tir-Na-Og, the promised land in the west. Fog was still rolling over the land, so I couldn't appreciate the scenery much, though the green fields and the gentle hills would certainly be lovely when bathed by sunshine. Land where the fairy folk would love to dance and play.

The train was mostly empty.

"Sure, aren't we going into the West to pick up all the poor lads and lassies who have to come back from their homes tonight to their jobs in Dublin?"

"Shorter trip than from New York or Chicago."

"Ah, but wouldn't many of them be willing to make that trip if they could?"

The real Tir-Na-Og was America as it always was. Poor kids. But with a 15 percent unemployment rate, what could they do?

I returned to guidebooks about Galway that had turned up in my computer bag. It sounded like a grim, gray city which had seen its best days before Cromwell had paid his genocidal visit to Ireland and had never quite recovered from that visit.

I was distracted by images of the fair Sara Anne, who must really be fair. And I worried about Rae, damn her. I opened the Aero, turned it on, and gave the usual instruction.

>**Go Rae**
Go away, Toby.
>**Paddy**
All right. Go away, I'm busy.
>**I'm worried about you.**
WHAT?
>**You said that you were fragile. I know angels die eventually, but you're a young angel with a husband and kids, uh, a companion and**

progeny. I don't want you taking any chances for my sake. Is that clear?

Nothing for a moment.

You are such a sweet, thoughtful boy, Paddy Tobin, that you have made me cry.
>Gosh!
Give me a moment to bring my emotions under control.
>Sure.

I gave her a moment.

So now you know that you can make a Seraph weep as well as blush?
>It makes you all the more attractive.
Stop that Irish blarney! As to your question, I will not take foolish chances. I never do. There is not much that can actually kill us short of our time. Random bursts of energy, a few other such things. My progenitor was killed by one such burst. My life bearer has another companion, of course: We cannot live alone. It was long ago, but we all still miss him.
>You expect to see him again.
We hope to. The Other is good and loving.
>What was his name?

Pause.

I will tell you his name, but I will tolerate none of your foolish human folklore. My progenitor was a great and wonderful spirit. He died protecting humans. The stories about him are slanderous. You should remember that in the book of Job even Satan was a member of the Other's court. Understand?
>Sure.
All right. He was called—and I'm sure still is called—the Carrier of Light.
>Lucifer. And he was one of the good guys! I

bet he and Michael were close friends.
*Now you've made me cry again. If that Sara
Anne bitch doesn't adore you, I'll break her little neck.*
>No you won't.
*Of course not. You are too sensitive for a mere
human, Paddy. And much too tender. But it
makes you very likable. She'll like you. She'll
have to like you. Just remember that you can
never be too tender. End.*
>I want no risks taken, Rae. None, do you
hear? You're too important to get hurt taking
care of me.

Silence.

*I can take care of myself, Paddy. But I prom-
ise I won't take any unnecessary risks. Does
that not satisfy you?*
>No risks at all.
*Life is a risk, Paddy. I'll take no more than you
have taken and will take. Fair enough?*
>OK.
*Now, try to leave me alone for a little while.
End.*

I turned off the Aero. What the hell was I doing? Trying
to protect an angel? A Seraph? Someone who had been
around a thousand years? No, thousands of years? How
dumb could a guy be?

Yet she said that I had made her blush and made her
cry. I also had made her smile and laugh. That was not
the advance billing for G. Patrick Tobin Junior. He was
no good with women, tongue-tied, clumsy, stupid.

Well, that was with human women. With ET women
maybe I was a little better. Would I be able to play the

same game with the fair Sara Anne as I had played almost
instinctively with Rae?

Probably not, but it was worth a try.

I was emotionally exhausted. How had that happened?
Had Rae's emotions transferred to me? Was I in love with
her and she with me?

Well, hardly. Or not in the ordinary sense of the word.
But we were linked to one another in some strange and
wonderful pattern of love. She was not a mother or a
daughter or a wife or a date. She was what? A guardian
angel, of course. Why fight it, even if it was emotionally
exhausting? Enjoy it while you can.

Enjoy the fair Sara Anne while I could?

Why the hell not?

Then, as the fog lifted and sun seemed to be considering the possibility that it was safe to shine on Ireland
again, I felt suddenly confident in my quest. Like Tobias,
I had learned a lot about human women in the last couple of hours.

Damn it, that was the point of the whole business! She
had deliberately taught me some lessons. Let me teach
myself some lessons.

Tobias was the lucky one. He got to swim in the nude
with her for his lessons. All I got to do was encounter her
emotions. And feel them.

No, come to think of it, I was the lucky one.

Had she been making love with her "companion"
when I interrupted her the last time? What a goof I must
have seemed to both of them. They probably had a good
laugh at my expense as they kept on screwing.

Or was she in the railroad car with me? Maybe with
him. Making love in a public place. On a train. Terrible
creatures, those Seraphs.

And terrible Patrick Tobin, having those obscene fantasies.

But the companion was a lucky fellow indeed.

>Rae, I don't want to bother you again if you're busy.

That's all right, Paddy.

>It's taken your kind a long time to end the conflicts here. And you've not really ended them yet.

They are a difficult and contentious people around here, G. Patrick Tobin Junior, however admirable they may be in many ways. They are good at loving and good at hating. We've been working on it for seven hundred years, if you must know. And those who have oppressed them are no bargain either, to put it mildly. We make progress. As I said, we can't do everything. And I will say once again that you are too perceptive for your own good.

>Were you involved in stopping that explosion in Pearse Street last night just because you were here with me? And why didn't you save the one man's life?

I decline to answer the first question because it implies metaphysical assumptions that are beyond explanation. As to the second, I have told you before there are many things we can't do.

>You always say "we." Are there others with you working on my case?

I'm not alone if that's what you mean. We rarely work alone. But there are not a legion of us either.

>Speaking of legions, when Jesus was talking to Pontius Pilate . . .

There were legions available then, you'd bet-

*ter believe. But the signal was never given.
The Other had different and, as it turns out,
much wiser plans.*
>Does your family travel with you?
*We are intensely social beings, Paddy Tobin, as
I think I have told you already. "Travel" is not
the appropriate word. However, you should
not add to your burden of concerns the possibility that I am separated from my companion
and my progeny. We are bonded together
much too powerfully for us to permit that to
happen.*
>Good. If, ah, if I should interrupt you at the
wrong time, like I think I did before, brush me
off.

Silence. Was she laughing at me?

*You have a dirty mind, G. Patrick Tobin Junior.
As you must know, that is an utterly inappropriate, if characteristically well-intentioned,
remark. My intimate life should not concern
you. When I'm really busy in various matters, I
will inform you that you should try to contact
me later. I will also ask you to restrain your
obscene imagination, since it seems to be
functioning at any and all times. You should
note that there are many different concerns
that might occupy my attention other than
mating.*
>You're laughing at me?
But affectionately.
>Do I get to meet them?
Who?
>Your family. He's a lucky person, that Seraph
companion of yours.
*I will tell him that. He'll be delighted to know
that you approve his taste.*
>But do I get to meet him?

Maybe. We'll see.
>*Yes, Mummy . . . What did he think of your caper with Tobit?*
I will not, I repeat, not tolerate your intrusions into my personal and intimate life. I am the Seraph, the guardian, you are the guarded. Now, keep your horny human fantasy life under control. Understand?
>*Yes, ma'am.*
As a matter of fact, I was not bonded then. Moreover, he thought it was a somewhat unusual, but in the event, highly effective, strategy. Our kind is little troubled by jealousy. My companion trusts me completely. As I trust him completely. Clear?
>*Yes, ma'am.*
Now devote your fantasy life to the fair Sara Anne until we arrive in Galway. Get it?
>*Yes, ma'am. And all you guys stop laughing at me, hear?*
End.

The screen went dead. So I closed my book and my eyes as we (the train and I and all possible passengers, including Seraphs) lurched on towards Galway and the fair Sarah Anne and ten million dollars.

I had hardly thought about the money. She was important. The money didn't matter.

How could I think a woman was important when I had never met her and knew nothing about her? Another pipe dream. Like the battles in the medieval room on Internet.

Were the Seraph bunch actually on the train? She'd said "till we get to Galway," had she not?

I could not sleep, and no images of the grail woman

came into my head. So I returned to my guidebooks. And wondered about the threat of explosions like the one last night at the Widow Scanlan's Pub. Presumably Rae read the Irish papers too, so there was nothing really to worry about.

Was there?

❦10❧

At Athlone on the Shannon River, the gate to the West of Ireland, the real Ireland (everything to the east being West Britain), two young women boarded the train and bounced into the seat across from me, tall, late-adolescent types (maybe a year or two older than Meg), one blond and fair and the other auburn and dark. Clad in jeans and T-shirts (which proclaimed their affiliation with UCG—University College, Galway), innocent of makeup, carrying student backpacks, and vigorously chewing gum, they giggled at me and, not distracting me at my programming work on my notebook, decided to ignore me and to continue their babble with one another.

One wanted to be a teacher, the other a journalist. They were going back to school for the final tests. Both would work in Europe during the summer. Neither was satisfied with her current gentleman friend, and both swore they had no intention of "living in sin."

The latter phrase was spoken with a derisive snort.

"Are you the new fella who's going to teach the course in computer programming this summer?" one of them said.

They were talking to me, but I pretended to ignore them.

"You're a Yank, aren't you?"

I gave it up.

"Irish-American actually," I said. "And no, worse luck for me, I'll not be teaching at UCG . . . My name is Pat Tobin."

One of them was Neve and the other was Fionna.

"We noticed you were working on a program," Neve, the blonde, said, now very shy.

" 'Tis true," I said, saved my work, and turned off the Aero. "I'm working on a program for the Internet."

" 'Tis too difficult to use altogether," Fionna insisted.

"Absolutely."

I explained DABEST to them. They actually knew what I was talking about.

"You wouldn't be a relative of Sara Tobin, would you now?"

"Sara Tobin?"

"She's a year ahead of us in school, finishing her second year."

My intended couldn't be this young, could she? And did she chew gum?

"Most beautiful woman in the university."

"Really?"

"And terribly talented. And sweet, too. Most of the time."

"Unless she's in one of her moods."

"Or too much of the drink taken."

"She went to the convent up at Kylemore. Maybe the

change to UCG was too much for her."

"She's doing a line with that eejit Oisin, isn't she?"

The name was pronounced Oh-SHEEN. I learned the spelling later.

"He's doing a line with her. Or trying to. She doesn't fancy him at all."

"Fair play to her. He's a frigging amadan."

"Doesn't she have a terrible temper too?"

"Doesn't she now?"

"Beautiful and troubled, hot-tempered and named Tobin?" I summarized the conversation.

"And fierce at soccer too . . . Would you want to meet her?"

"If I'm in Galway long enough, I'm sure I will."

They both giggled at that.

We talked about the two countries, schools, employment opportunities in Ireland, and the terrible blow to Galway when Digital closed. No fool either of these young women, halfway between Meg and Sara in age.

I had charmed them. How had that happened?

The Irish Rail train from Dublin limps into Galway from the south. You catch glimpses of the fabled bay, blue in the afternoon sunlight (7:00 P.M. in June is still early afternoon). Bathed in a warm springtime glow, the approaches to the city are quite impressive, not the gray city I had been led to expect, but colorful and picturesque with row upon row of new and attractive town houses.

A lot better, I told myself, than Chicago when you come in from around the south end of the lake. I would suspend judgment on Galway city.

"Would you believe the change in the last year?" Neve asked her friend.

"Frigging brill."

"How so?" I asked.

"Isn't it the fastest-growing city in Europe?"

"And doesn't it get more beautiful every month?"

The railway station, dark, dirty, and smelly, was not prepossessing, and the kids waiting to board the train for the return to Dublin were grim-faced and quiet, not what one expects from a crowd of young Micks. On the other hand, it was Sunday and their weekend at home was over. The yuppie bars in Chicago were not all that cheerful on Sunday night either.

I helped my two young friends off the train and promised that I would see them "around" in Galway. I hoped that Rae had watched me turn on the charm.

I climbed down a flight of steps to the Great Southern Hotel, built a century and a half ago next to the station (and hence called locally, I would learn, the "Railway Hotel"). It was a dour Victorian building, made of somber gray granite, which, when it was raining, might well look like a prison. However, the sunlight shining on the John F. Kennedy Park outside the hotel illumined it and the quaint old square (Eyre Square), which I would have to explore if I stayed long enough.

Let the charm of the city work on you, I told myself sternly.

There was a lot of charm at the reception desk.

"Good afternoon, Mr. Tobin," the pretty redhead said. "It's from Chicago, you are?"

Her nameplate said she was called Nuala. She wore a red suit and black and white polka-dot blouse, apparently a uniform.

"Home of Michael Jordan and the Chicago Bulls."

Behind her was a painting of the wives of fishermen from the Claddagh (as in the "moon comes up over" in Galway Bay) in bright red shawls.

"Isn't he playing for the White Sox now?"

"Isn't that the truth?"

Serves you right, Paddy Tobin. Don't be fresh with the local colleens. They're quicker than you'd ever dream of being.

"A suite, is it, Mr. Tobin? For two weeks? Facing the square? And your man's statue?"

Two weeks! How long did Rae expect me to stay?

" 'Tis." I sighed. "I'm looking forward to falling in love with Galway."

"Isn't that an easy thing to do? Is that all your luggage?"

"I travel light."

"You do that, don't you?"

She was so cheerful and pretty that I couldn't find it in my heart to be angry at her for the damn Irish interrogative sentences.

She conducted me to my room, opened the drapes, pointed out JFK's statue at the far end of the square, next to the "Brown Door" (taken from the home of one of Galway's famed merchant families before it was leveled), the new cathedral in the distance (at which she turned up her pert nose), and High Street running at a slant away from the park and into Shop Street.

"You might want to do some shopping there tomorrow," she said. "There's some fine bookstores and a couple of very good jewelry stores."

"The books at least."

"Have a pleasant stay in Galway, Mr. Tobin."

"If all of it is as pleasant as the first five minutes, it will be very pleasant indeed."

She laughed cheerfully. "You must have stopped in Cork and kissed the stone on the way up."

Well, the banter I had practiced with Rae and tried out

on Neve and Fionna had won me at least one radiant
smile. Not bad for starters.

I put my roller bag on the bed and retrieved my Aero.
>Go Rae.
*You did charm that one, Paddy, without half
trying. To say nothing of those poor children
on the train. I wonder if we have created a
Frankenstein monster for ourselves. Now, turn
this off and go find Ronan Tobin's house.*
>I don't know where it is. What does this ad-
dress "Across Salmon Weir Bridge" mean?
*Do I have to tell you to find a taxi? Stop stall-
ing. Faint heart, etc.*
>My heart isn't faint. It's beating like crazy.
Hormones, no doubt. Move! Now!
>Wait. One more question. What was the feud
about?
*I said stop stalling. Maybe you and fair Sara
Anne can learn about it for yourselves. Give
you something to do besides mooning over her
and feeling sorry for yourself.*
>How?
*You might try a thing called Internet. I hear
there's an access program called DABEST. End.*

The screen went blank. I had worn out my welcome.

I was hungry. Perhaps I should eat supper.

Oh, hell. Rae was right. I fished the large manila enveloped out of my bag and went down to the lobby, left
my key on the desk, waved at Nuala (who was busy reg-
istering a Japanese couple), and found a waiting taxi. It
was necessary to wake the driver after I got into the car.

"Where to, sir?" he asked briskly.

"Across Salmon Weir Bridge."

He started the car and backed out of the diagonal parking.

"And when we get across the bridge, sir? Do you have a street address?"

I looked at the manila envelope. Joshua McAdam's spidery scrawl provided no street address.

"I'm afraid not."

"Who would you want to be visiting, sir?"

"A man named Ronan Tobin."

"Ah, sure, sir, why didn't you say so in the first place? But I couldn't be taking your money now, could I? And it being within walking distance?"

"Why don't you drive me the long way around?"

"Well, now, that's not a bad idea at all, at all. Would you be wanting to see our famous cathedral? You can walk across the bridge from there. It's a lovely way to approach Ronan's house."

"Would they have Mass at the cathedral this late?"

"Mass, is it? Don't they have it all day Sunday?"

"You can drop me there."

The driver steered his way carefully down narrow one-way streets and across at least three bridges. Galway really seemed to be the "Irish Venice," as the guidebooks I had glanced at claimed. The seven branches of the Corrib River did necessitate a lot of bridges as, Irish-like, the river chose intricate and convoluted escapes to the sea.

"Aren't them Galway hookers racing out there?" said the driver. "Them broad boats with the red sails."

Against the blue sky and the blue waters, the black hulls and red sails seemed like objects in a water color.

"From *hoeckboot*, which is a Dutch word for a fishing boat."

He chuckled. "Aren't you well informed now?"

"And isn't the sculpture in the middle of the square

back in front of my hotel based on their sails? And didn't the poor people over there in the Claddagh have their fishing hookers too?"

So I had won that one.

We drove along the docks and the Spanish Arch and the Spanish Parade. The town houses along the river were either brand-new or freshly painted in dazzling colors of pink and blue and green and red. Some of the newer homes seemed to have been built on or around the ruins of older homes.

"Isn't it amazing the way the old city has changed?" the driver said to me. "All in just a couple of years?"

" 'Tis gorgeous," I said.

"Isn't it now."

He explained that we would drive along the canal to Presentation Road (named after the "sisters," of course) and instead of crossing over to Nun's Island (sure, you'd want to walk on that, wouldn't you now?), cut over to Newcastle Street, go by the university, and come at the cathedral from the other direction.

Fine, I agreed.

"Isn't your man entitled to that splendid new house he has just across from the Yacht Club? Isn't there no one in the West of Ireland that is as honest or as hardworking as he his? And himself a poor lad from Mayo who got into the university because he was so smart? And his wife, isn't she a lovely woman now? Isn't she one of the Burkes who have been running the courts around here for a hundred years? And wasn't it the little bit of money she inherited from her father, that gave your man his start? And the daughter, isn't she a sweet and pretty little thing, even if something of a hellion?"

All the gossip about the Tobins free of charge.

"A hellion?"

"So they say, but it isn't anything serious yet, is it now? And herself even more lovely than her mother, which is saying a lot, isn't it?"

" 'Tis." I sighed in agreement.

Hellion, huh? I had no ambition to tame a shrew. Terrible temper, according to Neve and Fionna.

"Still, doesn't everyone say that your man is as good as his word and his word is his bond?"

I wasn't quite sure of the logic of that argument, so I let it go.

"Now, isn't that our cathedral? Built on the site of the old Galway County jail? What would you be thinking about it? The Cathedral of Mary Assumed into Heaven and St. Nicholas. Sure, it's big enough to need two patrons, isn't it now?"

"It's big, all right."

The cathedral, opened in 1965, was a vast gray pile of stones, a gloomy Romanesque monstrosity that even the bright sun could not make more cheerful.

"Didn't Cardinal Cushing pay for most of it, and himself bankrupting his own archdiocese before the end of the day?"

"Big."

"And didn't the Anglican bishop offer to sell Dr. Brown—our bishop then—St. Nicholas Collegiate Church for a cathedral at less than a quarter of the cost? And didn't Dr. Brown, himself hating Prots if you take me meaning, sir, refuse even to answer his letter?"

"Big," I said for the third time, unsure whether the cabbie wanted me to praise or bury his cathedral.

"Now, won't you be taking that road to the right and crossing the bridge and seeing Ronan's white house with all the glass to the left? It'll be three punt, sir, won't it?"

I gave him a five-punt note, for which he was very grateful, and hopped out of the taxi.

"Ah." He sighed. "Thank you very much, sir. Wasn't it a good thing there were no poor people in the County Galway for whom the money that built that place could have been used?"

"Indeed it was." I winked at him.

Let him figure out my meaning.

Inside the huge mausoleum an early evening Mass—in Irish, I supposed, because it certainly wasn't in English—was in progress, the homily already over, thank God.

Technically as a traveler I was excused from my Sunday obligation, which, as my little bishop had told me, "doesn't mean that you're forbidden to celebrate the Eucharist with the ordained priest."

He's very good at using the liturgically correct words (equivalent in the Church to politically correct). But the effect is spoiled by the leprechaun gleam in his eye.

I wasn't sure of the subject matter of my prayers. Success or failure in the joust ahead? A quest that won the fair Sara Anne or one that safely escaped this lovely and ill-tempered young hellion?

I asked God as I had asked myself repeatedly what I was doing here. I didn't really need the money and I didn't really want the woman and I really wasn't "ye parfait knight" type.

Was I?

My sexual hormones had driven me thus far, as, according to Rae, hormones had driven other pilgrims. Now, however, they seemed to have deserted me. None of the nicely dressed young matrons in the cathedral excited my fantasies—though they did remind me of their counterparts at St. Hilary's and made me feel homesick again.

I noticed that the congregation was singing the mysterious, mystical melody for the "Lamb of God" in both English and Irish. Neat to have written it in such a way that it was a bilingual hymn. I hummed it to myself as I went up to receive Communion.

After Communion I slipped out of the church, risking the baleful glare of the young priest who was lurking in the vestibule. Emerging into the sunlight from the cathedral made me feel like I was rising from a tomb. Then I remembered that I had left the manila envelope addressed to Ronan P. Tobin on the pew. I returned to the pew and found it quickly enough.

Great knight errant, G. Patrick Tobin.

I discovered the Salmon Weir Bridge right where my map said it should be, crossed two more of the Irish Venetian waterways, and saw a pleasant enough modern home at the corner of Waterside Street. I put my map into my hip pocket and strode with more confidence than I felt towards the house. As modern homes go, it was tasteful enough and not too big. The broad, floor-to-ceiling windows opened to a view of the glittering river just before it divided itself into those seven channels.

My pounding heart betraying my sangfroid, I knocked firmly at the front door.

It opened and disclosed a great giant of a man with a broad smile.

"Jesus and Mary be with this house." I said the approved greeting in Irish.

"And Jesus and Mary and Patrick be with those who come to visit it," he replied with a grin that was bigger even than he was—and he was three or four inches taller than my six feet.

"Good evening, sir," I said, switching to English smoothly enough. "I'm Pat Tobin and—"

"Paddy Tobin, is it, and from America? Well, come

right in and welcome to the city of Galway. You'll be having supper with us, won't you now?"

"I don't want to trouble you . . ." I began hesitantly.

"No trouble at all, at all. Don't say another word. Edna, hasn't young Paddy Tobin come from America to have supper with us?"

Edna would, of course, be her name—the same as the name of Sara's mother in the older version of the story.

My exuberant and friendly giant was a young and handsome man in his very early forties, with bushy black hair, an open face, dancing black eyes, broad and strong shoulders, a solid stomach, and, as far as one could judge, beneath his doubled-breasted navy blue blazer, arms like Irish oak trees. His smile was as wide as the River Corrib, rushing enthusiastically down from the lake. He was wearing white slacks and a white shirt open at the neck.

Far too young a man, I thought, to have a daughter as old as the fair Sara Anne. And I wouldn't want to have to wrestle with him for her.

"Paddy." He had dragged me into the house. "This is me wife, Edna."

"How do you do, Mrs. Tobin."

"Isn't it Edna, Paddy Tobin?" She smiled graciously and extended her hand.

"Edna says we should dress up for Sunday night dinner, even if it's only for ourselves," Ronan explained, putting his arm around his wife's shoulders. "And sure, isn't she absolutely right?"

If I were married in the middle years of life to a woman as striking as Edna, I'd say she was absolutely right all the time too. Slender but full-figured, with blue eyes and jet black hair like her husband and a smile to match his, she was wearing a pleated white dress with a deep V neck, a thin red belt at her narrow waist, and red shoes. Her face was almost unmarked by age, and her deep and mysterious eyes hinted, as she leaned compliantly against her husband's chest, of the capacity to share wondrous sensual pleasure.

If the fair Sara Anne's mother was this dazzling, what would Sara Anne herself be like? I must be careful not to seem to be gaping at her boobs, in line with Rae's advice to me, but that would be very hard indeed, especially since her dress was designed to emphasize her nearly perfect body.

I'm sure I gulped when we shook hands.

"You really must stay for supper, young Paddy," she said softly. "And yourself surely being a cousin with the Tobin look all over you."

"Nothing wrong with that woman of the house, is there?" her husband bellowed happily.

"Won't it do till something better comes along?" She patted his chest. "But we'll figure out the relationship as we eat."

"Eighth cousin, once removed," I murmured. "Really, I don't want to—"

"It really won't be any trouble, Paddy," she insisted with an inviting smile that would melt the heart of a polar bear. "Our daughter just rang us up to say that she wouldn't be dining with us tonight. We don't want to waste any food, do we now?"

"No, ma'am."

They invited me into the parlor—tastefully decorated modern and looking out on the purple waters of the Corrib—and constrained me to sit down while Ronan went to fetch me a drink of the "real stuff."

"Is that one of your daughters?" I asked Edna as she seated me in a chair "with the best view of the river."

The photograph on the wall near the door was of a

young woman in her middle teens, dressed in a navy blazer and a blue blouse—school uniform probably. She was pretty enough but not yet as glorious as her mother.

"Ah, isn't she all we have, poor thing? That's four years ago when she was at Kylemore Abbey school, with the Benedictine nuns, you know. Isn't she pretty?"

"Yes, ma'am."

She sighed. "She was so happy up there, such a sweet and helpful little lass. Then she came home to live with us while she was at the university—she could have gone to Trinity, but she wanted to go to the same university as we did and live at home with us. Now she hardly speaks to us much of the time. We worry about her. As I said, she's all we have, and she's so gifted and bright. And she's still her sweet self some of the time. Then she gets into her moods and we try to stay out of her way . . . It's hard to be a young person these days, isn't it now?"

"How old is she?"

"She'll be twenty in August. She really is a very good young woman."

That meant she was still nineteen and would be nineteen if I married her to collect Uncle Gerry's bequest. Twenty might be old enough. Nineteen was still too young. Two months make a lot of difference, right?

"I'm sure she'll grow up just fine," I said, relieved that I wouldn't have to face this young hellion tonight. "Kids generally do, you know."

"And don't old people like you and me need to remember that?" Her mysterious eyes glowed with fun. "We find it hard to recall what it was like when we were young such a long time ago."

I was being teased by a woman who was perfectly at ease with her own intense sexuality. My face became very warm.

"A long time ago for me, Mrs. Tobin, uh, Edna. I'm sure only yesterday for you."

She clapped her hands. "Ah, sure, didn't I say you were a Tobin?"

Ronan arrived with a tumbler (Waterford, of course) of the "real stuff"—a deep brown liquid—and a bottle to back it up.

"Don't ask me where it came from and I'll tell you no lies," he said as he filled the tumbler to the brim.

"Now, then." He gave me the tumbler. "This is what you need on a cold spring evening."

"Except that it isn't cold, Ronan." Edna laughed.

"Not yet anyway. Now, let's hear all about yourself and your family, Paddy Tobin from America."

Whatever other uses the "real stuff" might have, it certainly cleaned out the sinuses. After a few sips of it, I decided that I could stare (with some discretion, of course) at Edna's boobs all evening and she wouldn't mind.

She certainly didn't seem to. I was already classified as a nice young man with a quick tongue who was a "real Tobin" and whose adoration, on occasion openmouthed, was amusing.

I had placed my manila envelope on the end table next to my chair with the intention of beginning the discussion of Great-Uncle Gerry's will at once. But I was distracted by the whiskey, by the racing conversation, and of course, by Edna's striking beauty. Anyway, I realized dimly that the Irish never did business till they got to the dessert and brandy.

We talked about the state of the Irish economy (Galway had been hard hit when DEC—"Digital," as Ronan called it—had closed its local plant and made twelve hundred people redundant), the Catholic Church (sure, we'd have reelected Bishop Casey no matter what he did twenty years ago, if they'd given us half a chance. He's a grand man, isn't he, Edna?), about my interests in Anglo-Irish literature (Edna's university major and a subject that made her animated and intense—and thus even more appealing), our relationship (Edna confirmed that her "man" and I were indeed eighth cousins once removed, "though you're so much like himself, I'd think you were first cousins"), my family (They must visit Galway the next time they came to Ireland), and my own employment and prospects.

I learned that Ireland had the highest GNP in Europe, the best balance of payments rate, and the lowest inflation rate. It was well on its way to becoming a prosperous country. Except for the unemployment. Ireland had lost a half million agricultural jobs since 1960. Moreover, because of the birth rates two decades ago, Ireland had to find twenty-five thousand new jobs every year. This year they hoped to have twenty-eight thousand.

"All things considered, aren't we doing pretty well now?"

"Astonishing."

"You teach Irish literature, do you now, Paddy?"

Were they already evaluating me as a potential son-in-law? What the hell was the rush? But sure, wasn't I a nice young Yank who could help their beloved daughter out of her moods? And didn't I have the look of a Tobin about me?

"I do not," I said as I accepted a dangerous refill to my "real stuff."

"I did my master's paper on your man from Dublin who married the Galway woman, and himself showing good taste to do that, and I'll probably try to get a Ph.D., maybe writing on herself, eventually. But it's not what I do for a living."

I almost gave my usual job description—a hacker and a nerd.

But wanting to impress the fair Sara Anne's parents, I upgraded my title. "I'm a computer programmer and consultant."

"Consultant, is it?" Ronan frowned. "Now, who would you be consulting for?"

"Mostly for medium-sized and large companies in Chicago who are trying to consolidate their systems which were never meant to be consolidated and get themselves into big messes."

"It sounds like it would be a good living, Paddy," Edna said with a nod of approval.

"It's all right," I said, giving away nothing.

Then I sympathized with their concern for their daughter and decided to tell them a little more.

"You must promise never to tell this to my parents if they should drop by because they would have a hard time believing it. My father is the dean of the College of Business Administration at an important university and thirty years older than me. Yet I make more money than he does. I don't tell my parents because I don't want to embarrass them."

"Sure, you're a sensitive young man, aren't you?" Edna nodded in approval.

I noted that a touch of lace had appeared at the bottom of the V of her V-neck dress. My hormones increased their competition with the alcohol that was rapidly entering my bloodstream.

"Well," Ronan added, "I always say that 'tis the wise young person who gets into computers these days. Our young Sara Anne is quite good with them."

"Really?" I said cautiously.

"She revolutionized our office," Edna said with a touch of astonishment in her voice. "And myself the office manager and having to ask her permission to use my own computer!"

They both chortled enthusiastically about their daughter's cleverness.

"Mind you," Ronan said, "only till you got the hang of it."

" 'You're an intelligent woman, Ma,' doesn't she say to me, 'as well as being beautiful. If you just would be patient with yourself and with your pushy daughter, you'll do just fine.' "

They laughed again.

Instead of my having to wrestle with them for my grail, they were trying to auction her off to me.

Fortunately, Edna pronounced dinner ready at just that moment.

The little brat, I told myself, must be a serious problem if her family is so eager to get rid of her.

The dinner, served on Irish linen bedecked with fine china and acres of Waterford, was of the sort I might have eaten at home on a family Sunday afternoon, though more tastefully presented—soup, roast beef, potatoes, vegetables. The meat here was not so well done as to be capable of bouncing off a basketball floor, which my mother and father agreed was the only way roast beef should be served. Red meat, you see, is not good for you.

Nor at home would they have served both white and red wine.

"Doesn't our Sara Anne buy our wine for us?" her mother said proudly, as Ronan and I helped her clear the table.

"A young woman with good taste in everything, beginning with her choice of parents."

My tongue was now very loose indeed. I'd have to be careful.

And they were too eager to parade their daughter's virtues. They had a quest of their own, which converged with my supposed quest. And that worried me.

We ate apple tart with heavy cream and drank tea so strong that I was afraid to stir it when Edna poured in a splash of milk, for fear the tea would bend the spoon. Then Ronan produced a bottle of what looked like very expensive brandy, and I brought my manila envelope from the end table in the parlor.

"I do have some business to transact," I began.

"Weren't we dying to know what was in that envelope, young Paddy?"

"Shush, Ronan." Edna reproved him with a total lack of conviction.

I opened the envelope and removed the smaller one.

"It's not bad news, heaven knows." I put the envelope on the table and picked up my Waterford liquor glass.

"My great-uncle, Gerry Tobin, died earlier this year. His will charged me to bring this letter to you, Ronan. I have no idea what is in it, though I should say that, not to put too fine an edge on things, Great-Uncle Gerry was a bit strange. Apparently he wanted to settle some family feud which dates to 1807. You apparently are the titular head of the other side of the feuding Tobins."

I passed the letter across the table to him.

"Feud." Ronan sounded confused. "I never heard of a Tobin family feud. Have you, Edna?"

"Not a word," she said. "You Tobins fight often enough, the good Lord knows, but you always make peace at the end of the day."

"Don't we now?" he said with a grin, and he slit open

the envelope with one of the silver knives that remained on the table. He removed the sheet of paper and the check I had seen at Heathrow and a yet smaller envelope that the Brits must have missed. Edna, producing glasses from somewhere, bent down and read over his shoulder.

Outside the sun was finally beginning to set, but night would be mostly a long twilight. The river had turned rose-gold. The top button of Edna's dress had somehow become undone, revealing a lot of bra and breast as she read the letter. I grew angry at my hormones, which were weakening my concentration at this critical moment. Not that the two glasses of whiskey and the two bottles of wine and the half glass of cognac had left me with much concentration.

"Holy Mother of God," Ronan exclaimed as he stared at the check.

"Oh, Ronny, you'll be able to start that project for the Digital programmers now."

"And have some left over, at that," he said, shaking his head in astonishment.

Unemployed programmers, the little of my brainpower that was still functioning, informed me. Just what you're looking for. All you need is ten million dollars to make it go. Well, you're giving half the money away, but a quarter of it would serve the purpose. All you have to do is to tame this little brat.

I am not Richard Burton, I remind myself, and I suspect she's no Elizabeth Taylor either.

"Listen to the poor man, will you: "Dear Cousin Ronan, the unfortunate Tobin family feud has weighed on my mind for many years. My grandfather, who was born in 1830, told me when I was a lad much about it, and I know of the violence and the murders and the hatred. I cannot recall whether he told me of the cause of the feud, but that is not important today. He did say that he always thought our side of the family was in the wrong—a very fair man, my grandfather always was.

"What is essential today, it would seem to me, is that the feud be brought to an end. While, to the best of my knowledge, there has been no violence in this century, I know enough about the Irish to understand that such family conflicts can always arise again, even after long periods of peace. Therefore I am enclosing a check as reparation for all the sufferings my side of the family may have caused your side of the family. I suggest, but do not demand, that you use some of the money to provide employment for those who need work in your part of Ireland. I am asking my grandnephew, G. Patrick Tobin Junior, to bring you this letter along with the enclosed materials. He is the male heir to our side of the family and a fine young man. I trust that you and he can make peace between our branches of the family. Will you please present him with the enclosed small envelope in which my lawyer will have placed a check drawn on my estate. I believe that he deserves it for his fidelity to an old man's last request. My lawyer, Josh McAdam, and I have, I am confident, honored the laws of both countries, and neither of you will have to pay much tax on my bequests.

"I am, Cousin Ronan, in full possession of all my faculties when I make these grants. Mr. McAdam in East Bend, South Dakota, will have evidence certifying to this fact. The materials he will enclose will answer any questions you or your lawyer or your accountant may have.

"I hope that I can die peacefully now in full confidence that you and my grandnephew will end the terrible conflict that has rent our family so long. I entrust to you and him the future of our family and ask that you both be

kind enough to say an occasional prayer for the repose
of my poor troubled soul.

"Sincerely,

"G. Patrick Tobin the Fourth."

Ronan passed the small envelope to me. With shaking
fingers I opened it. Two hundred big ones. I closed my
eyes. Enough to begin the advanced programming for
DABEST. A consolation prize if I should fail to win the
dubiously fair Sara Anne.

"We should say our first prayers for him right now,"
Edna instead.

So, over our tea and apple tart and cognac, we said five
paters and aves and requiescats for the repose of the soul
of G. Patrick Tobin IV (which must have made me V).
We took turns leading the prayers, a fine democratic pro-
cedure which Edna had mandated.

"May his soul and all the souls of the faithful departed
rest in peace," she finished the prayers.

"Amen," Ronan and I agreed.

"I don't know that I should take this, Paddy." Ronan
stared, peering at the check. "It somehow doesn't seem
right. The poor man was round the bend altogether."

"There's documentation in East Bend which says he
was not. Besides, any money that is left when the estate
is settled will go to the United States government, which
will use it to buy some parts for a B-Two bomber."

He rubbed his chin. "What do you think, Ma?"

"I think Toby is right, dear."

I reached across the table. "Ronan Tobin, let there be
peace between my family and yours from now until the
end of time, just as poor Great-Uncle Gerry wanted."

It was the drink that made me eloquent.

He shook hands firmly. "Indeed, let there be peace
between us, forever and ever. Amen. Not, mind you, that

I ever knew there was anything but peace between us."

"Or that we even existed."

The peace didn't last very long.

The front door of the house slammed shut with a loud bang. Edna and Ronan immediately became tense. Ah, enter fair Sara Anne, rampant.

"Sara Anne, dear," her father shouted, somewhat anxiously, "come in and meet your cousin from America."

The young woman who shuffled reluctantly into the dining room was dressed in a baggy sweatshirt (on which a coat of arms and the words "Galway Hooker" were emblazoned), tight-fitting jeans (long unwashed, it seemed to me), and sandals (with dirty feet). Her face was twisted into a scowl of scornful disdain.

"This is Paddy Tobin from Chicago, dear." Edna took over the formalities. "He is a very nice young man."

Wrong words! I knew that even before the explosion.

"Ms. Tobin." I stood up and bowed politely, the drink still giving me what I thought was charm. "Your parents have been telling me wonderful things about you."

Not a Richard Burton line, I admit.

"Another frigging Yank," she sneered.

"I'm afraid so . . ."

"Go shite," she yelled, and then fled the room sobbing.

This is what the Holy Grail looks like?

☙11☙

Back at the Railway Hotel, I pondered the
obligation to call home and report on my encounter with
the Galway Tobins. I decided that I would not tell them
about either my check or Sara's outburst.

I wanted no part of consultation with the Seraph crowd
just now. They had known all along what Sara was like
and still had led me on.

A dirty, smelly drunk.

Maybe not a drunk. There was no smell of the drink
on her. She could be nasty cold sober.

Was she as beautiful as everyone had said she was? Perhaps. It was hard to tell. But raw hatred obscures beauty
almost completely.

Why the hell did she hate frigging Yanks? What had we
ever done to her? Did she have a lover who worked for
Digital?

The lively dinner party had come quickly to an end.

The embarrassed Galway Tobins had apologized for their daughter, who, they assured me, only a few years ago was the sweetest child I could imagine. I had told them that I was not offended. Young people, I had observed pontifically, were entitled to occasional angry and rebellious moods.

"Not almost all the time," Edna had murmured through her tears.

"She's so many different people," Ronan had added. "We never know which one will come through the door. The one tonight is the worst of all."

"I'll be looking forward to meeting the real Sara Anne," I had lied.

I had left as soon as I could without giving offense. They had promised we'd get together for dinner tomorrow night. Ronan would call me in the morning.

Without Sara Anne, I had fervently hoped. I could not abide permanently angry women. Worse still, I usually became contentious with them.

"Ah, wasn't it good to meet you, young Paddy?" Ronan had shaken hands at the doorway. "And us ending the feud finally?"

"You're a very sweet boy, Paddy." Edna had brushed her lips against mine, rather slowly, to tell the truth, a surprise that had almost knocked me over. "I hope we'll be friends."

"Woman of the house," I said, "that's a given."

Arm in arm, indeed clinging close to each other, they had watched from the doorway as I had walked away in the twilight, two grieving lovers framed in the glow of their once happy home.

They would make love soon, I had told myself. Probably before I had arrived back at the hotel. Good enough for them. They would have gone up to bed much earlier if I hadn't shown up with all my surprises. Now they would couple because they needed strength to endure their humiliation. They must have feared all through the evening that their beloved daughter, the sweet little child in the school uniform, would come home while I was there and disgrace them.

I had never noticed such a sexual spark between my parents, though to be fair to them, they were a good fifteen years older than their Galway cousins and not nearly so exuberant. Besides, if the spark was there, I probably would have missed it.

Despite Sara Anne, Ronan was a lucky man, I had told myself.

I punched in the family number in Chicago, was informed by an operator that I had done it wrong, and tried again.

The phone on Virginia Avenue rang once.

"Toby! What's she like?"

Megan, of course, haunting the phone so she might get the first word in.

"Pretty enough and unspeakably nasty," I replied.

"Good! It should be fun making her unnasty."

"Now, Toby," my mother cut in, "you must not make any hasty judgments. Give the poor girl a chance. I'm sure she's really a sweetheart. Probably just a little shy with an American."

"It took you long enough to call, Toby." My father had picked up the phone in his office.

"Dad!" Megan the romantic enthused. "Toby says she's like totally gorgeous."

A somewhat generous rendering of my verdict on Sara Anne.

"Don't be precipitous, son," my father warned me.

"There's more important things in the world than physical attraction."

Don't I know it.

"Yes, Dad."

"You must give her more time." Mom continued her line of thought. "Never judge on the basis of a first meeting."

"Never judge a book by its cover," my father insisted.

Having received slightly different input, my parents were talking at cross purposes. It had happened before and they had never noticed. I let them continue talking because there was nothing I could say to present a different picture of the Tobin family and the evening at their house.

"Where you been, asshole?" Nicole on the line. "Dad and Mom have been sitting here all day worrying about you."

The family finally had a stance on which they could all agree.

"I said I'd call as soon as I got back to the hotel from visiting the Tobins. That's what I'm doing."

"What time is it over there?" Maureen joined the attack. "Nine o'clock in the morning? Did you spend the night?"

"No, Mo, it's eleven o'clock at night. They insisted I stay for dinner. I could hardly use their phone for an overseas call."

"Toby, if you would only apply yourself a little more, you wouldn't do thoughtless things like this."

"We were so worried about you, dear." Mom was sniffling. "Why don't you have any consideration for us?"

So it went, interrupted only by an occasional romantic foray from Megan: "Are you going to take her out tomorrow, Toby? You really should, you know. Get her away from her parents."

By now Mom was sobbing.

They were absolutely wrong about my failure to phone. But as so many other people do, they had confused the time change. My patient attempts to correct their mistake were wasted. By definition I had been thoughtless and inconsiderate again. It was my fault that mom was crying.

You should know what a really rotten kid is like, I thought.

There was only one way out of it. I had to apologize and sound like I was both wrong and contrite. It was the scenario and it had to be played that way.

No one ever apologized to me, even when they were patently and blatantly wrong. Especially my mother and my sisters. Women, I had decided, never apologized. You always apologized to them, even when they were wrong and knew deep down that they were wrong.

So it went. I apologized and promised them that I would call them on Monday night about six o'clock Chicago time.

"Write that down," I said, "six Chicago time."

"We can remember times, dear." Mom began crying again.

Instead of speaking the truth—that patently they could not—I apologized again. They never did get around to asking about Ronan and Edna Tobin. But that interest was not on their agenda and probably never would be.

"Don't give up on her, Toby," Megan pleaded, getting in the last word.

When I hung up I was fuming with rage, as I usually was after such sessions. I loved them and they loved me. I missed them. They meant well. But sometimes they drove me out of my mind.

With these happy thoughts, I threw off my clothes and fell into bed. Despite all the Tobin liquor, I was still on Chicago time. It took me hours of fretful and angry tossing and turning to get to sleep.

I woke up with an unpleasant start. Sunlight was streaming through the window. I looked at the clock next to my bed: 10:10! I might as well go back to sleep. I had nothing to do today.

Then I realized there was someone else in my room, herself sitting nonchalantly on the end of my bed in a dark blue business suit and a light blue blouse.

"I don't want to talk to you," I snapped. "Can't you leave me any privacy?"

"Actually, Paddy, you did rather well last night, all things considered. You ogled that woman for most of the evening. But she did not seem to mind."

"She was flattered."

"You were a trifle crude, but I must remind myself that you are in your reproductive years with no sexual outlets, so I suppose I cannot be too harsh on you. And the woman is quite devastating, I admit. And knows it too."

"That's wrong?"

"No, that's right. I thought the way she kissed you was quite skillful . . . You know, of course, you interrupted their preparations for intimacy?"

"After supper?"

"Before supper. Actually those who keep their passion alive are very fortunate. It sees them through crises and anneals their suffering. In this case as in most it is the woman who is responsible. The good Edna's beauty, by the way, is more the result than the cause of the phenomenon."

"So?"

"Young people who are raised in such an environment

of passionate love are likely to be excellent sexual partners."

"You people will stop at nothing!"

"That's true." She smiled genially. "We can't guarantee you happiness, Paddy, because we don't know the future. But, as I have said, we're pretty good guessers. It is our considered opinion that, while the two of you have character weakness which could be disastrous, on the whole you are the best chance either of you will ever have."

"I would rather curl up with a cobra."

"You might end up doing just that . . . Why don't you consider the possibility that this might be a transient problem for her?"

"Why didn't you tell me that Sara is a bitch on wheels?"

She raised her right shoulder in her now familiar shrug which dismissed what I had said as largely irrelevant. "I will concede for the sake of the discussion that the circumstances of your first encounter were a bit unfortunate."

"That woman is not the Holy Grail, not even close to it."

"You're being precipitous in your judgments, Paddy. Most unlike you."

"It is too like me."

The phone rang. I grabbed it and snapped, "Pat Tobin."

"Nuala at the desk here, Mr. Tobin. I hope I didn't wake you?"

"Not at all, Nuala. I'm wide-awake." I gave my Seraph guest a dirty look. "And just ready to order breakfast if it's not too late."

"Of course not, Mr. Tobin. We'll send it right up.

Would you ever mind taking a phone call?"

"I'd be happy to."

Rae rolled her eyes at my burst of charm.

"Pat Tobin."

"Good morning," a faint, little-girl voice said at the other end of the line. "This is Sara."

"Ah," I said curtly, "Cousin Sara."

Rae pointed a finger at me in solemn warning.

"Me da says that I should call and ask if you'd ever want me to take you to see the house of your man's wife."

"Nora Barnacle, is it?" I said evenly.

" 'Tis," she replied, her voice low and sad. "Sure you don't have to do it."

Rae was wagging her finger at me, a dire threat of permanent excommunication. I was free to make my own choices, was I?

"Quite the contrary, Sara Anne, I'd love to do the walking tour with you. What time?"

Rae smiled and nodded approvingly.

"Would half eleven be too soon?" Her voice, actually quite melodious, was still diffident, but it had picked up a little strength.

"It would be perfect."

"I'll meet you in the lobby then?"

"You will. At half eleven. I'll be looking forward to it."

The line went dead. The poor child would now go off and have a good cry for herself.

"There are times, Paddy," Rae said, standing at the door, arms folded, "when you really do rise to the occasion. That was very nice."

"Uh. She sounded, well, fragile. I didn't want to hurt her."

"Very good. Now, remember what I said about tenderness. Tons of it today, as human progeny would say. Tons of it, understand?"

"Yes, ma'am . . . You'll be watching, of course."

"Naturally. We try not to miss a thing. See you at the end of the day."

She dissolved into mists, the first time I had ever seen her do that.

Then she reappeared, though this time only in a kind of hazy outline.

"You should wear your blue slacks and the white shirt with short sleeves. It'll be a hot day. If you put on a jacket with a sweater, won't you be perishing with the heat? And your new walking shoes."

"I don't have—"

"Sure you do." She gestured towards the bed and vanished again.

Of course, my new, brand-new, shirt and trousers were neatly arranged on the bed, and a pair of the most expensive Nike walking shoes were next to the bed. Now they were my fashion consultants too.

So Sara Anne's parents were not about to let her pass up a nice young Yank without stern warnings to her. The game was back on.

At 11:28, clad in my perfectly fitting shirt and slacks and wearing my featherlight walking shoes, I emerged from my second-floor (first-floor in their strange system) room and walked down the stairs to the lobby. Real men, Nike-clad men, don't take elevators.

As I turned in to the lobby I heard two young women laughing. As soon as they saw me, they stopped abruptly. Nuala and Sara Anne, naturally.

"Isn't your cousin Sara here to take you around Galway, Mr. Tobin?" Nuala said briskly, trying to cover up for the two of them.

"Is she now?" I said, giving her the key to my room. "Good morning, Cousin Sara Anne."

"Good morning, Cousin Patrick." She extended her hand cautiously.

I shook hands with her and didn't—couldn't—say a word.

Sara Anne Elizabeth Tobin was the most beautiful woman I had ever been close to. She was wearing dark brown slacks, a beige blouse of some silky material with two of the buttons at the top open, and a faint touch of makeup. She smelled of very young spring. Her only jewelry was a silver Brigid cross pendant.

You dress up nicely for the nice young Yank, do you hear me, Sara Anne?

The pictures had not done the young woman justice. By my standards of taste, she was the perfection of womanly beauty, not as statuesque as her mother, but trim, compact, graceful. Her body suggested energy, much of it sexual, but lots of other kinds of energy too. Her eyes were a bewitching shade of dark blue, her forehead high and intelligent, her oval face classically lovely, her lips mobile and challenging. Her jet black hair fell cleanly to her shoulders, every strand in perfect position.

You are in trouble, boyo, I told myself, real trouble. Cobra or not.

"You look very lovely this morning, Cousin," I said finally—and hoped that my jaw wasn't still hanging open.

"Better than last night anyway." She lowered her eyes. "Would you be wanting to see more of Galway or just the home where the poor woman grew up?"

"Wouldn't I want to be seeing as much of Galway as you'd be wanting to show me?"

I took her arm and steered her towards the door. Nuala was enjoying the scene too much.

Out in the sunlight we paused at the bottom of the hotel steps.

"Won't we be perishing with the heat?"

"I'm used to hot weather," I said inanely.

"I want to say something to you, Paddy Tobin." She was staring at her long and supple fingers.

"All right, Sara Anne Tobin."

"I want to apologize for being such a bitch last night." She continued to examine her fingers. "I was a disgrace to meself and me family and me country and me religious faith. I was a terrible eejit and I'm humiliated altogether. I have no excuse. I wasn't fluttered or anything like that. It was just one of me black moods. There's no reason to forgive me, but I hope you will."

I thought my heart would break.

"Everyone is entitled to an occasional mood, Sara Anne, though to tell the truth, I don't have them myself, except in one set of circumstances."

She changed from her hands to my face, with just a touch of a smile. "And what would that be?"

"When I walk into a room where two young women are laughing loudly and they stop laughing instantly because they have been laughing at me."

"Go 'long with you." She pushed my arm, very cautiously. "Besides, wasn't Nuala saying such nice things about what a grand gentleman you are?"

She looked away from me again, head lowered and now near to tears. I had not, it would seem, been tender enough. Well, try again, eejit.

I took both her shoulders in my hands and turned her so she was facing me. Then I cupped her chin, delicate, it seemed now, like thin china, and lifted her head so that my eyes were looking into hers.

"Look, Sara Anne, you've just apologized to me. That

breaks all the rules of relationship between the genders. No woman has ever apologized to me in all my life. I have to be the one who apologizes, even at the times when the woman knows she is wrong."

Her eyes began to fill up with tears.

"Not only that," I continued, trying to absorb her in my very best smile, "you also apologized with charm and grace, which tells me that you are a charming and graceful young woman. So, Cousin Sara Anne, I expect that's the way you'll be ninety-nine percent of the time. Of course I forgive you. But only on one condition."

"What's that?" she asked, sniffling and trying to hold back the tears.

"That you forgive yourself."

Her jaw tightened in my hand for a moment. She took a deep breath. "All right," she said softly.

"Say it."

Another deep breath. "I forgive myself for being a gob-shite."

It seemed that her whole personhood leaned against mine as her chin kind of surrendered to my hand. An inital conquest. Fersure, as Meg would have said.

"Fair play. Last night is rubbed off the record and we're two distant cousins trying to find out a little more about each other's world. Fair play?"

The tears brimmed over for a moment; she grabbed a tissue out of her large (and expensive) leather shoulder bag, and grinned at me.

"Fair play, Cousin Paddy. But don't count on the charm more than fifty percent of the time," she said dabbing at her eyes.

"Fifty-one percent."

Finally she laughed. "I'll try," she said, pushing my arm a little less gently, "and sure, didn't me ma tell me you were a sweet boy?" She hesitated and then continued, "Thanks, Cousin Paddy. Thank you very much."

"My pleasure."

I wanted to kiss her then and there, but, I told myself, that would not be right. I'd be taking advantage of her shame. Still I felt that I had been hit over the head with one of those Irish pikes that the Finians and the other revolutionaries had used. This young woman was overwhelming. I was in love with her already. A tiny voice in the back of my head demanded to know what caused the moods, but I told it that I wasn't worried about them anymore. I had found my Holy Grail after all.

Hadn't an earlier Tobias not only fallen in love with an earlier Sara but married her the day he met her?

She also had begun to admire me. A woman's candid admiration is a heady aphrodisiac, if there ever were one. How had I managed to say the right words to her? Was that pushy, nosy Seraph whispering in my ear?

Our tour began. I didn't have to call her Sara Anne. Sara would do. No, she didn't mind if I liked using both names, she liked it herself. That was her da's office over there on the right-hand side of the square, Eyre Square. The park was named after John Fitzgerald Kennedy, poor man, and God be good to his wife, who had just died, a living saint if there ever was one. The statue is of Padraig O'Connor, the great West of Ireland poet. The doorway is called Brown's Door, from the house of one of the old merchant families. The cannon represents Galway's days as a great seaport which traded with Spain. Cromwell put an end to all that.

When we would pause in our walk for her to give a lecture, she would fold her arms, cock her head to one side, watch me out of the corner of her eye, and recite the appropriate information with a little self-deprecating smile that said in effect, "This is what I'm supposed to say, Cousin Paddy. If you think it's all ridiculous, just tell me to stop and I will."

I would smile back in approval, and she, having won approval, would continue talking.

Would I want to be looking at Shop Street? There were fine bookstores and a couple of nice jewelry stores, where I could buy presents for my young women friends back in America, couldn't I now?

No beating around the bush for this one.

"I'm afraid I don't have any young women back in America, Sara Anne."

"I don't believe that at all, at all."

" 'Tis true. I'm awkward and clumsy around young women. I always say the wrong things to them."

"Would you stop it?" she said with considerable determination. "Not you of all people."

"Would you stop it," I would learn, means something like "Cut it out."

"I admit that I've become a little better since I've been in Ireland. Maybe it's the air or the water or the loveliness of Irish women."

She stopped and examined my face very closely. "You are telling me the truth, aren't you now? Sure, whatever it is about Ireland, it cured you in a hurry."

"I guess it did."

Actually, Sara Anne, and you wouldn't believe it at all, at all, but it was a pushy, nosy, bossy Seraph that cured me.

"Well, you can look at the jewelry anyway if you want."

The Claddagh ring, I was told, was an ancient wedding ring from the old Claddagh fishing village on the quay (*claddagh* in Irish) across the mouth of the Corrib from Galway city. It had a culture and a language and even a "king" of its own. The last king had died in 1934, and the eejit government tore down the old thatched huts and replaced them with "council homes" (public housing), and that pretty much distroyed the Claddagh and all it stood for. Her gram remembered the times when the fishermen's wives used to paddle across the river and sell fish under the Spanish Arch, poor women. The ring stood for two hands of a marriage under the crown of a sacrament holding the single heart that man and woman had become.

There really wasn't much to see in Galway, I was told, a couple of narrow old streets with damp stone buildings that was all that remained of medieval Galway. Still it was her home and she loved it. She hoped she'd never have to leave. The West of Ireland didn't have much really. It was an empty stage from which all the fabulous actors had long ago departed—the O'Connors and the O'Flahertys and the O'Shaugnesseys and the de Burgos (Burkes, you'd call them) who took away all their land. And the fourteen fine merchant families who ran the city when it was a great place took it away from the Burkes (and that being the name of me ma's family) with a royal degree— the Browns and the Lynches and the Blakes and the rest of them, most of them Welsh, not Irish; now they were all gone too. Cromwell destroyed the city altogether, and it's never been the same since. Galway, like the rest of Ireland, had only land and rocks and scenery and ruins, and a lot of all of them.

"And people, Sara Anne. Some of the grandest people in all the world."

"And don't we have to export them, just like they were bottles of Bailey's, because there are no jobs for them?"

Much of Ireland, I was told, was reasonably prosperous, men like her father who worked hard and had something to start with because they were intelligent and educated and had good wives with a bit of money of their own. But one out of every seven men was unemployed, one out of six here, a fifth of the children were born out of wedlock, mostly to women in stable relationships.

I was introduced to the elderly grandmother of the bookshop, the son who administered it, and the smiling children of the house, who hugged my guide. I was shown old books, rare books, new books with no sales pressure (that I could recognize). My guide determined the kinds of books in which I was interested—anything about Joyce or Yeats or Synge or Brian Merriman, and old books. She discreetly advised me on what to buy and what not to buy, told me she was glad that I knew about one Irish language poet, and gasped a little bit when I ended up with a bill for more than two hundred Irish punts.

Her advice was gentle, no orders given, no purchases insisted on, no judgments about my taste made. Yet she watched my every move closely. What kind of man was this smooth-talking Yank cousin who claimed that he was a failure with women?

Of course, I wasn't evaluating her at the same time. No way.

"Are you a schoolteacher, Cousin Paddy?" she asked when we had emerged from Kenny's with arrangements made to ship the books home to America.

"Woman, I'm not. Did you're ma and da tell you last night that I was a computer hacker?"

"They didn't tell me much of anything." She laughed easily. "You mean you're one of those eejits that break into secret computers and mess them up?"

"That's against the law." I then explained to her what it meant to be a consultant and a programmer. Finally I took a big risk and told her about DABEST.

"It will make that frigging Internet thing work, will it now? Haven't I been driving meself crazy trying to figure it out?"

"Why do you need Internet?"

"Because it's there, you amadan! Wouldn't I run the risk of missing something if I didn't learn how to use it?"

"I'll show you how DABEST works, if you'd like."

"Ah, wouldn't that be fun!"

It might or might not, depending on whom you met on the Net.

And she wanted to know about it because it was there! Intellectually curious. I was sinking deeper into the swamp. Not only was she gorgeous, she was intellectually stimulating.

"I hear you're pretty good with a computer too, and yourself ordering your poor mother around."

"They told you that about me, did they now?" she said with a rich, happy laugh. "Ah, didn't we have a grand frigging time arguing? As me ma says, there's nothing like a good mother-daughter rivalry, so long as it is within limits. We bond when we fight."

In some families, I thought.

"So you're working in your father's office during the summer, but what do you study in school, Cousin Sara Anne?"

"Composition." She looked up at me shyly.

"Irish or English?"

"Musical," she said, and looked away. "I'm thinking that maybe I can become a composer, which shows what an onchuck I am."

An onchuck, I would later learn from Nuala, is a woman amadan. Roughly the equivalent of an eejit. Only worse.

Somehow I knew that she wrote music. How could I

have possibly known that? Her parents had not said a word about it last night.

"And your teachers, what do they think?"

"You ask a lot of questions, Cousin Paddy," she said, the scowl of last night returning to her face.

"Well, at least I didn't ask you how many boyfriends you have."

The scowl was instantly replaced with a smile that lit up the whole of Shop Street. She shoved me again, this time hard.

"Haven't you already figured out how to deal with me? And yourself clumsy with women indeed! All right, my teachers at Kylemore said I had talent. So do the teachers at UCG. My parents think I may be the greatest composer since Mozart. I don't know really how good I am." She waved her hands in bafflement. "I'm pretty good, all right, but I don't know whether I'm a real composer or not."

"And how will you know?"

"By taking the risk of trying."

"Well?"

She glanced at me again like she was about to lose her temper and then permitted her smile to return.

"I can't get angry at you, Cousin Paddy, even when I try . . . It's not meself I'm worried about. I can always earn a decent living in the family business, at which I'm already pretty good . . ."

"A woman of property?"

"The old biddy that loves to buy and sell? I'd be very good at that."

"What do you write?"

"So far, popular songs in Irish and . . . I'm blushing again, Paddy Tobin, and it's all your fault."

"And?"

"Masses."

"Masses?"

"I'm a liturgical composer." She threw up her hands in dismay. "Can you imagine that?"

"In which language?"

"Both of them. I try to write Masses that you can sing the main parts—'Lord Have Mercy,' 'Holy, Holy,' and 'Lamb of God'—in either language or both languages, and sing easily too. There's no point in writing a frigging Mass that the frigging people can't frigging sing, is there now?"

"Do they sing it in church?"

"Me da would give the bishop no peace, until they tried it in the cathedral."

Now, this is a real challenge for you, Paddy Tobin, boy knight errant. I tried to recall the haunting melody.

"Something like this?"

I began to hum the melody. She pulled back in fright, hands over her mouth.

"Glory be to God! Are you an angel or something? How did you know about that?"

"I heard it at Mass last night. I thought it was wonderful."

"They all say that," she said, easing back next to me. "But it's only because they don't want to offend me da."

Her eyes were shining brightly. Rae, stop putting these words in my mouth.

"I thought it was beautiful last night before I met you or your da."

Silence, broken only by a sigh.

"Do you use a computer to write the music?"

"I do NOT. Wouldn't it be a terrible thing for me to pay out almost three thousand punts for a special computer and a special program? How could I do that to me parents, and themselves doing so much for me already!"

So her fear was letting down her parents. Taking a risk and failing would be all right so long as you didn't fail THEM. For a kid as exuberant and creative and loving as my Sara Anne was, that would be enough to make you very moody indeed.

"I made a shareware program for my sister Megan, who wants to write music too—she's my youngest sister, the only teenager left in the family. I'd be happy to give it to you and teach you how to use it."

"How much does it cost?" she asked dubiously.

"Shareware is free, Sara Anne. Registration is twenty American dollars, thirteen punts or something like that. But for relatives of the owner like Megan and yourself, it's free."

"Thirteen frigging punts!"

"It won't do everything that dedicated machines will do, but unless you're planning to write opera, you can do just as well with MEGSONG, as I call it."

"Someday I want to write opera too. But, Cousin Paddy," she said, clapping her hands, "it would be so wonderful to have MEGSONG. Would you really teach me how to use it?"

"Woman, I would. So long as you're nice to me. That and Internet too."

"Well, I'll have to be careful of my moods, won't I now?"

"You will."

We laughed together, old companions sharing an old joke.

"Can I say something about your parents on the basis of just one night with them?"

"At your own risk!"

"I don't think you'll ever disappoint them or let them down."

She rubbed her hand across her forehead. "Poor dear people. Last night when I was a worthless gobshite—"

"What's that?"

"A gob of shite, you eejit. What did they do but come up to my room and tell me that it was all right and that I shouldn't sob and that you were a nice young man and they were sure I could make it up to you. If it were a daughter of mine, I would have slapped her face and told her to find lodgings of her own."

"No you wouldn't."

"You're probably right," she said listlessly. "They'll love me whatever I do. They'll put up with anything. Well, almost anything."

Now, what did she mean by that?

"They are very handsome people," I said carefully, aware that their patience with her was a burden.

"Are they ever now? Didn't one of me young men— former young men; I don't have any just now, Cousin Paddy—and himself a nice boy though a bit of an eejit, say that if he lived in the same house with me ma, he'd want to frig her every night?"

"And you said?"

"Well." She took a deep breath. "I don't want to shock you now."

"You won't."

"I reckoned I could either be offended or complimented. So don't I say, just as bold as brass, me father does, sometimes twice a night!"

I broke up in laughter. "That fixed your poor eejit, all right."

"Did it ever! And then I realized that it might just be true or close to the truth, and I was proud of them. Not that I could live that way meself."

Why not? I wondered. But I didn't ask.

"Ah," she said sadly, "I don't deserve parents like them. Not at all, at all . . . Well, Cousin Paddy, I thought we'd double back and look at the Collegiate Church and Lynch's Castle and Lynch's Window and then go over to Bowling Green where the poor woman was raised and then maybe walk up to UCG—that's University College Galway, in case, like a dumb Yank, you don't know what the letters mean—and wasn't it founded in 1845, and then maybe have a sandwich and a pint at me pub."

Sounded fine to me.

"Och," she said, stopping short as we turned down an alley, which was in fact a medieval street. "Am I not the terrible eejit? I was supposed to tell you me parents would pick you at half eight for dinner. Won't they be taking you up to Ardilawn House, which is a lovely place, especially on a hot summer night?"

"No," I said flatly. "I won't be going out with them tonight."

"And why not?" She scowled at me, and not a mood scowl either but a fighting scowl.

"Well, I will on only one condition."

"And that is?"

"That you're included."

"I don't think that's the drill, not after meself being a nine-fingered shite hawk last night."

What a marvelous combination of words! I didn't ask what it meant.

"You tell them that I said I won't have dinner with them unless you come along."

She hugged my arm. "Won't they be glad to hear that! Sure, Cousin Paddy, you're a desperate man altogether!"

"Desperate" is pretty hard to translate into American

English. It means wonderful but in a kind of outrageous way.

She hung on to my arm for a few more moments, tears welling up in her eyes again.

"No one excludes my lovely cousin Sara Anne Elizabeth from dinner, no matter how much of a gobshite she is!"

She thought that was very funny and hugged my arm more tightly.

I wish, Rae, I said to the lurking Seraph, that these were my words instead of yours.

Should I kiss her now, right here in the middle of Market Street? It probably wouldn't be a good idea. What if she kissed me first?

Lucky me.

⚜12⚜

So I was shown Lynch's Castle and Lynch's Window, from which James Lynch Fitzstephen, the mayor at the time, hanged his own son in 1493 for murdering a visiting Spaniard. Then we entered St. Nicholas Collegiate Church—which doesn't mean that it was affiliated with a school but that it was administered by a group of priests instead of by one pastor. It had been built by the Anglo-Normans in 1320 right at the center of town. The Protestants took it over during the Reformation, as they did all the major churches in Ireland.

"Why haven't we taken them back?"

She recoiled in horror. "Wouldn't that be a terrible thing to do! Aren't they as Irish as we are? Poor people, they don't have enough money to keep it up, and I think we should help them. Maybe even have Mass in there on Sunday. What would be wrong with that?"

"Do they sing your Mass at their own services?"

"Me da didn't give them any choice."

This young woman was already a major figure in her home city. Did she know it? Probably. She didn't miss much. She coped with her celebrity status by attributing it all to her father.

And didn't your man stop here for Mass and to read about St. Brendan before he sailed to America?"

"The Italian fellow?"

She nodded. "Sure, didn't St. Brendan get there almost a thousand years before?"

The Collegiate Church was indeed beautiful, too small to be a Gothic cathedral and too big to be just a parish church. There was scaffolding inside, as a repair project was under way, the young man in a soutane who was selling postcards and guidebooks told us.

"Isn't it a long project, Sara?" he said with a sigh. "There are not many of us left."

"The two churches are foolishness, Tony," she replied. "All they do is give us twice as many bishops."

They both laughed. Of course, he knew Sara. Didn't everyone?

I bought a half dozen postcards, gave him a twenty-punt note, and told him that I thought she was right. He was very grateful and my cousin beamed proudly.

"You really are a desperate man, Paddy Tobin," she said, clinging to my arm again as we left the church. "Terrible desperate."

It was the Seraph again. I never gave people twenty-dollar tips before, especially for Protestant churches.

We wandered around the back streets, visited the Druid Theater in a medieval hall (it's the best theater in the West of Ireland and maybe the best in the whole country), where herself, now clinging to my arm all the time, proudly introduced me to the whole company, who were taking a break from the rehearsal.

She also introduced me to a couple of artists who were wandering around the medieval streets with bright paintings. I promised I'd come back later in my trip and look at their work, in a tone of voice that suggested maybe I'd buy something.

Herself squeezed my arm more fiercely.

Instead of riding the cloud to which one is entitled when a transcendentally glorious young woman hangs on to your arm, I began to feel guilty. I had overplayed my hand. The poor child now adored me. That damn Seraph again. I didn't want or need adoration. Not this soon anyway. What would happen when I disillusioned her as I surely would?

Then we turned down Bowling Green, a street with tiny nineteenth-century row houses. Halfway down the row we stopped at Number 8, the house in which Nora Barnacle, the companion and eventual wife of James Joyce, had lived as a child and young woman.

"She dedicated her life to that poor amadan," Sara said, shaking her head sadly.

"So small and cramped, Sara," I said as I looked around the parlor on the first floor. "How could people have lived in such a crowded space?"

"More room than they had in the farmhouses or the caves before that, she murmured. "Poor woman. It wasn't much to leave behind when she moved to Dublin to work at Finn's Hotel. But it was still home. She gave it all up for your man—home, family, friends, country, religion. He was a genius, all right, but a filthy-minded drunk too."

"She loved him, Sara Anne."

"She did that, God knows."

We stood in the minute and crowded parlor for a few silent moments.

"As long as people read English, they'll know about her. Ulysses was written about the day that he met her. And she's all his women—the seabird woman on the beach, Gertie, Gerda, Molly, Anna, Livia, Plurabelle. Love can pay no greater tribute to a woman than to immortalize her in stories. Even if he was a pathetic drunk who died long before his time. She kept him alive long enough to finish his work."

"Ah, aren't you the romantic, Paddy Tobin?"

"Me?"

"You . . . It's all right. I kind of like romantics."

No one had ever called me a romantic before. If there is one thing that I am not, it's a romantic.

"Let's say a prayer for both of them," she whispered, and made the sign of the cross. "Sure it can't hurt."

So I prayed silently that peace and rest and joy be granted to James and Nora Barnacle Joyce.

"Even the Church has made peace with him." Sara Anne sighed, after making her second sign of the cross and thus indicating that our period of prayer was over. "Doesn't my literature professor say that he was the greatest Catholic novelist ever, and the Church not knowing it at all, at all, in those days?"

"I'm told that you can buy his books in the bookstore at the entrance to the Vatican."

"Somehow I don't think your man would have liked that."

"Ah, he would have, though. Didn't he live to read only one review of *Finnegans Wake*? And wasn't it in *Osservatore Romano*, the Vatican paper, and wasn't it favorable? And wasn't he pleased as Punch with it?"

She captured my arm and led me out of the door of the little row house with all its bittersweet memories. "And haven't we got you talking like an Irishman already?

Come on, let's leave the dead and go up to UCG where the living are, too frigging many of the living if you asked me."

"At your service."

"Do you like being a computer consultant, and yourself loving literature so much?" she asked me as we walked along the river towards the Salmon Weir Bridge.

"Do you like working in your father's office, and yourself writing music?"

She laughed again and patted my arm approvingly. Her laughter came easily now and sounded as musical to me as the bells of St. Nicholas Collegiate Church chiming behind us.

"A woman can't win a single exchange with you, can she, Paddy Tobin?"

"They win them all," I insisted with full regard for the truth.

She laughed again.

"God designed you to laugh, Sara Anne Tobin."

"Little enough to laugh at these days . . . But now tell me about your family."

I described my parents and my three sisters and our wolfhounds with as much sympathy as I could muster. I thought the presentation was pretty favorable.

"So you don't like them, except for the hounds and poor little Megan?"

"Megan can take care of herself."

"They never leave you alone, do they? I know Irish families like that. They have no patience for the wayward son."

"I'm not wayward!"

She leaned her head against my shoulder. "But, poor things, they think you are. They're wrong, of course, but they love you and they mean well. Eventually you will have to shut them up, you know."

Again I wanted to kiss her. But I didn't, not just yet.

"I suppose you're right. It won't be easy."

"Dealing with parents never is."

We crossed the Salmon Weir Bridge in silence. She was now hanging on me as if she would never let me go. I freed my right arm and extended it around her shoulders, drawing her even closer.

" 'Tis nice, Paddy Tobin." She snuggled against me. "Very nice indeed. A little forward, but still nice."

"I have no immediate designs on your wondrous body, Sara Anne Tobin."

"I know THAT . . . but sure when we get near UCG you must stop lest all me friends think I've been seduced by my Yank cousin the first day I met him."

"Second day."

She laughed again and snuggled even closer.

We were moving too fast altogether. But the feel of her against my body was too delightful to give up.

We walked by the cathedral.

"Ugly frigging place," she murmured. "I shouldn't let them sing my music inside it."

"Yes, you should."

"I know THAT."

We crossed two more branches of the river on University road. Sara Anne disengaged herself. "Now, I'll be introducing you as me cousin from America, like I'm very proud of you—which I am—and won't they all be wondering if there's anything between us, and I won't tell them a thing, will I now?"

"Is there anything between us, Sara Anne?"

"How would I be knowing that so soon? All I know is what me parents said: You are very sweet and gentle. Would that be enough of a preliminary comment?"

"Fine."

We stopped at the university chapel, built off the campus grounds because Irish law required that there be no church or theological faculty on any of the campuses of the National University of Ireland. It was a lovely little place, the sun shining through the stained-glass windows, painting it rose and purple and gold.

Hadn't Dr. Casey built it for the students when he was still bishop? And wasn't he a fine man even if he'd had a woman for a while when he was younger? Was he the first Irish bishop who had done that? Or the last? At least he found women attractive, which you couldn't say for most of those eejits. And at least he wasn't playing with little boys, was he? Wasn't he a great man even if he had the occasional faults of a great man? And hadn't the Irish media been terrible cruel to him?

Her hands were clenched into tight little fists as she defended him. I'd want her by my side in any crisis. Even if there wasn't a crisis.

"Do they sing your Mass here?" I asked as we walked up to the main building of the college, a Victorian structure with a great tower and an interior quadrangle.

"Do they have any choice? And me da being one of their major benefactors?"

"That may be true, Sara Anne. But it's lovely music and I suspect you damn frigging well know that it is and are very proud of it as you should be."

"Sometimes," she admitted. "Sometimes, Cousin Paddy. And sometimes not. I'm no Mozart."

"And he was no Sara Anne Tobin who could write music that everyone could sing in the language of their choice."

"Me ma and da are terrible proud of it."

She wasn't giving away much.

It being a day when one could "perish with the heat," most of the students were wearing T-shirts instead of sweatshirts, and the girls were wearing shorts and an occasional tank top. School was finished for the term, but there were still exams, though Sara Anne was finished with hers.

I thought the kids were quite attractive and very serious about their studies beneath their flip words. How many of them would be able to get a job when they graduated? How many would have to go into exile? Damn Cromwell and his followers for what they had done to this country and its people.

"Isn't that one as good as naked?" Sara complained in mock disapproval at a young woman in abbreviated shorts and a thin and scanty tank top.

"Not quite. And not as attractive as you fully dressed."

"Would you stop with your compliments," she said, slapping my arm. "As much as I like them, they make me blush."

Virtually everyone we passed as we ambled through the university grounds—a mix of dark gray nineteenth century and bright concrete twentieth century—greeted my Sara Anne, and she responded brightly to them.

But how could you not know the name of this radiant young woman?

She introduced me only to a select few.

"Aren't you all dressed up for such a hot day, Sara? Sure you look great, but won't you perish with the heat?"

"Me da is making me take my American cousin around the city, so he insisted I should dress. I don't think me cousin Paddy Tobin even noticed what I was wearing."

"I did too!"

Her friends would cautiously size me up and conclude that I was probably all right. For a frigging Yank.

"How could he not?" a young man would murmur.

"Will you be staying long, Paddy Tobin?" a young woman would ask.

"Until Sara Anne and her parents say they're tired of me."

"Are you still in university in America?"

"Isn't he an expert on Irish literature and a computer consultant too?" she would demand proudly.

"That makes sense," a young man would say. "Sure doesn't it take a computer to figure out what Irish writers are saying!"

General laughter.

"Aren't those eejits all wondering whether we're sweethearts?" she said, her nose tilted skyward. "Well, let them wonder, says I."

"Are we, Sara Anne?"

"Haven't I told you it's too early to decide that?" She stamped her foot. "Haven't I said you're a nice frigging amadan? Isn't that enough?"

"If you don't want them to suspect that we are sweethearts, you shouldn't act so proud of me."

"But I AM proud of you, Cousin Paddy. Can't I be proud of you without being your sweetheart?"

She stopped and stared at me with a frown that suggested she wanted me to accept her distinction.

"Yet."

"Right. Yet."

More musical laughter.

I patted her delicious rump ever so lightly under the guise of setting her in motion. She giggled but did not complain.

If I continued to say the right things Rae was whispering in my ear, I really could have this troubled, gifted, lively, beautiful young woman as my bride. Moreover her parents were so eager to find the right man for her—and thought I might be just that on the basis of a couple of hours of conversation—that they would not object to a marriage in only three weeks.

And I'd have a wonderful bedmate and ten million dollars.

Somehow it didn't seem fair. I'd be exploiting her fragility and fear, wouldn't I?

"That's the library." She gestured at a grand, gray limestone building. "Don't they have all the archives of Galway from 1485 to 1818? No one destroyed them here as those eejits did at the Four Courts in Dublin during the Troubles."

"Maybe we can find something in there about the Tobin family feud," I murmured.

"What feud!"

"Your da and ma didn't tell you last night why I'm here?"

"They did not. Sure, didn't they have a hard enough time even talking to the little gobshite?"

"Nine-fingered shite hawk."

More of her wonderful laughter. But she had not quite forgiven herself. So I told her about Great-Uncle Gerry and the family feud and his will and the crazy letter and his gifts. I did not tell her, of course, about the bequest to me.

Why not tell her up front? I could cover that up and still collect the money.

But that would not be fair to Great-Uncle Gerry. I'd have to keep my end of the implicit bargain I had made when I let my family talk me into coming to Ireland.

"How much did he give to me da?" she asked as soon as I was finished with the story.

"I don't know, Sara Anne, and if I did, I couldn't tell

you. He did say that he would use it for his plan to hire unemployed computer people."

"Glory be to God!" she exclaimed joyfully. "Wasn't I hoping for that? But, Cousin Paddy, was the poor man daft altogether?"

"I think he knew what he was doing, Sara Anne. A little daft maybe. Indeed, a whole lot daft, but he knew what he wanted to do."

"And that was?" She took my arm again.

"Heal an old wound that still existed even if no one knew about it."

"And why?"

"Because someday someone might find out about it and open the wound again . . . It might not make much sense to us, but it made a lot of sense to him."

She nodded thoughtfully. "Maybe he was right."

"Maybe."

"And why do you want to find out more about it?"

"Because it's there. And because if I don't, I'll always think I'm missing something important."

"Do you remember every word I say so you can turn it against me?"

"I do."

"Well." She sighed loudly. "I see your point and I'll help you search if you want."

"We're the last living members, if you are to believe him, of both sides of the feud."

She didn't challenge the inaccuracy of my statement. "Isn't that true . . . Now, here's me pub. Around the corner here on Newcastle Road. It's a shite house, but it has wonderful sandwiches."

The pub—The University Arms, it presumed to call itself—was a small, crowded, noisy, smelly hole in the wall. The smell was worse than the noise—the stench of sweaty young bodies and stout permeated it as if it had been part of the atmosphere for a couple of centuries, along with other nameless aromas, the origins of which one didn't want to know too much.

Sara Anne returned the greetings of her admirers and threaded her way through the tables until she found us a place for two in one of the far corners of the room.

"Hi, Rae," she said to the woman behind the bar.

"Hi, Sara," the latter replied.

No mists at all, at all. Only herself, now a few pounds heavier and with strands of gray hair.

The damn Seraphs were everywhere. I knew she'd been following me, telling me what to say and restraining my lustful impulses. But why show up in the flesh, so to speak, at Sara Anne's pub?

I was beginning to suspect that sometimes your Seraphim did some of their tricks for the pure hell of it.

"I'll buy lunch," I insisted.

"It's me own pub," she said hotly.

"And you're my tour guide. Don't give me an argument, Sara Anne. Fair is fair."

"Sure, if I'd know you were paying, wouldn't I have found a much more expensive place?"

I was told that I merely walked over to the bar and ordered two ham and cheese sandwiches on a croissant and two pints.

"Of what?"

"Of Guinness. What else?"

"I'm new around here."

I presented the order to Rae, and without even a wink of her eye, she presented me with the two sandwiches and the two pints, which had been waiting for me.

Was it really Rae? I wondered as I walked back to our table.

Of course it was Rae.

"Well, that was fast, wasn't it now? Rae must have liked the looks of you."

"How long has she been working here?"

"Rae?" Sara Anne hesitated, puzzled. "I don't know. Not long, I guess. She's very nice, though."

Just like in the Manchester police station. Rae could confuse people apparently with a twitch of a thumb. Or whatever organ was represented by the thumb in her analogue.

"Don't you smoke, Sara Anne?"

"I do not. I used to smoke something terrible up at Kylemore because it was against the rules. But I stopped when I came home because I didn't want to worry my parents . . . Eat your sandwich."

"Hey, it IS very good," I admitted after the first bite.

"They're always good," she said, "but today for some reason they're better than usual."

Naturally, if a Seraph made them, they were better than usual. I took a cautious sip of the thick black stuff I had poured into a glass. Well, it wasn't too bad.

"So what do you think, Cousin Paddy?" she asked me as she munched on her sandwich. Her unfathomable eyes stared straight into mine.

"I think it's a neat little city. Truly the Venice of Ireland. Fascinating. A little bit of everything. Nice people."

"As you well know, I didn't mean Galway. I meant your gobshite cousin."

"Isn't it a little early for me to be forming an opinion?"

"And yourself watching every move I make and remembering every word I say and looking at me half the time like I had all my clothes off."

"Only some of your clothes, Sara Anne."

I had seen her with all her clothes off, had I not?

No, of course not. Where did I ever get that crazy notion. Seraphs at work again.

"It depends on which ones you leave on . . . I want to know what you think about me and not just about me body."

She was not fishing for a compliment. She wanted my real opinion.

"Well, now." I took her hand. "Let me think about that."

She pulled her hand abruptly away. I recaptured it, and she didn't resist the second time.

"Cousin Sara Anne Elizabeth," I began

"Sara Anne Elizabeth Moire."

"Right . . . Well," I said, playing with her graceful fingers, "let me see."

She waited, her eyes relentless.

"First of all, we'll take it as a given," I said lightly, "that she is the most beautiful woman around whom I ever put my arms. Arm, singular, to be exact. Or whose lovely ass I ever patted, however lightly. Or ever met, in fact. Her beauty is not unimportant—"

She tried to pull her hand away. I clamped my paw around it like a vise.

"Secondly, she is charming, lively, funny, gifted, and a delight to be with. And her smile would melt an iceberg."

She stopped tugging. Her eyes did not waver.

"Thirdly, she is bugged by some emotional problem that I do not understand, but I'm sure it will go away eventually."

She lifted her shoulders ever so slightly in a skeptical gesture.

"Fourthly, her most endearing trait is a wondrous combination of energy and enthusiasm, which I'm sure will last at least till she's eighty-five. Moreover she has the rare ability to excite energy and enthusiasm in others. So on the whole, as we Americans would say, she's a keeper."

"What does that mean?" she asked solemnly.

"It means that I'm looking forward to getting to know her much better in the couple of weeks I'll be in Ireland."

"Couple of weeks?"

"Two weeks from Saturday."

"Ah, sure, by then won't we get to know each other so well that we'll be fighting all the time . . . and you can let go of me hand now."

"Not until I tell you that I think it would be fun to fight with you."

Only then did she blush and pull her hand away. "Thank you, Paddy Tobin. I'm glad you like me . . . Now I'll go get us some more nourishment. More of the same?"

"Two more sandwiches and a glass of mineral water or something of the sort."

She seemed surprised by the request.

"Ballygowan? It's kind of an Irish Pelegrino."

"Fine."

As she went off to do business with Rae, I relaxed for a moment and considered my performance thus far. I had not done all that badly. She liked me, indeed by her own admission was proud of me. I still had a long way to go in two and a half weeks to lure her into a marriage bed. But we'd made a good beginning. The chemistry, whatever that was, certainly existed between us. Now I had to ask myself whether I really wanted her. After all, she had some sort of serious problem, as I had told her. Moreover would such a hasty marriage to a woman so young and so fragile be fair to her?

"Who the frig do you think you are?"

Someone yanked me to my feet.

"And what the frig," the big man who had gripped the back of my neck continued, "Do you think you're doing here?"

I evaluated the possible opposition. He was a couple of inches taller than my six feet and maybe forty pounds heavier. But he was fat and drunk. No big problem, except I didn't like barroom brawls.

"My name is Pat Tobin and I'm eating a couple of sandwiches and drinking a pint."

"You're a relative of Sara?"

"Distant."

He was typically black Irish, a typical black Irish drunk, in fact. His thick black hair reached almost to his eyebrows. His red face and red nose partially covered pale white skin. His jaw jutted at me as if he were ready to start a fight.

"You clear out, you hear," he demanded, "or I'll beat you to a bloody pulp, you understand? She's my woman, understand?"

"Funny thing," I said, brushing his paw away from my neck with a single sweep of my hand, "she didn't mention that. And I don't quite think she'd pair up with a fall-down drunk."

As soon as I had spoken the last sentence, I regretted it. It was an invitation to a barroom brawl, which I didn't need or want.

"Be careful, Oisin," someone shouted. "The Yank might break your arm all over again."

Was this Asmodeus, the Destroyer? They grew their demons pretty pathetic here in Ireland.

He turned away from me and peered through the smoke, looking for his other tormentor.

"You shut your pissant face, Nial Raftery, or I'll destroy

you after I've finished with this frigger."

"Leave him alone, you frigging amadan." Sara Anne had reappeared and charged my would-be assailant.

"Get away from me, woman." He sent Sara flying with a quick shove. Her eyes became little pinpoints of black light and she clenched her fist.

"I'll break your other arm, you bastard," she screamed.

She tensed for another charge. She might just break his other arm, I thought. No one messed with Sara Anne or her family.

He paid no attention to her. Instead he slammed me against the wall and pulled back his fist, ready to strike.

"Didn't I tell you to clear out?"

"You did."

"And to stay away from her?"

"You did."

Sara had picked up an empty Guinness bottle and was waiting for the opportunity for a second charge. Grace O'Malley, the pirate queen, was alive and well and living in Galway city.

"Well, what are you waiting for?"

"For you to fall on the floor where a drunk like you belongs."

The mists were beginning to gather. About time, Seraph person.

With an angry growl, he swung and I ducked. His fist crashed into the wall next to me. He let out a terrible yell.

"It's the hand you'll be losing this time, Oisin me boyo," a young woman yelled.

Still screaming in pain, he nursed his right fist in his left hand. I took the opportunity to remove myself from the wall. I noted with some relief that Sara had put down the bottle.

"I'll kill you," he bellowed, and lunged at me.

He missed me completely and crashed into the table. He tried to straighten up but instead fell to his knees. The mists were thick now and I noted that Rae was approaching from a distance, a wild gleam in her eyes.

"Hit him again, Oisin," several people cried out. "Hit him hard this time!"

"There's so much fog in here," he said, pulling himself to his feet, "that I can't find the frigger."

Hoots and laughter from the masses.

He swung again, missed by at least a yard, hit the wall again, and fell on his face. Our table overturned on top of him.

"Get up and finish him off, Oisin," a woman yelled. "Put him away for good!"

He shrugged the table away and struggled to rise. He fell on his face again.

"The Yank destroyed Oisin altogether."

General applause from the audience.

"What's the matter, Oisin? Smoke get in your eyes!"

No, friend. Mists. Seraphic mists.

Speaking of that kind, Rae was among us. For a moment she seemed ten feet tall.

"You get out of here, Oisin O'Riordan. And never come in here again or I'll call in the Gardai. I don't give a good shite whether your father is a member of the Dáil or not."

A member of their parliament, was he?

She picked him up by the scruff of his neck and dragged him to the door. A couple of the lads, relishing the humiliation of Asmodeus—whose eyes had been blinded by smoke as in the older version—helped her throw him out on Distillery Street. On his rear end, I presumed.

"All of ye, listen to me," Rae shouted. "If he ever comes back, won't I call the Gardai first thing? So ye'd better keep him out, if you don't want this place closed for a week."

Her Irish accent had become a ridiculous caricature. A little overdone, my Seraph friend, but still impressive.

Shouts of agreement from the crowd.

I turned our table over and moved to it the three sandwiches and the two bottles of Ballygowan herself had left on the table next to ours, and guided her to her chair.

Still tense and glowering, my cousin permitted me to sit her down.

"Thank you, Paddy," she said through clenched teeth.

"Woman, if I ever see you looking at me with that look in your eye and a bottle in your hand, I'll get the hell out of wherever I am as fast as my aging legs can carry me."

She touched my hand. "I'd never lift a bottle to you, Paddy."

A number of folks came over to congratulate me on our triumph. Sara Anne introduced me as her cousin Paddy from America.

Behind the bar, Rae was grinning complacently.

"Why didn't you hit him, Paddy?" Sara asked, sipping from her Ballygowan.

"I don't like barroom brawls," I said. "So I don't hit people until it is absolutely necessary."

"You could have destroyed him altogether."

"Sure," I said with a shrug. "What would that prove? He's a fall-down drunk and bully of whom no one is afraid anymore."

"Most men would have hit him anyway."

"I'm not most men . . . Are you disappointed in me?"

"Oh, no, Paddy," she said, her eyes widening in surprise. "Am I not proud of you?"

She reached out impulsively and touched my hand and then pulled away quickly.

The adoration in her marvelous eyes destroyed me altogether.

"Why did you have only one Guinness?"

"Two drinks in a place like this is my upper limit. So I usually stop with one so as to not take any chances."

"Two?"

"Well, last year I had four one night and went on a rampage."

"I DON'T believe it."

" 'Tis true."

"Tell me about it."

How had I dug myself into the hole? How was I going to dig myself out? I didn't want any more adoration, did I?

Yeah, I did, as a matter of fact.

So I told her a sanitized version of my encounter with the two men at the automatic teller machine. I tried to make myself look like a lucky fool. So I concluded with the mayor's comment.

"Did he really say that?"

"He did."

"Didn't he give you a medal too?"

"Kind of."

"You would have done the same thing sober, Paddy Tobin."

"That's what the good Megan says."

"I'm dying to meet the child. I'm sure I'll love her."

"You will that."

"You saved the woman's life!"

"Maybe. Still, I should have called the police first."

This time she slapped my fist. "You were a hero, Paddy, and I'll hear nothing else about it."

"Well, at least I wasn't a hero today."

"By nightfall you will be. Won't everyone in Galway be saying that the Tobins' Yank cousin beat the living shite out of Oisin O'Riordan."

"But I didn't!"

"Ireland is a land of storytelling, as you must know by now, Cousin Paddy. Most people, meself NOT included, would think that is a much better story than the truth. Sure, do we ever let the truth get in the way of a good story?"

"I guess not."

We finished our sandwiches—I ate half of hers, thanked Rae, who still looked very proud of herself, and left the pub. We walked back to Eyre Square, both of us locked in our own thoughts.

She insisted that I visit their new shopping mall, a vast series of corridors tucked back between High Street and the Square, some of its walls built into old medieval walls. It was swarming with people, not all that many of them tourists, and on a Monday afternoon. Whatever its unemployment rate, Galway city was bursting with prosperity.

How long can a man face those adoring eyes, I wondered, and not fall irreparably in love?

Perhaps, I hoped, Sara Anne was thinking that she must be cautious about this big Yank cousin of hers. She didn't want to fall instantly in love with a man she hardly knew.

"I'd better stop in me da's office to see if there's any work for me to do," she said when we had finally arrived at the great granite pile that was the Great Southern.

"You'll be there tonight or I won't get in the car with your parents."

"There's no danger that I won't." She smiled happily. "Not at all, at all."

"Where did you say we're going?"

"Ardilawn House out on Taylor's Hill. Isn't it a brilliant old place with wonderful food?"

"I should dress up?"

"If you'd wear a jacket and a tie, it'd be nice. We'll eat in the garden where it will be pleasantly cool this evening. But any friend of Ronan Tobin's can come as he pleases."

"You and your ma will dress up?"

"Och! Will we ever! Me ma is already planning the sensation we'll create. She loves sensations."

"So she knows that I'll insist you come along?"

"She had more confidence in you than I did. But sure, hasn't she known you longer?"

"I'll dress as one who knows he'll be in the presence of two gorgeous women."

"Would you stop it?" She tapped my arm again and turned towards her dad's office.

Then she turned back to me, embraced me, and kissed me. With firmness and determination and warmth. It was perhaps a brief kiss, but I was too overwhelmed by her affection to time it.

Without a word, she turned her back on me and ran over to her father's office.

A passionate kiss?

Well, not quite. But not far away either.

"Did you have a nice time today with your cousin Sara, Mr. Tobin?" Nuala asked me as I floated into the hotel.

"It was all right now, wasn't it?" I replied.

"She's a beautiful woman, isn't she?"

"Ah, she's not bad, not the worst of them, if you take me meaning," I said, hurrying away from the inquisitive little chit.

By tomorrow morning everyone in Galway city would have heard of Sara and her big cousin from America and of how he had destroyed Oisin O'Riordan altogether.

And they'd be asking the same questions my reception-ist with the red hair was asking, however indirectly.

I expected, half expected as they would say around here, that my Seraph friend would be waiting for me. She was not in the room, however; and I didn't feel like trying to call her up on the Net. There were a lot of interesting questions over which I should puzzle and agonize.

Instead I swam in the pool on the top floor overlooking the bay (in an addition added to the hotel long after 1857), basked in the sauna, went back to my suite, took a shower, wrapped a towel around myself, and permitted myself a well-earned nap.

I don't remember the dreams, but I'm sure they were about my cousin and therefore very pleasant dreams.

13

I woke up about half past seven, rolled over, and wondered where I was.

It took me a while to remember. Then I became angry at myself because this long nap would keep me awake into the morning hours again.

Where was herself?

Nowhere to be seen. Well, I'm not eager to talk to her either.

Why did I think I had seen Sara Anne in the nude? I certainly had not, save perhaps in some anticipation of the future, a delightful anticipation at that.

Probably in one of my dreams. She had been wearing gray underwear, which was not particularly erotic.

Crazy dream. Crazy knight errant. Horny, aging quester for the grail. You don't screw the grail, you admire and reverence it. Well, maybe you could do both.

I'm supposed to have supper with them tonight. Half

eight. Too late an hour for supper. The hours I spent with the child today were exhausting. Too much of her in one day. Why not take it easy?

I only have a little more than two weeks.

So what. I don't need or want the money. Why not go home?

I'll probably be a half hour late calling home tonight too. It doesn't matter. They'll still have it screwed up in their heads.

Right, just go back to sleep. Tell them you're a little under the weather. Right.

Then I remember the taste of Sara Anne's lips against my own.

All right. I'd better take another shower.

So I struggled out of bed and into the shower. I didn't feel much better when I emerged. My clothes were laid out for me, naturally. Blue. Color-coded with my eyes— light blue shirt and slacks, dark blue socks, jacket, and tie. What did Rae do with all these elegantly fitted garments when I had worn them once? Or were they all the same clothes, which she had transformed temporarily?

I dressed but left the jacket off and tried to read some of Tom Flanigan's *The End of the Hunt*, a book about the "troubles" of 1916 to 1923. Five minutes before half eight, the phone rang. I thought the Irish were never punctual.

" 'Tis Nuala, Mr. Tobin. Isn't your cousin Sara Anne waiting down here with your family to take you up to Taylor Hill for supper?"

"They're early."

"You don't have to come right down."

"I'll be there in a moment."

"Wait till you see your cousin, Mr. Tobin."

"Would she be a sensation now?"

"You won't believe it."

I really didn't. Mother and daughter would have stopped traffic on any street corner in the world. They were both wearing "slip" dresses, which were in fashion this year for those who could wear them, and these two could. The dresses are modeled on mostly outmoded lingerie from the past—unadorned dresses with short skirts, thin straps, lots of shoulder and tit (though very discreetly revealed), and a silky sheen that shimmered as they moved. Edna was in green, Sara Anne in virginal and more daring white.

Plain and simple dresses for a warm evening in the County Galway, right?

I'm sure I gulped. What else? Nuala was grinning complacently in the background. The two women looked quite content with themselves and their sensation.

"Ah, Ronan Tobin, aren't we the lucky fellas that we can be seen in public with such beautiful women?"

"And won't I not be outnumbered at least this one night?"

"We're outnumbered, Ronan. Totally."

Edna kissed me just as she had the night before. Then, hesitantly but with eyes dancing with mischief, didn't Sara Anne do exactly the same thing?

"Sensational," I murmured into her sweet-smelling black hair.

"Wouldya stop it?" she said, grinning wickedly and then drawing back from me.

I was two down in the kissing game.

Her parents beamed with pleasure. Just now I was their designated hitter, the prime candidate for a son-in-law.

We entered her da's car, an older model Mercedes (before the time when they ruined the profile with a hump-back trunk). Sara Anne and I were assigned to the backseat. Her parents sustained the conversation by asking what we had seen during the day.

Herself was about as far away from me as she could be and still inside the car. Out of the corner of my eye I watched as she became tense; her back stiffened, her fists clenched, a frown descended on her face. A black mood in the making? Because of her parents' chatter? That didn't seem likely.

I reached for her hand. It was stiff and unyielding. I insisted with a tightening grip. She resisted and then capitulated. Her hand became submissive, even eager to give itself to me. I felt the tenseness easing out of her body. She relaxed against the back of the seat and enveloped me in the benediction of her very best smile. I caressed the palm of my captive hand with a gentle movement of my thumb. She sighed happily and snuggled closer to me.

I ought not to have such magical power over any woman. Not even a wife.

Well, maybe a wife.

"Sure, haven't you figured me out perfectly?" she whispered as I helped her out of the car. "Thank you, Paddy."

I wanted to say something clever, but the extra glimpses of breast and thigh as she climbed out reduced me to absolute silence.

We were to eat dinner in a lovely garden, surrounded by trees and smelling of roses. There were only three other couples scattered around the tables when we arrived. Naturally every set of eyes turned when our two women appeared.

"Sensation indeed," I whispered to my date.

She giggled. "I told you the woman loves sensations."

"So does her daughter."

Ronan ordered a glass of Bushmills Green for each of us.

"Ballygowan for me, please," the princess said. "I'm driving."

Ronan smiled proudly. "See what we have to put up with, Paddy? We never get fluttered when we go out to eat, but the young one, having read about it in some American magazine, insists she is the designated driver."

She flicked her long black hair and then smoothed it into place, a sign, I was beginning to learn, that Sara Anne was prepared to score points.

"Isn't your night vision already deteriorating, Da? It happens to everyone over forty."

"Don't I feel ancient already?" her mother sighed. "And meself with a grown-up daughter?"

"You don't look ancient, Ma," she said, touching her mother's bare arm, "not at all, at all."

Both parents beamed again. Sara Anne's trouble couldn't be a generational problem, not directly. There was too much love among the three of them.

I know that I had two glasses of whiskey, a half bottle of wine, and a sip of Bailey's at the end. But I have no idea of what I ate. The food was almost as sensational as the two women, but my hunger that night was not for food.

I could not take my eyes off my young cousin. I stared at her, drank her in, absorbed her, delighted in her. She was pleasantly embarrassed by my attention. She would look down, bite her lip, turn away from my gaze, and then peek at me out of the corner of her eye. Her pale skin would turn pink and she would laugh happily.

"Something happened today that you ought to know about, Da." She straightened her luminous shoulders.

"Your man Oisin tried to pick a fight with Paddy at me pub."

"The poor eejit," Ronan said, shaking his head sadly. "Won't he ever grow up?"

"What happened, Paddy?" Edna asked anxiously.

"Nothing much. He seemed to think I had no right to be in his pub with his woman. He took a poke at me and missed. Banged up his fingers when he hit the wall. He's a fall-down drunk. No threat to anyone."

"Rae threw him out," Sara Anne continued, "and warned everyone that if he came back she'd call the Gardai and they'd close the pub down for a week. Paddy had the good sense not to fight with him, but by now most everyone in Galway city will have heard how the Tobins' big cousin from America beat the shite out of that fat bully."

She patted my arm as she talked, approving my restraint.

"Good stuff, Paddy." Her mother echoed Sara Anne's support.

"The poor fella," Ronan continued. "His parents are good friends of ours. His father is a grand man, a T.D.— a member of the Dáil, as we call our parliament—and one of the richest men in Galway. Oisin is not bad, mind you, just a little wild long after the time a boy can be a little wild and no one minds."

"Superannuated child," Sara Anne snapped. "I am NOT his woman and I never will be."

"Sure, haven't we given up that idea long ago?" her father said. "He hasn't turned out right, though he may eventually."

"Not a prayer of that," Sara replied sharply. "He'll always be a little boy that his ma spoiled rotten."

"I'm afraid you're right, dear," her mother agreed

"She has always been too indulgent with her children. Thinks they're perfect."

"Thank God me own ma and da don't think I'm perfect."

General laughter and more wine poured.

"Just practically perfect," I agreed. "Save when she's in one of her black moods."

More laughter from everyone, including Sara Anne, whose practically permanent blush turned a deeper shade of scarlet.

"Paddy's not a coward," she insisted, "Just because he wouldn't destroy a drunken bully. Didn't the Lord Mayor of Chicago personally decorate him for heroism?"

"Mayor," I muttered. "We don't have Lord Mayors in America."

"A Waterford man, isn't he now?" Ronan asked.

"That's where his ancestors are from. His wife's family, however, is from this very county. The Corbetts from up around Keerannuageeragh, up at the far end of your lake."

"Glory be to God!" Ronan exclaimed. "A Galway woman and from my part of Galway."

"No man will ever be wrong if he marries a Galway woman," Sara Anne said flatly as if her statement were revealed as truth against which there could be no argument.

"Would you ever tell us your story, Paddy?" her ma asked politely.

"No."

"I'll tell it because he'll try to make himself sound like a bloody eejit."

So Sara Anne told my story, making me look more like a hero than I ever was or ever could possibly be.

"Like I told the mayor, I was fluttered altogéther."

"And tell them what he said!"

So I told them. They all laughed.

"Ah, he must be a grand man," Ronan said, nodding his head in approval.

"Did you bring your medal with you, Paddy?" Edna asked. "Sure, aren't we dying to see it?"

I hadn't brought it, but heaven knows that the Seraph might produce it on demand.

"Don't I sleep with it every night?"

More laughter.

I almost said that I wanted something better to sleep with. The drink was getting to my tongue. Fortunately what I did say was, "No, I don't travel with it. I'm kind of ashamed of the whole affair."

The women argued briskly that I ought not to be ashamed of it. Not at all, at all. I basked in their generous admiration.

Then I noticed mists on the other side of the garden. Rae and a tall, handsome blond guy, built like an NFL linebacker, were sitting at a table. They both raised wineglasses to me and bowed ceremoniously.

Now, what the hell did all of that mean?

Rae, never to be outdone even in her analogue by mere human bearers of life, was clad in something pink and ravishing, but she was too far away for me to see the details of her costume.

Could everyone else see this handsome couple or was it a vision intended only for me?

"By the way, Sara Anne, who was this Rae who threw poor young Oisin out of the pub?"

"She's the bar person, Da. She's been there awhile."

"I don't think I know who she is."

"And yourself not being in that terrible place for twenty years and more, Ronan."

He put his arm around his wife's naked shoulders. "We won't be saying, will we now, who was the very proper judge's daughter, and herself with a century of lawyers in her family, that I met in that terrible place?"

"And wasn't it a good thing for me that I went into it just that once?"

"Ah, sure, Ma, weren't you in there for weeks trying to get me da to notice you?"

"WELL, he finally did, poor dear man."

More laughter.

I looked across the garden again. The mists were gone; so apparently were Rae and her "companion."

Over dessert I listened to a discussion about the Poolnarooma Golf Club in Salt Hill (a resort suburb just beyond Galway) to which the Tobins belonged, about how good Sara Anne was at the game (in her parents' minds she was good at everything), and what a nice swimming pool they had. In my judgment these were not invitations but statements of facts.

"Are you that good, Cousin Sara Anne? At golf, I mean?"

She ran her fingers through her black hair, tilted her nose in the air, and announced, "Well, I'd wager I could beat you, Cousin Paddy, and meself willing to give away a stroke a hole."

"No bet."

When we left the garden of Ardilawn House, Rae and the guy were back at their table. I was able to walk a straight line, though only just.

"Good evening, Mr. Tobin, Mrs. Tobin, Sara Anne." The guy bowed politely. "I hope you had a nice dinner."

"Oh, we did indeed, did indeed," Ronan sputtered. "But isn't that the way of it here at Ardilawn House?"

"You and Sara Anne look lovely tonight, Mrs. Tobin,"

Rae said with a perfectly straight face, "as always."

"Not as lovely as you," Edna replied.

"Who are those handsome people?" Edna asked as we waited for the Mercedes.

"I don't know them at all, at all, dear. Otherwise I would have introduced them to Cousin Paddy."

"Come on, Da, you know the name of every beautiful woman in the whole County Galway."

"As you say, Sara Anne, I must be getting old."

More laughter.

I could have introduced them.

"Cousin Ronan, Cousin Edna, Cousin Sara Anne, I'd like to introduce the Archangel Raphaella and her companion. Actually they are both Seraphs. Aren't they taking care of me on this trip? Just like they did a kid named Tobias two millennia ago. Except I had to come to Galway city and not Ecbatana to collect my fair bride and inheritance. Shall we sit down and talk about it?"

What would Rae have done? Probably create a thick mist and make the others forget what I had said.

Finally we boarded the Mercedes that a young attendant, eyes bulging at the sight of our two women, brought us. Sara Anne took over the wheel and directed me into the front seat with her.

"Won't we let me ma and me da sit in the back in privacy and hold hands like teenagers?"

"Good idea."

I was bemused by the whole evening—women, drink, music, conversation. I didn't know what the program was for the morrow. Maybe it was my turn to invite Sara Anne somewhere for the day. Or maybe Tuesday was to be a day off.

I was too tired to try to think it out. Sufficient to the

day was the evil thereof. Or the good.

Speaking of Sara Anne, I glanced over at her as she drove the car with brisk efficiency. She was tensing up again, a black mood in the wind. Both of her hands were on the wheel. What was I supposed to do now?

Well, her knee and a substantial section of her thigh were exposed, both encased, of course, in white nylon.

So I settled for her knee.

She gasped and drew her knee away. Then she chuckled softly and moved her knee back. Again the tension ebbed from her body.

"Sure, don't you already know all about me," she whispered.

"What did you say, dear?"

"Wasn't I telling Cousin Paddy that he shouldn't be afraid of me and the gearshift between us up here?"

"I don't think Cousin Paddy is afraid of you, dear. Not exactly."

"Yes, I am."

Uneasy laughter from the rear seat, since they weren't sure whether I was serious.

"But not much afraid." I added as I moved my hand above her knee to the lower part of her thigh.

She sighed contentedly. My hand did not explore any farther, though it surely wanted to.

At the hotel, I thanked them, shook hands with Ronan, and permitted the two women to kiss me good night. Perhaps they were a little more affectionate than they had been at the beginning of the evening. I was in no shape to be certain.

Fortunately for me, my red-haired friend Nuala was not at the reception desk. Thank heaven they gave the poor child some time off now and again.

But Rae was waiting for me in the parlor of my suite, dressed now in some kind of pink satiny pajamas and long, matching, smartly tailored robe.

"You planning on staying the night?" I said, sinking in the couch.

"Certainly not. I merely intend to convey to you that I need some sleep and propose to take it."

"Seraphs sleep?"

"Of course we do. We are creatures who need periodic rejuvenation as you do, not as much and not as often, but nonetheless we must on occasion sleep."

"With the blond guy, I suppose?"

"That is an impertinent question . . . Did you like him?"

"A real charmer. And he must have the patience of a saint."

"Of a Seraph, more precisely. I add that I need some rest after this arduous day of work with you and that child."

"Whispering into my ears what to say to her."

"I was afraid you'd think that. In fact, that would be a violation of your freedom. We are not above intervening if you were about to do or say something outrageous. But there was no need to do so. You did everything intelligently and skillfully, including that delicate little *pas de deux* in the front seat of the car while you were coming back."

"No way."

"No way what?"

"No way that it was all me."

"Yes, it was, Toby, uh, Paddy; you were remarkably adroit, save perhaps in that self-serving account of your heroism last year. But you didn't have much choice. The child was adamant in her demands.''

"So?''

"So we progress.''

"I don't want to exploit her. She's so fragile.''

"Did she act like she was being exploited?''

"I don't know. I don't think so. I couldn't figure out a lot of her reactions.''

"Try the model of a young woman with a very severe crush on an attractive and tender young man. That will account for most of the variance.''

"I'm not sure I want her to have a crush on me.''

"Don't be absurd!'' she said, dismissing my qualm with a wave of her Seraphic hand. "What else could you expect?''

"And I have a crush too?''

"Oh, no, Paddy, you are but one step away from falling in love with her. Perhaps I use the wrong participle. I should have said 'one step way from being in love with her.' ''

"No way.''

"Yes way... Continue to be gentle and tender with her, but continue to court her, not that, given the state of your admiration for her and your hormone count, you are likely to do anything else.''

"For the money.''

She waved her hand again. "You barely thought about that today.''

"You can't read my thoughts.''

"Of course not, but I can read your eyes.''

"I've never been good with women.''

"Attribute your success this time to the Irish air... Now, call your family.''

"Shite. I forgot about that. I'll be an hour late.''

But they'll have confused the time again.

It was the usual routine. I explained that I had just returned to the hotel from dinner with the Galway Tobins. That cut no ice.

"What did they wear, Toby?" Megan screamed.

"Slip dresses, I think you call them. Edna green, Sara Anne virginal white."

"Ohhhh!" Megan shouted. "Were they like totally gorgeous?"

"Attractive enough."

"Have you changed your mind about Sara Anne?"

"She has her good side," I admitted.

Again she shrieked.

"Now, Megan dear, that's enough . . . Toby, they sound like they are a little common, maybe even coarse."

"Not at all. They both have university degrees. Edna's family has been in the law for several generations. They're not common at all. Very refined and dignified."

"Refined women don't wear slip dresses for dinner," Nicole insisted. "That's vulgar."

"Depends on the women and on the dinner."

"What does Sara Anne do?" Megan again.

"She's still in university, Meg. Studying music. She's a liturgical composer."

"Really, Toby." My dad now for the first time. "Isn't that a bit of an exaggeration?"

"They sing her Masses in the churches over here, both Catholic and Protestant, and in both Irish and English."

"That sounds rather presumptuous for one so young."

"Young and talented."

"You must be careful about what you're getting into, son. You shouldn't let them turn your head."

"My head is not turned."

I had lied and Rae laughed at me.

"What are their teeth like?" Maureen demanded. "Do they have bad teeth? All the Irish have bad teeth."

"They still sound coarse to me." Mom was closing in for the kill. Here we go again.

"Their teeth are excellent, and, Mom, I know them and you don't. They are NOT coarse."

"You sound like you love them more than us," she replied as she began to cry.

We went through the whole routine. The others reprimanded me for hurting Mom, who had waited so long for my phone call. Dad told me that I was being thoughtless again. There was no point in my calling every night if I intended to hurt Mom's feelings each time. I apologized for being thoughtless, though I did not agree, as I was doubtless expected to do, that our Galway cousins were "common." Nor did I promise to call the next night.

Rae was scowling when I finally hung up.

"This won't do, Paddy. It won't do at all. They love you indeed and they mean well. But you must draw the line. You have been the family whipping boy and ink blot long enough. It has to stop."

"They're my family."

"Regardless. Given half a chance, they will destroy Sara Anne and ruin your marriage."

"If I marry her, which I don't think I will."

"If you *do* marry her," she said, amending her words, "they will pick and pick and pick away at the poor fragile child so there's nothing left of her. They'll keep her in tears every day of her life. They'll mean no harm because all they are trying to do is to make her the kind of wife you *should* have. But they'll ruin your marriage just the same. You will have to stop them."

I knew she was right, but I didn't say anything.

"Explicitly and repeatedly until they finally get it. Then they'll be very nice to her and begin to take her side against you. She won't let them do that."

"Uh-huh."

"And *if* there be a wedding two weeks from Saturday, they will arrive and take the whole celebration away from Sara and her parents. For their own good, of course. You will have to stop them."

That's exactly what they would do.

"I'm not very good at stopping them once they get rolling."

"You will have to be very firm and direct. Any other strategy would be a betrayal of your wife—always assuming the possibility, not yet confirmed, that there will be a wedding two weeks from Saturday."

"A long time till then," I said again.

"You are not being very realistic, G. Patrick Tobin Junior. If the civil and ecclesiastical norms are to be honored, the decision must be made by a week from Saturday."

"That soon?"

"Absolutely."

She stood up and tightened the belt of her robe. Time to leave.

I was too tired and too dizzy to argue or even to comprehend the implications of what she had just said.

"Well, at least you blew smoke in the eyes of Asmodeus this afternoon. That's one thing we don't have to worry about."

"Don't assume that too readily, Paddy. The demons are not yet exorcised."

Having said that, she faded away in the mists.

"Give my best to the guy. Have fun with him."

Not wanting to think about any of my new or newly uncovered problems, I shed my clothes, dove into bed, and into a deep and heavy sleep.

Without any pleasant dreams.

14

Another phone ringing. It must be judgment day. I turned over in my bed, wrapped a pillow around my head, and tried to go back to sleep.

It kept ringing.

Oh, hell.

"Yes?"

"Isn't your cousin Sara Anne down here with her golf clubs, Mr. Tobin?"

"Are we playing golf today?"

"Aren't you now? Out at Poolnarooma? Don't they have a lovely course out there? And a nice swimming pool too. And hasn't she been waiting since half ten?"

I squinted at the clock. It was after eleven.

I didn't want to play golf with Sara Anne Tobin today or with anyone else.

I glanced around the room. No golf clubs, thank heaven. But brown slacks, brown shoes, a brown Ralph

Loren polo, and brown socks. I sighed.

And brown and white golf shoes too.

And a red swimsuit.

Sure I was free to disagree with the damn Seraphs, but a fat lot of chance I had to do that.

Then it occurred to me that I would see Sara Anne in a swimsuit. That might be worth all the effort.

"Tell her I'm sorry. I must have overslept. I'll be right down.

I took a quick shower, donned my new golfing togs, grabbed the golf shoes and the swimsuit, and rushed down the stairs.

"Isn't she in the dining room ordering breakfast for you? And hasn't she already called out there to change your starting time?"

"I'm sorry, Sara Anne, I didn't know we were playing golf today."

"Sure you had a lot of things on your mind last night," she said, rolling her eyes and grinning. "Didn't you?"

"And pleasant enough, they were too," I said, draining a glass of orange juice.

She was in powder blue today, shorts and a tight-fitting tank top, the sort of costume that she had dismissed on another woman yesterday as "practically naked."

"We did definitely agree on a round of golf and a swim in the pool. And weren't you saying you wouldn't bet me?"

"I remember that, but . . ."

"You don't have to play golf."

I dug into the cornflakes and heavy cream. She buttered a thin slice of toast, smeared it with raspberry jam, and silently handed it to me. I swallowed it whole and she handed me another. I drank a large gulp of Irish breakfast tea (strong enough so that a submarine would not be able to descend through it) and ate another slice of toast.

Silently she filled up my cornflake dish and poured more heavy cream on it. If she was upset with me, she showed no signs of it.

"Damn! I know what happened, Sara Anne. It's the cultural difference between the two countries. What sounds to you real Irish as a firm date for golfing sounded to me like a vague hint that it might be nice to play some-day."

"Ah," she said, looking very guilty. " 'Tis my fault al-together for not being more explicit."

" 'Tis not your fault, woman," I said, touching her chin. " 'Tis your country and I'm the visitor. I'm the one who should adjust to your styles of speech, not the other way around."

She did not seem persuaded.

"The good host adjusts to her guest and not the other way around."

"Well, no harm done. Would you ever fix another piece of toast for me? You do it so much more charmingly than I do."

She giggled and, her guilt at being a poor host at least somewhat healed, she fixed another raspberry-coated slice for me and, very gently, shoved it into my open mouth.

I should always have it so good.

Outside the day was gray and muggy.

"Will it rain?" I asked.

"Only a little, I reckon," she replied, "and don't I have an umbrella and me da's golf raincoat in the trunk along with his clubs for you to use? I'll open it and put in your golf shoes and swimsuit."

"You'll be swimming too?"

She tilted her head back and ran her fingers through

her hair. "I might just do a lap or two. We'll have to see about that."

There were two sets of clubs. The shorter ones were in an expensive red leather bag.

How did I know beforehand that she had a red leather golf bag?

She closed the trunk and turned and faced me.

"Now, Cousin Paddy, I have a lot of faults, but there are some I don't have. I don't sulk and nag and coax; I don't complain much; and I don't try to manipulate men; and I don't get angry when someone doesn't want to do something that I thought they wanted to do . . . Course," she added with a shrug and a leprechaun grin, "I may lie a little now and then."

"Indeed!"

"So we can play golf or not play, swim or not swim, eat dinner at the Norman place out beyond or not. We can do whatever you want to do or we can do nothing at all. Sure, don't we maybe owe you a day off?"

How wonderful!

I put my arms around her, pulled her firmly against my body, and kissed her—and a solid and aggressive male kiss, it was.

She gave herself over completely to the exercise. Neither of us paid any attention to passersby—though there didn't seem to be any just then.

"Well, now," she said with a gasp for breath, "wasn't that nice? Was there any special reason?"

"Only that you are so wonderful. I warn you that there may be a few repetitions on the golf links today."

"Wonderful, am I now?" she replied skeptically. "Wouldya stop it? We'll be playing golf, is it?"

"Only if you promise to swim."

"So you can ogle me in me skimpy swim costume?"

"You wouldn't have brought one along unless you wanted me to ogle you."

"Come on, Paddy Tobin," she said, running her fingers through my curly hair, "let's go play golf."

I was all for it.

We climbed into the Mercedes. She drove skillfully and easily through the streets of the center of Galway city.

"You look very nice in your brown golf togs, Cousin Paddy."

"As do you in your powder blue outfit."

"Thank you," she said, beaming complacently. "You must have brought a lot of luggage with you."

"One carry-on bag. And my computer bag."

She frowned. "Wouldn't you be having a lot of changes of clothes?"

"They were all packed by an expert."

"Who?"

"My travel agent."

She seemed satisfied with that perfectly true answer.

"Now then. May I lay out for your approval our plans for the rest of the week—direct and Yank fashion?"

"Please do."

We crossed the Wolfe Tone Bridge, the last one before the Corrib, gathering all its channels together like wayward children, plunged into the Atlantic.

"There's the old Claddagh over on the right. It's only a park now, more's the pity . . . Well, we'll play golf today and swim if you insist. Tomorrow we'll take me da's boat for a ride up to the head of the lake and have lunch at Ashford Castle, so be presentable, but you won't have to wear a jacket and tie for lunch. Then we'll come back to our house and you'll show me how to use your computer toys."

"DABEST and MEGSONG?"

"Indeed, then—"

"I'll take you to supper at the Great Southern's grill."

"Ah, won't that be nice, now? I accept on the spot. Then the next day, Thursday, we'll drive up through Connemara, have lunch in Clifden where there's the best pub food in all the world, and climb to the top of Maumene, where there's a grand shrine to your patron—"

"And end up swimming either at the club or in the pool at my hotel, which we'll also do tomorrow. I'm terribly out of condition."

"Ah, is that the reason?"

" 'Tis."

"Friday morning, if the weather isn't too bad, won't we have a go at flying out to the Aran Islands? 'Tis only a fifteen-minute trip."

"In a plane?"

"Or a helicopter if there's one around. Sure, isn't it the best way to go? No one can get too sick in fifteen minutes."

"You haven't seen me yet with motion sickness."

"Go 'long with ya," she said, dismissing my protest as if I were joking. "In the afternoon we could always go over to the archives and see if there's anything in them about the feud."

"We'll try to find something on Internet when I'm installing it on your computer. A 486 DX 80, is it now?"

We turned left on the road to Salt Hill. Galway Bay was quiet and grim under the dark sky.

"How would you be knowing that?"

How did I know?

"I just guessed."

"Anyway, on Saturday we'll take in the Galway races, the great social and sporting event of the year. As one of the priests at Maynooth wrote, you don't understand Ireland if you've never been to the Galway races."

"I take your word for it."

"And won't we be seeing it with the ordinary folk and not with the swells in the boxes like me ma and da?"

"As long as you're with me, I won't feel ordinary."

She ignored my comment.

"That night we'll go to the young people's dance at the St. Catherine's hotel here in Salt Hill. 'Tis a grand night. And jeans and T-shirts are fine all day long."

"And Sunday?"

"Well, won't we go to Mass at the cathedral where they'll be singing a new hymn of mine, and then, if the weather is nice, won't we make me ma and da take a leisurely ride on the lake with us and eat supper at our house like you did last Sunday?"

"And if you get in one of your black moods, I'll hold your hand under the table."

"Or me knee!"

"Or your knee . . . Your parents left out till then?"

"Ah, aren't they terrible eejits. You young folk have a good time by yourselves for a couple of days."

"Not a bad idea."

"Is me schedule all right with you? Tell me now if it isn't."

"It sounds wonderful."

"Even if I tell you I'll pick you up at half eight every morning, even on Sunday?"

"So long as it's you picking me up, I won't mind at all, at all."

"Silly!" she said, removing one hand from the wheel of the car to poke my arm.

The clouds seemed to be sinking lower and lower towards the bay. We'd never finish eighteen holes.

"How good are you on the links?"

"I can beat me da most of the time."

"That sounds pretty good."

"I play more often than he does, poor dear man."

"And how many championships have you won?"

Silence.

"You think you know so damn much!"

I'd made her angry.

"I'm just a good guesser."

"Well." She calmed down. "I did win the woman's cup last year."

"It looks like I'm in for a long day."

"I'll give you a stroke a hole for a punt on each hole. Isn't that fair?"

"I doubt it, but I suppose I can afford to lose eighteen punts."

Ah, the woman was a fierce competitor too, was she?

Well there was nothing wrong with that.

"Do you play much golf, Paddy Tobin?"

"Woman, I do not."

"You don't belong to a club?"

"My father is an academic. We no more belong to a country club than do the families of your teachers at UCG."

Actually, with the income Dad earned from his consultation work, we probably could have, but that would not have been "respectable."

("It's all right, Toby Junior, for your father to have part-time work because he has a regular job. You don't have a regular job." Never mind that I made more money from my irregular job than he did from his regular and his "irregular" jobs combined.)

"Sorry, that was a dumb and rude question from a spoiled rich child."

I touched her bare shoulder. "You are certainly not

spoiled, woman, and yourself working in your da's office all summer long . . . There are a lot of good public courses in Chicago, one quite near to where I live. I used to play but ran out of time a few years ago.''

"I'll give you two strokes a hole instead of one, all right?''

She pulled up to a grotesque Victorian limestone building and parked the car in front of it.

"I still won't have much of a chance against the champ.''

She smiled ruefully at my remark but did not reply.

"This used to be a place only for the gentry. Now they'll let anyone in. So it's almost all Catholic . . . There's no one here. We should be able to shoot around in a couple of hours. "I'll go in and sign us up.''

So the poor academic's kid from Chicago wouldn't see how much it cost.

"I'll see you on the first tee after I look at the pool.''

"You have a one-track mind,'' she said as she entered the building.

"But such a lovely track.''

There were no golf carts and no trolleys with which to pull our clubs. It was going to be a long day.

She rejoined me at the first tee.

"I think it's a shame for someone as young as me to hire a caddy, don't you? It's easier for me to carry the clubs than it would be for him.''

"It's how they earn their living.''

"Oh, don't I leave something for them, so they don't feel cheated?''

I wanted to kiss her again, but thought better of it. Not on the first tee.

She teed her ball up firmly, addressed the ball with her club, and without any practice shots, hit it straight down the middle of the fairway about 180 yards. It was going to be a long day for the veteran from Chicago.

But not an unpleasant one since he could admire the grace of her swing, the quick flick of her wrists, and the changing shapes of her astonishing body as she swung the club.

"Shorter than the last time," she murmured. "I'm probably distracted by the boy who is staring at me."

"If you didn't want stares, you wouldn't have worn that tank top."

"Ah, 'tis true enough, isn't it now? I didn't say I didn't like it and I didn't tell you to stop staring, did I?"

"Woman, you did not."

My drive soared maybe 250 yards, half of it in a mammoth slice that aimed directly at Galway Bay. It landed, however, in the rough.

"I'll help you to find it," she said promptly. "Sure, didn't I mark just where it fell?"

"I'm sure you did."

It has been said, with perhaps some exaggeration, that in Ireland the greens are like American fairways, the fairways like American roughs, and the roughs are like abandoned farm fields. I knew that my golf ball (Ronan Tobin's golf ball, to be precise) was lost forever.

Naturally the woman walked directly to where it lay, in five inches of thick grass.

"You wouldn't want to be shooting out of there," she said, judiciously weighing the situation. "Better to take the penalty strokes and shoot from the fairway."

"Yes, ma'am . . . It's going to rain in a few minutes."

"Only a few drops," she replied as we trudged back to the fairway. "And it'll be brisk and clear tomorrow for our boat ride."

"On the *Sara Anne*?"

She stopped in her tracks. But this time she laughed.

"I suppose that had to be her name . . . but she's a docile boat, not at all a bitch like her namesake."

So I kissed her again. And again she gave herself to the kiss.

"You're just trying to distract me from my game, Paddy Tobin, but sure, you're a good kisser, aren't you now? A lot of experience at it?"

"More in the last two days than in the last year."

"I don't believe you."

In fact, she wasn't quite sure. But that was all right too.

She pared the hole. I had an eight. She diligently noted the scores on her card and we trudged on to the next hole. She was indeed a fierce competitor, single-minded in her grim determination to beat me (no great challenge), the course, and herself. After each shot, she would sling her heavy golf bag over her arm and mutter a reprimand to herself for not having done it right. The rain was "not serious at all, at all," and we didn't even bother with the raincoats and the umbrella.

Nor did we go into the clubhouse for lunch "with the eejits who are in there getting fluttered." She had brought an egg salad and a salmon sandwich and a bottle of Ballygowan for each of us. This golf was a serious business.

"I know you Yanks like ice in everything, but this is Ireland, isn't it now?"

" 'Tis," I sighed loudly, imitating her own loud sigh, which sounded like an onslaught of a serious asthma attack.

I don't mind a woman who likes to compete and is honest about it. Nor one who has solid calf, thigh, and arm muscles. In fact, I kind of admire them. This child, whatever else she might be, was not passive-aggressive.

Rather she was blatantly and unapologetically active-aggressive.

So I fell ever more under her enchantment. I only kissed her four or five times during the round of golf. She seemed to enjoy every one of them.

"Do you mind some advice from a pushy and competitive woman?" she asked me as we teed up for the tenth hole.

"The woman in question is fiercely competitive but not at all pushy," I replied. "And I'll take the advice of anyone who is as good at this game as you are."

"Well," she observed with clinical detachment, "don't you have a brilliant natural swing, but aren't you going about it all wrong? You've got to stand about here and move your front foot just a little back and keep your elbow close to your side on your backswing and keep your head down, which you almost never do."

She rearranged my hips and my knees and my chest and my feet and stood back to consider me. "Well, you'll do, I suppose. Take a practice swing."

I did just that. It felt smooth and powerful.

"Not all that bad. Now address the ball . . . No, you've still got your rear foot in the wrong place."

She moved my body slightly and then patted my rump approvingly. Fair is fair.

"All right, now remember to keep your head down when you swing."

I did, not that I had any choice in the matter.

My golf ball, now straight as an arrow, sailed down the middle of the fairway, perhaps 225 yards.

"Haven't you got the hang of it now? Sure, won't we make a good golfer out of you yet?"

"Why didn't you correct my swing earlier?" I asked, immensely pleased with my shot.

"Didn't I want to make sure that I had won enough holes to beat you before I turned you into a serious rival?"

She was grinning smugly. So I had to kiss her again.

"Isn't the truth of it that you weren't sure how your Yank cousin would take advice from a woman?"

She nodded and leaned her head against my chest.

"I kind of knew, but I wasn't sure."

A couple of more times during the rest of the round (I won't call it a match, because it surely wasn't that) she rearranged my stance, always with positive effect on my ego (because her touch was so pleasant) and my game.

She won only two of the last nine holes. We tied on six (by the grace of my two-stroke-per-hole handicap), and I won one hole when she missed a five-foot putt by a half inch.

"Shite!" she shouted, and whirled the putter around her head in dismay and rage.

"I win," I announced modestly.

"Only because of the two strokes I gave you," she said as she strode furiously around the green.

Then she laughed and relaxed. "Sure, Cousin Paddy, don't you know now that I'm a terrible sore loser?"

"At least you didn't throw the putter at me."

"Oh, I never throw me golf clubs. You might break one that way."

Mystery, wonder, surprise, delight—she was all of them.

"Well," she said as she tallied up her score, "shouldn't I bring you along every time I play a round? Isn't it my best score of the season?"

"The kissing is what does it."

"Sure, maybe it is . . . but mind you now, none of that at the swimming pool. Won't the eejits inside be watching us?"

Inside the oak-paneled clubhouse, however, with its old-fashioned leather chairs and its thick maroon carpet, there were only a couple of eejits, and all of them far too fluttered to notice anyone.

"See you at poolside," she said, waving the slight bits of black and white fabric she had removed from her golf bag just as she entered the door of the women's locker room.

"No, I'll see you."

I thought I heard her laughing as the door closed. She loves every minute of it. Then, as I put on my trunks and wandered out to the pool, I returned to my agonizing. I had known her only two days. She was an innocent and fragile child. To lead her into a hasty marriage, however willing she might be, for millions of dollars would be ruthlessly exploitive. I simply could not do it, regardless of the haste with which the first Tobias had bedded his bride.

The rain had ceased, the clouds were breaking up, the sun was threatening to return, and Galway Bay in the distance had turned from gray to a shimmering dark silver.

"Well?"

She was standing behind me, wrapped in a towel.

"Well?" I turned to face her.

She tossed the towel aside.

"Well?"

"Well!"

She was standing, patiently awaiting my inspection and approval.

Her bikini, black with white trim, was much more modest than the ones the models wear in *Sports Illustrated* or that young women wear in the pictures I had seen of Brazilian beaches. It still revealed a lot of Sara Anne, all of her paralyzingly attractive.

"Is my mouth hanging open?"

" 'Tis."

I groped for the right words.

"Sara Anne, you are an awe-inspiring young woman, but your physical beauty is just a hint of the wonder and the mystery and the surprise of all that you are."

"Oh, Paddy," she said, lowering her head and beginning to cry. "Don't you say the sweetest things?"

Encouraged by my verbal success, I began to trace designs on her firmly muscled belly. She looked up at me with wide eyes and took a deep breath. But she didn't try to fend me off. Then she closed her eyes and her mouth fell open.

"Paddy," she said weakly, "aren't you driving me out of me frigging mind?"

"Should I stop?"

Were the Seraphs watching? Would they approve? Who cared?

"Only when you want to," she whispered as her shoulders sagged in surrender.

Finally I stopped. "I think we'd better swim now."

"Sure, don't we need the waters of Galway Bay to cool us off instead of this warm pool?"

We dove in, she more gracefully than I, and began to swim, she more powerfully than I.

Since there're no eejits watching from the French windows in the club, we also frolicked as young men and women do, wrestling with and dunking one another. Since she was far more agile in the water than I, the ratio of dunks against me was at least two to one.

When I came up from one of the longer dunks, sputtering and gulping, she attacked me with a passionate kiss that took my returning breath away. She pushed her body against me, and me against the side of the pool, and consumed me with her lips as if she were grimly determined to subdue me and make me her own.

I was astonished by the ferocity of that kiss. Modest young women like Sara Anne don't do that on the second day they know a young man. I had no intention, however, of resisting. Indeed, I gripped her rear end and held her in place.

So we were competing even in kisses, and she had won again.

So what? Let her subdue me and make me her own.

Finally she broke away and swam swiftly to the other side of the pool.

"Don't come near me," she shouted.

"I'd be afraid to. Can I swim?"

"Silly!" she yelled. "Of course you can."

So I swam up and down the pool in a leisurely backstroke. In a few minutes she joined me.

"I always wanted to kiss a man that way, just to see how he reacted."

"I'm honored to be the first victim."

"Men surrender to women, do they now?"

"Sure. Sometimes. Depends on the woman. And the man."

"I wouldn't be trying it with just anyone, would I?"

"I hope not."

She seemed very satisfied with herself.

A huge crush, Rae had said. Where was Rae, by the way? Who cared?

Finally she announced, " 'Tis time to stop if I'm to be getting you back to the Great Southern for a nap before I pick you up at half seven."

"It will be a nap filled with pleasant dreams."

"Go 'long with you," she said as she climbed out of the pool.

"How many more bikinis do you own, Cousin Sara Anne?"

"Sure," she said, wrapping herself again in the towel, "if you've seen a woman in one of these obscene things, haven't you seen her in all of them?"

"No. Not if it's a woman like you."

"Eejit." She walked briskly to the door of the women's locker room. "Let's just say I have enough of them to keep your dirty mind occupied for the rest of the week."

" 'Tis not really dirty," I said, trailing after her.

"Wouldn't I know that?"

The door closed. I ambled uncertainly back to the men's locker room. The woman was a hellion, all right, an attractive, fragile, competitive hellion. I had never met anyone like her in my life and did not believe that there could be anyone like her in the world.

So I had been wrong.

A couple hours later I was sitting across the table from her in a beachfront restaurant, out near An Spidel, the center of an Irish-speaking district. The restaurant, specializing in Norman French cooking, was built on rocks on the bay side of the road, so at high tide we were looking directly down on the waters glittering in the moonlight, but sheltered from the wind that was blowing across the bay.

She was wearing a simple, short-sleeved white knit minidress with a sweater over her shoulders against the cold.

My nap had indeed been filled with pleasant dreams. Rae did not appear at the Great Southern, so presumably I had done well, or well enough. No querulous phone calls from home. Not even the marvelous Nuala to raise her eyebrows when I came in.

Sara Anne had been thoughtful and reserved while we drove out to the restaurant and even as we ordered ocean trout and white wine. "Only one glass for meself," she warned me. "So you'll have to drink the rest."

Then she lapsed into silence again. I was reluctant to break into her thoughts. She had much to think about, and so did I.

"You love me, don't you, Paddy Tobin?" she asked suddenly, as her fingers smoothed her hair.

In hearing her words, I realized for the first time that I did.

"How can you tell?"

"Oh," she said, waving her hand, " 'tis easy. The way you treat me, the way you touch me, the way you look at me."

"How do I look at you?"

"Like a thirsty man looking at a pint of Guinness. You absorb me, drink me in, consume me."

"Isn't that just desire?"

"Men have desired me before, Paddy Tobin, but they don't look at me with the respect and admiration that is mixed with your desire."

"And what does this do to you?"

"Ah, sure," she said with her most radiant of smiles, "doesn't it disconcert me altogether? Don't you take away all me defenses?"

"You have nothing to fear from me, Sara Anne."

"Don't I know that, eejit? And doesn't that make you even more disconcerting? But I don't understand how a man can fall in love with a woman he's only known for two days."

" 'Tis easy, if it's the right woman."

"You hardly know me. And you don't know any of me terrible faults."

"I know a lot of them and they don't matter."

She shook her head. "I don't want to hurt you."

"You haven't . . . but, fair is fair; what do you think about me?"

She shrugged her shoulders. "I don't know what to think, Paddy. I've never met a man like you before. I don't understand me own emotions at all. Sure, don't I have the biggest crush in all of Ireland? And don't you take me breath away altogether?"

We were on very dangerous ground now, a minefield with thousands of booby traps. I must steer my way cautiously.

"That's not necessarily bad."

"If," she said as she groped for words, "I were ever going to marry, it would be a man like you. So I could easily fall in love with you. But since I'm not going to marry, I'll not be going beyond a nineteen-year-old's biggest crush."

Rae, where are you when I really need you?

"Not going to marry?"

She shook her head firmly. "I'm not the marrying kind, Cousin Paddy. I don't want to sleep for the rest of my life with a man. I don't want his paws all over me. I don't want him thrusting into me every night of the week, if you take me meaning."

"You yourself have said your mother doesn't mind."

"And good stuff for her. But I'm not me mother."

"You don't seem to mind my paws."

"That's different."

What do I say now?

I didn't say anything. Rather I refilled my glass with the nice Moselle she had chosen for us and took a bite of the trout, drenched as it was in a marvelous sauce.

"You see, Paddy," she continued. "I think I'm going to become a nun. I've talked to Mother Petronillia up at Kylemore about it for more than a year. I hope to enter after I graduate from university next year. The Benedictines have a grand tradition of liturgical musicians, you know."

"I see."

Passionate and beautiful women had become nuns before, often in the long course of Catholic history—and with impressive benefits for humankind. Why not my cousin Sara Anne?

Why not indeed?

"You've told your parents?"

"Not yet. I don't want to worry them."

"How will they react?"

"They'll think it's wonderful altogether. Isn't that how they react to everything I do? And Kylemore is not so far away as America if I should marry an American husband and go live with him."

Did she mean me? Maybe.

"And there's nothing wrong with being a nun, is there now, even if most young women don't think of it anymore? And if I don't like it, I can always leave, can't I?"

She drank a small sip of white wine.

Nuns were a lot more liberal these days than they used to be. In a convent Sara Anne would not have to live under the restraints that her predecessors suffered.

"I would be the last one to try to talk you out of it, Sara Anne. I don't want to get in a tussle with God."

"It would be so easy to fall in love with you, Cousin Paddy, even after only two days."

"No one has ever found it that easy before . . . All I'll say is that you should become a nun for the right reason—serving God and the Church and other humans or something like that. Not because you find the thought of sexual intercourse for the rest of your life repellent."

"I know that," she said sadly. "Oh, I know that!"

Did she really?

Why hadn't the damn Seraphs told me about this problem? Did they doubt the authenticity of her vocation? Should I try to fight it? And how do you go about fighting it if you should? I looked around the dimly lighted restaurant. No sign of herself tonight just when I need her.

And why were my caresses, so far rather mild but also patently pleasurable to her, "different"?

As I pondered these thoughts, she took my hand in hers.

"Thank you for being so understanding. Didn't I know you would be? I had to talk about it, don't you see?"

"So I shouldn't continue to be in love with you, actually to love you?"

"I can't tell you that, Paddy. Not at all, at all. But didn't I think I should warn you?"

Well, I'd continue my pursuit a little longer. If God wanted her, He wouldn't let me get in her way. Besides, He would have restrained those angelic beings who were reputed to stand before His face, wouldn't He? She. Whatever.

"Thanks for the warning." I kissed her hand lightly.

Despite her alleged vocation, she kissed me enthusiastically when she dropped me off at the Great Southern later that night.

I reminded myself that women who like to kiss men are not excluded from the ranks of potential consecrated virgins.

I fully expected Rae to be waiting for me. But she wasn't anywhere in my suite. What the hell good is a guardian angel if she's not around when you need her?

I flipped open the Aero.

>**Go Rae.**
Yes, Paddy.

>You know what I'm worried about now.
*The young woman's alleged religious vocation,
I presume?*
>Why didn't you warn me?
*Did you think we would set you in pursuit of a
young woman who was destined to be a consecrated virgin?*
>She doesn't have a vocation?
*I didn't say that exactly. We think it most im-
probable. Beautiful and passionate women, as
you well know, can become consecrated virgins, but not those with as much sexual hunger as the fair Sara Anne experiences, without
quite recognizing what it is. The result, I dare-
say, of being raised in a passionate home.
Nothing wrong with it.*
>She is sexually hungry?
Surely you have perceived that by now.
>She says the thought of intercourse repels
her.
*I am well aware she takes that position. Did
you feel her repelled by your, ah, modest sexual advances?*
>No. She says they were different.
*What do you think could be different about
them?*
>I don't know.
*Consider, Paddy Tobin, the possibility that she
loves you as much as you love her. While she
is terrified by her sexual longings, she's not
terrified by you.*
>I'm considering it. Why should she be terri-
fied by sexual longings and afraid of sexual
union?
You mean of being screwed?
>If you want to put it that way.
There's mystery in the child, Paddy Tobin. It's

*your job to sort it all out, and you don't have
much time. End.*

The screen turned dark.

Damn.

I turned it back on.

>**You mean it is all right to pursue her?**
*Didn't I say that already? Do you love her,
Paddy, as she alleges you do?*

I hesitated. Did I really?

If I didn't love her, what would love be like?

>**Yes.**
*That's your answer. Now, go away and let me
have my nap. End.*

Nap? Angels nap?

Well, there wasn't much doubt what Rae wanted me to
do.

Would I do it?

I'd have to decide that in the morning.

☙15☙

Before I went to bed, I copied DABEST on three diskettes for Sara Anne and called down from Internet a copy of MEGSONG. The Seraphs had arranged things so that I didn't need a modem for any transaction with the system and not merely my conversations with Rae. Why not? She had claimed that the system was their invention.

Surely there were ways electronic pulses could be carried through the air without the need of a modem. There were primitive systems that could do that already. Eventually Internet would be a radio system, wouldn't it?

I felt guilty about how little attention I had paid to my task of improving DABEST during this trip. Well, I was busy with other things.

I fell to sleep promptly. I think it might have been a relaxed and pleasant sleep. But I don't know for sure because the phone rang in the middle of the night. Three A.M. to be precise.

"You haven't phoned us yet, Toby, and it's already three in the afternoon over there."

My father.

"I didn't promise to call every day."

"We assumed you would. If you had any consideration for your mother, you would realize how much she is concerned about you. I don't understand why you cannot apply yourself to ordinary human courtesy."

"Dad, it's three o'clock in the morning over here."

"It can't be. It's already nine o'clock here."

They would not, could not, ever get the time difference right, even though they'd been to Europe themselves.

"Look, Dad, this daily argument about time change isn't getting us anywhere. Meg is on E-mail. I'll send a message every morning and every evening, and you can reply if you want. Meg can take care of it."

As an academic who used E-mail in his office all the time, he couldn't argue with that.

"It's not like hearing your voice."

"Look, Dad, I have to get some sleep. We'll use E-mail from now on. Besides, it's cheaper."

"Your mother's peace of mind is more important than money."

Rae was right. I had to put a stop to this stuff. Why had I been patient with it for so long?

"The E-mail will be more frequent than the calls, and that should ease her peace of mind. Good night. I'm going back to sleep."

They were good people in every other respect. Why had they been on my case so long? Because I was the only son and I didn't measure up to their expectations. Their own mild neuroses reinforced each other when the subject was me. They both expected the other to do something to straighten me out and used the welfare of the other as an excuse to harass me.

They wouldn't like my Sara Anne either. Well, too bad for them. She was mine and was going to be mine for the rest of my life, and that was that. They'd get used to her eventually and would, of course, take credit for her.

But, as Rae had warned me, it would be a fight in the early stages.

"Shite," I muttered as I rolled over and tried to go back to sleep.

But sleep came slowly because my woman was on my mind.

I had told myself out at the restaurant that she'd make a grand nun, a dead frigging grand nun, to use her idiom. But that did not seem to be true, according to my good friend Rae. Some personalities are better suited for the religious life than others, are they not? While my woman was doubtless virtuous and dedicated, she didn't quite seem to fit the mold. Right?

So the convent more likely was an escape from her fear of sex—which did not seem to include a fear of me, did it?

So I should continue my gentle campaign to win her and see what happens, right?

Maybe if we made love soon, that would cure the problem?

No way, I warned myself. That would be crude and cruel and wouldn't do any good at all. Besides, you wouldn't really like it either.

One does not try to force a fragile woman, even if she would be mostly willing. As Rae had said, there was a mystery there about her alleged fear of sex (which did not seem to include me). I would have to probe tenderly to find out what it is. Not today, however.

Yes, I did want her. I didn't care if it took two weeks or two years. And no one was going to take her away from me.

Why?

Because I love her, that's why.

My cautious programmer mentality took over.

How can you know that you love her after three days? Aren't you just horny and nothing more?

A reasonable question.

You'll never find another one like her, G. Patrick, I told myself. Not a chance. She's not perfect and neither are you. But you can't blow this chance by letting the precise and careful programmer in you take over.

No way.

Aren't you after her for the money?

"I already said that I didn't care if it took two years, didn't I?" I had spoken the words aloud to confirm their validity.

It would still be nice to have her in bed with me in another couple of weeks. In bed with me and naked and content and happy.

At that pleasant thought I went back to sleep.

Nuala awakened me at eight o'clock, right on time.

"Isn't herself on the phone?"

"I wouldn't be surprised. Please put her on."

"Won't I do that right away?"

"Good morning, Cousin Paddy; isn't it a grand day for a ride on the lake?"

"Good morning, Cousin Sara Anne. I'll take your word for it since I haven't looked out the window yet."

"Sure, isn't the air as brisk and clean as a brand-new dress? . . . Would you ever walk over to our place? I have moored the boat temporarily across the street, and won't

I be making breakfast for you there?"

Her voice was lively and happy. Not a trace of the grim seriousness of the previous night.

"An offer I can't refuse. See you in a few minutes."

I drew the drapes back for a peek. Sure enough, small puffs of vanilla ice cream were racing across the brilliant blue sky, and the dark clouds and drizzle of yesterday had been banished—for a few hours anyway. ("Sure, if you stay long enough in Ireland, Paddy Tobin, won't you get used to being a little wet from the rain?")

I looked around for the clothes that were usually laid out for me. Sure enough, white jeans, a black sweatshirt with "CYC" on it, a red and black Chicago Bulls windbreaker (with a hood), and white deck shoes. No socks.

I guess you didn't have to wear socks at Ashford Castle for lunch.

My fashion consultant had also chosen a boating cap with a gold anchor and gold braid. Well, why not?

I dressed quickly because I was hungry as I always am in the morning. Besides, I wanted to see her again.

Should I bring my 3.3-pound Aero? Why not? It might be useful when I installed the programs on Sara Anne's 486.

Just the same, I'd better send an E-mail to Meg now.

>Meg and family,
Sara Anne and I are going to take a ride up
Lake Corrib (Lough Corrib around here) this
morning and explore some of the islands
around the lake. We're having lunch at Ashford
Castle, which is supposed to be one of the
grandest hotels in all the world. Then we're
coming back to Galway city and I'm going to
install MEGSONG on her system. Maybe we'll be
able to send some of her work to you in an Internet file.

> The plan tomorrow is to drive around Conne-
> mara and climb the mountain to a shrine in
> honor of my namesake up at a place called
> Maumene. Sara Anne assures me that I can
> wear shoes.
> Am I in love with her yet, Meg?
> She is an attractive and fascinating young
> woman. And mysterious. Or as they say around
> here when they want to pay a compliment,
> sure, she's not the worst of them.
> The boat, by the way, is called the *Sara Anne*
> as you might have guessed. It's an immense
> white cruiser and safer than the QE2.
> :-)

That should hold them for a while.

I was right about the *Sara Anne*. It was a big boat, maybe twenty-seven feet with a roomy cabin, two bedrooms, and a small but efficient galley.

Sara Anne, in a red sweatshirt with a gold crown on front and white jeans like my own, helped me climb on the boat.

"Be careful now, lad," she said with a smile, her top-quality smile. "It doesn't look to me like your seamanship is any better than your golf."

"Well, maybe I'll prove as apt a pupil at the former as I was at the latter."

"Welcome aboard." She kissed me modestly.

"Ah, woman, that's no real welcome, at all, at all."

I kissed her much more insistently. She went limp in my arms.

"Aren't you assaulting me now?" she said in a weak voice.

"Not as furiously as I was assaulted in the swimming pool yesterday."

" 'Tis true . . . Well, come on in and have your breakfast and take your mind off me."

Her hair was tied in a ponytail and she wore a white baseball cap with gold braid trim and the letters SARA ANNE printed on it in red. Ready for boating action.

" 'Tis the name of the boat, not the temporary captain." She sat me down at the table in the cabin and poured me my first cup of tea. "And what does CYC stand for?"

"Chicago Yacht Club," I said, removing my Bulls windbreaker, which wouldn't be needed till we were under way. "I don't belong. A friend gave it to me."

She began to prepare chunks of bread, lathered with butter and raspberry jam. She popped them into my mouth with the same delicacy that priests use when they put the Eucharist on the tongues of the older folks who don't want to receive it in their hands. No priest ever smiled at a communicant like she smiled at me.

She loved me as much as I loved her.

Her breakfast was immense—grapefruit juice, fruit slices, "rashers" and scrambled eggs, raisin bran with strawberries and heavy cream, toast, brown bread, and an immense pot of tea.

"I reckoned that we won't get up to Ashford till about half one, and won't you be perishing with the hunger by then and the huge appetite you're having?"

"The brown bread is the best I've had yet in Ireland, Sara Anne, and still warm. Were you baking it only this morning for me?"

She lowered her eyes shyly. "I was," she said in a tiny voice.

"So you're a good cook too."

"Me ma says I'm not the worst of them."

"Better than your ma?"

"I don't have the variety yet she has. But I think me brown bread is better."

She popped a slice of it in my mouth with the usual coating of butter and jam. "Eat up now, Cousin Paddy. I don't want you complaining about having a grand frigging hunger out on the lake. Drink another cup of tea. There's a head on board if you were wondering."

"I wasn't. I assumed there would be . . . Now, tell me, Cousin, do you race on the Galway hookers too?"

"Didn't I crew on one of them last year? Won't we be seeing some of them practicing on our way to Clifden at the far end of Connemara tomorrow? I'm not sure I'll have time this summer."

Not if I can help it. We'll be on our honeymoon together in America, which you will be seeing for the first time, as I will too.

"Would you want to take a run on one of them?"

"Let's see how I do today. My inner ear does not like too much motion."

"Ah, today won't be a problem at all, at all. The bay's another matter altogether. Look what I have," she said, bouncing to a cabinet and pulling out another red sweatshirt. "Wasn't I scared of wearing it, for you'd get the wrong idea 'bout me?"

The sweatshirt was the same color as the famed dark red color of the hookers. The letters proclaimed "Galway Hooker!"

"I'd never get the wrong idea about you, Sara Anne. It's a grand sweatshirt. I'm not sure you ought to be wearing it at Ashford Castle, however."

"Ah," she said, "wouldn't it give the stuffy Yanks up there a shock?" She draped the shirt across her chest. Then, very quickly, she jammed it back into the locker.

"Come on," she continued, "let's clear off the table

and get this craft under way!"

We cleared off the table, she put on a navy blue wind-breaker and started the boat. It's engines, unlike all the boat engines I know, purred instantly.

"Would you ever cast off the mooring lines, Paddy? Bring them into the boat. Be careful of the tug of the river. It wants to pull us out towards the ocean. And don't fall in the water. 'Tis terrible cold."

I managed to fulfill my assigned tasks, however clumsily. The boat eased away from the dock.

"I really shouldn't be mooring there," she admitted. "But 'tis only slightly against the law . . . We have to move slowly until we get out of the river and into the lake."

"I'm in no rush," I said, extending my arm around her waist. She did not resist.

"Lough Corrib," she informed me, "is thirty miles long and is the second largest lake in Ireland. For hundreds, maybe thousands of years, it was the major means of transportation down to the sea for what we now call Galway and Mayo. It's fed by an underground river from Lough Mask a couple of miles above it in County Mayo. The Brits tried to dig a canal—weren't they great ones for digging canals?—because that would provide water transportation almost up to Castlebar. But didn't the water sink into the limestone rocks and back into the underground river where it belongs? Most of the year it's empty, but sure, it provided lots of jobs for poor folk during the famine, including some of my Tobin ancestors. We'll stop by O'Flaherty's Castle where them folk fought off the Normans and the Brits for a couple of centuries and terrorized Galway whenever they had too much to drink. Sure, isn't there a sign on a wall in town praying for deliverance from the wrath of the O'Flahertys? And didn't Granne O'Malley herself rule up there for a long time? And won't we also stop in Inchagoil, the largest Ireland on the lake, where there is a shrine to your patron?''

"He must have been an important man around here at one time."

"Och, isn't most of it legend? Me teachers at UCG say it's doubtful that he ever got out to these parts."

"Does anyone really sleep overnight on this boat?"

"Not I surely. Me ma and da do sometimes during the summer. You can imagine what they do anchored out on the lake under the moonlight."

"I'm too polite to imagine."

"Me ma just turns pink when I ask her about it, but she doesn't deny a thing. And doesn't she give me some good advice too, though terrible indirect even for the Irish?"

We finally emerged from the serpentine river and plowed into the lake. The chill wind was coming straight down from the north, and there were two-foot waves on the water. Nothing by Lake Michigan standards, but still enough to worry my inner ear a little. The wind howled around the boat, singing in the various antennae that presumably kept us in touch with the world. Both of us zipped up our jackets and huddled together to stay warm.

Sara Anne opened up the boat, and for a couple of minutes she (the craft) road deep into the waves. Spray splashed around us and into the cabin. My stomach threatened to turn queasy any moment.

"Isn't it glorious?" she shouted above the wind.

" 'Tis grand!'' I shouted back. It was a lie, but I was not yet ready to beg her to slow down.

"There's no rush, I suppose." She throttled back the engine. "It's supposed to be a leisurely trip . . . You look a little green, Paddy. You were serious about your inner ear. I'm terribly sorry."

"It's all right now," I said bravely.

"Were you sick on the flight over?"

"Was I ever. But it was a rough flight. I'm fine."

I wasn't fine at all. If she had driven a few more minutes at top speed, I would have been vomiting all over her carefully burnished cabin.

Then a hand touched my forehead, and it wasn't Sara Anne's hand.

"God Heals" is what her name means, the name we use anyway. Very quick cure. Thank you very much, Rae.

"Ah, sure, haven't you got your color back now, and wasn't I a terrible eejit for thinking you were only joking about motion sickness?"

"I should probably invest in some of those little patches. I'm told they give you nice dreams."

"Tell me if you feel the slightest bit sick. It's no weakness to be prone to motion sickness," she said firmly. "Not at all, at all."

"Yeah, it is a weakness, Sara Anne, but not a fatal one . . . I'll probably need a lot of tender, loving care all day long," I said, hugging her more closely.

"Ah, well, wouldn't you be getting that anyway?"

So we consumed midmorning tea (and scones, also smothered in butter and jam) at a pleasant lakeside hotel near Oughterard, and visited the O'Flaherty ruins and the mysterious little churches on Inchagoil—which seemed to be a permanently soggy island. The newest of the churches and the only one that was not in complete ruins dated to the ninth century and was supposed to be the burial place of St. Patrick's navigator, a certain Saint Nimian. What was left of it was strangely attractive. Sara Anne informed me that the Latin inscription on an obelisk a couple of feet high was supposed to be the oldest Latin inscription in Ireland. The island wasn't spooky so much as sad. A melancholy, bittersweet sadness hung over it, despite the thick growth of trees, the sound of birds singing, and the blooming wildflowers.

"Even if himself were never here," Sara Anne, arms folded, said, continuing her lecture, "it's still a holy place. You can feel it in the air, can't you, Paddy Tobin?"

She took my hand into hers and held it firmly.

"Indeed yes. Great faith and great skill went into building it out here on this island. The people are now gone and we don't know who they were or what they did or why they chose to bring all this granite out here."

"Sure, isn't that true of most of the Irish in years gone by? They're all forgotten, despite their work and their faith. And Cromwell destroyed what was left over. But sure, there's no good to be done by feeling sorry for ourselves, as me da always says. But don't we Irish love to feel sorry for ourselves?"

"I've never seen a bit of self-pity in you, Sara Anne, my love," I said as I kissed her. It was a long and very tender kiss.

"Now, that was very nice, Cousin Paddy," she said with her usual rueful sigh. "The nicest kiss yet. You're getting better as you figure me out."

"I'll not hurt you, Cousin Sara Anne."

"Sure, don't I know that?"

"But I do want you."

"Don't I know that too? And it frightens me and flatters the hell out of me."

"What I want to know is whether I'm going to get assaulted in the pool again this afternoon like I was yesterday."

"As to that, I make no promises either way . . . Come

on, now, let's get off this island before it spooks us altogether."

I saw a chance to score a point or two, an opportunity never to be passed up with any woman, even one so little domineering as my cousin.

"Maybe we should say a couple of prayers before we leave, for the poor people who lived here and for the poor people in Ireland who have suffered so much for such a long time, but still sang and danced and told stories and laughed."

"A grand idea," she agreed.

So we both made the sign of the cross and bowed our heads and prayed.

This time I made the final sign of the cross before she did. She smiled slightly as she watched that out of the corner of her eye.

Silently we went back to the little pier where the boat was tethered. I helped her climb aboard and with more skill than before, hauled the lines back into the boat.

"Think of what Ireland might have been like if it were not for all the invasions and struggles. It was the most civilized place in Europe up till the ninth century."

"Sometimes I think we'd be indistinguishable from the frigging Belgians if that had happened."

Ashford Castle came into view at a quarter past one. We were right on schedule. Naturally.

Well, that was a habit that would stand her in good stead once she joined the Benedictines.

The castle loomed in the distance like a Hollywood version of a royal resort—long, graceful, and dominating with its turrets and battlements and its gray solemnity.

"Quite a place," I said to the captain.

" 'Tis said that it's the kind of castle God would build if He had as much money as a Philadelphia millionaire—

or as Walt Disney Incorporated," she replied, readjusting her cap. "But 'tis somewhat authentic just the same. The part on the left really is a medieval castle, and the center parts are seventeenth and nineteenth century additions. And on the right is the new construction, which doesn't look so bad at all, at all. 'Tis a great place for rich Yanks to spend their honeymoons, especially after their second marriage."

"No pool?"

"No, you amadan, no pool. So I guess you're safe here from me attacks."

"Worse luck for me."

The boatmen at the pier waved to her and shouted greetings. I tossed them the lines and assisted her out of the boat. The boatmen helped her onto the pier. No one assisted me and I almost fell into the water, but they were too busy with her, and she was too busy being the charming precinct captain to notice me.

When we got to the low entrance of the hotel, she became rather a countess, an experienced woman of the world, entering a church—reverential and respectful but still very much in charge. She bowed and smiled and returned everyone's polite greetings without disturbing the solemnity of the place.

It was very much like a church inside, albeit an Episcopal church, big, tall rooms with vast windows, stairways, and galleries, deep leather chairs, expensive paintings on the paneled walls, and a devout quiet that made me want to pray.

"It would be a quiet honeymoon at that," I observed to my captain.

"Sure the bedrooms are huge, aren't they now? And quiet. And isn't there singing and drinking downstairs at night?"

The manager, a charming and silver-haired person called Mr. Murphy, appeared in the lobby, led us into the bar, and insisted on buying us a drink. Two dry sherries, it was, one of them on the rocks, because that's the way the Yanks like it.

"Only one of them drinks for herself," I insisted. "If she drinks two of them, won't I have to be driving the boat back, and won't that be ruination of the boat and of us?"

"And of Lough Corrib," herself added.

We chatted a few minutes over our drinks, and I made the decision that I would not mind frolicking with herself in a vast bedroom in this place for a couple of weeks. Not at all, at all.

We were shown into the dining room, an ornate place with gleaming china, snow white tablecloths, polished silverware, neatly and formally dressed personnel, and the smell of good food. The room was half-filled, young rich Yanks, older rich Yanks, Yank tourists who were not so rich, but scarcely poor, Japanese and Germans with their cameras at the ready, and a few well-groomed Irish fat cat types.

Every eye turned to watch as we sauntered in. Naturally my tour guide was the object of their interest.

"I'm starved," I informed her.

"I'm not surprised. Didn't I order the meal last night so you wouldn't have to wait?"

"You seem to have clout here."

"No, me da has."

But the smiles of everyone were for Sara Anne and not for her da.

I couldn't be sure because in the far corner of the dining room there was too much mist, but I thought I saw the ineffable Raphaella with two serious-looking blond tykes. I suppose they had come up the lake on the boat and watched my every move.

We were served with a half bottle of Jesuiten Garden wine, scallop mousse, poached salmon with a wondrous wine sauce, roast leg of lamb with mint jelly, and a sherry trifle with heavy cream. To say nothing of Irish brown bread, which was not as good as that made by my love, but still sensational.

"It'll do," I said, sighing contentedly after I had finished the remnants of her trifle. "Do you think I could have some hot apple tart with heavy cream like your man at the next table has?"

She laughed and summoned the waiter.

"This will hold me till half eight at the Great Southern tonight . . . Do you think that nice Mr. Murphy will buy me a glass of Bailey's?"

So in the lounge we had another pot of tea and I had my Bailey's (on the rocks because I'm a Yank), courtesy not of Mr. Murphy but of Ms. Tobin.

While I was putting away the drink, Rae and her two children, oops, progeny, drifted by.

"Good afternoon, Ms. Tobin," they said, nodding politely. I was favored with a pleasant smile for someone who really didn't belong at Ashford Castle.

"Who are those people?" I asked my beloved.

"I don't know, to tell the truth. I mean I've seen them around, but I don't remember their names."

Why does my Seraph friend do things like that? Maybe just for the pure hell of it. Or maybe to let me know she hadn't lost interest in this crazy grail quest of mine.

"Are you going to stay here all afternoon?" she asked as I put aside the empty Waterford liquor glass and considered ordering another. "We could get a room for you to sleep in."

I sighed loudly and stumbled to my feet. "Ah, no, I wouldn't want to sleep in this grand place in a bed with no other person in it. I'll have to wait for my honeymoon."

She slapped my arm in mild protest. "You get more outrageous every day, Cousin Paddy!"

"And you more beautiful, my dear," I said, covertly slapping her delicious derriere.

She did not protest. Quite the contrary, she kissed me affectionately after *Sara Anne* had pulled away from the pier.

"You were so wonderful in there, Cousin Paddy. They have more than their share of obnoxious Yanks and some nice ones, too. But rarely does someone like you walk into Ashford Castle with all your warm and natural charm."

She followed that compliment with a second kiss.

Warm and natural charm? Me?

Yet it was nice to be adored—and a rare enough experience in my life.

She permitted me to drive the boat for ten minutes or so.

"We're going with the wind at our backs, and the waves have calmed down anyway. Just keep an eye on where you're going and don't get too close to any of them islands."

"No, ma'am. Well," I said, "sure, isn't the boat a lot easier to handle than her namesake?"

"Isn't that the truth now?"

Standing behind me, she put both arms around my chest and hung on to me like her life depended on it. Her firm breasts pushed against my back, were a challenge and an invitation.

But not, I thought, yet enough of an invitation to raise the question of an early marriage.

It would truly have been grand to have retired after lunch to one of the bedrooms of the castle with her in my arms.

Well, it might still happen.

I excused myself so I could compose an E-mail message to my family that I could plug into the Net at her house. I didn't think she was yet ready for Internet without a modem.

>Megan, Sara Anne and I are coming back from Ashford Castle on the boat named after her. It's been a glorious day, though it's clouding up now and looks like rain. Sara Anne is an excellent boat pilot, though she got me a little seasick on the way up. The lake is only about thirty miles long and is laced with all kinds of fascinating little islands, each one of which you're sure has a story behind it. I disgraced myself and captain/tour guide/hostess by eating too much at lunch, including an apple tart with heavy cream after a sherry trifle with ditto. And herself with the good manners and taste of a very refined and poised countess. I'm sure I embarrassed her altogether, but what can you do about a big and crazy Yank cousin who eats scallop mousse, poached salmon, roast leg of lamb, and Irish brown bread like he doesn't know where he's going to get his next meal? The poor girl is bearing up well enough under the strain of having me around her pretty feet.

In fact, I am going to have my next meal in the highly touted grill room of the Great Southern at half eight tonight with herself, if she can keep me sober till then. I suppose tomorrow, when we climb the mountain to my patron's shrine, will be a day of fast and ab-

stinence. Then the next day it will be off on a
fifteen-minute flight to Inishmore, the largest
of the Aran Islands. My lady Sara Anne tells
me that no one can get sick on only a fifteen-
minute plane ride.
I think she's in for a surprise.
After we get back to Galway city, I'm going to
install MEGSONG on her 486 DX. Maybe we'll be
able to send you some of her work on the Net.
Love to all,
Toby

"Can we really do that? I mean, send some of my music
to Megan on the Net."

I feigned surprise and horror. "You mean you've been
watching over my shoulder all along?"

"You knew that I was. But can we send some of my
music home to your family? What will they be thinking of
it?"

I was not going to answer the second question.

"Of course we can send your music to America, though
we'll have to send something you've composed on MEG-
SONG."

"And don't I have a melody that's been running
around in me head for the last couple of days? . . . Why
Toby?"

" 'Tis a nickname that my father's friends gave him
when he was a kid. I guess it stuck to me. My real name
is G. Patrick. The *G* for Gerard. Just like my great-uncle."

"I like Paddy better," she said with a sniff.

"So do I."

"What will your family think of that letter?"

"They'll think I'm out of my mind . . . or maybe in
love."

She touched my face with her cold hand.

"You don't get much support from them, do you, Paddy?"

Her kindness and concern almost broke my heart.

"Not a lot. Except from Meg. I'm the only son, and I haven't lived up to their expectations."

"Then they had the wrong expectations."

That settled that.

"Put a PS on the note before you save it. Tell her that Sara Anne told you to tell them that you were at all times a perfect and charming gentleman, though you did eat a terrible lot. Go on, Paddy Tobin, or I'll start calling you Toby."

She smiled as she gave her order, but it was an order nonetheless, and I dutifully typed it before I saved the letter and terminated the session.

"I hate to mention this, but I think it's raining," I said.

"Just a mild drizzle. You shouldn't come to Ireland if you're afraid of getting a little wet."

The rain had ended, temporarily, when we pulled up to the dock at the marina where the Tobins usually parked their boat. We washed the breakfast dishes by hand, gathered the remnants of our trip, and climbed on to the pier at the yacht club. This time I made it with some elegance.

"The little red Ford is me ma's. We'll carry everything up there."

And her ma and da used it at work when Sara Anne wasn't cavorting around all of County Galway in it with her Yank cousin—the big eejit with the warm and natural charm.

"It's going to rain again," she said as she entered her home. "I'm afraid there'll be no pool for us today."

"I won't be assaulted then."

"I didn't promise that you would be or you wouldn't be or that you will be or you will not be . . . Now let's put these things away."

"We could use the pool at the Great Southern."

She ignored that possibility. But she hadn't said no.

The kitchen was spotlessly clean. Was Sara Anne or Edna the neatness freak? Or both of them? It was all right with me. I liked to know where things are.

"Would you like a pint while we install your software?"

"If I did, woman, after my excesses up beyond, wouldn't I have to stay the rest of the evening and way into the night?"

"Well, we have a couple of guest rooms if it comes to *that*," she said as she led me up the stairs.

I had the sense of déjà vu again as I walked into her convent-neat room. I'd been there before, but I knew I'd never been there before.

"You keep a neat room, young woman, and yourself a picture of Michael on the wall."

"I played a little basketball at the abbey . . . and I like to know where things are. That will be some help when I enter the order, won't it?"

"It will."

First time that had been mentioned all day.

"Aren't you afraid of letting me into your room, and with no one else at home?"

"No. I'd never be afraid of you, Paddy," she said as she unfastened her ponytail and let her hair cascade back to her shoulders.

Then she turned on her 486. "Should I access the gateway over at UCG?"

"Not until I've loaded DABEST. All you have to tell it is the phone number of the gateway, and it will do the rest . . . Let me sit in the chair now."

She stood beside me as I loaded the three disks. It takes DABEST a while to decompress and sort itself out. Lest I find myself with nothing useful to do, I put my arm around her waist and drew her close.

Not once in our long relationship—well, it seemed long—had she resisted or protested my signs of affection.

My hand slipped under her sweatshirt and around to her belly.

She sighed deeply. "You're trying to drive me round the bend altogether, Cousin Paddy."

"That'll be the day."

DABEST created a number of weirdly colored lines on the screen, as it usually does.

Was Rae in the house, watching my every move? Well, so what if she was?

I moved my thumb lightly along the bottom of her warm and brimming breasts, delicately constrained as they were by a thin cotton bra.

She gasped, grew limp in my arm, and moaned softly.

"I'll stop if you want."

"Stop when you want," she said in a hushed voice.

I reached as far as a hard nipple pressing against her bra.

"Paddy," she said softly, "isn't the prompt asking us for the UCG phone number?"

"OK," I said, giving up my adventure. "You sit in the chair and tell it the number, and I'll give you instructions."

She slipped into the chair I had vacated, glancing at me with round and worshipful eyes as she did so.

She typed in the number. DABEST whirled and hunted and finally came up with a prompt.

Had I gone too far? She didn't seem to think so. She was right, I would never hurt her, all the more so because her trust was so powerful and her worship so deep. The trust, maybe I deserved, but hardly the worship. I forced myself to concentrate on the work at hand.

"Type 'Irish feuds.' "

She nodded and did so.

"Now give it the following criteria: nineteenth century, Galway, Tobin family. Let's see what it does."

My program went through its usual song and dance and announced it had five entries.

"Is it that easy, Paddy?"

"Sometimes a lot harder . . . Let's look at each one of them."

The first three were references to Galway archives, which were apparently pretty well cataloged. But the archives were not transportable files.

"We can look at them on Friday when we come back from Inishmore," she said. "Let's see what's in this one. It looks pretty long."

She moved the cursor down and pressed the enter key. The cover of what looked like an old pamphlet appeared on the screen.

"The Murderous Feud in the Tobin Clan: Another Story of Irish Primitive Morality."

The author was Rev. Timothy T. Huntington of the Collegiate Church of St. Nicholas in Galway.

"Press shift F-eight and it will tell you where the holding is and whether it's transportable, which I doubt."

The University of Chicago Library.

And an icon depicting a transportable file appeared. Someone else had called it up recently and asked that it be scanned into a file. Someone writing a dissertation? Maybe.

Or maybe someone else. I hoped Rae was watching this possibility. Well, she would from now on since she claimed that she eavesdropped on the Net.

"Just push enter and the file will FTP to us and print it out after it comes in. It looks like about twenty pages. That won't take too long. While we're waiting I'll send my E-mail to Meg."

"How can you do it at the same time?"

"It's a little trick of the program, one of the reasons I'm going to be in hot pursuit of Bill Gates at Microsoft in a couple of years. Basically it's a line-sharing arrangement. Is your Galway account free?"

" 'Tis."

"Good. We won't be cheating them then."

I inserted the diskette I had copied from my notebook, directed the program's attention to it, called up address system, and told it:

>**Go Meg**

First it searched for mail from Meg.

Toby, have fun with herself today. Does she really adore you? I bet she does. WELL, she has good taste. The family doesn't like this E-mail bit, but I tell them it's great, better then listening to their endless bickering with you on the phone. They're torn between fear that you and herself are going to like one another and fear that you won't. I tell them that if she has good taste, she certainly will.
AND I want to listen to her music. I bet it's TO-TALLY excellent.
Megperson

"The kid's an incurable romantic," I said apologetically. "Just like her brother."

"She sounds like a darling child," Sara Anne said enthusiastically. "I do want to meet her."

"She's maybe two and a half years younger than you, Cousin Sara Anne."

"Your family does give you a hard time, doesn't it?"

"All except Meg."

"They want the best for you. Just like me own parents."

"Yours are much nicer about it."

She nodded. "I know, they couldn't be nicer. That only makes it tougher."

"They want you to put some stability in your life?"

"Isn't that the truth? Why should I be ready for stability just because me ma was married when she was only six months older than I am now?"

"I know you don't plan on marrying, but don't you think that's too young in our time?"

She shrugged indifferently, as if it were an irrelevant question.

"The time to marry, if you're going to marry, is when the man comes along you couldn't live without."

A clear enough statement of values and also reassuring to me.

"It's coming off my printer now," she said, grabbing for the first page that her HP 4M spit out.

We read it in silence. Each page was more horrifying.

On the west side of Lake Corrib, just across the Galway boundary into Mayo, there lived in the late eighteenth century hundreds of Tobins on either side of a small mountain. They were divided into two clans, the Gerry Tobins and the Malachi Tobins. They were rough, brutal, uneducated men, often suspected of engaging in lawless resistance to the legitimate government (meaning London). To make matters worse, the author reported, they were under the superstitious control of the local Catholic clergy who were often more brutal—and more likely to be drunkards—even then their parishioners. Some of the Tobins, even in this modern age, spoke only the barbaric Irish language, and most of the others preferred to speak that language instead of respectable English.

Although they were related to one another, they nonetheless engaged in fierce gang fights at the annual "patterns," pagan feasts allegedly in honor of St. Patrick at the pagan shrine of Maumene in Galway. The weapons in these fights were clubs, sticks, athletic bats, and stones. Many men were injured in these brawls, and some died. Exact numbers were not available because the Tobins carried their dead and dying back to their mountain.

Eventually the savagery spread from the annual gang fights to violence on the Tobin's Mountain itself, as the place was vulgarly called. Hard-pressed government officials could not prevent the battles, because neither side would reveal grudge violence to the lawful authorities. "We'll take care of it ourselves," was the only law they knew.

Land was an important issue in the feud because both sides claimed they had been cheated out of its lawful property (by which was meant the miserable if traditional rights of tenants to work on Lord Mayo's land—the only property with which the bog Irish could be trusted) by the other. With such large numbers of humans crowded together on impoverished land, it was difficult to determine in a court of law which claims were valid and which were not. So, lacking patience and restraint, they settled land claims by the club, the pike, and the sword.

The leaders of the two clans were Malachi and Gerard Tobin—Mal and Gerry to their friends. They were the principal land farmers on the mountain and at one time had been great friends. There were even reports that they had fought with the "Ribbonmen," a masked and seditious group wearing green ribbons who for many years had terrorized the generous and hardworking landowners of Galway and Mayo. But they had fallen out over some minor dispute and no longer cared to keep their relations from doing violence to one another.

They were finally persuaded by a new and younger priest to bring their case to the proper and civilized tribunal of the English Crown in Galway. Throngs of ruffians from both sides invaded the town to await the court's decision. In the meantime a romance of a sort had blossomed between the only children of both leaders, young Patrick Tobin, son of Gerry, and Sara, the seventeen-year-old daughter of Malachi.

"My father's middle name is Malachi," Sara told me grimly, as she passed the page on to me.

Despite the anger that now existed between the two clans and despite the tinderbox they had made of Galway during the long and tedious trial, these two young people courted and were married secretly by the young priest—a most unwise decision on their part.

The court finally ruled in favor of Gerard Tobin. Upon returning to his lodgings after a violent night of drinking in celebration of his victory, he found his son and daughter-in-law sharing a marriage bed. He promptly beat them both to death with a club.

Hearing of his beloved child's death, Malachi Tobin gathered his family around him, found the now-sleeping Gerard Tobin in the room where the unfortunate young people's lives had been cut short, and butchered Gerard with a carving knife. According to eyewitnesses, there were no major parts of the man's body left in one piece when Malachi's clan was finished with him.

Thereupon ensued a fierce and bloody battle through

the streets of the city in which scores of men, women, and children were killed and many more seriously injured. Troops from the local barracks of the Royal Army were finally called upon to restore order. When the raging mobs refused to disperse, the troops were forced to fire upon them, inflicting more casualties on these savage native Irish people who patently are substantially less than human.

The narrow streets of Galway literally ran with blood as the troops, hoping to end the Tobin threat to the city, resolutely fired at the retreating mobs.

Finally what remained of them retreated on foot and in boats back up their mountain redoubt. Malachi was dead, the victim of a well-aimed English musketball that penetrated his spine.

Although Gerard Tobin had won his case in court, his relatives fled the country, leaving the land in possession of his cousin's relatives. Nonetheless, citizens of Galway remained in fear for some time of the return of the Tobins. There are even today reports of more killings in that remote region as Malachi's survivors and Gerard's survivors continue to dispose of one another.

"Why did your relatives leave the country when they had won the suit?" Sara asked sadly when she had finished the story.

Her face was drawn and pale, her lips tight, her voice haunted. But she had not wept.

"Perhaps because my ancestor had murdered the two young people, and everyone thought that was the worse of the crimes."

"My father owns all that land up there, you know. It's not worth much anymore, though there are stories of mining companies, English mining companies, poking around, looking for hints of gold."

"Gold?"

"Croagh Patrick is supposed to be a mountain of gold, though we won't let any of them bastards desecrate it. Wouldn't that be strange? Gold all over North Galway and South Mayo, and all the suffering there through the years?"

"Does your da think it likely?"

Her shoulders were slumped in discouragement and resignation.

"No . . . but he says nothing is impossible in that desolate country. Practically no one lives in the area anymore. Only one gravel road runs into it. But if the story is true, it is your property, not our property."

"Hardly, Sara Anne," I said, patting her head. "The law certainly would not respect those claims from so long ago, even were we of a mind to claim the land, much good that it would do us. The story is history, history that apparently no one in Galway knows."

"I vaguely remember a nun at the abbey talking about the gang fights. She said that no one tried to stop them because they felt that when Irish people killed other Irish people, it was a good thing for the English. They considered us apes. We never wanted to remember the gang fights. I'm sure no one in Galway remembers. But it is still dangerous."

"Why?"

"I don't know why," she said, scowling at me. "I just know that it is. And didn't they have the same names as us, poor dear things?"

"Family names have a tendency to persist for generations. I once saw a report which traced similar names among descendants of New England Puritans which survived for over two hundred years. It's a long time from beginning to end, but only a brief span of time for those who name their kids after parents and uncles and aunts and grandparents."

I was spooked, too, by the story. Yet I had to argue the case for common sense against her almost superstitious dread.

"I know. It still seems . . . well, haunted."

"Your da is not going to come home and find us in bed with one another. Even if he did, he wouldn't kill us."

"He'd probably celebrate that I'd finally captured you . . . and anyway, it was your side of the family that did the killing, wasn't it now?"

"Uncle Gerry wanted to make peace because he knew that was true."

"Indeed."

"You are not angry at me for something that happened two hundred years ago, are you?"

In response she smiled wanly and touched my hand. "How could I ever be angry at you, Paddy?"

"It's a terrifying story. I can understand why it upset you. Hell, it upsets me too."

"If you don't mind, I'll put it in me purse and shred it at me da's office tomorrow morning. I don't want them ever to see it."

"At least we know what Great-Uncle Gerry was trying to expiate."

"His family won the suit and then went to America and became rich."

"Some of them."

"Aye . . . only some of them. Would you ever mind if we went over to UCG tomorrow, no, on Thursday when we come back from Inishmore, and see what more we can find?"

"I was thinking the same thing, Cousin Sara Anne."

"Let the dead bury their dead, as the Bible says. And it doesn't have anything to do with us, does it?"

"It does not."

I wasn't quite as confident as I sounded. Who had dug up the old pamphlet from the University of Chicago? And why?

"Still," she said thoughtfully, "we'd want to be sure that there's nothing there someone can use to embarrass both our families."

"I know what you mean."

"Maybe there's still some uneasy souls that are waiting to be put at peace."

"That may be what Great-Uncle Gerry had in mind."

Particularly by trying to arrange a marriage between the descendants of the two bloody clans. That was silly, but it did not follow that the idea was absurd in itself.

"Let's say a prayer for them now and get on with your MEGSONG."

"Are you sure you want to?"

"Of course I want to," she responded crisply. "We have our own lives to live, don't we?"

We did indeed.

So we prayed for the second time that day for our Irish ancestors, poor miserable, suffering people that they must have been.

Shot in the back by British troops.

This time we said the prayers aloud, and Sara Anne led us. At the end she said the final requiescat in Irish.

I responded with the usual "Amen."

"Now." She rubbed her hands briskly. "Let's turn to MEGSONG."

I installed the program, called up the composition screen with its lined musical staffs, and typed in the first few bars of "Galway Bay."

"Glory be to God and His Blessed Mother!" she exclaimed piously. "Isn't it a frigging miracle?"

"Just a very simple program. I'm working on an advanced version of it, which will sell for a lot more than twenty dollars. It will even make suggestions for orchestration!"

"Spoil all the creativity." She sniffed. "Can I try it?"

"Sure. Do you remember that melody which was running around in your head?"

I vacated the chair for her. She bounced into it, flicking her hair out of her eyes with a deft move of her hand.

"Don't I now? It's just a sweet little lullaby. Maybe for Christmas . . . How do you do this?"

I told her to call up the "keyboard," a window that described how the computer keys had been converted into musical notes.

"Astonishing!" she exclaimed. "If I push Control-P, it will print it out?"

"It will indeed."

She studied the user-friendly key arrangement for a few moments, and began to bang away. The notes appeared on the screen as rapidly as though she had known the song for a long time.

She transcribed several bars of music and then sat back and hummed it to herself. It was a lovely, lilting melody, suitable indeed for the Christ Child at Christmastime.

"I'm thinking of maybe writing a whole cycle of lullabies," she said. "I hope they're the kind little kids will love. Sure, the songs are for them, aren't they now?"

"You love kids, Sara Anne?"

"Certainly I do." She erased a note and inserted a new one, without my having to explain how she should do it.

She loved children but planned not to have any of her own. I was not convinced of her "vocation" at all, at all.

"I'll print it out and go play it on the piano."

"You don't have to do that yet. Just do Alt-P and see what happens."

With the enthusiastic eagerness of a child with a new toy, she touched the keys. The computer beeped out her melody. It was indeed a lovely lullaby.

"You know, it's not half bad, is it now?"

"It's lovely."

She changed a couple of notes and played it again.

"Ah, now that does it, doesn't it? May I print it out?"

"Sure."

She saved it and printed it.

"Do you have any lyrics for it yet?"

"Only snatches of ideas," she said, gathering the sheets that the HP 4M had already spit out. "Ah, 'tis gorgeous. I mean the printing."

"Can I send it to Megan?"

She hesitated, frowned, and then said, "Sure, why not?"

So I fired off the melody on the Net. Rae, I presumed, had already heard it.

Sara Anne insisted on driving me back to the Great Southern.

" 'Tis the least I can do for you in the drizzle, and yourself giving me those wondrous new toys. You are a bit of a genius, Paddy Tobin, aren't you now?"

"No, ma'am, I am not," I replied firmly.

She tilted her head up and moved her fingers through her hair.

"Well, if I want to call you a genius, I will."

At the hotel I said, "There's a pool here."

"Don't I know that?"

"So we could swim in it."

"Could we now?"

"There's lockers up there. So you wouldn't have to change in my room."

"Isn't that convenient?"

She climbed out of the car with me and led me into the hotel.

"Your man insists we swim in your tiny pool," she informed Nuala as we strode in.

"Isn't it nice and warm now?" The receptionist rolled her green eyes.

Sara Anne's swimsuit today, red with white trim, was somewhat less comprehensive than yesterday's. Alas there were other hotel guests in the pool area, so our behavior was limited to swimming—and to my ogling.

"See you at half eight," I said back in the hotel lobby.

"If you still want me," she said dubiously.

"Now, why wouldn't I want you?"

"I'm such a mercurial person, if you take me meaning."

"Half eight promptly, do you hear, woman?"

"Yes, Cousin Paddy," she said meekly.

I waved at Nuala at the reception desk. "Herself will be here for dinner at half eight."

"I'd wager she'll look gorgeous again," that one replied.

Rae was not in my suite. Probably waiting till the end of the day to render her verdict. I'd have to thank her for the cure in midlake. Would it be, I wondered, a permanent service?

So I turned on my Aero and accessed the E-mail from Megan.

What an absolutely darling lullaby melody. I bet she won't tell you the lyrics, and I bet they are about you. She is certainly in love with you by now, Toby. You don't waste any

time, do you? She must be really neat, truly
excellent. I do want to meet her soon.
I played the melody on the piano for Mom and
Dad and Nicole. As you can imagine, they patronized it. Sweet, pretty. They wouldn't know
genius if it hit them like a truck. She is a genius, Toby. Marry her before someone else
does.
Megperson

I sent a reply.
>Meg,
She wants to meet you too. She may well be a
genius at that. She is certainly gifted. She is
also, to use her own word, mercurial. I'm taking her to supper in the grill room here (by all
accounts very elegant) tonight.
Assure Mom and Dad that I feel fine, though
I'm eating too much. I'll send another note tomorrow morning before we leave for Connemara.
By the way, they call me Paddy here, short for
Patrick. It's a name I kind of like.
Toby

There was time for a nap and a shower before eight
o'clock, when I would have to dress in whatever elegance
Rae would decree.

I asked Nuala to wake me at a quarter of eight.

"Taking a nap, are you?"

A fresh question.

"It never hurts," I said, hanging up. The woman was
too curious altogether.

At a quarter past eight, I had taken my shower, shaved,
and was half-dressed in the quite serious, dark blue, three-

piece suit Rae had chosen for the evening. The phone rang.

"Herself is on the way up," Nuala announced in a solemn tone.

"On the way up!"

"Wait till you see her."

"I presume I won't have to wait long."

I had buttoned some but not all of the buttons on my shirt when I heard the knock at the door of the suite.

"Come in, woman, and yourself being fifteen minutes early."

"Glory be, will you look at it now, and himself having a fancy suite. Sure, Mr. Tobin, you must be a terribly rich man to be able to stay in the honeymoon suite here at the Railway Hotel."

"Honeymoon suite?"

" 'Tis what they call it. Course, you don't have to be on your honeymoon to use it."

"My travel agent has a sense of humor."

She discarded her raincoat and folded it neatly on the sofa of my parlor.

"Well?" she said. "Do you like it?"

I gulped again, as any man would. Sara Anne was wearing an off-the-shoulder, black knit dress with a thigh-length skirt and a deep décolletage. She had replaced her St. Brigid cross with a string of pearls, real ones.

"Do you think it's too extreme?"

"Not at all, Cousin Sara Anne. Admiration, not shock, reduced me to silence."

She advanced toward me, slowly, hesitantly, touched my bare chest with obvious delight, then threw her arms around me, pushed me back against the wall, and smothered me with wild, hungry kisses.

"Fair is fair," she murmured as she paused for breath.

Then she resumed her attack.

I thought that I had better bring an end to this exercise because we were sliding towards thin ice. Then she stopped with an amused laugh.

"Was that as good as in the pool?"

"You get better every day."

"Do I now?"

She seemed quite pleased with herself.

"You do . . . Now, if you don't mind, I'll put on the rest of my clothes and we can go upstairs for dinner."

"Tomorrow we'll have to go back to the pool at the golf club."

"If you say so, my love."

She didn't argue with my choice of language.

A few minutes later we left my suite. She picked up her raincoat.

"I'll not be coming back here after dinner," she insisted.

"I'll not argue with you about that," I said, putting an arm around her waist. She snuggled close to me in the elevator going up to the grill.

"How many suits do you have, Cousin Paddy, and yourself coming with only carry-on luggage?"

"I don't count."

It was an honest answer, but, I admit, an obscure one. Would I ever be able to tell her about Rae? Not now anyway.

She disengaged as the elevator halted. I took her raincoat from her and checked it.

The grill room was perhaps three-quarters occupied with Yank tourists, German tourists, some affluent Micks, and some less affluent ones, celebrating a birthday or an anniversary.

A chorus of compliments followed us across the room

(accompanied by the delighted eyes of everyone).

"You look lovely, Sara Anne."

"What a beautiful dress, Sara Anne."

"Prettier every year, Sara Anne."

A few folks whom I had never met greeted me with remarks like, "Good evening to you, Paddy Tobin."

"Good evening to you too," I would reply. "I hope you enjoy your dinner."

"Your fame precedes you," she said with a giggle.

The whole damn Galway city was watching my courtship. Pulling for me? Probably. After all, wasn't I the big Yank with warm and natural charm?

We were conveyed to the far corner of the room where we looked out on the bay through both sets of floor-to-ceiling windows which lined two of the walls.

We both ordered sherry, one on the rocks. I extended my hand to a solid, nylon-covered thigh. As usual, she neither resisted nor protested.

"You must have clout to get us a table like this."

" 'Tis yourself that made the reservation."

"Everyone in the frigging hotel knew who I was bringing."

Another giggle.

"Sure from this spot, won't you be able to see the sun actually going down over Galway Bay and the moon rising, though not quite over Claddagh—if you don't distract yourself with other things."

"I can handle both."

"Can you now?" She gasped as I slowly moved my fingers up and down her leg, staying far away from the inviolate areas. For the present.

Had no one ever played with her this way before? Or had others tried and been rebuffed?

Galway Bay was indeed beautiful. The sun broke intermittently through the dark clouds. The bay was like a kaleidoscope, an ever-changing blend of black, gold, green, and silver.

"You must order the smoked salmon and the roast beef from the trolley and the strawberries with heavy cream."

"Yes, ma'am."

I relinquished her thigh when our drinks came.

"You must think I'm a terrible woman altogether, Paddy Tobin."

"That's not the adjective I'd use. Try beautiful, bright, gifted, mysterious, challenging."

"Would you stop?" she said with a blush. "But here I am being so forward with you, and meself telling you last night about my vocation to be a Benedictine."

"I think I'm the one that's being forward."

"I should really push your hands and lips away, and instead I act like I'm trying to seduce you."

"Is that what you're trying to do?"

"I don't know," she wailed, but softly. "I don't know what it takes to seduce a man."

"Sure, wouldn't you have to be a lot more forward?"

"I'm not sure I could seduce you even if I wanted to."

"Oh, I think you could, Sara Anne. But don't expect me to give you the details."

"I'm all confused," she said, draining her sherry glass. "You mixed me up something terrible."

"Are you driving tonight?"

"Didn't me da drive me over, and won't I be taking a taxi home? So please, sir, can I have another glass of sherry?"

"One more."

"So what do you think about us?" she asked, her blue eyes sad and fragile, gazing plaintively into my own.

What did I think about us? Good question, and with

the "about us" more specific than previous versions. I
wanted her, all right, no doubt about that. I didn't care
how long I'd have to wait. Yet, to tell the truth, I would
rather not wait long, more because I loved her so much
than because there were ten million dollars at stake.

I took her hand into mine.

"You're an intelligent and resourceful young woman,
Sara Anne, as well as passionate and attractive. I'm sure
you'll work out your problem. I'll help you however I can.
If you don't want to see me again, tell me and I'll disappear. If you want me to lay off the signs of affection,
I'll do that too. While I love you, as you so perceptively
observed, I'm not yet so far gone that you would break
my heart. If you want to talk to me about whatever it is
that's bugging you, I'll be happy to listen to you. If not,
it's your call."

She pondered my little speech.

"I don't want you to go away and I don't want you to
stop being affectionate . . . I don't know that I can talk to
you about . . . about my vocation and everything. Now or
ever."

"Fair enough."

"But I don't want to break your heart. You'd be wise,
wouldn't you now, to give up on me tonight."

"I'm not going to do that, Sara Anne. You can count
on that."

"I know, and I ask meself how you can have turned my
head in three days."

"Not the only head that has been turned in this relationship."

I squeezed her thigh again. Briefly.

"Isn't that our smoked salmon coming? Let's forget all
this serious talk and have a pleasant dinner."

So we did just that. She lectured me on Irish politics. I argued with her about films, though I admitted that the Irish had turned out a run of good ones lately. I told her about St. Hilary's and how much it meant to so many of us. She explained to me how the Irish universities worked and described her long-run ambitions in musical composition, adding piously that "of course, it will be up to my superiors in the order whether I'll do that line of work."

I told her more about my family and my problems with them. She said that it was a very Irish style. Parents, she observed, always worry about their children, they just do it in different ways. My parents, she insisted, had much less to worry about than her parents did. They thought that marriage to the right man would "settle me down," but that wasn't true at all, at all, was it?

We have to solve our own problems, I replied. A good marriage is a help but nothing more. And it depends on the man, doesn't it now?

We turned to the Irish sports scene. She analyzed at great length the Irish prospects in the World Cup, which opened in America next week (not as good as last time) and explained the differences between rugby and Gaelic football and soccer (which she called "football") and American football, which was a descendant of rugby.

Soccer, I told her, was a boring game, as exciting as watching grass grow. She hotly challenged this assertion. Wasn't everyone else in the world obsessed by it?

Just proves we have better taste, a comment that stirred up even more of her ire. How dare white Americans enjoy basketball when it was nothing more than a plantation sport? Sure now, aren't two of your best Irish soccer players of an African background? That stopped her cold because it established that I knew more about "football" than I was letting on.

"You're a terrible desperate man, Paddy Tobin," she said, as she squeezed my thigh.

Fair is fair, isn't it?

While we chattered and argued, the sun did set in triumph over Galway Bay, and the lights of the Claddagh, what was left of it, substituted for the moon.

Sara Anne was a great date, an endlessly amusing and entertaining companion—intelligent, sly, funny, opinionated, well informed, contentious (though never bitterly so), and a skilled artist of repartee.

It would not be a dull life. Not at all, at all.

I glanced occasionally around the grill room looking for a striking woman with chestnut hair, perhaps with a blond, linebacker companion. There were, however, no mists and no Seraphic analogues.

After dinner we rode down the elevator without stopping at my floor. I accompanied her into the lobby.

"Hasn't it stopped raining, Cousin Paddy?"

"It has. And, woman, I'm going to walk you home."

"You WILL not! Can't I take a taxi?"

"You cannot."

I took her arm and ushered her out of the hotel entrance and down its steps.

She sighed in mock protest but huddled close to me.

"I should put on me raincoat, shouldn't I? In a grill room this dress says one thing. On the streets of Galway it would say something else."

I helped her on with the coat and took her arm again. We walked up to her house in companionable silence. My love knew when to talk and when to be still. Our walk through the narrow streets of central Galway, wet and glittery in the dim streetlights, was a time for silence.

"It was a grand night, Cousin Paddy," she said when we arrived in front of her house. "I don't suppose you want to go out to Connemara with me tomorrow?"

We had come all too quickly to the door of the Tobin home.

"And climb up that mountain with you?"

"Not if you don't want to."

She was giving me an honest way out if I had wanted to take it. I removed her raincoat and kissed her—lips, throat, shoulders, chest, the visible tops of her breasts. She arched back from me and groaned, "Oh!"

Then she added, "Aren't you destroying me altogether?"

But she didn't try to escape.

Finally I stopped because if I didn't, all my discretion and restraint would have crumbled.

"Does that answer your question, young woman of the house?"

She glanced quickly up and down Waterside Street to be certain that no one was watching.

"Well, if you're coming along tomorrow, you should wear a warm sweater and a warm jacket because it'll be windy and cold after lunch and it will probably rain. But with any luck, we'll have the sun again by the time we get to the swimming pool. I'll pick you up at half eight."

Then she quickly ducked into her house.

I hurried back to Railway Hotel, where I was certain Rae would be waiting for me in my suite.

She was, this time wearing a light blue cocktail dress that compared favorably with my love's black costume.

"Nice," I said. "Blessed Mother blue. Appropriate for a Seraph who stands before the face of God. You folks are really vain, aren't you? I hope you and the kids, er, the progeny had a nice time on the lake today. They're attractive little tykes, a bit serious perhaps, but with nice smiles. Your progeny and your companion could pass for German tourists, but that's all right."

She actually laughed as I grabbed the initiative.

"More and more, G. Patrick Tobin, I feel like Dr. Frankenstein. To respond, I'm glad you like my gown; yes, we are vain; thank you for the kind words about my progeny, though I would rather think of them as Vikings; and, to your implicit question, when I am standing before the face of the Other, metaphorically in a certain sense, surely the Other enjoys my equivalent of your kind's boobs. Did not the Other make all His creatures to be beautiful? Would He not enjoy the special beauties of His most beautiful creatures? Why should you have a monopoly on ogling Sara Anne's admittedly lovely body? Satisfied?"

"Sometimes you call the Other He and sometimes She."

"She is both and neither. But She is certainly the life bearer of all, is She not?"

"You sing and dance naked before God?"

"Naturally . . . but enough chatter, Paddy. I must commend you on your words and deeds today. I thought you might have gone a little too far with her at the computer, but she did not think so, and it was her decision, not mine. Otherwise your performance was flawless. If it would not run the risk of enhancing your suddenly inflated ego, I might go so far as to say you surprised me with your sensitivity and skills. My progeny were impressed too."

"How old are they, Rae, I mean really?"

She lifted her bare shoulder. "No more than a couple of thousand years."

"Oh."

"Tomorrow it will be critical for you to demand of her that she tell you her problem. It is time that you take action against it. Understand?"

"She doesn't have AIDS or anything like that? She's not pregnant, is she?"

"Don't be absurd . . . You must absolutely insist on the whole truth even at the risk of putting the relationship in jeopardy for a time. Do not tolerate a refusal. Is that clear?"

"Yeah, but—"

"No buts."

She rose from the chair.

"I still don't quite understand why you spend so much of your time worrying about us."

"Don't you, Paddy? I would have thought it clear that our motive is the same as the Other's motive in creating us and watching over us. It's called love, a love far more intense for us, and infinitely more intense for Him, than the passion you feel for young Sara Anne. But," she added, lifting a finger, "the important point is that love is a continuum. When you love her, your love differs from ours for you, and the Other's for all of us, only in degree and not in kind."

"God wants Sara Anne like I do only more?"

"But not necessarily in the Benedictines, get it?"

"Yes, ma'am."

"Oh yes," she said, pausing at the door of my suite. "The Megperson, a very clever little child, is absolutely right: There do exist lyrics for the lullaby, and they are about you. Good night, Paddy."

I think that, instead of opening the door, she simply passed through it. In the mists I couldn't quite see what happened.

Show-off!

♣16♣

The next morning, under a bright sun and buffeted by a fierce Atlantic wind that shook Edna's little red Ford, we drove out to Connemara along the north shore of Galway Bay. The relatively lush region around Galway city and Salt Hill began to change when we reached the town of Spiddle, an Irish-speaking center. Rocks, mostly barren fields, peat bogs, little bays from the ocean, and lakes dominated the brown countryside.

"It was once mostly forest land," Sara Anne informed me. "The British tore down all the trees for their navy during the Napoleonic wars. There's not much left now except the bogs and the scenery and the Irish language."

"But the cottages are painted lively colors, pink and blue and yellow and red and gold."

"Sure, you give an Irish person a bucket of one-coat paint and won't he change the whitewash custom as quick as he can slap paint on a wall? The Book of Kells syndrome, if you take me meaning. Make a simple reality as convoluted and as intricate and as colorful as possible. Isn't that what we do with words?''

"The greatest storytellers and poets in all the world," I responded.

"Well, you can't eat stories or poems, but on the other hand, we Irish can't live without them."

I decided to look at the rough, rocky land of Connemara through the prism of the Book of Kells. It made a big difference.

We stopped at a tearoom in Spiddle for a cup of tea and a few scones to keep us going through midmorning. The elderly husband and wife who were in charge became ecstatic when they saw herself. Their faces glowed, their eyes brightened, and they made signs of the cross. Sara Anne embraced them both and kissed each on the cheek. The three of them babbled happily in a soft, musical language that was spoken gently and sweetly—Irish as spoken by the Irish speakers.

I was introduced and bowed politely when I heard the name "Padraig." The two older people bowed courteously in return. They seated us at one of the small wooden tables with red and white checked tablecloths and brought us tea and scones—with raspberry jam and clotted cream for me, accompanied by a smile and another bow. Doubtless they had been told that I was herself's latest "young man."

"Is Irish your first language?" I asked as she popped a piece of scone, layered with jam and clotted cream.

" 'Tis not, nor my parents for that matter. But they sent me to school as a little brat to learn it. I hated the extra school until I met some of the people out here and I began to love it. It's the most gentle and poetic language in all the world."

"Our Tobin forebears spoke it?"

"Certainly, and left to themselves, they were gentle people too, though perhaps not as gentle as these poor folks."

"Why don't you sing your new lullaby for them?"

"That's a good idea."

She summoned them to the table and wordlessly sang her song. The old folks clapped appreciatively. Sara Anne flashed with pleasure at their approval.

When we were back in the car, I said, "You didn't sing the lyrics for them."

She hesitated before she said, "Haven't I told you that there are no lyrics yet?"

"Sure there are. And about me, aren't they? I'm the boy child you're singing to."

She gripped the wheel tightly and stared straight ahead at the two-lane road ahead of us.

"You think you know everything, don't you?" she said bitterly.

"No, ma'am. I didn't even figure that out until the Megperson told me."

"Little bitch," she murmured with a trace of a smile.

"Can I hear it?"

"No."

"Never?"

"Well, not for a long time anyway."

"Why?"

She relaxed and laughed.

"Because it's a very personal song."

"Oh."

We drove on in silence.

" 'Tis a wedding night song, isn't it, Cousin Sara Anne?"

"We'll never have a wedding night, Paddy," she said with a sigh. "Never."

"But if we ever did, you'd sing the song for me, wouldn't you?"

"I just might, Paddy Tobin, I just might. Mind you, it isn't obscene."

"But it is erotic?"

"The Irish language is extremely erotic because, unlike English, its sexual allusions are all indirect and stir up the imagination something terrible."

"So I'm told. Well, now I have a number of reasons to look forward to the wedding night."

I was going pretty far now and not at all sure Rae would praise me tonight as she had last night.

"It's not to be, Paddy love, but it would be a grand night indeed. Dead frigging grand!"

And then she dismissed me with a laugh and began to speak of Cararoe, which was, she contended, the most perfect Irish-speaking village in all the world.

The young woman, however, had agreed to marry me. In effect, anyway. We just had to remove the problem, whatever it was. You don't go writing romantic and erotic lullabies for your man on your wedding night and seriously plan to become a consecrated virgin. Nor do you refer to the object of your sexual fantasies as "Paddy love." No way. I felt better about my prospects than I had since leaving East Bend, South Dakota.

There was still the problem of exploiting her for ten million dollars and her probable fury when she found out after the wedding. Sufficient to that day, as my priest would say, is the evil thereof.

Now I had to concentrate on solving the mystery of why she planned never to marry. Had her father abused her as a little girl? It seemed unlikely, but one could never be certain about that sort of thing. Or had she fallen into some lesbian relationships at school? Did she think she was gay? That she was gay was most unlikely given her responses to my highly tentative advances. But she might think she was.

"Paddy," she said suddenly, "I . . ."

"Yes?" I said after her voice had trailed off.

"I don't want to talk about it now."

"Fine."

But we will talk about it before the day is over, young woman, or I'll be in deep trouble with my angel.

It would not be easy. For all her sweetness, my love had a strong streak of Irish stubbornness in her. That was all right except if it operated in the wrong situations. There had been no need in this first week of my pursuit of her to face her down when she had retreated behind the wall of stubbornness. I wasn't sure how to deal with it. Perhaps appeal to her intelligence, but that sounded pretty weak.

One thing was certain: If we didn't develop the protocols for dealing with such problems before we were married—if we were married—we'd have a more difficult time doing it afterwards.

How did I know that to be true? My priest must have told me. I wish he were here. Maybe I could send him an E-mail message. No, too late. I had to deal with it today. Why didn't I think of him before?

She stopped the car in the middle of Cararoe, which was in fact little more than a lacework of narrow roads and white-sand beaches among lakes and small bays with wildly painted cottages strung along the roads amid tiny green fields separated by whitewashed stone fences. Some

women were working in the fields, some men were drag-
ging heavy carts or directing sheep down the road. An
occasional dog barked at our car with a notable lack of
enthusiasm.

"Wow!" I said softly.

"Like a picture postcard, isn't it?"

"Or a travelogue. Or maybe an argument for the belief
that a little bit of heaven fell out the sky one day."

"Or a Jack Yeats painting come to life like in that Japanese film *Colors*."

"Best metaphor yet."

"Yet they are very poor people and live a very hard life.
Their children must all move away to London or Liver-
pool or Australia or the States. It's not always this pretty.
It can be cold and rainy and gloomy out here for weeks
on end. Yet on days like this it may all be worth it. Anyway,
they're great natural poets and storytellers."

We stopped on the road a couple of times so Sara Anne
could speak to people she knew. In Irish naturally. I insisted she sing her new lullaby to one group. With only a
show of reluctance, she sang it for them, again wordlessly.
They applauded enthusiastically.

"Would they be shocked by the indirect eroticism?"

"These people? Not at all. The old Irish culture was
anything but puritanical. But wouldn't they be embarrassed if the obvious target of the song was evidently in
the car with me?"

"I see. You could sing it in Irish for me. I wouldn't
understand the words."

"I could, but I won't," she responded firmly. "It's bad
enough that I think them."

We then proceeded around the end of Connemara to
the town of Clifden out on the far end, a pretty little

village, with two church steeples soaring over the closely packed homes, in a saucer created by hills and a small bay. To the east the Twelve Ben Mountain chain hovered over us. Clifden was a prosperous little town with pubs and restaurants along its main street.

"We're going to eat at O'Grady's," she informed me. "It has the best lunches in the West of Ireland. Don't look at me suspiciously like you're doing. It's not like me own pub by UCG. Not at all, at all. None of your croissant sandwiches or that sort of thing."

The pub had a red and black front and a pleasant little dining room inside. A nice young man, casually polite, took our orders. His brogue was so thick that I could barely understand him. Herself ordered two poached flounders with white wine sauce and a "tad" of roast beef. And a carafe of white wine.

She was certainly right about the food. It was superb.

"That nice young man is the chef too," she whispered in my ear. "Didn't he study in Paris? And don't most of the hotels in this part of Ireland want him? And doesn't he stay out here with the young woman he's keeping company with because he likes to live here?"

"Like St. Hilary's."

"That's what it's like, is it now? Your Chicago parishes are like a West of Ireland village?"

"Something like that."

The "tad" of roast beef, with, mind you, red wine sauce, was far more generous than the word implied. Nonetheless, I ordered a second helping, much to the amusement of my tour guide, who had shed her heavy jacket and looked delightful in an Aran Island pullover.

I also had a second helping of the hot apple pie with heavy cream.

I grabbed the check despite her loud protests and left a big tip on my (Rae's, that is) Visa card. I congratulated the young man on his superb cuisine.

He modestly disclaimed any need for praise—so long as I felt I had a good lunch. When Sara Anne went off to the "ladies," he remarked, "A grand woman, that one, isn't she?"

"Everybody in Galway seems to know her."

"As well they might . . . Would you be as sweet on her as she is on you?" he asked with a knowing wink.

"More so."

"Well, good luck to you, though, God knows, you seemed to have had plenty of luck already."

"Isn't that the truth?"

We were now going to drive, she informed me when we were back in the car, up to the northern end of County Galway at Kilray Harbor, next round to Maumene and the sacred mountain, then through Maam Cross and Oughterard and back to the club for our evening swim. Dinner was to be at the Druid theater where they were doing *Riders to the Sea*, which would be appropriate considering that, if the weather wasn't too bad, tomorrow we'd fly on a plane or maybe a helicopter (pronounced "healycopter") to the Arans.

I had decided that I would confront her at the top of the sacred mountain. What better place? My throat turned dry at the thought.

"Do you have a different bikini for our swim?"

"Ah, now, wouldn't it be so tiny that you'll be thinking it obscene?"

"I doubt that I would ever use that word about you."

About ten miles north of Clifden, we pulled over at the side of a lovely lake set like a diamond among pine trees, a sheet of dark blue under the still persistent sun. On the far side of the lake, an elaborate white Victorian castle was set against the trees.

"Isn't that me school?" she said, her hands folded primly in her lap.

"The place where you're going to be a nun?"

" 'Tis."

"Do I get to see it?"

"NO! And they don't get to see you either. Besides, if any of me old teachers should see you, even in the little shop, we'll never get away from them. And you must climb that mountain to do penance for your sins of gluttony these last days—and other vices too."

"I probably do need the exercise."

A little later we pulled up at Kilray Harbor, a dark blue, somewhat sinister gash cut by the sea into the Connemara Mountains. This time I was permitted to leave the car to view the narrow bay across which maybe Warren Moon or Randall Cunningham or even maybe Erik Kramer could throw a stone.

" 'Tis thirty kilometers long and in the center forty-five meters deep. You could park the whole American navy in it, though why you would want to do escapes me."

"If you don't like one bit of the hodgepodge scenery in this place, wait a few minutes and it will change."

"That's why you have to be careful about judging Connemara by a couple of postcards."

"I keep remembering the Book of Kells, which, alas, I didn't see when I was in Dublin."

"Shame on you!"

We hopped back into the car and returned to the previous crossroads, and turned left into the Inagh Valley.

On the left were Lough Inagh and the Twelve Ben Mountains, and on the right the Maumturk Mountains. The valley was quiet and hauntingly attractive, a place of mystery and wonder and maybe spirits, more likely (but not certainly) good spirits than evil ones (which Rae had assured me she had never encountered).

"Is this valley haunted?"

Isn't every valley in the West of Ireland haunted? . . . And isn't your patron's shrine up there just beyond that big mountain on your right? But the best way to climb it is from the trail down below."

"Are you sure I can wear my shoes?"

"Of course you can wear your shoes. Aren't we Galway Catholics much more civilized than your people from up beyond in Mayo and Donegal?"

We emerged from the valley and turned right on the road to Maam Cross. Here the country was rough and barren again. My love pulled over on the side of the road and gestured at a barely discernible cow path that ascended at a sharp grade up the side of a mountain.

"This is it?"

"It's only fifteen hundred feet up," she said. "No big climb at all, at all."

We climbed out of the car and zipped up our jackets. Dark clouds were slipping over the mountains, coming right towards us. Sara Anne inspected my climbing shoes to make sure they fit properly. She didn't want to carry me down the mountain if I developed blisters on my feet.

"Nice shoes." She nodded her approval. "Leave your computer in the car. Isn't it a bit of a walk?"

Of course they're nice shoes. Didn't a Seraph pick them out for me?

"Yes, ma'am . . . It's going to rain."

"You're on pilgrimage, you eejit, you're supposed to be uncomfortable."

So we trudged up the mountainside, talking only to two young German tourists (man and woman), holding hands as they came down. They didn't look at all like Rae's companion and progeny.

"Just think, Cousin Paddy, pilgrim feet walked this path in the time of Abraham."

"And they didn't have shoes like we do." I gasped, pausing for breath.

My love didn't stop.

"An English traveler who visited one of the 'patterns' here in the eighteen thirties said there were seven tents filled with poteen and gang fights all over the place. Didn't the Mayo priests discourage pilgrimages here so they could promote their shrine at Croagh Patrick?"

"Shame on them."

"But wasn't it a Mayo priest, and himself a Jesuit, who restored the shrine? Won't you love the white granite statue he flew in on a helicopter? Come along with you now, Paddy Tobin. If you don't want to get wet, you'll have to keep up with me."

Her reprimand was an affectionate one, teasing the big Yank who had no experience climbing even small mountains.

"I'll get wet in the pool anyway."

I glanced back at Galway Bay, turning gray as the sun gave up to the now rapidly moving clouds. The view was spectacular, land, sea, sky, and lakes combining to produce a panorama of both beauty and threat. A great setting to confront one's beloved.

"You never climbed mountains, did you, Paddy love? Be careful of the rocks we're on now. Couldn't an inexperienced climber sprain an ankle?"

286 Andrew M. Greeley

"It's not the Matterhorn."

I stumbled and bumbled and finally, exhausted and panting, reached the top. A spectacular modern granite statue of my patron loomed ahead of me—a man of both great and solid strength and of intense pastoral concern.

"Very nice," I told herself.

"I knew you'd like it. Isn't it kind of like yourself?"

"I'm not that big."

"I mean metaphorically."

"Oh."

"It's all downhill, Paddy."

"Uh-huh."

Not yet, not by any means. The highest summit, albeit a psychological one, was still ahead of us.

The shrine consisted of the statue, a small wooden oratory of recent construction, the slab in the rock on which my patron (a braver man than I) was supposed to have slept, a holy well (actually a cistern), and a small round of stations of the cross. I glanced back again down the path we had climbed; Galway Bay looked even more ominous. On the other side of the pass it was already raining on the iron gray lakes.

"You must walk around the stations three times," Sara Anne told me, "to get your wish, and say three paters and aves each time. Sure, there are no guarantees, so it is not superstition, but it can't hurt."

Indeed it can't.

She led the prayers in Irish, and I responded in English.

The shrine was a rugged and crude place, which fit its rugged and crude setting. Yet somehow there was an atmosphere of holiness about it. A place where God might just be present in a special way for the stoic pilgrims who had climbed it since the time of Abraham.

No sooner had we finished the stations than the rains, racing up the other side of the pass, closed in on us. The clouds were so near that they touched the top of the peaks on either side.

"Don't I have a key to the oratory?" Sara Anne shouted over the wind. "There's no reason to get too wet even on a pilgrimage."

She opened the door and we stumbled into the oratory.

"It won't last long," she assured me as we sat shoulder to shoulder inside the snug little building as the wind roared by outside. "Besides, you probably need some rest before we walk down."

"I have to talk to you, Sara Anne."

She turned to look at me, doubtless surprised by my somber tone.

"Talk then," she said cautiously.

"I want to know what's eating you. I want to know it all."

·17·

"I don't want to talk about it," she said furiously, turning her back towards me.

"I know you don't, but just the same, you will."

"You have no right to pry into my private life."

"Yes I do."

"Well, I'm not going to tell you a thing!" she shouted, and struggled to get to her feet. She would leave me, rain or no rain.

I hauled her back down.

"We are going to stay here till you talk about it, even if it takes all night."

"I won't talk about it even if we stay here till Judgment Day!" she shouted, pounding my chest with fierce little fists.

What do I say now? Rae, please help. Even a suggestion.

But the help came from Sara Anne. She stopped hitting me and bent over her knees, sobbing piteously.

Should I put my arm around her and offer her comfort? Why not? What more did I have to lose?

She did not try to fight me off. Instead she leaned against me and continued to sob. Then she drew a deep breath.

"You're right as always, Paddy Tobin. I have to tell you. I owe it to you."

I patted her shoulder in reassurance.

"Nothing you could possibly say would make me love you any less."

She studied my face, examining it very closely.

"I've been raped. Twice."

So that was it. Terrible, but it could have been so much worse.

"Oisin?"

She nodded. "And a loudmouthed Yank he sold me to."

"Sold?"

"He told the Yank that I was his woman and if he wanted to fuck me, it would cost him a hundred pounds. Then he stood by and shouted taunts while the Yank beat me and humiliated me and finally, after the longest time, raped me."

As she talked, she drew back from me. Her eyes were dry now. She was under rigid self-control, her voice hard and cold.

"You haven't told anyone before now?"

"Who could I tell? Me parents? It would have broken their hearts. The Gardai? I didn't want a public humiliation for meself and me parents. I didn't want to be a great frigging martyr to Irish feminism. Besides, his da has so much power here that he might be able to cover it all up. And I'm sure I would be blamed . . . I don't know, maybe I am responsible. He said I was because I led him on. As

God is my witness, Paddy, I never meant to. I never went out with him. I only talked to him in the pub when he came and sat with me and me friends. I never liked him."

"If you don't stop him, he'll do it again."

"Don't I know that?" She flicked back her hair. "Hasn't he tried again?"

"What did you do?"

"Wasn't I the one who broke his arm? No one knows that. I won't tell and he could never admit it, a slip of a girl breaking the arm of the great rugby star Oisin O'Riordan, and himself hardly ever playing in an important game."

"You broke his arm?"

"Aye. Didn't the martial arts course up at the abbey finally pay off when I worked up the nerve to use some of my tricks on him? I stuck him with me knife too."

"Knife?"

She opened her shoulder bag and showed me a very wicked-looking switchblade. She flipped the switch. The blade, a good six inches long, leaped towards me.

"I carry it all the time. I told him when I stuck him— in the other arm, though not very deep—that I'd kill him if he ever tried it again."

"Would you?"

"I don't know. I might. He thinks I would, so he's being very careful."

"You live in constant fear of him?"

"How else could I live? Paddy, I was a virgin and a pretty innocent one. Now I feel dirty and vile and degraded and not good enough for any man, and meself not wanting a man either. And I feel that somehow I am responsible."

"You're not."

So Asmodeus was alive and well, despite the smoke Rae

had blown in his eyes. I would deal with him. But I must not let my rage interfere with healing for my violated love.

She was crying again, not hysterically this time but with sad resignation.

"The frigging bastard ruined my life." She dabbed at her nose with a tissue. "I might really kill him if he tries it again."

"You haven't talked to a counselor?"

"One of those at school? They'd report it to the administration and the story would be all over town. A lot of people would blame me. They always blame the woman. It would destroy me altogether."

"Is there a good psychiatrist in town, preferably a woman?"

"There is." She wiped her nose. "I know her socially. Her office is right across the square from me da's office. But I don't have the money to pay her, and wouldn't I have to tell my parents why I needed the money?"

The horror of the story would indeed destroy her parents altogether. Ronan would storm over to Papa O'Riordan and demand reparation. If the latter was as indulgent to his son as he seemed to be, he would instantly smear Sara Anne as the one responsible for what had happened. There would be enough people in Galway who would believe that version. When your worshiped princesses fall, there's a lot of folk who want to pull them all the way to the ground. Then the fat would be in the fire. She would be a victim again, and her parents with her.

"Have you ever called the psychiatrist on the phone?"

"Haven't I had the frigging thing in my hands a dozen times, twice already this week?"

What do I say now?

She watched me anxiously, expecting some sort of miracle from the big, crazy Yank who loved her.

Then I had a marvelous idea.

I grabbed her shoulders and turned them towards me. "Listen to me, Sara Anne Elizabeth Tobin, and listen to me carefully. I absolutely demand that when we stop at the club—and we'll stop there whether we swim or not—you call the psychiatrist woman across the square and you tell her you need an emergency appointment tomorrow morning. That's an order, do you understand, and I'll accept no arguments."

"But me parents . . ."

"You know very well that, for reasons that have to do with their excellent taste, they worship the ground I walk on."

"God knows that's true."

"Then you tell them after you made the appointment that it was my idea you call the psychiatrist woman, that I insisted, in fact, because I said you had to get rid of your moods. It's all true."

She considered the suggestion, then nodded and grinned.

"Sure, won't they be delighted? Won't they praise you for being so direct and forthright? Won't they say that's one more proof of what an excellent . . . man you are? And won't they be pleased with me for having the good sense to listen to you? Oh, Paddy love, aren't you a frigging genius?"

She collapsed into my arms again. She was crying again, but now with relief.

I wept a little with her. Also with relief. I had passed the test. I had earned my degree. The new program worked without any bugs. I had triumphed over fear, mine and her own.

A lot more remained. I might have to wait two years for her, but she would be mine.

"I'll do it, Paddy. It'll be hard, but I'll do it. For you and meself."

"Good." I kissed her forehead lightly. "I don't hear wind or rain anymore. So let's get down off this frigging mountain."

She stood up with me. She was unsteady on her feet, so I helped her out the door. The rain squall had swept through the pass, and the sun shone again. On the one side Galway Bay was as smooth and blue as Lake Michigan can be on a perfect day. On the other side the Galway lakes glowed silver and purple in the sunlight. I now understood why for several millennia men and women had climbed this pass to pray.

" 'Tis glorious," I murmured to my beloved. "Unbelievable. The sun is out again on your life, Sara Anne Elizabeth Tobin."

"Moire is my fourth name," she said with a chuckle. "In case you wanted to know . . . and, Paddy love, I'll never forget this day as long as I live. Nor the man who helped me. Now, take me hand and let's walk back to the car. I don't want you to sprain your ankle on the way down."

So hand in hand, just like the two young Germans, we scrambled down the mountainside. I explained to her that she had done the Irish "hat trick" because her name contained the names of the Lord's mother, his grandmother, and his cousin. I added that hardly an Irish woman existed in the world who didn't have at least one of those names.

She laughed. "Ah, we need a lot of saints to protect us, don't we now?"

"And angels."

"Angels too."

"I'll go swimming at the club," she told me as she

opened the door to the car. "I don't think there'll be any assaults this afternoon, if you don't mind, but we both need the swim."

"Fine."

I waited at poolside for her, huddling under a big terry cloth robe for ten minutes. I began to worry that something might have changed inside her head and she had run off without me. Maybe I had counted my chickens far too early.

Then she appeared in a burst of terry cloth, tossed it aside, and plunged into the pool.

"What are you waiting for, amadan? Jump in."

I did just that.

We both swam rapidly for a few minutes. Then she paused at one end of the pool and waited for me.

"I did what you told me to do," she said proudly, "and wasn't herself terribly nice? Isn't she going to see me at eight tomorrow and every morning for the next couple of weeks?"

"Good on her! . . . Did you tell her what happened?"

"Only that I had been raped twice, and the second time the first rapist sold me to another man. She was very gentle with me and told me that it would be all right, but it might take some time . . . Oh, Cousin Paddy! I'm so happy. I feel like I have been reborn!"

"As you have, Sara Anne. Death and resurrection. Just remember resurrection isn't supposed to be easy."

"I know that, but I'm a tough woman, Paddy Tobin, especially when I know there are people on my side . . . and yourself not saying a thing about me new gold and black swimsuit?"

"New?"

"Didn't I buy it last night, so I could please you?"

Dear God, she was resilient, wasn't she?

"Well." I contemplated the situation. "It's not exactly Brazil or *Sports Illustrated* yet. But it's still enchanting. You look wonderful."

"It doesn't leave much to the imagination, does it?"

"Ah, it leaves a lot to the imagination."

Actually it didn't leave much to the imagination, but what it did leave was critical. If Rae was right about God enjoying erotic beauty even more than I did, God must have reveled in my nearly (but not quite) naked love.

"And meself buying it even though I had decided to be a nun."

"You need better motives for a vocation than your horror at being raped."

"Don't I know that!" she said, exultantly, and brushed her lips against mine. "Now let's swim."

So we swam.

My love's emotions were unstable. As she dropped me off later at the hotel, she said, "Maybe we should skip the Druid Theater tonight."

"Maybe we should not."

"Why not?" she said with a frown, suggesting she was ready for another explosion.

"You go home and tell your parents that you called the psychiatrist woman . . . What's her name, by the way?"

"Isn't it Moire Fitzpatrick?"

"And tell them the reason, giving me full credit. They'll be overjoyed because, unless I'm mistaken, they've thought of suggesting it long ago but were afraid of your moods. Their joy will transform you for a while, but then get out of the house before you turn moody again and spoil it for them and for yourself."

She nodded assent. "You're right, Paddy Tobin, as always. I'm a terrible mess, am I not?"

"No, you're not. You're merely in a crisis situation,

which you are on the whole handling very well indeed."

"Only because a good man is helping me," she said, and kissed me. "Tonight at eight o'clock, is it now, Cousin Paddy?"

" 'Tis."

I kissed her back. She enveloped me in her wondrous smile. I climbed out of the car and stumbled through the lobby and up to my room. I fell on my knees at once and thanked God that I had made no fatal mistakes up there on my patron's holy mountain. I also gave thanks for the Seraph crowd, which had helped me so much. I was glad that Rae couldn't hear my prayers. It didn't suit our relationship that I should be obviously grateful. She could probably guess my prayers anyway. Then I dashed off a hasty note to Meg and family praising the shrine and the beauties of Connemara, stripped down to my shorts, and fell into my bed, exhausted by my efforts of the day.

My last thought was that there would probably be many more such efforts as I struggled to help my love out of the horror in which she had been trapped.

Later we walked from the hotel to the Druid Theater and enjoyed a pleasant meal and agonized through a fierce production of *Riders to the Sea.* The tragedy of the lives of Aran fishermen, told with all of Synge's power and superb acting, kept me on the edge of my seat through the entire brief play. Dear God, the human condition can be awful, can't it? We do what little we can to lessen the suffering, but it is so very little.

"Didn't he say that in the nine months he lived out there, he never heard English, save when they were talking to dogs and pigs?"

"I don't speak English. I speak American."

That truth earned me a light tap on the arm, followed by a firm grip on my hand.

My love's emotions had leveled off. She was a pleasant supper companion and reacted with tears and enthusiasm to the play.

"Wasn't it beautiful, Paddy?" she asked as we emerged into the fog-dense streets of the old city—the Irish weather having changed again.

"A terrible beauty, to quote someone."

"Aye, a terrible beauty. I guess I should stop feeling sorry for myself. My life is so much easier than their lives were."

"I'm not so sure of that. Different times, different challenges."

She took my hand as we walked towards the square and the hotel.

"I'm grateful to you, Paddy Tobin," she said softly. "I will be grateful for all my life."

"I love you, Sara Anne."

"And I love you too. And I think right now I'm going to assault you again because I haven't done it all day."

So she did, again pressing me against the wall. She drew one of my hands against her breast—still protected by sweatshirt and bra—and pressed it hard. I returned the fierceness of her kiss. My hand found its way under the neck of her sweatshirt. It pushed aside the restraints of her bra, and captured its prize. She moaned with joy.

"I love you," she murmured with her loudest sigh.

"And I love you."

Suddenly I was aware that there was someone else with us in the protective fog. I released my beloved and swung around.

"Cunt! Whore!"

Oisin O'Riordan, very drunk.

"Didn't I tell you to stay away from her, you frigging Yank bastard? You try to paw her again and I'll kill you."

I heard the flick of a switchblade behind me.

"If there's any killing to do, Oisin O'Riordan, I'll be doing it. All I'm going to do now is cut off your balls!"

She advanced towards him, knife at the ready. O'Riordan was so drunk that she might have been able to do just what she had threatened.

"Put that frigging thing away!" he begged, terror in his voice.

"You'll never rape another woman again." She lunged for his crotch.

He screamed and ran off into the fog.

The knife flicked shut.

"Scared him real good, didn't I, Cousin Paddy?" she said with an easy laugh.

"Me too."

"I wouldn't do it this time because he was too drunk to be a threat. Still, didn't I want to frighten him half to death?"

"You certainly did that."

"Aye, and it will give me one more good story to tell Moire Fitzpatrick tomorrow morning. Now, where were we before being so rudely interrupted?"

"You had me up against the wall."

"And you were doing wonderful things with my boob. Let's go back to it."

Naturally we did. Sara Anne was delighted with the proceedings, though she accused me once more of depriving her of all her sanity.

I was not displeased, especially because my love's passion had been reignited.

" 'Tis enough now, Sara Anne."

" 'Tis, Paddy love, for now."

We walked the rest of the way to the hotel, quite pleased with ourselves.

"Wish me luck tomorrow morning," she pleaded in the lobby.

"I do that, and I'm sure you and Moire Fitzpatrick will get along just fine."

"I hope so," she said, uneasiness in her voice.

In the suite my Aero was turned on and the screen was up, though it had been darkened by the screen-saver program, which displayed the starship *Enterprise* rushing towards the final frontier, wherever that may have been.

I touched the space bar and the screen returned.

> *Well, Toby, I suppose you are satisfied with your performance today.*
> >It's Paddy, and yes, I am satisfied.
> *I will admit, Paddy, that you carried off your responsibilities with no major blunders.*
> >I am praised with faint damns.
> *Color me laughing at that one . . . You realize that, while the fair Sara Anne has turned a major corner in her life, the road ahead will still present some problems?*
> >You mean she will be all right?
> *In time, surely. Yet I see no reason you two should postpone your wedding plans. Judging by the amusements in which you engage, you should not postpone them.*
> >You mean for two weeks from tomorrow?
> *Certainly.*
> >We haven't known each other very long, less than a week. She's terribly young. I don't want to exploit her for money.
> *Nonsense. Pure, uncontaminated nonsense. Neither of you is likely to find a better opportunity for the rest of your life.*
> >Indeed.
> *We will continue to watch over both of you. You must continue to take good care of her.*

Don't you dare hurt her.
>You don't have to worry about that.
It was, you must admit, rather unperceptive of you not to realize that rape was her problem several days ago.
>I knew you'd get around to that. Yeah, I should have guessed. I couldn't imagine anyone so evil as to want to hurt such a lovely child, especially when he damn well knew she was a virgin.
Many people do unimaginably evil things, Paddy. And you are not to seek vengeance on Oisin O'Riordan. Leave that matter to us.

That sounded ominous.

>If you say so.
I most certainly do say so. Now, forget about resting on your laurels. The fair maiden—and morally she is still that—is within your grasp. But do not waste your opportunity by giving in to either fear or crudity.
>Yes, ma'am.
Good. Now I believe there is a message from the adorable child who calls herself Megperson in your mail. End.

No reason to call her back tonight. Hope that didn't hurt her Seraphic feelings.

What was up with the Megperson?

>Paddy, the people around here kind of like your E-mail messages. They think you show some minor talent at describing scenes. I tell them that if they'd ever listen to you, they'd observe much more talent. Their praise is not unqualified because they're not capable of that yet. But it's a nice change, isn't it?
Mom even says that maybe Sara Anne will be a good influence on you. She's making you go on

pilgrimages and pray and good things like that.
We're making progress, aren't we, bro?
I hope you kissed her by now.
MEGPERSON

Little brat.

I'd better send a prompt reply.

Megperson,
Yes, I have kissed. Often. More to the point,
she has kissed me often. She started it.
You'll love her.
This message is for your eyes only.

I reached over to turn off the Aero. But herself was
back.

Paddy?
>Yes.
Do you not wonder that within a week, more
or less, you have progressed from being a nerd
and a hacker who was afraid of and clumsy,
not to say tongue-tied, with women to being a
bit of a romantic hero?
>Yes I do wonder.
Consider the reasons: (1) You are away from
your family's constant attacks on you and (2)
a beautiful, passionate, and terrified woman
has called forth from you the best of your humanity.
>You mean that she's made a man out of me?
Certainly not, and don't speak to me with cli-
chés like that. I meant what I said: She has
called forth the best of your humanity. Made
you human, if you wish to oversimplify. I trust
that you'll be able to generalize from that
truth.
>You're saying that I should marry her and
then protect her from my family?

Soon. End.
>But

The machine went dead. End of conversation with Rae tonight.

Yeah, I knew what she meant.

❧18❧

The next morning as I was eating breakfast in my room, Nuala rang to inform me that Sara Anne was outside in her da's car.

"She seems to be in one of her bad moods."

"I can cope."

Outside I observed that it was cold and a fierce wind was blowing. Black clouds and sunlight chased each other rapidly, one happily destroying the other when they caught up. Bad day for a flight.

Sara Anne paid no attention to me as I approached the shiny black Benz. She didn't open the door for me and didn't greet me as I jumped in.

"Well, Sara Anne?"

"I don't want to talk about it."

"Now or ever?"

"Now. Would you ever give me a little time and a little space?"

"Sure," I said, leaning up against the doorway so as to put as much space as possible between me and her.

"You know frigging well I didn't mean that kind of space."

But there was a touch of an amused smile on her lips.

We drove out to the Galway Airport without saying another word.

As she parked the car in front of the miniature terminal, she rested her hand on my knee.

"I'm being very rude, Paddy, and yourself so concerned about me. I'm sorry. I don't want to hurt you. Moire Fitzpatrick promises me that I'll be fine—and her kind don't give prognoses very often. Right now I need just a little more time with me rage. I don't want to turn it on you."

"Be my guest."

We went into the terminal. Ah, Sara, so happy to see you. No, alas, the helicopter will not travel to the Islands today. A minor part is broken and we had to order it from London. However, one of the Islanders will leave in twenty minutes, and we do have a reservation on it for you and your cousin. At this point you are the only passengers on the first flight, though we have many reservations for later in the day, so business isn't altogether bad.

No one in his right mind was flying out to the Aran Islands in a nine-passenger plane on a day like this. But I'd never talk Sara Anne out of it.

We sat side by side in the terminal lobby on uncomfortable plastic chairs and drank tea that was not strong enough (it didn't bend the plastic spoon) and ate scones that were not fresh enough.

"We'll do better out on Inishmore," she promised me, and then fell back into her solemn and perhaps sullen silence.

After ten minutes of this, she spoke up suddenly.

"Moire Fitzpatrick says he'll try again, especially with yourself being around."

"You told her you might kill him."

"Cut off his balls first. Prick too. One clean sweep of me knife blade. I showed it to her."

"How did she react?"

"She believed me and was impressed. Still, she said, isn't he very dangerous?"

"She thought you should go to the police?"

"She did not. I explained to her the reasons, and she thought that they were reasonable enough. She did say I should have come to see her long ago. I could have thought up something to tell my parents which would be true and yet not the whole truth."

"She's probably right."

"I won't argue with that . . . She said you had given me very good advice."

"You talked a lot about me?"

"Sure, why wouldn't we?"

"And she said?"

Sara Anne squirmed on the plastic chair and looked down at her Nikes. She shuffled her feet nervously.

"I won't tell you what she finally said about you. But I will tell you that it was a compliment and one that would make you blush."

"I can live with that."

She smiled wearily. "I'm to see her every morning at eight o'clock for the next two weeks. Then we'll see."

"Sounds reasonable . . . She didn't tell you to stop seeing me?"

"Oh, no, Paddy love," Sara Anne replied, grabbing my arm. "She never said that at all, at all. Not that I thought she would."

"So it wasn't the worst of such sessions?"

"I've never been in one before. It was worse than I expected and better than I expected. So I suppose you could say it was a grand session." She rested her head against my arm. "Dead frigging grand."

"I'm delighted to hear it."

She moved her head, still resting comfortably on my arm, up and down in assent.

I was also delighted to hear that I had not been dismissed from the playing field. On the contrary, reading between the lines, I suspected that Dr. Moire Fitzpatrick had been skeptical at first and then very much in favor of the big, dumb Yank cousin.

Whose humanity had been challenged to the fullest, as Rae would have said.

Air Aran's flight 103 to Inishmore was called.

"Let's go!" my guide said, bouncing off her chair.

"Yes, ma'am."

The ancient green and white Norman Islander was something more than an old Piper Cub. It had a low wing and two engines even if it lacked a retractable landing gear. Nonetheless, it was a lot smaller than the MD-11 monster in which I had crossed the Atlantic. I'm not afraid of flying, only afraid of getting sick.

The winds sweeping down the runway almost knocked me off my feet.

"Isn't this real flying?" my guide informed me. "Not like flying in them big, inhuman jets."

"I'll take your word for it, Sara love."

She cocked an eye. "First time you said that to me."

"So you'll know before we die on this trip."

The wind was rocking the wings of the Islander. Now I was truly frightened. The pilot was already in the plane, younger than me and herself a woman. Naturally she knew the fair Sara Anne. Didn't everyone?

"It'll be seventeen minutes over there today," the Viking pilot (blond with a permanently flushed complexion) informed us cheerfully. "A bit of head wind. Some moderate turbulence too. Nothing serious."

"Great!" Sara Anne exclaimed.

She was right about it being "real flying." As the Islander took off I felt like whichever of the Wright brothers took the first flight. The plane swayed and pitched on the runway and seemed determined not to take off in the face of the fierce wind that was battering it. When it finally did leave the ground—with half the runway still ahead of it—it seemed to hesitate in the air as if it were even less sure of the trip than I was.

The thing about the MD-11 monster was that, whatever it did, one had faith and confidence in its ability to triumph over the elementary forces—except perhaps things like wind shear. I had very little confidence in the pipsqueak Islander even if in its younger days it had flown from the mainland of Scotland to offshore islands, like the Shetlands.

Yet it did make it aloft and then pushed its way against the wind over the city, and towards the bay.

"Isn't it glorious?" herself shouted. "Look at the view. There's me da's house and there's the square and the Railway Hotel."

"I believe it."

Where else would they be?

"Look out the window!" she yelled.

I did.

"The ground looks awfully close."

"Sure, isn't it twenty-five hundred feet below us?"

"That's not very far."

Looking out the window was the mistake. Instantly I

became restless and immediately thereafter sick, very sick. From being afraid I was going to die (not seriously), I became afraid that I might not die. Just like over the Atlantic. Where was Rae when I really needed her?

The fair Sara Anne shouted information at me, not that shouting was required in the relatively quiet Islander.

I did not, could not, listen. But enthusiasm and her need to pummel my arm made me even sicker.

Several times the gorge rose in my throat, and I fought it back each time. I was sure that the next time would be too much for me. I would vomit all over the Islander and Sara Anne.

It might just serve the woman right.

"There's Inishmore." She turned my head to look out of my side of the plane. "We're about to land! Isn't it fun!"

The largest of the Arans looked like a postage stamp, and what might have been the runway was a watermark across the stamp. Now we would surely die and my agony would be over.

Where the hell was Rae?

As the plane descended I became even sicker. Out the window I saw the waters of the bay rushing up to meet us. The pilot would never make it to land, much less to the runway. I braced for the crash. Then the runway loomed up before us, but now we were too high.

Then the plane gently touched the ground and rolled to a leisurely stop. The pilot opened the door, pushed down the steps to the ground, and led the way herself. She extended a hand to Sara Anne, who accepted it gracefully. That she looked up at me and ducked.

Wisely. That's when I began to be sick, violently, pitiably, horribly sick. Fortunately, no one was in my line of fire, so I soiled only the parking apron in front of the tiny gray stone terminal.

"Och, Cousin Paddy!" the Viking pilot exclaimed. "What have we done to you?"

"Caused me to die a slow and painful death," I murmured. "But I forgive you if you promise to pray for the repose of my pour soul."

I vomited again.

"Poor Paddy love," Sara Anne said with compassion. "We'll bring you into the terminal and let you lie down for a few moments."

"I want a priest. I've been a terrible sinner. I'll promise God that there'll be no more women in my life."

The pilot, Sara Anne, the young lad who apparently was the airport manager, and the whole staff found my plaintive cries amusing.

Even my love laughed at me as she led me to a narrow bunk in the crowded terminal room and eased me into it. The boarding passengers, three elderly Islanders who looked like they had stepped out of *Men of Aran*, gazed at me sympathetically.

Sara Anne held my head, eased it into a reclining position, and then stroked my cheeks.

What the hell had happened to my guardian angel?

"You can keen over me if you want, woman. I'm not long for this world."

"Poor dear Paddy, and after meself being rude to you this morning."

"It wasn't you that destroyed me, woman, it was the frigging little airplane thing."

I closed my eyes. The final words I heard as I slipped into sleep were, "Paddy love, how can you be so funny when you are so sick?"

"Irish wit" is what I think I said.

I probably slept about forty-five minutes. When I woke up there was no one in the terminal. Here it was my wake and no one had come to mourn.

There was something I wanted to do as soon as I had a few minutes of privacy. What was it?

I remembered and turned on my Aero, which the pilot or Sara Anne must have salvaged from the plane.

She was waiting for me.

We'll take care of her, Paddy. We know there's danger. Last night was enough proof of that. We're watching him very closely. In fact, we have been watching her for several weeks, even before we established contact with you.

So I was a secondary player in the game. Had been all along. Made sense.

>Guarantee?

Nothing is ever absolutely certain, but she's safer than with a squad of professional body-guards around her every minute of the day and night.

>YEAH?

Oh, yes indeed. Nonetheless, you must continue to be watchful. We do make mistakes on the odd occasion.

>Like not healing me in the plane.

Oh, that wasn't a mistake. Don't worry, I'll take care of you on the way back.

>What was the point of letting me die out there? I did die, you know, and have miraculously come back from the dead.

Surely you can figure that out.

>Impress Sara Anne that I wasn't completely perfect or invulnerable?

Sympathy, my dear Paddy, is a hole through which you can drive a truck.

>You're a terrible cynic.

*And of course, you impressed her with your
humor. She adores you even more.*
>**Yeah?**
*Yeah . . . but there's no reason to ruin the rest
of her day.*

A cool and calm hand touched my head. All traces of
my illness vanished.

>**Not bad, Raphaella, M.D. But you gotta prom-
ise me that you'll take care of me on the way
back. Sara Anne's touch is wonderful, but she
doesn't do magic or miracles.**
*I've told you that we don't do magic or mira-
cles. We just know a little more science than
your kind does . . . Now, close this thing up
quickly. Herself is coming back with all the
medicine she could find in Kilronan and much
tender loving care. By the way, her interview
with Moire Fitzpatrick this morning went very
well. She's a brave and truthful young woman,
which you already know. I see no obstacles to
a wedding in the near future. Neither does the
good doctor, human doctor, that is.*
>**We'll see about that.**
End.

It was time that I terminated the conversation, especially because my love was entering the terminal, her eyes
wide with sympathy and concern, a paper bag of medi-
cines in her hand, and a green sweatshirt with "Man of
Aran" inscribed on it in gold letters.

I stood up immediately and swept her into my arms.

"Och, woman, wasn't it worth a little bit of sickness just
to see that loving sympathy in your eyes?"

"I've brought medicine . . ."

"All I need is some of that mouthwash you brought.

I'll clean out my mouth before I kiss you. The rest of the stuff will be good to have around for the return trip. But I'm fine now.''

I took the mouthwash, went into the tiny "gents," and cleansed my mouth. Also my hands and face. I took off my soiled Chicago Bulls sweatshirt, rinsed it out in the water to remove some of the smell, and became a Man of Aran.

I glanced in the mirror. I didn't look bad at all, at all. Kind of pale maybe. And just a little green.

I returned to the terminal room and, as promised, kissed her, though with considerably less fervor than last night because this was hardly the time or the place to get passionate.

Nonetheless, she surrendered herself into my arms.

This one won't object to a wedding in the near future, to use the term of Dr. Rae. How is it possible that she loves me so much?

"Well, haven't you recovered your health altogether?"

"Ah, no, I've only received a remission. I'm not long for this world."

"Silly."

She slapped my arm lightly.

"But, Paddy, you were so funny. I felt terrible sorry for you, but I couldn't help laughing at your jokes."

"Let it be said that he died with a smile on his lips. Come on, woman, let's get a look at these Aran Islands."

I patted her lovely rump and she squealed complacently.

Inishmore looked like the Aran Islands are supposed to look. And the people, while not as impoverished as in Flaherty's film, certainly seemed to be poor folk wrestling a living from a harsh land and a dangerous sea. And from the tourists.

Yet the place and the people were subtly different from my expectations. Both the island and the people in the morning sunshine seemed to be attractive, a strange beauty, but a powerful one nonetheless.

"It's beautiful, they're beautiful, Sara Anne," I said as the airport manager drove us into Kilronan, the town at this fishhook shaped end of the Island.

"Isn't it faith and love permeating the whole land like some wonder drug? Your friend J. M. Synge had their words, but he didn't understand the full meaning behind them."

"Faith and love but no hope?"

"Sure, if you have faith and love, don't you have hope too?"

"Might make a good hymn . . . Now, woman, am I not perishing with the hunger? There must be a place around here where a man could find some good brown bread and hot pot of Irish tea."

There was. And didn't a young couple, friends of Sara Anne, preside over it? We went through the usual ritual of my love buttering my bread, smearing it with jam (only strawberry out here), and popping it into my mouth. The young couple found it hugely funny.

We went to another shop, and under Sara Anne's critical supervision, I bought Aran sweaters for the rest of my family. "The designs," she said solemnly, "were different so they could recognize the bodies of dead fishermen. Thank God that doesn't happen anymore. They still fish in those tiny canvas boats, but the coast guard boat out there and helicopters pick them up when the weather becomes dangerous."

"They were made in the Republic of China, were they?"

"They were not, Paddy Tobin. They were made right

here. These folks wouldn't let anyone sell something that wasn't authentic."

Considering the mixture of gentleness and determination on their faces, I didn't think so.

We visited the heritage center, admired the old clothes, the canvas curragh, and the small hooker. Then we walked around Kilronan, admired the ocean as it waged its timeless war against the massive rocks, strolled on the beaches, said, "Jesus and Mary be with you" to everyone we passed, and accepted their response, which added my patron to the litany.

"I didn't know you had any Irish, Paddy," she said, hugging my arm—which she had rarely relinquished since my miraculous, or at least angelic, recovery—with even stronger affection.

"I just exhausted my vocabulary. Anyway, I like to watch the way your dark blue eyes light up when you're translating back and forth."

"And yourself not visiting Cork yet?"

"The Irish have the Blarney Stone down there not because they need it but because they deserve it."

After consuming roast beef and salmon sandwiches and our pints of Guinness at Sara Anne's favorite pub on the island, we caught the plane back to the mainland at a quarter past two. This time every seat was taken. I needed neither Dr. Rae's healing powers nor Sara Anne's medicine. Either the cure worked all day or, more likely, the winds had died.

I was asked once a minute whether I was still feeling fine.

"Dead frigging brill," I would reply.

It was still nice to feel the solid ground of Galway underfoot.

"Do you still want to go over to the library?" she asked

me as we walked from the terminal to her father's Benz.

"Do you?"

"Not to say I WANT to, but maybe we should."

"My sentiments exactly."

The elderly archivist recognized Sara Anne immediately and smiled as they conversed in Irish, and again when she introduced me as her "cousin Paddy from the States."

"I've heard of you, lad."

"Don't believe only half of it."

I had finally put together an appropriate Irish bull. They both laughed, though not as vigorously as I thought they should. We were shown to the dusty storeroom where the archives from the early years of the last century were stored, and left to search. The listings we'd picked up on Internet were accurate, and we found what we were looking up with little effort.

It was the record of a suit brought in 1818 by one Ronan Malachi Tobin against the descendants of Gerard Tobin, claiming that since those descendants had left the County Galway, they had forfeited their lease rights to the land and it should revert to those who lived on it. The court ruled that it was rare enough for Catholics to own land rights, even worthless land like the land in question. The fact that they had abandoned it did not, however, invalidate their right to the land, as established by this court a quarter century ago. As long as they paid their sharecropper's due to Lord Mayo, the present occupants might remain on the land at Lord Mayo's pleasure, but they had no claim to lease rights unless Lord Mayo thought it appropriate to remove these ancient rights from those who have always held it in accordance with the law.

"Lord Mayo was in London and almost never came

over here," Sara Anne explained to me. "The Tobins would not want to have been bothering him on the subject of their rights, because he might just throw them off the lands altogether. The local agent for his lordship was willing to leave well enough alone. Agents had a way of dying suddenly when they offended the farmers in those days."

"After that they apparently stopped litigating."

"We could check in the more recent court records, but I think you're right, Cousin Paddy. Then after the Land League War, when the farmers were permitted to own permanent leases on the land they worked, the Tobins that were still around, such as survived the Great Famine, undoubtedly claimed the leases for their own. Most likely in good faith, since only vague memories of the feud had survived."

"Did your friend out front say that anyone else had been looking at these files?"

"Just the other day, by which he meant three months ago."

I thought about it very carefully. Someone was obviously preparing to plant a story in one of the papers about the dubious title Ronan Tobin possessed. Perhaps they'd researched all subsequent court records. They could not make the claim stand up in the law, but they could notably embarrass Ronan and harm his cherished reputation for integrity. After a single leak, they would approach him and ask a reasonable price for the land, but not what it was worth if there really was gold in the mountain. Neat trick.

"It's his reputation they'll threaten if he doesn't sell them the land cheap," my tour guide said thoughtfully.

"They must think that old mountain up beyond is worth a lot of money to cook up such an elaborate ruse."

"Maybe it is. Maybe it at least might be worth enough to make a few trips to a couple of libraries."

I thought some more.

"I think we can easily solve this one, Sara love. My father and I don't always get along very well. But he is an absolutely straight shooter. Won't even let us take university pencils from his office. His son, he never understood, but integrity, he does understand. He'd never have any part of such a plot, no matter if all the gold in the world was under Tobin's Mountain."

"Maybe you are the legitimate heir."

"I hadn't thought of that and I don't know enough of our law to be certain. If anyone should try to launch a plot, he would sign a quitclaim as quickly as he could write his signature—and he would have done that even without Uncle Gerry and official peace between our families."

"Would he ever be willing to settle it now, before anyone makes a move?"

"I'm certain that he would. If our friends are around Galway now, they won't be happy to know that I'm here."

"There's not much they could do about it, though they're probably not giving any thought to the odd chance that we might poke around in the history of the feud."

Rae had told me the feud was unimportant. She had not, however, warned me not to snoop into it. On the basis of her performance, or rather her nonperformance this morning, she was quite capable of letting us discover the mystery and the plot because its resolution would enhance my standing with the Galway Tobins.

The Seraph would stop at nothing. Moreover she seemed to enjoy scheming. Well, this wasn't an altogether bad scheme.

"I'll send an E-mail to my father this evening. You don't happen to have kept the pamphlet on your hard disk, have you?"

She reached into her purse, pulled out the switch knife, removed a diskette, and passed it into my hand.

"I think we can take care of this from now on, Sara Anne. I'll have quitclaims from my father by early next week. All right with you?"

She bathed me with her specially radiant smile. "You're wonderful, Cousin Paddy. Now let's go out to the club and play nine holes of golf and do our swimming and have tea."

"A grand idea."

So we played the nine holes, and with a two-stroke handicap and her delightful attention to my body posture before I swung, I actually managed to win two holes to her three—with four ties. She was not pleased at losing even one hole, this one never would be. But she was pleased at my improvement.

"If we could only keep you here for a couple of months, we'd turn you into a decent golfer."

"That would be a good work."

"It's two weeks from tomorrow you'll be going back?" she asked sadly.

"I'm afraid so . . . but lots of things can happen between now and then."

"Whatever God wants."

"God and His holy angels," I added with a chuckle to myself.

"Her holy angels."

Then we adjourned to the now-crowded pool. My friend wore a white bikini today, more modest than even the first one I saw because "sure, with the racing season won't the pool be filled with people?"

Then we had tea to tide us over till late supper—a small glass of sherry, sandwiches (with the crusts cut off!), cones, rolls, our clotted cream, a wide variety of jams and jellies, choice of teas and pastries.

"They do this every day?"

"Certainly."

"A person could put on a lot of weight here."

"Only if he is totally lacking in self-restraint."

"I'm just a growing boy."

"You're the kind who puts on thirty pounds after marriage and never takes it off."

"You gotta drink a lot of booze to put on that kind of weight, but I don't."

Judging by her facial expression, she almost said, "Well, we'll just have to wait and see." But, uncharacteristically, she kept her mouth shut.

After she had driven me back to the Railway Hotel, we decided that our late dinner would be pizza for a change at Sev'nth Heaven right next to the Druid Theater, and then we'd go on to the Alley, a pub behind the Skeffington Arms Hotel in the new shopping center, or rather in the alley behind the shopping center but still part of it.

"Fine with me, but the only real pizza in the world is made in Chicago."

I noticed as I got out of the car that the square was crowded with people. So was the inside of the hotel. The racing season had already begun, and with it lots of very loud Irish men and women in varying stages of sobriety. Nuala was being hassled at the reception desk by some quite fluttered Irish women in the middle years of life. She didn't look up as I slipped by.

In my room I drafted a letter to Dad in which I explained the circumstances of the feud and made some very tentative recommendations. I then loaded the file

from the pamphlet about the feud, called up the Net, and
composed a note to Meg.

>**Megperson,**
**I am enclosing two files for Dad—a letter from
me and an ftp about Irish history in the last
century. Both are for his eyes only, and you
are absolutely not to read either of them. Do
you understand, young woman!**

I knew I was wasting my typing fingers. She would understand, all right, but she would read every last word.

>**Sara Anne and I went out to the Aran Islands
today. I didn't get too sick during the fifteen-
minute plane flight. It was a lot more interesting than I had expected. Beautiful people
and beautiful place, though an unorthodox and
weird sort of beauty. From the fields like a
design Piet Mondrian might have made if he
had turned from straight lines to curves. Sara
Anne says that, after long centuries, faith and
love permeate the rocks and the people. Still,
they're not giving anything away to the Yank
tourists.
I did make some minor purchases.
We're going to a pizza place tonight for dinner
and then to some kind of singing pub. It's the
racing season here (a long weekend) and Galway is filled with visitors, most of them drunk
and all of them loud. Sara Anne says it's the
high point of the Galway social season and
that I have to go at least one day if I want to
understand Ireland. Then she's taking me to a
dance in the basement of St. Catherine's (sic)
Hotel in Salt Hill, which sounds like a mating
game, something like the World's Largest**

**Block Party down at Old St. Patrick's in Chi-
cago.
I'll report more.
Sara Anne is very nice. I think she's leaving
her bad moods behind.
Best to all,
Paddy**

The pizza, though obviously not up to Chicago standards, was not all bad. Not the worst of the pizzas, as
they'd say in Ireland. I declined a pint of Guinness to
demonstrate that I wouldn't put on thirty pounds after
marriage and settled for a couple of glasses of Ballygowan.

"I was only joking," my date insisted. "You'll never get
fat. You like to exercise too much."

"Just like I climbed that mountain."

"Thank God you did climb it."

We had a "grand" time at dinner and at the pub, singing at the top of our voices, she on key and me off key.
Every fifteen minutes or so, we did "Galway Bay," which,
though it was strictly American pop kitsch in its origins,
had become the national anthem of Galway and particularly of the racing season.

Though it was cold, down in the fifties, men and
women roamed the streets, without coats, singing at the
top of their voices.

"Isn't it grand?" Sara Anne asked me as we joined the
walkers, though in tightly buttoned-up coats.

"They're all fluttered."

"Not all of them, Paddy. Most of them are less fluttered
than they look. Nothing like your college drinking on
weekends in the States."

"Touché."

"They'll be sober by racing time tomorrow."

"And they have to keep warm in this Galway spring weather."

She kissed me.

"Does that warm you up, Paddy love?"

"A little."

We paused at the entrance of the Railway Hotel.

"It's been a grand day, Paddy," she said solemnly. "One of the hardest days of my life. Yet you made most of the day fun for me. I'm so grateful to you for being so nice."

What had I done to make it fun? Get sick on the plane?

"Do you see Moire Fitzpatrick tomorrow morning?"

"At noon tomorrow. Then at eight every day next week. It'll be grand, Paddy. It really will."

"Your courage will make it grand, my dear."

She kissed me again, tears filling her eyes.

"You are such a good man, Paddy love. I didn't know there were any young men like you in all the world. I'll pick you up tomorrow at a quarter past one."

"Stay warm," I said as she got into her mother's Ford.

It might not have been the best way to say good-bye at the end of a "grand day."

A response from my father waited on the Net.

> I must congratulate you, Toby, on being very perceptive. Apparently that young woman is a good influence on you. In my judgment you are absolutely correct that someone is trying to develop a sinister plot against our Galway cousins. They do not know our branch of the family if they think that we would be part of such a plot. In fact, the assumption that we would is an insult to our integrity. As you have suggested, I will have our lawyer draft quit-claims on Monday morning and send it to you by Federal Express. You should have it by

Tuesday morning. You can use your discretion as to the manner of passing them on to Ronan Tobin. You may assure him that I will tolerate no attempts to injure his reputation, which, from what you tell me, he justly values.

I find myself wondering how much Uncle Gerry knew. Maybe he was approached by the plotters at the time he was making his will. Perhaps he concluded that a marriage between you and the young woman would not only reunite the two families but would cut the ground from under the plotters. It's an odd notion, but not totally bizarre. Clearly Uncle Gerry had read the pamphlet you sent me and brooded over it.

Viewed from that perspective, his strange bequest makes some sense.

Again I congratulate you on your sensitivity to the problem. And the young woman to the extent she was involved.

A dry, deanlike response. But compliments from my father were rare in my life.

There was also a brief note from the Megperson.

>What a terrible story! It made me cry for all the poor people who lived on Tobin's Mountain. But you and Dad and Sara Anne will stop the plot, thank God.

I know you can send pictures on the Net. Will you send us some pictures of her?

I replied immediately.

>I'm going out on their boat for brunch after Mass on Sunday. I'll bring along a camera, get the pictures developed on Monday morning, and send them off by FedEx that day.

I don't have a scanner with me to copy the pictures.

Then I went to bed and to a peaceful sleep. Tomorrow the Galway Races and St. Catherine's Hotel. Not much problem in those amusements.

I could not have been more wrong.

◆19◆

As is probably obvious by now, I liked Galway, city and county both. But even without the terrifying events in the evening, I can contain my enthusiasm for the racing season. But then I don't like horse races anyway.

It rained all day, sometimes a drizzle and other times a downpour. The local folk simply ignored it, my fair love included. Yet because I was deeply in love with her courage and her enthusiasm and her talent and her passion and her beauty, I agreed with her every time when she shouted (even when the rain suggested we might soon need Noah), "Isn't it grand, Cousin Paddy?"

That may be what love is all about. I'm not sure yet.

While she did wear a raincoat over her black jeans and black sweatshirt (no name)—apparently the required dress of young people her age during the "season"—and carried a vast colored umbrella, she rarely closed the former or opened the latter. As the day went on, she looked like a kid who had been thrown into a pool with all her clothes on by a gang of rough and arguably envious friends.

She knew everyone and had to greet everyone with a kiss, a hug, a handshake, an enthusiastic shout, a wave of greeting, a polite nod, all carefully graduated to be appropriate to the person and the situation. I trailed along after her, a knight errant, sometimes to be introduced (as "me cousin Paddy from America") and sometimes to be discreetly ignored.

There was no harm in it, at all, at all, was there now? She was having a good time and honing her social skills. She assumed that I would be tolerant of the game because I loved her. But if you can't feel dyspeptic self-pity under such circumstances—especially when your waterproof jacket turned out not to be waterproof—your Irish ancestry is in grave doubt.

If we did marry, and I was still not sure about that a good deal of the time, would I settle her down and put an end to all that nonsense?

Only if I were an utter fool, a terrible amadan, and a complete eejit altogether.

The "Races" were not merely horse races on a track and in front of a pavilion, both of which by American standards were tacky, it was also a reunion, a carnival, a pub outdoors, and a stage for singers and actors. The kids had a particularly good time. They raced from magic show to magic show, bet their shillings on games of chance, devoured ice cream, climbed into the grandstand, patted the horses, and crawled under the walls into the infield.

Some of the kids permitted me to join one of their games and emptied the coins from my pockets.

Some folks had come actually to watch the races, and more folks to bet on them without watching. The races, while not unimportant in themselves, were an excuse for a variegated social and recreational event.

Aren't you smart for figuring that out, Paddy Tobin? I told myself.

Then I had another brilliant thought, a horrifying one at that. If I were the Ulster Volunteer Force or the Ulster Freedom Fighters and I wanted to strike a mighty blow at the Republic and its people, I'd try to blow up the Galway Races. You could kill a lot of innocent people and make a powerful symbolic statement that what happened north of the border could also happen south of it.

"Isn't it a tribute," Cousin Ronan, in great good humor, told me, "to the historical and pre-Christian Irish addiction to horses—to the breeding, training, arguing about, and racing of horses, and betting on them? So here I am with no interest in the nonsense, sitting in this uncomfortable grandstand, all dressed up with other swells in a morning suit under me rain slicker, and pretending that I'm part of the tradition. 'Tis madness altogether!"

"And your woman with a lovely rose-colored dress and matching hat and a corsage, also covered by a rain slicker."

"Thank you, Cousin Paddy," that good woman said, beaming at me. "I rather like horse racing. I usually win too, which is more than poor Ronan does."

"Then won't I be going to a stuffy banquet tonight with stuffy people I don't particularly like, and me wearing a stuffy dinner jacket trying to pretend that I'm not bored to death? And the only consolation will be staring at me wife in a formal gown."

"Ronan!"

"Consolation enough, God knows," I agreed. "And won't I be going to the Salt Hill dance with the woman's daughter, and meself too old to pretend that I'm young people."

" 'Tis nothing more than a marriage market," Ronan said, with a noisy Irish sigh.

"Not that there is anything wrong with that," his wife quickly added.

"It is not true, is it, that they put the women up on auction blocks?" I asked.

"Sure, don't the women put themselves up for auction."

"Ronan!"

My date was laughing happily as this banter went on, greatly pleased that her love could match wits with her family. I cited this in vain as an argument in my favor when we broke up on Monday.

"Och, woman," Ronan replied to his wife, "weren't you terrible forward with me in the days we went out to Salt Hill during the racing season?"

She smiled complacently. "Don't listen to him, Cousin Paddy. He was the forward one."

"Sure, it would be nice to be out there tonight with you young folk."

My love was becoming nervous, eager to get on with her social obligations. So we left her parents with the promise we'd see them at Mass next morning.

Sara Anne said we were obliged to bet on each race at the long line of portable betting booths that the "turf accountants" (as bookies called themselves in the British Isles) set up alongside the grandstand.

I had secretly bought a tout sheet the day before and worked out a careful strategy of safe bets mixed with an occasional long shot. My love, for her part, followed her instincts, superstitious in this context, which dictated choices based on the names of the horses and wild, intuitive hunches.

I bet ten Irish punts on each race, she two punts. I won on a spread of the favorites in the first two races and put my new fifty punts on a long shot (thirty to one) in the third, a horse the sheet described as one that "might surprise us all." He did and I now had fifteen hundred punts to play with.

"You've got it all figured out mathematically, have you now, Paddy love?" She said, her eyes watching me shrewdly.

"More or less, but remember that all horse players die broke."

"Who said that?"

"Damon Runyon, I think."

In the next race she bet on the same horse I did and we both lost.

She'll be disillusioned with me now, I thought. But she stuck with my bets through the rest of the races and ended up with five hundred more punts that she started with. My take was well over three thousand punts.

" 'Tis almost sinful to earn so much money that way, Paddy," she said as we drove back to the Railway Hotel. "You're terrible good at it, aren't you, and yourself a grand mathematician with the odds?"

"My game theory is not to lose too much, Sara Anne love. When I win it's more a lucky day than anything else."

"I'm glad to hear that. Remember: All horse players die broke."

We laughed together happily. I cited that fact in my defense on Monday to no avail.

She'd be back at half eight to pick me up for the dance

at the St. Catherine's in Salt Hill. We would wear the same kind of clothes, though I could wear dry ones if I wanted.

In my room I peeled off my clothes, hung them up on the bathroom heater to dry, indulged in a leisurely shower, and then jumped in under the warm covers and went to sleep almost at once.

The woman wears me out altogether, I thought as I lost consciousness. It was a pleasant thought.

When I woke up at eight, brand-new black jeans had appeared on the bedroom chair and a new black T-shirt that announced, "Chicago—The City That Works."

No smelly clothes for someone under my travel agent's tutelage.

The dance was more fun than I had expected, mostly because I was able to hold Sara Anne in my arms for most of the evening—and this despite pleas from other men that she dance with them.

"Sure wouldn't that be rude to my cousin from America?"

She instructed me to dance with Nuala, who was there with a freckle-faced, pint-sized Mick with curly hair (thicker even than mine) and a wonderfully engaging smile.

"He's my young man," Nuala (Nuala Nora as she told me) explained shyly.

"A very nice young man."

"Ah, he is that, Mr. Tobin, and himself working so hard at a full-time job while he is at university."

"Paddy . . . Any prospects that he might be something more than a nice young man?"

"Well, we're not sleeping together if that's what you mean."

" 'Tis not what I mean at all, at all, and don't you know that?"

"Could I just say that I don't intend to let him get away?"

"Good on you, Nuala Nora."

I returned her to her young man and congratulated him on his good taste.

"That was very sweet, Cousin Paddy. She does admire you a lot because you are such a charming gentleman."

"More likely because I'm your eighth cousin once removed."

Smoking was forbidden in the pious confines of the St. Catherine Hotel, except in rooms on the single smoking floor upstairs. Nonetheless, the hall, crowded with people, without any ventilation, to say nothing of air conditioning, soon became stifling. It was doubtless part of the fun. There was a fair amount of the drink taken, as the locals say, but no one seemed to be fluttered. The hotel staff unobtrusively ejected a couple lads who had too much of the drink taken.

"Can we sit this one out, Paddy love? I need a bit of a rest."

"I'm having the time of me life," I said, guiding her to a chair in the far corner of the room.

"I noticed that. Ogling all the pretty Irish girls."

"Just admiring them, me love, and meself with the prettiest girl at the dance."

"Wouldya stop!"

I explained to her my theory that the Galway Races were in part very like the World's Largest Block Party at Old St. Patrick's Church in Chicago. She listened attentively and laughed at the right times.

" 'Tis amazing that some scheming woman didn't capture you at one of those things."

"No one tried. I only went once."

"I don't believe that. Sure, wouldn't they be after

throwing themselves at you?"

"Maybe I was too frightened to notice."

She frowned suspiciously, then shrugged. "Maybe the Irish air really has changed you."

"It's not the air."

"But it's the air in here which has made me dizzy . . . Paddy love, I'm going outside for just a wee breath of fresh air even if it's foggy air. Don't move. I'll be right back."

I was too exhausted to follow her. Despite my nap, I was ready for bed. I glanced at my watch. Midnight already.

Then I realized that I had permitted Sara Anne to go outside by herself. What the hell was wrong with me! I jumped to my feet and with an ominous sense of dread dashed out the entrance to the basement hall. The tableau a few feet away from the top of the stairs at ground level froze me for several critical seconds.

In the fog two masked men were pointing guns at Sara Anne.

My friends who are cops say that violence always occurs quickly, a couple of seconds and it's all over. I suppose it was that way at the St. Catherine, but for me everything went into slow motion.

"Kill the papist cunt!" one of them shouted.

UFF people, the guys that had planted the bomb at Widow Scanlan's Pub on Pearse Street in Dublin.

In a car at the rear of the tableau, a third masked man pointed a gun at her too.

"You kill the frigging whore! My frigging gun is jammed!"

Sara Anne was preparing to launch herself, headfirst, at the stomach of the man nearest to her. She must have remembered my tactics the night the Bulls won. It then occurred to me that it might be wise for me to do the same thing.

We hit them at the same time. Struggling vainly with their weapons, they weren't ready for us. They tumbled to ground. The man in the car began to shoot wildly. I had to protect Sara Anne. I struggled to my feet. The man I had knocked over rose with me and tried to shove me back on the ground. Suddenly he gasped loudly and went limp in my arms.

The car raced away up the street from the beach.

"He's dying, Paddy," Sara Anne groaned. "This poor man is dying."

"Mine's already dead!"

I heard a violent crash up the street. I looked up. The car with the third gunman had swerved into a concrete wall around someone's villa. Nothing happened for a fraction of second and then it burst into flames. Three dead terrorists.

"Paddy, they left a bomb down there!"

In the darkness at the bottom of the stairs was a dark carry-all, as they called them over here. If the bomb went off this time, it would kill or maim at least five hundred people. My thought process had shut down in the heat of battle. I dashed down the stairs, picked up the bag, rushed up the stairs, and turned towards the seawall and the beach.

"Stay here," I warned Sara Anne, and ran as fast as I could down the block between the St. Catherine and the beach. The unexploded bomb at the Widow Scanlan's had weighed nineteen pounds. This one seemed to me to weigh at least fifty pounds as I slogged, or so it seemed to me, through a swamp filled with molasses. It would take me an eternity to reach the bay road.

The bomb grew heavier, pulling me towards the

ground; my legs were weak, almost ready to collapse under me; my lungs ached from the effort of running; any minute now I would die. Why suffer anymore?

But I kept on running, frantically, desperately, through the thick fog and towards the road (Upper Salt Hill Road, I later learned). I possessed the courage of the damned. What better way to die, I thought, than to save Sara Anne—and five hundred other young people? Please, God, let me save them.

Suddenly, almost without warning, I was on the road, dodging an oncoming car. Get out of here quick, buster, I mentally warned the driver. This thing is about to explode.

The ocean was at high tide, the water had flowed all the way up the seawall. Maybe water would prevent the explosion.

With all the strength that remained within me I hurled the bomb out into the darkness where the sea and the night sky met.

I paused for a few seconds to savor my accomplishment and to draw a breath or two. Then I realized that if the bomb should go off now, it would probably kill me. Run, you frigging eejit, a voice screamed inside my head.

I turned and ran again, this time back to the hotel. Thirty or forty yards behind me, Sara Anne waited, arms outstretched.

I had been crazy to think she would not come after me. I caught up with her just as the bomb went off with a crushing blast. The force of the blast flattened the two of us. Looking back, I saw a huge plume of water soaring to the sky and then collapsing over the bay road—like the explosion of a depth charge in the submarine movies.

"Are you all right, Paddy?" she asked.

"I am, woman. Yourself?"

"Fine! Except you're on top of me."

"And meself too scared to notice my advantage."

The world was still running in slow motion. I was still thinking rapidly. I climbed off her and pulled her to her feet.

"The Gardai station is just round the corner. They'll be here in a few minutes. We don't want any part of it. We'll go around the back of the hotel next to the St. Catherine. In the fog no one will see us. Then we'll join the crowd that's pouring out of there now. Not a word to anyone."

"Right."

As we were ducking behind the other hotel—Our Lady of Lourdes—Sara pointed back at the bay road.

"Look, Paddy, the frigging thing buckled the seawall."

The fog had lifted momentarily. The seawall was bent and twisted and ready to cave in.

"It must have taken much of the force of the blast. Thank God for that or we both might be in heaven now, long before our time. Hurry." The blue lights came around the corner.

Having brushed off our clothes and our faces, we joined the back of the crowd just as the Guards arrived.

"What the frig is going on here!"

"Look, Kevin, two dead men. With masks."

"Call the special branch, Mickey. This looks like the UFF again."

The crowd was ordered back into the basement of the St. Catherine.

We joined them. Like everyone else, we expressed wonder about what the frig had happened. But we knew.

"I know you don't feel like it, Sara Anne. Still we'd better dance. We don't want to get publicity for being involved in this"

"I'll always like to dance with you, Paddy love." She nestled closely against me. "You're the bravest man in all the world."

"More likely the worst frigging amadan in all the world."

"Not at all, at all."

Finally I realized that the fog, the jammed guns, the misdirected shots, the car crash, and maybe even the delayed explosion were Seraph work. We'd never been in any danger. I must have known that subconsciously all along. That explained my gratuitous folly. Nice going, Rae et al.

"I've never been that close to a man who was dead, Paddy, one that had just died. I don't feel anything at all about that, and maybe I should."

"You didn't kill him, Sara Anne. His friend did, and he was aiming at you. Lucky he didn't shoot straight."

"Oh, he shot straight enough. But the fella just sort of loomed up to go after me right when the shot was fired. Same thing for you. He killed both of his friends and then killed himself trying to get away. Poor men."

"Better them than us."

"Some poor mothers will weep tomorrow, and themselves so loving the little babies they brought into the world."

My woman's compassion was universal.

Later the manager of the hotel made an announcement on the public address system.

"The Gardai tell us that the three dead men were Unionist terrorists from the North. The first blast you heard was the escape car hitting a wall and exploding. The second explosion was a bomb out in the bay. The force of that blast tore apart a section of the seawall. If it had exploded in the stairwell where the Gardai feel that it had been left, most of us would now be dead and the rest of us maimed for life. We should all of us offer prayers of gratitude to St. Catherine before we go to bed tonight.''

A gasp of horror rumbled through the crowd. Sara Anne squeezed me tightly and rested her head on my chest.

"The Gardai say you're free to leave now. If any of you saw anything outside, they ask you to report to them on the way out. Thank you very much.''

"How the frig," a young man next to us asked his date, "did the bomb get from here down to the bay?''

"Maybe an angel carried it away from us," she replied.

Pretty good guess, young woman.

"Maybe an angel did," Sara Anne whispered in my ear. "Maybe."

Soon I would have to tell her about Rae. I'd better get permission first.

Theoretically the basement of the St. Catherine was a private club, so drinking could continue after closing time. There had been a lot of drinking since the explosion. The hotel management apparently had decided that under the circumstances, they could not very well object. We left the dance hall a little after one.

"I'm glad we finally got out of there," my love said, holding on my arm for dear life as we walked to her car.

"It's been a long day, Cousin Sara Anne.''

"Hasn't it been, Cousin Paddy.''

We stopped at the seawall where a crowd had gathered to inspect the damage. Sara Anne peered over the side of the wall.

"Holy Mother of God, Paddy! It's destroyed the wall altogether.''

I risked a peek. The tide was ebbing. The explosion had bent the top of the wall back over the Upper Salt

Hill Road and torn the bottom of it apart. Water had seeped through under the highway. Sunday or not, the lads would have to be at work on it as soon as the sun came up or the road itself would be undermined.

"How the frig did it get down here?" a teenage kid, the smell of the drink on his breath, asked us.

"Maybe an angel did it," I suggested.

"I didn't used to believe in your frigging angels. But now maybe I should."

"A good idea, a very good idea."

"Do you believe there are angels, Paddy love?" my date asked as we reentered the car.

"Sure I do. No doubt about it."

We kissed each other good night at the Railway Hotel and promised that tomorrow would be a grand day.

"The weather will be better tomorrow." She smiled affectionately as I left the car. "I promise you."

My Aero was open and on in my parlor. I pressed the space key to activate the screen.

> *Sorry, Paddy.*
> >Sorry for what?
> *We blew it. I'm so ashamed of myself that I can't face you with my analogue.*
> >What did you blow?
> *The affair with the UFF tonight. We simply did not expect them and were unprepared when they arrived. We will have to monitor their behavior as a matter of routine in the future. There is always too much work on this island.*
> >You didn't jam their guns?
> *They jammed the guns themselves. They are, or I should say were, very sloppy terrorists.*
> >You didn't cause the driver to run his car into a concrete wall?

He did that on his own. Too much of the drink taken, I fear.

>You didn't delay the explosion of the bomb?

We did not. We were too late for that. We did have plans to draw you into an . . . another plane of being, but that would have been a risky venture. All I was able to do was shout at you when you tarried too long at the wall. We would have saved your cousin, however.

>That's nice.

I told you we were not infallible, Paddy. We make mistakes. We don't know everything, we can't do everything. We are not always prepared for random interventions into the system.

>Yeah?

Come now, Paddy Tobin, if you really thought we were involved, you would have left the bomb disposal to us. Your only thought, in fact, was to save your love and all the people in the hotel. Be candid about it, you're a hero.

>I don't want to be a hero.

Sometimes, as you well know, there's little choice about it.

>I'll take your word for it.

You can rely on us to keep an eye every hour of the day on Oisin O'Riordan.

>I'm glad to hear that . . . I hope you're watching your UFF thugs. I thought this afternoon that if I were them, I might want to blow up the Galway Races.

Prescient of you. But you need not worry. We have already discovered the rest of their plots for tomorrow and guarantee their failure.

>I'll count on it.

Again, I am sorry to have put you at such risk, Paddy. It's the kind of mistake guardian an-

gels are not supposed to make. We will do better in the future. Now go to bed and get some sleep.
>All right. If I can.
You will . . . Good night, Paddy. End.

I shut off the computer and closed the screen.

What about my family? Since no one had been killed besides three Irish terrorists, the events in Salt Hill would hardly be Sunday morning news in Chicago. They were not likely to hear about it. If they did, Mom would blame me for not being considerate enough of her feelings.

Well, I wouldn't tell them.

I slept instantly, surely because of the work of Dr. Raphaella.

But I was awakened in a few hours by my friend Nuala.

"Mr. Tobin . . ."

"Paddy. Did you get any sleep at all?"

"I did not . . . I thought you ought to know that three Gardai are coming up to your room."

"What . . . ?"

"I suppose it's about the bomb last night. Good luck with them, Paddy. I think they're Special Branch."

"Frig 'em all!" I said, hanging up.

Almost immediately there was a knock on the door. I threw on a robe and tied the belt. Then I opened the door. There were three of them, a man about forty, another man about thirty-five, and a woman a little older than me, with flaming red hair, green eyes, and a wedding ring. None of them wore the blue uniform of the Civil Guards.

"What the frig are you frigging bastards doing bothering an honest tourist at this hour on Sunday morning? Go away. I won't talk to you."

I slammed the door in their faces.

I was truly angry. I had also decided that the only tactic to use with them was a hardheaded refusal to talk.

They kept knocking on the door.

"Go away."

"We insist, sir. We wouldn't want to have to break down the door."

"You wouldn't dare break down the door. I know that and you know that."

"Please," the woman begged, "we'll only take a few minutes. Then you can go back to bed."

"All right." I flung open the door. "Come in. But note that I intend to complain to both the American ambassador and to your Ministry of Justice, if that's what you call it."

"May we sit down?"

"Having forced your way into my room, you can do what you frigging please. But I'm not inviting you to sit down."

The older man introduced himself and the others. He was Superintendent O'Meara, the other man was Inspector McGrath (pronounced McGraw), and the woman, Sergeant Ryan. All of them extended their hands. I ignored them.

Without my permission they sat down.

"I note that without my permission you sat down in my parlor." I made a few marks in a notebook I had snatched from my desk and flipped open.

"We're only doing our duty, sir," Sergeant Ryan said pleasantly.

"That's what the Gestapo said and the KGB."

She flushed and the others tightened their lips.

"I want to see your warrant cards."

I had no idea what a warrant card was, but it was mentioned often in British detective stories.

Superintendent O'Meara collected the three cards and handed them to me. I looked over them suspiciously, as if I knew something about them.

"They don't say you're Special Branch." I threw the cards on the floor. "But obviously you are. Only secret police wake a man at this hour of the morning."

"There's no call to be rude, Mr. Tobin."

"When I encounter rude people, I treat them rudely."

These were tough cops. They needed some answers to finish a satisfactory report. I was serving notice on them that they wouldn't get such answers from me, not at this hour on Sunday morning (when they hoped to catch me off guard), nor any other time. They were tough, were they? Well, I could be tough too.

Generally I like cops. We have a bunch of them in our softball league. But I didn't like these cops.

They were very polite, very indirect, very cautious. I ignored their Irish indirection and spoke bluntly as a true American barbarian would. They did a lot of wincing at my responses.

I translate their questions into American.

"We have some questions about the incident last night in Salt Hill."

"If you frigging amadans were doing your job instead of harassing innocent American tourists, you would have prepared for last night's attack from the North. Anyone but a bloody fool secret police person would have known they were going after the Galway Races. What the frig would you do if you were a Protestant terrorist? And you should be out searching for their next bomb. If I were you, I'd look under the grandstand at the racetrack. Or at a turf accountant's booth. Or maybe where the children's games are. It's always better terrorism in this frigging island to kill children."

They shuffled their feet nervously because they knew I was right.

"We are taking adequate precautions, sir," Inspector McGrath said so softly that I barely heard him.

"We'll know about that before the day is over, won't we? Now ask your frigging stupid questions and get out of here."

I glanced at my watch and made another notation.

"You attended the dance last night with your cousin, Sara Anne Tobin, did you not?"

The woman had been assigned to ask the questions in the hope doubtless that her youth and her red hair and her attractiveness would calm me down. She opened her own notebook.

It was a little more difficult to be rude to her, but I managed it.

"Is that a crime in Ireland? She's far beyond the borders of ecclesiastical consanguinity."

"Eighth cousin, is it?"

"You can't even get that right, can you? Eighth cousin, once removed."

"If you would just please be a little bit more courteous, Mr. Tobin, sir, we could get this over more quickly."

I looked at my watch, made a note in my notebook, and waited.

The woman began again. "It was certainly not a crime to accompany Ms. Tobin to a dance, sir. It might even disclose your good taste—"

"I don't give a good frigging damn about your judgments about taste, Sergeant."

"Sir," she said, her face crimson and her voice high,

"we're only trying to find out some of the details about last night."

"All right, yes, I did accompany Ms. Tobin to the dance, and no, I'm not sleeping with her, not that it's any of your frigging business."

God forgive me; I was beginning to enjoy baiting these cops.

Slowly and painfully, with much effort to contain their anger, they extracted from me the additional information that we had arrived at the dance in Ms. Tobin's car about nine o'clock and left after one. She had presumably gone home to her family house.

"And you bastards wouldn't dare bother her at this hour of the morning. Ronan Tobin would have thrown the gobshite lot of you out of his house. So you decide to pick on the dumb Yank tourist."

No, despite what they had heard, Ms. Tobin and I had not left the dance hall together at any time. After considerable confusion they finally got around to asking whether it was true that she had left first and I followed her shortly thereafter.

"Why did she leave, Mr. Tobin?"

"That's none of your frigging business. If you want to know, go hassle her."

"What happened after you joined her?"

"We didn't screw if that's what you want to know."

"Two men were killed about the time you were standing in front of the hotel."

"I did not say we were standing in front of the hotel . . . Who were the men that were killed, masked men, according to an announcement made last night at the dance hall? Indeed the announcement said they were UFF terrorists."

She glanced at the super, who shrugged his shoulders.

"We have reason to believe that they were, sir."

"You think I killed them?"

"Oh, no, sir. We're only asking for a description of what happened."

"Who did kill them?"

The super shrugged his shoulders again. I think he knew that he'd met his match.

"We have reason to believe that they were shot by the driver of the escape car, who subsequently was killed when his car hit a wall. Apparently in his haste to escape he missed a curve in the street. We theorize that in the fog he did not see his targets clearly."

"Really? Ballistics tests?"

"Not finished yet, sir, but it is the same kind of gun."

"Were these, ah, alleged terrorists armed?"

"Yes, sir. Both their guns were jammed."

"Really? How unfortunate for them."

"There was some sort of scuffle with the two men in front of the hotel before their colleague shot them. In that scuffle we believed their guns jammed."

"How fortunate for the scufflers that the guns jammed—of course, they would never have been in danger in the first place if you frigging morons had sent a few guards up from the station to protect the St. Catherine from the UFF."

"We have reason to suspect, sir, that you and Ms. Tobin," Inspector McGrath said in his soft and threatening voice, "were witnesses to this event."

"You have proof of that?"

"No, Mr. Tobin," the super said, breaking his long silence, "merely well-founded suspicions. Now, may we please end this charade and have a description of what actually happened."

"No."

"No?"

"You heard me: no, spelled N-O."

"We could take you into custody and hold you unless you answer our questions."

"You gotta be kidding, McGrath. You wouldn't dare do that, and I know you wouldn't dare. It would be headlines in every paper in American, and Galway's tourist industry would collapse."

"After the shootings," the green-eyed woman persisted, "someone took the bomb, which we have reason to believe was left in the stairwell, carried it down to the seawall, and threw it into the bay. The subsequent explosion badly damaged the seawall."

"Better kill half a thousand people than permit that, eh, Sergeant? Maybe the frigging eejit who did it should have brought it down to the Gardai Station and left it there. That would have been a good work."

"No, Mr. Tobin." The super spoke again. "You misunderstand us. Whoever removed the bomb risked his own life to save the lives of hundreds of other people. He or she is a true hero; in this country we like to honor our heroes."

"Before you kill them, like you did Michael Collins? Look, Inspector, if anyone was frigging dumb enough to fight men with loaded weapons and carry the bomb away, do you believe that the person would also be frigging stupid enough to talk about it and make himself and his family a target for the UFF just so you assholes can finish up your frigging report?"

The cops had not a word to say.

The super kind of smiled. "It looks like you win, Mr. Tobin. Perhaps we should have anticipated that."

"Get out of my room."

"We're leaving."

They left, the sergeant last of all with a bit of her own smile for me.

I tore up my notebook pages and threw them away. I still didn't like the bastards because they were willing to make Sara and me targets for the UFF just so they could do their report.

Should I call her and warn her? No, they wouldn't risk Ronan Tobin's wrath. I'd tell her at Mass.

I flipped on my Aero.

A message from Meg.

> >Paddy,
> I just heard the report of the bombing at-
> tempt in Galway on CNN. It's too late to make
> the Sunday papers, and the rest of the family
> doesn't watch CNN. I won't tell them I saw it.
> Since no one at the dance was hurt, I guess
> you and Sara Anne are all right?
> Were you the one who threw the bomb in the
> water? I bet you were. I won't tell anyone.
> MEGPERSON

I responded promptly:

> >Megperson,
> Destroy your last message to me promptly and
> this reply. I'll tell you about the dance when
> next I see you. It is absolutely essential that
> you erase this correspondence from your ma-
> chine as I am doing from mine.
> Love,
> Paddy

Then I went back to bed and slept till eleven o'clock.

๑20๑

Hungry as I was, I wondered during Mass how the brunch Edna and her daughter would serve us on the *Sara Anne* would differ from the breakfasts the daughter had prepared for me several days before. There certainly ought to be more food, shouldn't there?

I need not have worried. In addition to Sara Anne's menu from the other day, they offered steaks, smoked salmon, a touch of caviar, and an entire apple pie. And an apparently limitless supply of heavy cream.

"Give your man his raisin bran, Ma," Sara said with a flick of her hair, as she put the steaks on the broiler. "Or won't he be eating one of these raw?"

Later, however, she did furnish me with my ration of brown bread, butter, raspberries, and clotted cream to the approving smiles of her parents.

They really wanted to get this adored but troublesome child out of their house, didn't they?

The three Galway Tobins wore to the Eucharist (at which indeed Sara Anne's Mass was sung) white cotton slacks, white sweatshirts, and red windbreakers. On the jackets, *"Sara Anne"* was inscribed in white in modest letters above the pocket, and on the sweatshirts in red and gold in the same place. The women both wore scarves over their heads in church—I was assured that the bishop approved of boating clothes at his final morning Mass, though the "young priest" vigorously disapproved of the irreverence.

On the boat they donned red baseball caps with the same insignia and tied their hair up in ponytails, Sara Anne after she started cooking the steaks.

I was wearing my Man of Aran sweatshirt. Naturally. Rae didn't have to lay it out for me, I would have done it anyhow.

As a prelude, Ronan opened two bottles of champagne, filled our Waterford goblets, and proposed a toast to "our previously unknown American cousin, Paddy Tobin, may he stay here as long as he can and come back often!"

I responded, "And to my newly known Irish cousins, whose hospitality exceeds even the very high standards the Irish set for themselves. I hope to get to know them much better in the years to come."

Sara Anne blushed and winked at my mild double entendre.

On the walk over from the cathedral, I had whispered to her, "The Special Branch came to see me at six this morning. They were snooping for details about last night."

She had nodded.

"I didn't tell them a thing. All they were trying to do was finish up their report. They pretended to think I was a hero. I told them I was not about to make myself and my family a target for the UFF just for their frigging report. I suggested they'd be better occupied if they went out and combed Ballybrit Race Course for more bombs."

"Were you really rude to them, Paddy?"

"Really rude."

"Good stuff!"

"Don't mention it to your parents, who are worried enough about last night. But if the Guards should show up at your house or anywhere, don't say a word to them. I don't think they will because they'd be afraid of your da and your ma's people."

She nodded and squeezed my arm and blessed me with her marvelous smile.

So I had reason to feel that I was adored, didn't I?

Ronan eased the boat away from its mooring off the rowing club and slowly up the river to a place inside the entrance of the placid lake and dropped anchor so we could eat our brunch without any movement of the boat.

While I was finishing off my cereal, my Sara Anne entertained her parents with the story of my suffering on the flight over to Inishmore. She remembered all the "funny" things I said.

"We shouldn't really laugh at you, should we now, Patrick?" Edna said, wiping the tears of laughter from her eyes.

"Why should you be different from anyone else? Would you please pass me some more of that caviar? It's beluga, isn't it?"

Nothing but the best for the future son-in-law.

I unlimbered my camera, concentrating more on the scenery on the boat than on the scenery along the shore.

The day had started out calm and warm. It was now becoming hot. The heat of the broiler made the cabin even hotter. In an unspoken agreement and with no show of either modesty or exhibitionism, the women removed their sweatshirts and went on cooking and chattering as if nothing had happened. Both were wearing swimsuits, Edna an aquamarine maillot and Sara Anne her red bikini, the most modest of the three I'd seen so far.

They ignored my camera, though they damn well knew I was taking pictures.

Cousin Ronan rolled his eyes.

"The woman drives me mad," he whispered to me in a mock complaint. "I can't keep my hands off of her and I can't get enough of her. The witch knows it too."

"Lucky you."

"Aye," he said complacently. "Lucky me. Though sometimes she's a terrible distraction."

"Like now."

"What are you two whispering about?" Sara Anne demanded.

"We're wondering if we're ever going to have any of those steaks."

"Just be patient."

The steaks were served in short order, with a béarnaise sauce that Sara Anne had made, her mother told me proudly.

I continued to click away with my camera.

"What are those pictures for, Paddy love?" she asked lightly.

"For me sister the Megperson."

"Well, she'll certainly be able to guess our bra sizes."

"Dear!" Edna protested.

"That's the general idea."

More family laughter. I could do no wrong.

Or so I thought that afternoon.

We ate the steaks, I finished off half the apple pie with heavy cream, naturally. Ronan turned on the motor and steered the boat out into the lake.

"You brought your swimsuit, Paddy love?"

"Am I not wearing it? But you're not going to swim in that lake?"

"Oh, I think we are eventually," Edna said. "So you'd better put some more film in your camera."

"You'll perish with the cold, woman."

"Just wait and see." Sara Anne tilted her head skyward and touched her ponytail. "You just wait and see."

We slipped by Oughterard out into the widest part of the lake.

" 'Tis about time now for our little dip, Ma, isn't it now?"

"After all that good food and champagne?"

Sara Anne was the more energetic of the duo; her mother, the more sensuous and lazy.

"All the more reason to go. Come on, woman, you don't want to get fat, now do you?"

She swatted her mother's rear end, something that none of my sisters would have dared to do to our mother.

"All right, all right, you young hellion. You win. We'll show off for young Paddy."

They peeled off their slacks, reached into a locker and brought out the most elaborate wet suits I had ever seen—cap, leggings, bootees, gloves. Only a tiny circle of face was exposed when they had put on the whole skin-tight outfit. I continued blazing with my camera.

"It's hellish for the first two seconds," Sara Anne explained to me. "But then it's quite cozy."

"Paddy, dear," Edna asked, "would you ever get the skis and the ropes from down below? The slalom skis, if you don't mind."

"You're going to water-ski in that water?"

"It's great fun really."

So I fetched the skis and the ropes, attached the ropes to cleats on the back of the *Sara Anne*, and threw the ropes into the water. With practiced ease, they tossed the skis in the water so they landed near the ropes, and then dove in themselves. Gracefully.

They shrieked in immediate agony as the cold water hit them, and then quietly put on their skis. The layer of water near their skin had warmed and they were now quite comfortable.

Still I wouldn't do it, not at all, at all, at all.

"You'll be keeping an eye on them, won't you now, and let me know when they drop?"

"The idea is that I keep an eye on them."

They waved that they were ready.

"Hit it, Ronan!"

As graceful as two geese taking wing from the lake, the two women emerged from the water, waved at us, and began to engage in complicated maneuvers as they crossed paths, sprayed each other with water, shouted and screamed and howled. I was spellbound, but not so spellbound that I didn't switch to my telefoto lens to catch close-ups of my cavorting women relatives.

"Isn't it a show and a half?" Ronan asked me.

"Is it ever."

Finally they dropped the ropes together, I shouted "down," and Ronan turned the boat to pick them up. I made myself useful by putting down the ladder and helping them into the boat.

Both of them zipped down the front of their wet suits as the came up the ladder. The suits were unbearable, I was assured in justification for this unveiling.

I managed to get even more pictures as, laughing and rejoicing, they removed their wet suits—with much agreeable squirming and contorting—and huddled in big terry cloth robes.

" 'Tis your turn, Paddy," my love challenged me. "Fair is fair."

"I don't have a swimsuit."

"You said you were wearing it."

"You don't have a wet suit that's my size."

She reached in the locker and removed one.

"Brand-new and just your size."

"I can't get up on one ski."

Both these beautiful women were laughing at me.

"We have a two-ski set."

I was trapped.

"You both are trying to humiliate me."

"Ah, now, Cousin Paddy, don't we both love you?" Edna said. "Aren't we just giving you a chance to say that you skied on Lough Corrib?"

I will not detail my humiliations. I died when I hit the water, then fell on my face four times before I was able to get up. I barely managed to drag myself out of the water. However, the skills came back to me and I performed credibly if not spectacularly. Finally I threw the rope, eased into Lough Corrib, and pushed the skis towards the motionless boat. The cold was, as they always say, not so bad when you get used to it.

It was, however, pretty bad.

"Try the slalom," my love yelled, throwing the ski into the water. "We'll teach you."

"I can't slalom," I yelled back.

"Sure you can. Listen to my instructions. I learned from a great instructor."

Her ma doubtless.

"Not without a lot of fighting," Ronan shouted.

I listened to her instructions and gave it a try.

Miraculously, I made it up the first try amid delighted screams and cheers from the boat. Indeed I managed to stay up for a presentable amount of time. I was applauded as I climbed up the ladder, and hugged when I collapsed into the boat.

"Grand, Paddy!"

"Brilliant!"

Ronan rolled his eyes again.

"You'll both be the death of me," I complained.

But I was very proud of myself and pleased with my success. I had shown them, hadn't I?

The women went below to change out of their suits. They were wearing blouses, white for Sara Anne and pale blue for her mother, when they came back. My love was not wearing a bra beneath her blouse.

"Shameless hussy," I whispered as I went below to put my clothes back on.

She giggled, but did not seem at all embarrassed.

When I returned, they had found another bottle of champagne and proposed another toast to me, this time to my success as a water-skier.

"Sure, wasn't it the instructions that did it all?" I responded to the toast.

Every muscle in my body was shouting in protest at what I had done to it.

"You'd better put more film in your camera, Paddy love." She handed it to me.

"I just put film in it!"

"Didn't I shoot it all during your triumph? Now, don't you dare destroy the film."

We trolled slowly around the lake for another couple of hours, sipping champagne, eating bits of salami and cheese on crackers, and listening to Mozart and Irish folk music on the CD player. I attended to Ronan as he explained that the best salmon-fishing time was not in June when the salmon ran but in May when the mayflies were all over the lake.

"She's just like she used to be, Paddy. Serene again. 'Tis amazing."

"Serene" was not the adjective I would have used to describe my beloved. But perhaps it fit now. She was certainly happy.

I would have dozed off had it not been for the special attraction of watching Sara Anne's exquisite breasts.

Finally we returned to their house for another drink and an "Italian" dinner at which I was toasted again and stuffed with food that, even by Chicago standards, was more than acceptable.

I insisted on walking home because, as I said, I needed the exercise. No one in the family, I thought, should be at the wheel of a car tonight.

Sara Anne walked with me down to Mary Street and kissed me good night. Chastely, I thought, but that was all right too.

"Tomorrow, Paddy Love, we'll go over to Clare and see the Burren and the Cliffs of Moher."

"Grand," I said.

Riding up to my room, I was proud of myself. In a week I had won the most beautiful and the most exciting and most challenging woman I had ever met. Not bad.

I was presumptuous, alas. We did not go to Clare together the next day. Or ever.

❧21❧

The next morning there was a MEGPER-SON message for me:

>Paddy (if that's what you want to be called,
and I like it a lot more than that awful Toby
thing),
Messages destroyed as this one will be after I
sent it.
I know you threw the bomb in the water;
that's the sort of thing my brother Paddy
would do.
I want to be woman of honor and toast person
at the wedding next week.
Love,
MEGPERSON

I chuckled at her request. Fine, so long as my bride didn't object. That sure was I that everything was over except my moral problem about the money. Maybe I'd just tell

Sara Anne about Great-Uncle Gerry's strange bequest and forget about the money.

I brought the four roles of thirty-six shots of ASA 200 film over to a photo shop on the square. They promised to have the prints in an hour, four copies of each print (one for me and one for her and one for each family). That would be ten o'clock, a quarter of an hour before herself showed up for our ride to the Burren.

The weather was "dull," to use a favorite term in weather forecasts in Ireland—a gray, listless day on which nothing would happen, either good or bad. However, it would not rain and it would be pleasantly warm. From what I had heard about the rocky Burren, a dull day would be an appropriate time to visit it.

I walked back to pick up the pictures. They were ready on time.

"Nice pictures," the woman behind the counter said, smiling pleasantly. "The Tobins are certainly attractive women, aren't they? And didn't you show them how to water-ski?"

Apparently there was no privacy in this place.

"The water was frigid," I replied.

Her Benz was already waiting for me. Early again.

I ran over to the car, eager to show off my photographic work, which I thought was pretty good.

She rolled down the window on the driver's side and glared at me.

"These are the pictures we took yesterday."

"I don't want to look at your frigging pictures."

"OK, maybe out in the Burren."

"We're not going to the Burren, today or ever."

Trouble, perhaps big trouble.

"Why?"

"Because I don't want to see your frigging face ever again."

What do I do now?

"I'm sorry if I've offended you, Sara Anne. Can you tell me what I've done?"

"What haven't you done? You've patronized me and my family. You've patronized Ireland. You've treated us like we are a bunch of ignorant country bumpkins. You made fun of the dance at Salt Hill, you ridiculed the Galway Races. You disapproved of our drinking. You laugh at our scenery. You are not sympathetic with the poverty of our poor people. You treat our children with contempt. You sneer at our heritage. You're ungrateful for our hospitality. You hold your snob Yank nose up in the air all day long. You trailed around after me like you were the patient hero who was bored to death with all our fun. Sure our racecourse isn't as good as those you have in the States, but it's ours. Sure our dance at Salt Hill isn't like your frigging block party, but it's ours. Can't you understand that we're a proud people and we don't have to put up with the likes of you, if we don't want to?"

She had just left her session with Moire Fitzpatrick, obviously a tough session. I was the first one she had encountered and thus the legitimate target of her anger. The enormity of her accusations nonetheless devastated me. With her fine memory for every word I had said during the past week, she could make a pretty good case against me.

"I'm sorry I've given those impressions, Sara Anne. I'll try to do better in the future, but I do think my words are being taken out of context."

"Frig your frigging contexts."

Not a word about our scene in the oratory at St. Patrick's shrine, her assaults on me in the swimming pool and elsewhere, the bomb at Salt Hill, or her braless breasts yesterday. I had a feeling that if I mentioned any of those events, the final curtain would go down.

Nonetheless I tried to defend myself against her assaults and to explain what I *really* meant when I said the words she was quoting against me. She wouldn't listen. All she wanted to do, it seemed, was to vomit her rage on me. When she was finished she would leave. Nothing I could say would change her mind. She was trying to provoke me, but I managed, just barely, to control my own temper.

Finally she'd had enough. I had been sufficiently destroyed to satisfy her.

"I don't want to listen to any more of your shite. Frig off and leave me alone."

She slammed the gear into forward and roared away.

It hadn't turned out to be such a dull day after all. I half expected the Seraph to be in my room, but there was no sign of her, and I'd be damned if I'd beg for her help. If I had not played the scene right, she'd let me know soon enough.

I examined my conscience carefully. Maybe I had said the wrong things sometimes. Maybe I hadn't been as sensitive as I should have been to Irish pride. Maybe I should have joined the fun at Ballybrit with a little more enthusiasm. I certainly enjoyed the dance up to the encounter with the UFF. The kids with whom I had played games at Ballybrit were not offended by me. In fact, they seemed to like me. Nor had she mentioned our success with the "turf accountants."

No matter what I said or did, she would have twisted it to her new view of me. Why? She was afraid of sex and afraid of love. Well, welcome to the club, Sara Anne.

I went over all her accusations again and concluded

while my behavior might have left something to be desired, the apparent breakup was not my fault. That judgment didn't make me feel any better. Well, to hell with her. I didn't need a crazy bride or ten million dollars of Tobin money. Still I felt like all joy and all hope had been drained from my life.

I sorted through the prints. A lot of them were pretty good. You shoot enough film and you're bound to come up with some winners. Also some real losers that you didn't want to look at yourself and you'd never dare show to your models.

I finally cut the 150 shots down to thirty that ran from pretty good to excellent (only a few that would make that category). I put one batch into my roller bag, a second in a Railway Hotel envelope to send home by FedEx tonight, a third in another envelope which I would deliver to Ronan's office on the morrow along with the quitclaims, which should arrive late this afternoon.

The fourth? I thought about throwing them away. That was a silly idea, however. Instead I put them in a fourth envelope, wrote her name on it, and put it next to her father's envelope. Maybe they'd do as a peace offering. More likely she would accuse me of objectifying herself and her mother.

The little bitch.

Maybe she would get over it. Maybe she'd come crawling back as she had done last week. So what?

Did I want to spend the rest of my life with such explosions possible when least expected? No way.

I wanted out. I'd leave on Wednesday.

What would I do today? I grinned as I thought about what I'd do.

I went to the reception desk, where, thank heaven, Nuala was not present, and asked if I could hire a car and

driver to take me out to the Burren and the Cliffs of
Moher. I spent the rest of the day taking pictures of that
rocky, barren, grimly beautiful land—where it was said
that God had dumped all the rocks left over after the
creation of the universe (and of which the Arans were a
geological extension)—and returned home to a solitary
supper in the hotel restaurant (NOT the grill room,
which I never wanted to see again).

Well, I had shown her that I could see the West of
Ireland without her help. That thought didn't make me
feel much better.

After dinner I found the FedEx package Dad had sent.
There was also a note from the Megperson.

>Paddy,
Dad was really impressed with the way you
handled that thing I wasn't supposed to know
about. He didn't mention it, of course, but he
asked me whether I thought that we had un-
derestimated you. I told him exactly what I
thought, and he listened. He didn't agree, but
he didn't disagree either. Then the next day he
gave us all one of this dean lectures that we
probably hadn't noticed how much Toby had
matured and what a responsible and perceptive young man he had become. No one disagreed, of course. They never disagree with
the dean's lecture. I cackled to myself all the
way through it. Three cheers for our side, and
remember that I have first dibs on being person of honor and toast person.
Love,
MEGPERSON

No wedding, I'm afraid, Meg dear.

What the hell, I thought, and dialed the Tobins' number. Edna answered.

"Pat Tobin here, Edna. I wonder if your daughter would ever come to the phone and talk to me."

"I'll ask her, Paddy," she said dubiously.

She returned to the line almost at once.

"I'm sorry, Paddy, really sorry. But she said she never wanted to talk to you again."

"OK."

"Please don't give up on her, Paddy. Please. Neither of us has any idea what's going on."

"Neither do I, Edna. Neither do I."

I thought about talking to Moire Fitzpatrick the next morning. That would never work. Maybe Sara Anne had poisoned her against me.

I strolled around the city, drank a Guinness at Blue Note, a jazz pub on West William Street, listened to the jazz, which, like the pizza, was pretty good for not coming from Chicago, and walked back to the hotel. Nuala waved sadly at me from the reception counter. You engage in a love affair with Sara Anne Tobin and everyone in the frigging city knows in detail about its ups and downs.

The next morning at ten, after dropping off the FedEx of my photos to be sent to the Megperson, I took my father's pack and my two envelopes of snapshots and ambled over to the Tobin office. Edna and Ronan beamed when I came in and then their expressions turned sad.

"She's not here, Paddy," Edna said sorrowfully. She came home yesterday and screamed at us that we were trying to sell her off to you like a countryman selling a prize heifer."

"A heifer would be much less of a problem," Ronan added.

"She said a lot of terrible things about you which didn't make any sense at all."

"I'm not here about Sara Anne," I said briskly. "Do

you mind coming into the inner office?''

I told them in brief and sanitized outline about the Tobin family feud, the court decisions, and our suspicion that there was a plot to force him to sell the land cheaply or have his reputation ruined.

"There's no gold up there." He snorted uneasily.

"Some think there's a good enough chance that there is to cook this scheme up. I informed my father and made certain recommendations. This package contains a letter from him and certain legal documents.''

Ronan opened the pack and read it carefully. Edna peered over his shoulder.

"By God, your father is a decent man!''

"That's the highest compliment Ronan can pay, Paddy."

"Ah, sure, he's not the worst of them . . . Oh, by the way, here's some of the pictures I took on Sunday. I hope they don't offend you.''

They shuffled the prints rapidly.

"Aren't they glorious, Paddy!''

"Brilliant, Paddy, brilliant!''

"You've got us all perfect, dear. And isn't this a grand picture of yourself on a slalom every bit as good as us?''

"A little better maybe.''

"You've made my woman a little more vain than she already is.''

"Ronan!''

"By the way,'' I said as I was leaving the door, "here's a set for herself. Give it to her whenever you think it safe to do so.''

Back at the hotel, I called their house. Sure enough, that's where she was.

"Yes?''

"It's Paddy, Sara Anne. Can we—''

She slammed the phone down.

Well, that message was pretty clear.

I'm getting out of here tomorrow. She's history.

What about today?

As I remembered her schedule, this was the day we were to drive up to Mayo as far as Achill Island. Fine. I'd do it myself. I'd show her. I called my driver. He came by in fifteen minutes. The fog was thick when we left, but it cleared away to a mild and sunny day. I learned why those from the County Mayo say, "Mayo God help us!" Mayo land is beautiful and barren. No wonder most of the people have left. However, Achill on a sunny day looked like films on the Travel Channel of the Bay of Naples, a sparse and somewhat cooler Capri or Ischia. Come to think of it, I would have to visit those places someday.

I enjoyed scampering around the Mayo countryside with a camera in my hand, but as much as I told myself it wasn't, my heart was breaking. I had loved and lost, which was not better than not having loved at all.

I had lost her. No, she had lost herself. But the result was the same. My love was lost.

So back at the hotel I tried ringing her home again. This time Ronan told me that she wouldn't talk to me.

I began to pack for my return trip.

"Young man, what do you think you're doing?"

She was wearing what I took to be an angel dress, a long white robe tied at the waist with a golden cord.

"I thought packing would stir up your attention. No time to phony up something from a fashion magazine, huh?"

"I'll do the packing. You'll never get it right."

"I want to go home tomorrow."

She sat on the edge of the bed where I had been shoving my present wardrobe into the roller bag.

"Wednesday?"

"That's what tomorrow is."

"There is," she said, considering the possibilities, "a Ryanair plane that leaves from here to Manchester at six-thirty A.M. You can connect there with a plane to the States and be home in Chicago in early afternoon."

"Fine. Make it so."

"You have more hair, Paddy, than Captain Jean Luc Picard."

"You watch *Star Trek?*"

"Of course. They're splendid morality plays . . . I can't say I blame you for wanting to go home. The poor child is acting like an utter fool. It is herself that she hates, not you. One must permit such rage for an hour or two after a painful session with the good Dr. Fitzpatrick, but no one should enter an intimate relationship with a person for whom such periods of regression seem habitual. They may diminish and soon, but one could hardly expect you to wait for that to happen."

"Right. She's history. I'm out of here tomorrow."

"I will arrange that."

I had expected an argument from my usually contentious Seraph, but she seemed to agree with me.

"Fine."

"Paddy, do me a favor."

In Chicago that is a line we cannot ignore. The Seraph was about to give me a marker.

"What?"

"You're supposed to say, 'Name it!' "

"All right. Name it!"

"Wait till Thursday. Give her another day."

I slumped to the chaise. No harm done, I suppose, if I waited another day. Maybe she'd change back to her old self and we could at least separate as friends with the door open for the future.

"You'll owe me a marker?"

"I understand how you Chicagoans play the game," she said, chuckling amiably.

"OK, I'll wait till Thursday. But then I'm out of here."

She rose from the bed. "I understand."

"The angel dress looks kind of nice on you."

"Thank you, Paddy."

She disappeared in the mists.

What are these lounges for? I wondered. Probably for the bride to recline on when she was doing her nails. And for the groom to spread out the bride when he was making love to her. That's not going to happen for me next week, as I thought. And I was looking forward to marriage. My love would be gorgeous spread out on this thing, compliant and eager.

I reveled in feeling sorry for myself.

Then, disgusted with my morose fantasies, I went down to supper. Afterwards I sent an E-mail home. There was nothing waiting for me on the Net. I tried to return to my program improvements for DABEST, but my programming skills were rusty and my heart wasn't in it. I went outside for my regular solitary nightly walk and my lonely pint at the Quays, a pub in Quay Street. All the young people there seemed quite happy. Indeed I had two pints.

The second pint didn't help me sleep. I spent a restless night, tossing and turning and dreaming that the quarrel never happened. When I stirred out of bed in the morning, my bag was neatly packed and the tickets were on the coffee table in the suite.

I drew the drapes. Another lovely day. It would have been a "grand" day for golf and swimming.

After breakfast I rang the Tobin office.

"Edna, I'm calling to say good-bye. I'm leaving for Manchester and Chicago at six tomorrow morning."

"Oh, Paddy," she said with a sob in her voice, "we'll miss you something terrible."

"I'll miss you too, Edna. You and Ronan both."

"Sorry it had to end this way, lad," Ronan added from another phone. "Damn sorry."

"I'm sorry too."

After more sorrow at both ends of the line, we promised we would see each other again soon. All three of us knew, however, that the magic would be gone the next time we met, if there ever was a next time.

I sat down on the sofa in my parlor, fiddled with the airplane tickets and made some notes for DABEST. I would not wait much longer for a knock on the door.

Finally I gave up on the knock and struggled out of the sofa. I reached for my jacket and wondered where I would visit today. Back to Connemara? Up to the shrine again? Or maybe the shrine to Mary at Knock up in Mayo?

Then the timid knock at the door. My heart jumped. I opened the door. It was herself in jeans and sweatshirt and a raincoat she didn't need today. Her hands were jammed in the raincoat pocket and her head averted so she wouldn't have to look at me.

Penitent now? Fine, but too late. She was history and that was that.

"Yes?" I said sternly.

"Me da gave me the pictures you took on Sunday, Paddy, and I wanted to thank you for them before you went home. They're brilliant altogether."

She risked a quick glance at my face and then turned away again.

"I'm glad you like them. You shoot a hundred fifty

times, the law of averages says you end up with a few adequate shots."

"Would you ever let me come in, just for a minute?"

Don't do it, Paddy Tobin. You let her in this time and she'll never be history.

"I suppose so."

I stood aside and let her in the room. I closed the door and turned around towards her. She was kneeling in front of me.

"Hey, you don't have to do that," I said, trying to raise her off the floor.

"Let me, Paddy. Please. I have to remember what this is like."

She grabbed my right hand, kissed it, and sobbed.

What the hell am I supposed to do now?

I rested my right hand reassuringly on her head. Big deal Lancelot du Lac forgiving his woman.

How terrible it was that such a woman as my Sara Anne should be reduced to such misery. Damn Asmodeus.

"I've done the most terrible thing I have ever done," she said, trying to fight off the sobs, "to the finest person I've ever known. I hated myself, but I shouldn't have hated you, Paddy. You shouldn't forgive me. You should throw me out of this room and tell me you never want to see me again. Still I beg for your forgiveness. Please give me another chance. I'll try never to be that way again . . . I don't want to lose you."

What does a severe and self-reliant man do when he is presented with such a situation? When he faces a plea to renew a relationship that he has already consigned to the archives of history where it belongs?

Obviously he lifts the woman off her knees, leads her to the sofa, sits her next to himself, wraps her in his arms, and says sternly, "Of course I forgive you, Sara Anne. Did you think I could possibly refuse? And, woman, you'll never lose me."

The mists shimmered behind Sara Anne. Rae materialized briefly, today dressed in a severe gray business suit (and vest!), gave me a thumbs-up sign, and flitted away again.

"It's not like me," Sara Anne pleaded. "Not at all, at all. I don't rage and I don't sulk and I don't hold grudges and I don't rip what people say out of context. I really don't."

"I know, Sara love, these are bad times for you, but they won't last long. Anyway, I probably was a little inept in some of the things I said."

"Only if you have to watch every word you say because you're with a crazy woman. None of it was your fault, Paddy, none of it."

She no longer sobbed, but she still clung to me for dear life.

"If it happens again, how should I react?"

"Please God it will never happen again. But if it does, react just like you did. Keep after me for a couple of days. Then give me an ultimatum like you did this morning. I promise you, Paddy Love, I'll come running, just like I did this morning."

"Ultimatum?"

"Didn't you call me ma and me da and tell them you were going home tomorrow? And didn't me ma give me these brilliant pictures? And then tell me you were going home? And didn't I know that was an ultimatum? And didn't I come running?"

And wasn't that what I had in me mind?

She sat up straight and pulled back from me so she could examine my face closely.

"You're not going home tomorrow, are you, Paddy? Tell me you're not!"

I glanced at the coffee table. The tickets had disappeared. Rae was not about to permit second thoughts.

"I had reservations, but my travel agent will cancel them."

"Is this travel agent here or in America?"

"Oh, she gets around a lot."

"Am I really your love again, Cousin Paddy?"

"You never were not my love, Cousin Sara Anne. You will always be my love. Don't ever try to get away from me again because I won't let you."

I kissed her and caressed her and she purred softly with happiness. Then I reached under her sweatshirt and probed for her breasts.

"Och, isn't this too awkward altogether?" she said, straightening up and yanking off her sweatshirt. "Haven't I been wanting to do this for the last couple of days? And there's no better time than the present, is there now?"

She folded the sweatshirt neatly and placed it next to her on the sofa. Then she unhooked her plain white cotton bra and tossed it recklessly on the floor.

My love had no idea how to be lascivious, however; she folded her hands on her lap, hunched her shoulders, and waited.

She was mine now, all of her. I could take her to bed and she would not protest. I could propose marriage and she would accept. But we'd both regret the first tactic, and it wasn't quite time yet for the second. So I kissed her and played with her and nibbled at her and told her how wondrously beautiful her womanliness was and how much I loved her. She closed her eyes, pressed my hands harder against herself, and moaned happily.

Finally it was enough. I put her bra back on her breasts, hooked it clumsily, and then helped her on with the sweatshirt.

"Promise you will do that to me often, Paddy Tobin?"

"You can count on it," I said, arranging the sweatshirt.

"Would you ever want to do anything with me today?"

She realized that she had said something absurd and turned quite red.

"I mean besides what you've already done?"

She knew that wasn't quite right either and became redder still.

"I mean," she said with a giggle, "I mean like going over to the Burren."

"Didn't I do that on Monday?"

"Or up to Achill?"

"Didn't I do that on Tuesday?"

"Good on you, Paddy Tobin! Showed the crazy little bitch, didn't you?"

"I did . . . Why don't we play golf, swim, have tea, and then go back to that restaurant on the bay where you guys wore the slip dresses last week?"

"Can I wear the same dress this week or maybe me ma's?"

"Would I ever dare to tell you what to wear?"

"You can tell me what you like."

"I'd like to see you in your ma's slip dress."

And so it was, though we began with a stop at the Bewley's on Middle Street for our midmorning pot of tea and scones. Sara Anne beat me three to two on the links, but described my improvement as "brilliant" altogether. She looked even more glorious in her mother's slip dress than she had in her own. Our day of reconciliation was a festive experience.

Until we left the restaurant to return to Galway. Then Asmodeus intervened.

❧22❧

We were driving back to Galway along the bay road, deserted at this late time of night. Thick fog was rolling in from the bay. We were both happy and silly because we were happy. Neither of us had consumed more than two glasses of wine all day (not counting a single sherry during tea at the golf club), so what I'm about to describe was not the dreams of two people who were fluttered altogether.

Sara Anne was teaching me to sing Irish folk songs and laughing at my terrible pronunciations of that ancient and sacred language (as she called it). Suddenly she slammed the brakes. The Benz, screeching in protest, ground to a halt.

"Glory be to God, Paddy! There's a body in the middle of the road!"

Stupidly, foolishly, I left the car and stumbled through the fog to the body. It was a man, a big man. I knelt down and rolled him over. He was wearing a ski mask and pointing a gun at me.

"Gotcha, frigger!"

It was Oisin O'Riordan.

Then something hit my head and everything went dark, very dark.

Later a splash of ice-cold water hit my face.

"Wake up, gobshite. We don't want you to miss the little entertainment we've prepared."

I opened my eyes, blinked, and saw Asmodeus, still in his ski mask and still carrying the gun. Two other men in ski masks stood behind him, both of them holding some kind of automatic weapon, Uzis maybe, though I knew nothing about such things. We were in a wooded place, near the bay to judge from the tart smell of fish and salt water. Flashlights mounted on tree branches shed sinister light on the scene.

I tried to move, but could not. My hands and feet were tied. The pain in my head made it impossible for me to think. What had they done to us? What were they going to do us?

Sara Anne! Where was she?

I tried to focus my eyes. My vision blurred. Then I saw her, also bound hand and foot, and propped up against a big oak tree. Her dress and bra had been torn away from the top part of her body; her face looked like she'd been beaten.

"Bastards!"

Asmodeus kicked me in the groin. Unbearable pain spurted through my body.

"Keep your frigging mouth shut, frigger, or you'll get worse than that . . . Now, let me tell you what we're going to do for entertainment. I figured it out so there'll be a maximum of entertainment for us and a maximum of pain for you. A computer type like you should appreciate me calculations.''

"You won't get away with this."

"Oh yes we will. It's all figured out. First of all we're going to kneecap you. My two friends here with the automatic weapons are going to cut your legs to pieces with a spray of bullets. Even if you live, and I kind of think you won't, you'll never walk again. Your whore over there is going to watch you bleed to death. And you're going to watch us rape her till she's almost dead and then cut her up with this knife of hers.''

He flicked Sara Anne's switchblade.

"When we're finished doing artwork on her, no man in the world will ever want her. But you won't be dead yet. So you'll enjoy every scream of hers. We'll let you die and we'll probably let her live so she can enjoy life when men turn away in disgust every time they look at her. We might cut out her tongue too, just so she can't tell what happened here.''

Asmodeus was insane. Sara Anne could still write out an account of what happened. The Gardai would pretty much guess who was responsible. He'd made enough threats before witnesses. He'd be finished.

I'd be dead and Sara Anne would be permanently disfigured. He'd be out of jail in fifteen years. Maybe less.

Out of the corner of my eye I saw Sara Anne tensing for an attack on him, a headfirst charge into his gut, the same strategy as at Salt Hill.

"So what do you think of my entertainment scheme?''

"I think you're a frigging lunatic!''

He kicked me in the head, doubling the force of my headache.

"That ain't respectful at all, at all. Won't we have to teach you some manners?''

Sara Anne hit him in the gut, but she stumbled at the last moment and the blow was only a glancing one.

"You frigging whore!" he screamed. With a brutal sweep of his massive arm, he knocked her to the ground. She fell next to me, our heads only a few inches apart.

"We're going to have to teach you some manners that those frigging nuns forgot about. I'm going to cut off a bit of your tittie, just so you know what's coming after we kneecap this frigger."

He knelt over her, cruelly grabbed one of her breasts, and cut away a small peace of flesh. She screamed in agony. A stream of blood flowed down her body.

"See, you're learning what happens to those who don't have good manners."

"I love you, Paddy," she said through gritted teeth. "I'll always love you."

"I love you, Sara Anne. I'll always love you too."

"Isn't that sweet! Lads, kneecap him now! Let's see how sweet he feels after that!"

The two men moved silently through the dim light. The fog was thickening.

"Shite, O'Riordan, I can't see him in the fog!"

"He's right here! God damn you! Do it now!"

Then fog obliterated the lights. All three of them were stumbling around in the dark. Then mists seeped into the fog, lacing the darkness with white spots.

My head hurt so much that I had forgotten about herself.

Suddenly she appeared, a radiant being ten feet tall, in a gleaming white robe with a rich crimson cape and a gold crown on her head. In her right hand she carried a sword that glowed red and silver. As she stood there surveying the scene, she pulsed with light, silver and blue and snow white light.

Angel light.

Sara Anne screamed again, this time in terrified awe.

"Do not worry, child, I am on your side."

"Holy Mother of God!"

"I'm not Her, though I know Her well."

She lifted her sword and pointed it at Asmodeus.

"Kill them all," he shouted.

"It's too dark to see any of them!"

A beam of light sped out from her sword, hit Asmodeus and illuminated him.

"I can't see a frigging thing! I'm blind! Kneecap him now!"

"Smoke gets in your eyes!" I sang the Jerome Kerns song just for the hell of it. "Never mess with Seraphs, guys. They're dangerous people."

Two more beams flowed from her sword. The gunmen fired swift bursts from their automatic weapons. The screams and curses were not mine. The gunmen had shot Asmodeus by mistake.

The fog had not lifted, but I now saw through the fog and mists. Oisin O'Riordan was twisting and squirming on the ground. He tried to grab his wounded legs, but that seemed to make his agony worse.

The angel Raphael in the old story had first blinded Asmodeus (using poor Tobit as his instrument), then bound him in Egypt.

"Sorry about that, Oisin, but better you than me."

Next to me, Sara Anne was vomiting.

The two gunmen, unlike us, were still in the dark. My Seraph friend pointed at them with her sword, and two more light beams flashed from the tip of her fiery swift sword. Immediately they turned and fired bursts of automatic weapon at each other. Blood spurted from their legs; bones, muscles, sinew, and flesh burst apart in small pieces. They dropped their weapons and fell to the ground, screaming in terrible agony.

Sara Anne vomited again.

Then two beams of angel light enveloped both of us. My hands and feet were freed. My headache vanished. My genitals no longer hurt. Next to me, still radiant in angel light, was Sara Anne, her dress back in place, as I presumed was her bra, now protecting an undamaged breast. The bruises on her face were gone and the vomit had been wiped from her face and body. Even the smell of vomit had disappeared.

Keep the Seraphs on our side, kid. They're good at what they do. I stood up and helped Sara Anne to her feet. She glanced at herself and gasped in surprise. The wounded men were still howling and cursing.

Then the two of us were gently picked up off the ground and whisked through the night to a dark place.

"Where are we?" Sara Anne asked.

Light glowed all around us, angel light.

"You're in the watch tower at Kilmacdoagh, dear. I find it useful because it taunts the memory of Lord Protector Cromwell."

She was now wearing a long, white evening gown with a red mantle over her bare shoulders. No sword.

"I will explain to you what we have done. Your car, my child, is safely back on Waterside Street. Your parents think they saw you go to bed an hour before this regrettable incident, just as the adorable Nuala thinks she saw your young man go up to his suite. The Gardai have been summoned and will shortly discover three masked men, two of whom they will recognize as members of the UFF, on the ground bleeding to death. They will halt the bleeding and arrest them on whatever charges they can find, assault with deadly weapons perhaps. It will develop that they will tell the Gardai that Mr. O'Riordan hired them to kneecap a rival in love and rape and mutilate the object of his affections. They will be unable to recall the names. They were promised ten thousand pounds for their cause in return for these services. As best as they can remember, they argued about prepayment and in the darkness and fog shot one another. The Special Branch will find the story odd, but they'll cheerfully accept it. Mr. O'Riordan, who has been temporarily blinded by a mysterious flash of light, will say nothing. Even he will not be able to remember who the targets were supposed to be. Neither will anyone in Galway remember his obsession with you, Sara Anne, my dear. His father will scream loudly tomorrow morning about Special Branch plots, but by afternoon he will have to retire from the Dáil in disgrace. That should take care of everything."

"Those poor men!"

"All suffering is to be regretted, child. But any hope of salvation they might have begins now. Moreover, their days of tormenting and killing other humans are finished. I should also note that we indeed deceived them about the targets, but they fired their weapons of their own free will. They maimed themselves with their own malice."

"What kind of a creature are you, woman?" Sara Anne asked in fear and trembling.

Rae sighed loudly, mimicking the West of Ireland trademark sigh.

"As your young man will testify, I am merely a Seraph, one of those seven who stand, metaphorically, before the face of God. In this instance I am his guardian angel and, by extension, yours."

"You're no frigging Seraph!"

"Oh yes, my dear, I am a frigging Seraph . . . For sweet charity's sake, come dance with me in Ireland."

With that quote from an old Irish poem, Rae turned into a revolving, pulsating pillar of red and gold and white fire which soared to the top of the round watchtower, a radiant plasma of angel light, brighter than the sun itself. The light filled the whole round tower, Sara Anne and I were swept up in it, and, for sweet charity's sake, danced and sang on the stars over Ireland.

Or so it seemed.

I don't know how to describe what happened next. Though Sara Anne and I had lost our clothes—and she was very beautiful—the experience was not erotic, not in the ordinary sense of the word anyway. Rather it was ecstatic. As we soared and dipped and pirouetted through the heavens, choirs of beings danced with us and carried us through mystical lands where light and shadow alternated in waves of goodness and reassurance that engulfed us, bathed us, annealed us. We swam in lakes and rivers and rich purple seas, all of them delightfully warm. We luxuriated in bathtubs and then sailed back into the heavens where we sang with the finest choirs in the universe, often Sara Anne's own songs and under her direction. Songs that she had already written and songs, I somehow understood, that she would write someday.

Everything would be all right, we knew that. We saw the whole of creation and our place in it and knew that all would be well, all manner of things would be well. We were filled with joy and hope and love and light and laughter.

And all the time we danced, sometimes slowly and gracefully in elaborate waltzlike movements, sometimes wildly in demented rock and roll enthusiasm. The beings dimly around us danced with us and sang lovely choruses in tune with our dance steps.

Our movements were are own. We determined how we

danced and what we sang, but we were supported and somehow led by our friends who filled the skies.

Choirs of angels?

I don't know.

Rae danced with us too, also devoid of clothes, sometimes with the two of us and sometimes with one or the other. She was unbelievably attractive. This is better than some dirty pond in Syria, I said or thought. She must have heard me because she laughed happily.

Angels are very vain creatures, you know.

Then we glided into a large and multicolored grid, not unlike a computer board, though one far advanced beyond our own time. Each time we touched a piece of the grid with our dancing feet, lights blinked on and off all through the system in a giddy eruption of red and blue and green and yellow lights, accompanied by electronic musical syncopation. With no effort I absorbed the patterns of light and the sounds of the music.

Then hand in hand, Sara Anne and I, our madcap dancing ended, ascended ever higher into the sky, out beyond the planets and the galaxies and the universes to a region that was both radiant light and total darkness. Here is where it all originated, I thought, the big bang or the big bangs, whatever. The place where infinity starts, and perhaps the place where the Other only just begins.

We savored the holiness of that place only briefly because, I understood, too much of it would prevent us from ever returning to our own time and our own world. Then, lying happily in each other's arms, Sara Anne and I gently floated back to the holy land of Ireland over which, for sweet charity's sake, we had danced.

Then we were back in the round tower, now only dimly lit. I was standing and Rae was sitting on the ground with

Sara Anne huddled in her arms. We had all somehow reclaimed our clothes.

"Nice show," I said.

"You are a frigging Seraph," Sara Anne whispered reverently.

"Oh, yes, my dear, I am a frigging Seraph . . . Do you think you can remember the melodies you heard tonight?"

"For the rest of my life."

She nestled more closely into the arms of her angelic protector and sighed peacefully.

"They are your songs, child. Everything that you and himself"—a brief nod in my direction—"experienced when, for sweet charity's sake, you danced with me in the holy land of Ireland came from inside yourselves, though not merely from there. The melodies are already in your head. We just took the slight liberty of bringing them to your consciousness early. They should keep you busy for many years."

"Yes, ma'am," she said docilely, not understanding yet that the proper way to deal with Seraphs is to argue with them.

"Would you ever mind leaving us alone, Paddy, for a few minutes? Herself and I have a few things to talk about."

She jerked her head in the direction of the door of the round tower, as Chicago politicians do when they refer to "your friends out on the West Side" (meaning the Mob).

I took the hint and left, fully aware that if I tarried, I ran the risk that I would be flung out on my rear end.

Outside there was no fog; it had either blown or had not come inland as far as the ruins of the great abbey of Kilmacdoagh ("gh" being pronounced in this strange land like "ff" if you happen to have a cold).

I watched the stars, silent and implacable above us. Had we really danced among them or was it all in our heads? The answer was probably that both suppositions were true in some way or the other.

I marveled at the complexity of the human brain and the complexity of the universe which it reflected and revealed.

Then, perhaps after fifteen minutes, I realized that the grid on which we had danced, and which was imprinted indelibly on my imagination, provided not only the answers to all the problems of DABEST, but enough computer insights to make my company a huge success. Bill Gates of Microsoft would not be able to compete with me in my own area.

Too bad for him.

I reviewed this prospect in my head. I'd still have to do a lot of program writing, but I knew where it would all lead. Rae had said it was all in my head, but now it was not only in my head but vividly in my imagination as well. Programming, as everyone knows, is more creative imagination than anything else.

Finally Rae appeared with the version of the Irish sigh that said a good night's work has been done.

"She's sleeping now," she said, rearranging the mantle around her shoulders, "in her own virginal bed. You will be sleeping in your room at the Railway Hotel shortly."

"Thanks for the help and the joyride, Rae."

"Did you really think it possible that we would not be there in full force?"

"My head hurt so much, I couldn't figure anything. But you guys do put on a good show."

"Naturally."

"Herself?" I gave the required jerk of my Chicago

head, this time in the direction of Galway city.

"She is fine, Paddy. You understood, of course, that I was instructing her and healing her?"

"Naturally."

"She is mostly healed, Paddy. I'd say ninety-nine percent. What remains will add to her character by providing her with a level of compassion that she would not otherwise have possessed. She should continue to see Dr. Fitzpatrick for the present and perhaps consult occasionally with someone like her for the rest of her life. However, her mad moods are likely to last only a few moments in the future instead of several days. So essentially she is healed. Poor Dr. Fitzpatrick will doubtless think it is her most astonishing case."

"You explained who you are and what you're up to?"

"As much as she needs to know. I also gave her some good advice for the rest of her life, most of which she already intuits but which needed some validation."

"I see."

It's between you two women. I'm not so dumb to ask questions.

"And now, Paddy, I think you need a good night's sleep."

And that was that.

❧23❧

As I was eating breakfast in my room the next morning, Rae materialized again, this time in her professional woman modality, dark blue suit, beige blouse, nylons, sensible shoes, even rimless glasses.

She did nothing without reason, but there was no way I could figure out the rationale for her wardrobe changes. Vanity, by her own admission, was an important consideration (but perhaps not so much as she implied); but there was more to her costume choices than that.

"Well, Toby," she said complacently as she sat on the edge of my sofa, "I mean, Paddy, we seem to have made it in the nick of time."

"What do you mean?"

I poured myself a second cup of tea.

"I mean it's only a week to your wedding."

"We haven't agreed on anything yet. I'm not sure we will, and as I count, it's ten days. What's the big rush?"

"Nine to be precise. But you must begin your plans today because nothing gets done on the weekends anywhere in the North Atlantic world, as you well know, and very little gets done on Friday. You have to give your family a decent amount of time."

"Shite!"

"How so?"

"I'm not sure I want to do it."

"G. Patrick Tobin, there are times when I simply can't understand you. You are hopelessly in love with the young woman; she adores you beyond all reason; you are desperately hungry to possess her as you must assume she is to possess you. You have survived several interesting adventures together, there is no serious objection, not from her family or my kind and only perhaps some from your mother and your elder siblings. What's to wait for? You should propose to her today."

"Today!" I shouted in alarm.

She lifted her hand to moderate my voice. "Please, Paddy, not so loud!"

"I don't want to exploit her."

"You're still worried about the ten million dollars? I assure you that she will not be troubled in the slightest. Have you not seen the adoration in her eyes? It will go to your head, I'm sure, Paddy, but from her point of view, you are incapable of doing anything wrong."

"It's my own point of view that I worry about. I'm in a bind, Rae. Caught between desire and my own tattered integrity, which I inherited, I guess, from my father."

She tapped her foot on the floor and frowned thoughtfully.

"I wonder if this is the result of your integrity, Paddy, or of a normal fear, especially on the part of the male, of the challenge of marriage and of the sexual encounter."

"I won't deny the second is part of it. But the first is more than an excuse."

She nodded. "I can see the problem of marrying a young woman for her money. But this isn't her money, and you would marry her if there were no money involved, would you not?"

"I guess so," I said miserably. "But it still doesn't seem right."

"As you know, our 'prime directive,' to use the *Star Trek* jargon, is that we do not deprive any of our clients of their freedom. I certainly don't intend to do that now. Nonetheless, I would urge you to propose marriage to that young woman today. At lunch. At the Ardilawn House."

"Do they serve lunch?"

"They do and it's a very nice lunch."

"I'll think about it. Or rather I'll think about a way to resolve the problem."

"That's all I can ask."

She dissolved into the mists, a bit impatiently, I thought.

All right, the male of the species is reluctant to lose his freedom and does so only because of a passion to sleep permanently with this particular woman. Moreover, he realizes his male ego is very much at stake when his ability to perform sexually is at issue.

So I was concerned about those things, though not all that much. Take away the other problem and I would not be reluctant. Well, not as reluctant as I am now.

I thought about it and thought about it and thought about it. I replayed it a couple of times as though it were a computer programming problem.

Yeah.

I put on a shirt and a blue sport jacket and left the

hotel after giving my room key to a smiling Nuala and walked over to Shop Street where I made a purchase in cash, using my winnings from Ballybrit. It was already a quarter to twelve.

Then I walked back across the square to the offices of R. M. Tobin, Estate Agent.

"Good morning, Ms. Tobin," I said to herself. "Are your parents in the office at the present time?"

"And good morning to you, Mr. Tobin. I trust you slept well last night?"

"Yes indeed, Ms. Tobin. And you?"

"Peacefully, thank you very much . . . Me ma is out on a job, but me da is in the office."

"Would you ask him if he could spare me a minute?"

"I'm sure he can, but to be perfectly proper, I'll ask him."

She was back in moment.

"You may go straight through, Mr. Tobin."

"Thank you very much, Ms. Tobin."

"Terrible thing about young Oisin, isn't it now?" Ronan said as soon as I had walked in.

"Terrible indeed."

"Your man was making all kinds of noise this morning about a Special Branch plot. But he won't get away with that. He'll have to resign this afternoon or in the morning regardless."

"I'm told it's all his fault because of the way he spoiled the poor lad."

"Sure, those who say that won't be far from wrong, will they?"

That idiom was of the same sort as "Sure, he's not the worst of them."

As Rae had predicted, everyone in Galway, including the journalists, had forgotten completely about Oisin

O'Riordan's pursuit of the fair Sara Anne, even her own father.

Ronan and I talked about my plan to open one branch of my electronics firm here in Galway in the very near future. He was delighted and made some useful suggestions about the practicalities of it.

He asked me what name I would give to the firm. He seemed to be quite pleased with the answer and my explanation.

We went back to the outer office, where Sara Anne was working on a stack of correspondence.

"Ms. Tobin, would you be good enough to phone Ardilawn House for me and make a reservation for two for lunch for one o'clock?"

She giggled.

"For yourself and your man?" She nodded towards her father.

"As you well know, young woman, for meself and yourself."

"Och, Paddy," she said, gesturing at the stack of letters on her computer station, "I have so much work to do. Haven't I been irresponsible all week long?"

"I can't imagine that . . . but, Mr. Tobin, did you not promise me that I could borrow your daughter for lunch?"

"I did indeed."

"Young woman," I said, pointing a finger at her, "ring them up."

She made the booking, as it is called in Ireland, and then held her hand on her mouth with horror.

"Paddy, I can never eat at the Ardilawn House dressed the way I am, and meself in jeans and a T-shirt."

"Then we'll stop at your house on the way home and give you a few minutes to change."

"You can use me car," Ronan said, handing her the keys. "Won't I not be needing it for the rest of the day?"

She grabbed the keys and ran down the steps, a happy young hoyden. I followed her.

"Wasn't that a grand night, Paddy? Isn't she a wonderful woman?"

"Wouldn't she be the first to tell you that?"

"I can't believe it all happened, and herself a Seraph that's your personal guardian angel."

"Travel agent."

"So she's the travel agent you're talking about all the time?"

"Isn't she now?"

"We had such a grand talk last night; she healed me, you know, Paddy. And wasn't Moire Fitzpatrick surprised this morning at me progress?"

"I'm glad of that."

"And she told me all kinds of things about life and how to be happy."

"I'm glad of that too."

"She certainly thinks the world of you."

"Really?"

Now, that I wouldn't have expected.

"Isn't it astonishing that she has made everyone in Galway forget about poor Oisin being after me so long? How does she do it?"

"I think she sprinkled forgetfulness dust over the whole city last night."

We both laughed. Yet Rae's trickery was more astonishing than the forgetfulness dust of fairy tales.

"I'll be out in a jif." She kissed me and hopped out of the car.

"I'll come with you and make sure you don't take too long."

"And watch me change me clothes?"

She seemed startled and even embarrassed by the prospect.

"Yeah."

She relaxed and grinned. "Well, I suppose after last night there's nothing wrong with that, is there now?"

She put her arm around me as we climbed the stairs to her room.

"Did you like me last night, Paddy?"

"You were heart-stopping, Sara Anne love, though it was different from a naked body here on solid earth, more ecstatic than erotic . . . Did you like me?"

"Ah, Paddy," she said, hugging me, "are you not the most beautiful man in all the world?"

An exaggeration, but I didn't intend to fight it.

I sat on the edge of her bed and watched her change her clothes, a delightful ballet.

She was modest but neither embarrassed or prudish. She kicked off her Nikes, lifted her sweatshirt off her shoulders and over her head, and hung it up neatly on a hanger. Then, facing me so I'd get the full benefit of the show, she tugged off her jeans. She was wearing white cotton lingerie, skimpy but hardly immodest.

"Sure, if I'd known this morning you'd be coming home with me, wouldn't I have worn something more provocative?"

"Sara Anne love, aren't you wonderfully provocative?"

"Thank you, Paddy," she said, absorbing me in her radiant smile. "You're always so sweet."

Had I not seen this all before?

But there was no way I could have seen it.

She hung up the jeans neatly and bounced towards the bathroom.

"I must spray meself with the proper scent for the Ardilawn House."

She bounced back and considered a number of dresses on the hangers in her closet.

"How about this one?"

She held a plain white shift (thigh length) in front of her.

" 'Tis grand."

She slid it over her head and smoothed it out.

"Would you ever mind buttoning me buttons?"

"I'd be delighted."

I kissed the back of her neck as I did so.

"That's very sweet, Paddy dear . . . I don't have to wear panty hose, now do I?"

"Certainly not."

She grabbed a white purse, transferred the essentials from her shoulder bag, and dashed down the steps in front of me and out into the Benz.

"Five and a half minutes," she shouted triumphantly. "Does that prove I'm not a slowpoke when it comes to changing me clothes? Sure, you didn't have to come in to check up on me, did you now?"

"Woman, I did not."

"But I'm glad you did."

I kissed her as tenderly as I could.

"I'm glad I did too."

We were the only ones in the garden at Ardilawn. It was easy enough then to slip my hand under the table and up her thigh. Far up indeed, but not yet all the way up.

She merely smiled at me.

I freed her from my caresses when our food came. She seemed disappointed.

We ate our poached salmon and rice, drank a glass of

wine, and finished off our apple tart with tea.

Over the tea I got down to business—because it's only at the end of the meal that the Irish ever get down to business.

"I stopped by an establishment on Hill Street this morning and made a purchase."

"Did you now?" she said guardedly.

I opened a small box and placed it in front of her.

"Oh, Paddy. Isn't it lovely now? A Claddagh ring with the biggest emerald in all the world!"

Without taking the ring out of the box, she examined it carefully, then closed the box and passed it back to me. "Grand!"

She must know what it represented. She couldn't help but know. Yet she was afraid to know, frightened of being too presumptuous and wary of the challenge it presented to her. I understood the latter fear very well indeed.

" 'Tis for you, Sara Anne love."

I flicked the box open and pushed it back across the table.

She stared at it hesitantly.

"I don't know, Paddy, I don't know. I'm probably too young and certainly too confused, and we haven't known each other long enough."

"You're only a few months younger than your ma when she married your da. After your session with Dr. Raphaella last night, you're not confused anymore. And how long would you have to know me?"

She shifted her glance from the ring to me and back again. Then back to me.

"I don't know, Paddy. I'm confused something terrible."

"I don't want to rush you, my love; I can wait for an answer. Take your time and think about it."

I moved the ring box back to my side of the table.

"Don't you dare!" she exclaimed with a hoyden whoop. She jumped across the table and grabbed the box away from me. "If I take time, you might change your mind, and wouldn't I be a terrible eejit altogether if I let that happen!"

She removed the ring from the box and gave it to me. I slid it on the appropriate finger. Then we both wept and embraced one another.

"When shall we be married?" she said, nuzzling her face against my chest.

"Saturday a week?"

"Saturday a week! That's no time at all, at all . . . but sure, my love, why should we be waiting?"

"No reason at all, at all."

But we still would have to face problems, a few of them serious. Very Serious indeed.

❦24❦

By the end of supper that night at the Tobin house on Waterside Street, we'd cleared away the easiest problems. Neither Sara Anne nor her mother was prone to the panic that had characterized the six months in our house before Maureen's marriage.

We'd be married at the cathedral "across the way" at high noon on June 25. Edna had checked and the time was available. My priest, the Most Reverend John B. Ryan, Ph.D., would preside over the ceremony. Edna's youngest brother, Peter Burke, would be the best man. The Megperson would be woman of honor and toast woman, as she had insisted. Sara Anne would wear her mother's wedding dress, which, it was said, would fit her almost perfectly. We'd find Meg's size and order a dress for her that both women were sure she would love. The reception would be at Ashford, where Edna was fortunate enough to make a booking at just the right time. The rehearsal dinner would be on Friday night at Ardilawn just for the two families. They would invite all their friends to the wedding but would understand if some of them could not come because of the short notice. We would honeymoon in America and return in September so Sara Anne could finish her courses at the university, and our new programming firm, Tobin and Tobin, would open its Irish operation (the Chicago branch having been established in the summer). After that we'd maintain two homes, one in Galway and the other in Chicago. In St. Hilary's naturally. We'd come back and forth often.

"We're not losing you at all, at all!" Edna exclaimed happily.

"But you are getting rid of your most troublesome heifer!"

Laughter all around.

"The point is," Ronan insisted, "there's no need for a lot of fuss and bother during the next week. You two can enjoy your brief engagement, don't you see?"

He didn't know my family. The noses of my two older sisters would be seriously out of joint because Meg had been chosen over them. My argument that we had decided to have only two attendants because of the shortness of the time (and they'd know the reason for that) would not defuse their sense of outrage. Neither they nor my mother would like the Galway Tobins at all.

I would have to shut them up, as Rae had warned me, but it wouldn't be easy. As it turned out, it was virtually impossible.

After supper my fiancée and I walked across the bridge and over to the cathedral to make arrangements with the Church. It was an unpleasant encounter.

The young priest did not shake hands with me when

Sara Anne introduced me and did not even ask us to sit down.

"Wouldn't we like to be married at noon a week from tomorrow, Father?" Sara Anne asked tentatively.

"Absolutely impossible," he snapped. "Out of the question!"

"We were told that the time was available," I murmured softly.

The young priest was a thin, mystical-seeming young man with hollow eyes that shone in a fanatic's glow.

"I will determine what is available and what is not available. Moreover the question of available time is not the primary issue. In Ireland, Mr. Tobin, we do not permit young people to rush into marriage. There are a number of requirements that you must meet. The banns must be announced. You will have to provide documentation and releases from your own parish and your own diocese.

"Archdiocese."

That was irrelevant. He would have to instruct both of us about the meaning of the "Holy Sacrament of Matrimony, which is not merely sex, though I'm sure you both think so." His schedule was crowded with responsibilities at the present time. He could not possibly think of such instruction sessions until the fall. Moreover there were serious legal requirements that had to be fulfilled. We could be married perhaps at Christmastime.

"Oh," Sara Anne said, her shoulders slumping in dejection.

"How long have you known each other?" he demanded.

We were still standing at the door of his office.

"Two weeks," my love replied meekly.

"Two weeks!" He exploded. "Do you think that we would permit a young Irish woman to marry a man from

America about whom we know nothing in two weeks? You both must have taken leave of your senses!"

"He's me eighth cousin, Father."

"Once removed," I added.

"That is not of itself an impediment to marriage. But we will not permit this marriage to take place a week from the day after tomorrow."

"But, Father—"

"No 'buts,' young woman. Your are a spoiled rich girl with no concern for the poor or the oppressed. That in itself is reprehensible. But you show not the slightest awareness of the sacredness of the Holy Sacrament of Matrimony and the care and reverence with which it should be approached. Good evening to both of you."

Sara Anne wanted to beg, but I took her arm and steered her to the door.

Then I turned to the priest. "Father, I know a man of your great virtue does not gamble. But I'd be prepared to wager you any amount that you would care to name that this marriage will take place on Saturday a week at high noon whether you like it or not."

Then I walked away without giving him a chance to reply.

"Whatever will we do?" Sara said plaintively when I caught up with her outside the cathedral offices.

"I'll take care of it, Sara Anne, don't worry. Skull Face in there doesn't know it, but this institution happens to be one in which I have some clout."

Her parents were distraught by the young priest's verdict. Distraught and furious.

"I could go to the bishop, I suppose," Ronan said. "He's reluctant to overrule one of his priests, which is generally a good policy. But he would be reluctant to offend both our families too. It would be awkward, however."

"They'd marry us at St. Nick's."

"They're not Catholic, dear."

"They're a lot more Catholic than that frigging bastard is."

"Not to worry, good people. I'll take care of it with one call to America . . . Sara Anne, pick up the other phone. I want you to hear this."

I dialed a credit card call (Rae's card, of course) to America and directed it to 312–743–9343. I asked the young person who answered if I could speak to himself.

There was no doubt in her mind who that was.

"Father Ryan," said the sleepy voice at the other end of the Atlantic.

"Bishop, this is Paddy Tobin, formerly known as Toby Tobin."

"Ah, yes, Paddy. I had heard about the name change, which I think is quite appropriate. I heard it from a certain Meg Tobin, a student at Saint Ignatius College Prep, I believe, who purports to be your sibling, which for all I know may well be the case. She also informs me that you are involved in some romantic relationship of which she enthusiastically approves. Not doubting her wisdom in these matters, I have been trying to reach you to offer my congratulations. I'm glad I was finally able to contact you."

"I'm calling you, Bishop."

"Really! How convenient!"

"Sara Anne and I are to be married at high noon in the Cathedral of Mary Assumed into Heaven and St. Nicholas, Saturday a week. We would like you to preside over the ceremony."

"I will check my schedule. Hmm . . . my staff insists that

is the time of my holidays, as I believe they are called on your side of the Atlantic. With God's help—and that of the Holy Angels, of course—I'll be there. I may even remember to bring my Episcopal robes, which may brighten that awful mausoleum."

"My bride is a liturgical musician, Bishop. They sing her Mass here every Sunday because it is easy to sing and lovely."

"Easy to sing and lovely? That makes her rare in that profession, which is normally devoted to exactly the opposite goals. I look forward to meeting her."

"And I you, Bishop."

"I assumed, Sara Anne, that you were on the line. Some things do not change in our common culture. Let me congratulate you. You are a very fortunate young woman as, ah, Paddy, you are a very fortunate young man."

"Thank you, Bishop," both of us said. Sara Anne was grinning broadly. This was her kind of priest.

"There is one problem, Bishop. The young priest here absolutely refuses to tolerate the marriage. He says that by December we may have fulfilled all the ecclesiastical requirements."

"Dear me. As I read the Code, you both have a right to the Sacrament. Well, I shall call your prince bishop, with whom I am not unacquainted, and inform him that Bishop Ryan from Chicago will celebrate this nuptial Eucharist at his cathedral church of whatever and whatever at high noon on Saturday a week, and I trust he will be good enough to protect Cardinal Sean Cronin's auxiliary from all penalties, both civil and ecclesiastical. I think that should suffice, don't you?"

"Thank you very much, Bishop Ryan," Sara said tearfully.

"You're quite welcome, my dear. I should tell you, by

the way, that for reasons which arguably have to do with my middle name, I am generally known as Bishop Blackie."

The next night Sara Anne and I had dinner at the bishop's house, where everything was quickly arranged and all problems settled.

"If Bishop Blackie says you're all right, son, then you are definitely all right."

Clout.

As the saying goes in Chicago, "We don't want nobody that nobody sent."

So we had solved one problem. But now the most serious problem remained to be faced.

Which is exactly what Rae said to me at the hotel the night of our engagement. She was wearing, for reasons of her own, a glittering old-fashioned white nightgown and matching robe.

First of all she hugged me and kissed me and warmly congratulated me.

"You'll never regret it, Paddy, never."

It's an odd experience to be kissed by a Seraph. Not unpleasant but a little strange.

"You took care of that insufferable fanatic nicely, Paddy. Your mother and your elder sisters will be a much more serious difficulty. Given a chance, they will slice your bride up in little pieces, and her parents too, under pretext of being helpful, naturally. Do you understand?"

"Yes, ma'am."

"And you must establish the new rules from the very beginning."

"Yes, ma'am."

"If you take that stand, in due course they will come to love the child and to take credit for her."

"Fine."

"And if you are actually planning on living in St. Hilary's, and I have no objection to that, then look as far away from them as possible. Understand?"

"Yes, ma'am."

"I'll investigate the real estate situation over there."

Not only my travel agent but my real estate agent too.

It would be a tough fight, but I'd have to do it for my beloved.

"Do you mind telling me, Paddy, how you resolved your quandary about the money?"

I told her.

"Well," she said, rolling your eyes. "I must admit that you certainly are a credit to your Jesuit training."

"Naturally."

"Again my warmest and most loving best wishes and blessings to you, Paddy. I speak for my associates and my, uh, family. We are all very proud of you."

That was a strange thing for an angel to say, wasn't it?

There was a message from Megperson waiting for me.

>**Paddy,**

What bitchin' shots! They're both simply gorgeous. Wow! What marvelous boobs! And your Sara Anne looks so sweet. You're really luckier than you deserve to be. And if you're not nice to her all the time, I'll never forgive you.

Dad thought they both looked charming and said that Sara Anne was a very attractive young woman and clearly intelligent. I don't know how he found that out. The others complained that, yes, they were both quite attractive but a little common and vulgar, don't you think. Not much taste, if you know what I mean. They should have boobs like that!

And congratulations on the slalom skiing, though I bet Sara Anne deserves credit for

that. Kiss her and tell her I love her already.
Love to you too,
MEGPERSON

Well, there'd be one ally, and maybe Dad would be a
second.

I sent a reply:

>Dear Mom, Dad, Maureen, Nicole, and Megan,
Sara Anne and I will be married in the Cathedral of Galway at noon on June 25. Bishop Ryan
will preside, arguably, he tells us, in full robes.
Peter Burke, Sara Anne's uncle, will be the
best man, and I'm asking Meg to be best
woman. Because of the haste of the wedding
(the reasons for which you know), we felt that
it would be impossible to arrange for more
than two attendants. I've also asked Meg to
be the toast person because she'll be giving
toasts all night anyway.
I will arrange for first-class tickets from Chicago to Manchester on American Airlines and
from Ryanair directly to Galway City. I suggest
you leave on Wednesday night so you can arrive on Thursday and have supper with the
Galway Tobins here at the grill room of the
Great Southern that evening. The rehearsal
banquet will be at the Ardilawn House on Taylor Hill just outside of the city, and the wedding dinner at the legendary Ashford Castle up
in Mayo. I will make reservations for you here
at the Great Southern.
You can come before Wednesday if you want.
But I hope you can make it by then at the latest.
I will arrange for limousines to pick you up at

**Galway County Airport. It is not, by the way, anything like O'Hare.
See you soon.**

That would raise bloody hell in the family.

On Sunday we attended the Eucharist at the cathedral. They sang Sara Anne's Mass again. It being the second lovely Sunday in a row, we went out on the *Sara Anne* again. I skied before the others and did reasonably well, though not as well as my adoring bride insisted that I had. My Irish cousins were fixated on the screen of the portable television. Replays of the Irish World Cup victory over Italy the day before were at least as important as our marriage, even to Sara Anne.

But she did take me aside for a brief chat at the interval.

"I spoke to our travel agent and told her that we'd probably leave on Wednesday for the States. To Manchester and Chicago, like you came. She thought that was fine."

"*Our* travel agent?"

"Well, didn't she say she was my guardian angel by extension? . . . We wanted to make sure you approve."

"Sure . . . what do we do the first four nights?"

"You mean, Cousin Paddy, that you haven't figured that out yet?"

I felt my face grow warm.

"I mean where do we do it?"

"Well," she said with the grin of a sly conniver, "didn't I think that we might leave from the Ashford like we were heading for Shannon and then go down the other side of Lough Corrib to Oughterard, where no one would look for us, and then back to the hotel on the boat and park it at the dock? They'll leave a door open for us so we can sneak in. They'll let us have the bridal suite for four nights and we can get all our meals from room service at no extra charge. Won't we never have to leave the bridal suite except to sneak out on the boat if there are any moonlit nights, which there might be?"

"Sounds delightful. I gather you intend to exhaust me."

"Absolutely . . . and won't it be fun to make love on the lake under the stars?"

"You're driving me into delirium, my love. And sure, couldn't we find a quiet cove somewhere during daylight hours too?"

"That's an interesting idea," she said judiciously. "Sure, I don't know why not."

Was my future wife really so sexy? You'd think Ireland would be the last place in the world you'd find such a woman—you would think that if you didn't know Irish language literature.

One afternoon we stood on the Long Walk beyond the Spanish Arch and stared at the park across the mouth of the Corrib where the Claddagh used to be. Sara Anne had shown me a collection of photos of that quaint and attractive village of thatched cottages and appealing people.

"Sure, it smelled and it had sanitary problems, but they never should have torn it down. They destroyed the whole culture along with the cottages. Someday I'm going to write a choral lament for the Claddagh."

"Poor people."

"Their men were fishermen. They would bring their own style of hookers into the fish market by the Spanish Parade, and their women, dressed in red petticoats and blue jackets, would sell the fish to the people of Galway."

"Ah."

"Didn't me grandfather's grandfather do a line with one of them?"

"Courted her?"

"In a manner of speaking. He was eighteen and she was sixteen. He wandered down to the fish market one spring morning to buy some fish for his ma. Didn't he see her, wearing no shoes and having only the Irish language, but as proud and as bright as the finest young woman in the county, and didn't he listen to her singing in a voice like an angel? He fell in love with her at once, and she with him.

"They half courted all summer and then he went off to Dublin to study to be a doctor at Trinity College. It was the time of the famine. Here in the city there was enough to eat and the fish were still in the bay, waiting to be caught. But some kind of infection was sweeping the Claddagh. When he heard about it, he went down to the fish market to see if his Eileen was there. Sure, hadn't he left for Dublin without saying good-bye? Well, she wasn't there, and the other women saying that her whole family, parents and six children, had all died. So didn't my grandfather's grandfather, Michael Burke, run across the Claddagh bridge and down the lane where they lived, a lane in which no living being survived? And didn't he find the dead bodies of the whole family in their cottage? And didn't he burst into tears at the sight of his dead love?"

"What a tragic story!"

"It didn't end that way, Paddy love." She held my arm tightly. "While he was sobbing, didn't she stir? And didn't she say that he'd come too late and would he ever leave her alone so she could die in peace? And didn't he pick her up in his arms and rush back to the bridge and over to his own house on High Street, and didn't he and his mother save her life? And didn't she become my grandfather's grandmother? And herself having only the Irish language and not being able to read or write and never having worn shoes!"

"But she could sing?"

"And dance and play the harp and tell stories. And laugh. And sure, didn't she learn English and learn to read and write and even to wear shoes and become a grand lady? And my grandfather saying that she never lost any of her Claddagh laughter and wit. She lived into her nineties and died only in the nineteen twenties, and didn't she sing every day?"

"An Irish love story with a happy ending."

She sighed loudly.

"Isn't this one of your daguerreotype things when she and me grandfather's grandfather had their first baby?"

I looked at the picture. The very young mother in it already looked like a grand lady, though the glint in her eyes and the slight upturn of her lips hinted that she was still a laughing hoyden from the Claddagh.

She also was a dead ringer for my Sara Anne.

So that was the point of the story?

"So I'm really going to marry a throwback to a Claddagh woman?"

"You are," she said sadly.

"Well, they're not the worst of them," I said, hugging her.

She sighed again. "That's what me grandfather always said."

The two of us by implicit consent cooled displays of affection for the week before the marriage. Passion was important, as my future wife said to me, but so was restraint. I didn't disagree. It was my idea, however, that we receive the Eucharist every morning at seven-o'clock Mass and pray that God would bless and protect our union.

Rae, who materialized and dissolved frequently, said she was impressed with our piety. I fear angels and themselves bearing compliments. She seemed as concerned about the wedding as did Sara Anne's parents.

My family was another matter.

The first E-mail was from my father.

>**Toby,**
First, in the name of the whole family, let me congratulate you on your engagement to Sara Anne Tobin. Judging by the pictures you sent, she is a sweet and charming young woman as well as being very attractive. Her parents appear to be delightful people. Moreover, your future father-in-law in his letter to me after the matter of the quitclaims was settled (but apparently before the engagement was announced) revealed himself to be a decent and honorable man. You appear to be fortunate in both your future wife and your future in-laws. I am, as I may have said before, enormously impressed by your transformation. I suspect that your future wife had something to do with it.
However, I must say I don't approve of your extravagance in flying us over to Ireland. Even if you have or shortly will have the money for such prodigality, it still is more than a little inappropriate. We will fly on Aeroflot, which has the advantage of flying nonstop from Chicago to Shannon as well as being much cheaper.
Also, our guidebook says that the Skeffington Arms, which is also on Eyre Square, is as good as the Great Southern.
We have made all our reservations accordingly. We would appreciate it, however, if

you'd provide us with cars at Shannon on arrival.

Dad

Shite!

Then one from the Megperson.

>Paddy.

I will not sleep in the same room with that pig Nicole, especially since she and that hog Rob that she's going to marry will want to screw all the time. I'll take the reservation at the Great Southern. They'll never miss me.

Love,

MEGPERSON

I answered the latter first.

>Meg,

Your reservation stands. A cute redhead named Nuala is one of the receptionists. She's coming to the wedding with her young man. Tell her you're my sister and you'll own Galway city.

Talk them out of Aeroflot.

Also send me the appropriate measurements for your dress. Sara Anne plans on a pale green dress, off the shoulder with a green lace mantle. If you don't like it, we can make a quick change.

Love,

Paddy

Then to Dad.

>Dad,

Thank you for the good wishes and the nice words. I'm sure you'll love both my bride and her parents.

I urge you to reconsider Aeroflot. Their international safety record is all right (unlike their domestic record), but they are the most un-

comfortable airline in the world. You'll arrive
here for a busy weekend, exhausted and nervous and angry at the damn Russians. Please
come on American.
The Skeffington is nice but not as nice as the
Railway Hotel, and there's a lot of singing in
its pub at night, to say nothing of the Alley, a
pub behind the Skeff which is the most popular pub for adolescents in this city. You'll rest
better at the Great Southern.
Please change your reservations.
Also I'd be very grateful if you warned everyone NOT to reveal the secret of Uncle Gerry's
will. I think the letter of the will would not be
violated, but the spirit would be dishonored. I
am grateful to Uncle Gerry for his generosity
and am increasingly persuaded that he knew
very well what he was about.
Paddy

I was strongly tempted to flame them for rejecting my
generosity. But that would violate etiquette and make
matters worse. I'm sure it was Mom who had objected.
The wedding had to be a painful experience for everyone.

The reply from Dad insisted on his plans. Meg, in addition to the proper measurements (which I will not repeat out of deference to her modesty), added:

The dress sounds bitchin'! If herself likes it, so
will I. Up the Republic!
Love to herself,
MEGPERSON

The most serious problem to emerge on the Irish side
of the Atlantic was that Ireland would play Mexico in the
World Cup the night of the rehearsal dinner. The three

Galway Tobins were horrified. I assured them that most of the match would be over before the dinner and that Ireland would surely be way ahead. They agreed they would soldier on. Besides, there would surely be a TV in the bar at Ardilawn and they could sneak back and forth.

"We couldn't do that," Ronan protested. "Wouldn't that be terrible rude to your family?"

"All right, I'll do it."

On Wednesday Dr. Fitzpatrick dispensed Sara Anne from any more sessions till our return from America in September. "You're doing very well, dear. You'll be fine."

I don't think Sara Anne would have believed her unless Rae had told her the same thing after our ride to the stars.

So Thursday morning at four o'clock Sara Anne and I were in one of our two limousines, driving down to Shannon to meet Aeroflot Flight 330 at six o'clock, an Ilyusin 62 that stopped in Ireland only because it didn't have the fuel capacity to make it to Moscow without a stop. (Approximately twenty-five hundred Aeroflot flights landed at Shannon each year.)

Before I had left my room in the Railway Hotel, Rae showed up to warn me again about my family.

"I've got to be candid about my family, Sara Anne," I said in the car. "Megan is wonderful, as you well know. Dad is coming around. He is already favorably disposed to your father and to you. My mother and my other two sisters are bitches . . ."

"What a terrible thing to say, Paddy. Shouldn't you be ashamed of yourself!"

"It is terrible and I'm not ashamed of myself because unfortunately what I said is true. They'll pick at you and gnaw at you and try to remake you so you'll be on their side. They'll want you to remake me so I will live up to their standards. They'll go after you and your mother about the wedding and pressure you to change everything. Do not give them an inch. I am going to tell them to leave you alone. If they violate that warning, tell me and I will attend to it. Clear?''

She looked frightened. ''It can't be that bad, Paddy.''

''Oh yes it is. On the way back from Shannon, I want you to ride in the car with Meg and the men. Fran, Maureen's husband, and Rob, Nicole's intended, don't matter. They're hollow men, though my mother thinks they're wonderful because she likes hollow men. But Dad does matter, and as I say, he's on your side. He's got blind spots like this Aeroflot business, but he is, as your father says, a decent man. Even if his integrity is insufferable at times. You don't have to fawn over him, but I'm sure you can charm him without half trying.''

''I'll be nice to him, Paddy love.''

''I'm sure you will. I'll take the other women in my car and I'll warn them. I remind you again that if they begin to work over you or your mother when I'm not around, you are to tell me at once. Understand?''

She watched my scowling face and pondered.

''It is really that bad, isn't it, Paddy?''

''It really is. Our friend Rae warned me that if I don't stop them early, they'll destroy you and ruin our marriage. They're subtle and ingenious. They'll pretend to take you under their wings and then they'll crush you.''

''I'm sure they have the best of intentions, Paddy.''

''I suppose they do, but I'm tired of hearing that.''

''Don't worry, Paddy.'' She held my hand tightly and leaned against my shoulder. ''I won't let them hurt you anymore.''

I reflected that it was a very subtle and very perceptive answer.

We learned at Shannon that SU 330 would be three hours late. It was as I feared; they'd be in a thoroughly vile mood when they finally escaped from the mare's nest that these flights were reputed to be.

Sure enough, when they came through the customs gate, they were six grumpy people plus an ecstatic Meg, who spotted the two of us, flew across the arrivals room, and embraced Sara Anne and then me.

"You two will make common cause against me," I said with a laugh.

"Be careful of them, Paddy," Meg whispered in my ear. "They are in a very bad mood. Except Dad."

I introduced Sara Anne to all of them. Dad was very gallant. "I'm happy to know you, my dear. My son is very fortunate."

"I'm the fortunate one, Mr. Tobin."

"How very nice of you to say that."

The other women mostly ignored my bride. They found it more important to complain to me about their flight over.

"Don't blame me for that. You should have taken American, like I said."

"You were right, Toby," Dad agreed. "Absolutely right."

Then the women turned on Sara Anne.

"We were so happy to meet you, my dear," Mom began. "You certainly have your work cut out for you to make something out of our Toby."

"And you won't have much to work with either," Maureen added. "Was a Claddagh ring with an artificial emerald the best he could do? Typical Toby."

"But I'm sure you will be able to remake him," Nicole said. "You can count on us to help you."

Behind them our guardian angel appeared, glowering

angrily. I hoped she had left her sword at home.

"Wouldn't that be a terrible thing to do? Sure, don't I love Paddy just the way he is? Why would I ever want to change him? And by the way, the emerald is real—three and a half carats."

She spoke with a smile and a laugh, but she'd drawn a line in the sand. The Megperson nudged me with her elbow. With a thumbs-up sign, Rae vanished.

Also, by the way, I had never told her the size of the emerald. Trust the estate agent's daughter to check it out.

We spent a half hour loading and unloading luggage in the big trunks of our two cars. My passengers insisted that all their luggage—enough for a month's stay—be loaded in the car in which they were riding.

"The other car might be delayed, Toby dear."

I was being punished for the unpleasant ride in Aeroflot. My bride, chattering with the worshipful Meg, watched the proceedings with horror.

The ride back to Galway was hellish.

"Your little sweetheart is very attractive, Toby," Mom began. "Not really beautiful, of course, but quite pretty."

"What was that funny dress she was wearing? She doesn't have any taste at all."

"Not a brain cell working in that pretty little head."

"Someone ought to do something with her hair."

"She needs a lot more makeup."

"She certainly won't fit in our neighborhood."

"Are you sure you know what you're getting into, Toby, dear? She does seem, well, a little common."

"Is she in good health? She's awfully skinny."

I let them finish their barrage.

"Are you all finished? Good. Now, listen to me and listen me carefully. She will soon be my wife. I am deeply in love with her. I will not tolerate any of these criticisms ever again, do you understand? I don't give a good goddamn what you think about her. Moreover I warn you to leave her alone. If I find you belittling her or her parents or interfering with the plans for the wedding, I'll give you a second warning; if you go after them again, then you're out of my family. Is that clear?"

"Toby, dear, we were just trying to be helpful."

"Mom, I don't want that kind of help."

"You have a lot of nerve," Nicole snarled.

I almost said that my woman was not a hollow person, but that would be playing their game.

"Why don't you get some rest," I said, terminating the conversation. Almost.

"This car is quite uncomfortable, Toby dear; how can you expect us to sleep? What make is it?"

"It's a brand-new Mercedes limousine, Mom."

Nonetheless, all three of them slept.

I was knotted up in rage. Why had I put up with this all my life? I must not let my fury explode and ruin the wedding celebration for everyone.

But I would protect my woman from them.

We unloaded the luggage from the two cars at the Skeffington Arms and sorted out rooms and luggage. Sara Anne, still horrified and dismayed, watched from a safe distance. Tears glistened in her eyes.

"Take Meg over to the Railway Hotel. She's staying there. Turn her over to Nuala Nora. No one will miss her here. No one has ever missed her."

"Won't I be coming back afterwards to talk to you?"

I didn't like the sound of it.

After everyone else had gone to their rooms, Dad cornered me.

"Well, son, thank heavens we finally got all of that straightened out . . . I must congratulate you once more on your choice of wife. That young woman is pretty and sweet, but she also possesses a first-rate mind and a quick tongue. She gave us a wonderful lesson in Irish history, politics, and economics on the way up here. Very soft-spoken and diffident, but also very precise and wise. You have done very well indeed for yourself, young man.''

"Thank you, Dad . . . Did you tell her that?"

"In no uncertain terms. She blushed shyly and then kissed me on the cheek and said I was a grand man and now she knew why you were so nice."

"Yeah, that's what she would do and say, all right."

I waited outside the hotel for her return.

"Meg's grand," she said listlessly. "I left her in charge of Nuala Nora, and we're going to see about her dress after lunch."

"You certainly won over my dad."

"Did I now? Well, he's a very nice man. I don't know how he puts up with those women. Was it terrible in your car?"

"It was. I laid down the line. They are to leave you alone and not mess with the wedding plans. If they try when I'm not around, you and Edna should tell me at once. They have to learn that their old game with me is over."

"I couldn't believe me eyes and ears, Paddy," she said. "They get off the plane and you introduce them to your woman and they tell her what a terrible person you are. They tore you to pieces by pretending to sympathize with me. Do they know how horrible they must seem to everyone who hears what they say?"

"No, Sara Anne, they live in their own world of respectability where their personal perceptions constitute reality."

She embraced me and rested her head on my chest

while tears streamed down her cheeks.

"Oh, Paddy love, what a horrible life for you!"

So she was more sorry for me than for herself.

"I don't think it was all that horrible. I learned to tune them out. Anyway, now I have you!"

"You're crying too, Paddy!"

"Tears of joy!"

"I adore you and you know that. It may embarrass you a little, but I don't care. Now I adore you even more."

"Ah, woman, sure, you're not the worst of them!"

The fight was not over, however.

"I don't like it, Paddy, not at all, at all," Rae informed me during a brief visit to my suite at the Railway Hotel. "They're mean-spirited, nasty people. Your father is a coward. He knows what's going on and he won't shut them up."

"He quit trying long ago . . . How am I doing, by the way?"

"So far not too badly, all things considered, but you must not let down your guard."

"Don't unsheathe your sword just yet."

"I'm tempted."

Later Megan came down to my suite, another lovely young woman in tears.

"I don't care, Paddy; it's a bitchin' dress, and if I can't wear it, I won't be best woman . . . It's not immodest at all, better than the prom dresses they didn't complain about, and it fits my figure perfectly. Mom was terrible, you know, so sweet and so mean, especially to poor Sara Anne and Edna. She absolutely forbids me to wear it. They're trying to figure out where to get me another dress."

I patted her curly head and reached for the phone.

"Edna, this is your future son-in-law. With all my solemn authority, I decree that the Best Woman and Toast Person is to wear the dress that you and me woman selected. Unchanged. Is that clear?"

"But . . ."

"If she doesn't, I'll grab me woman by the hair and storm out of the cathedral. And me friend the bishop will come along with us."

Edna laughed.

"Ah, well, wouldn't that attract more attention than the World Cup? . . . What we were thinking of doing, Paddy dear, is making one or two minor changes so we could claim that we had honored their wishes, sure, without honoring them at all, at all."

"I'll put the Megperson on the line and you can tell her about the changes."

That latter child, tears now banished, took the phone.

"That's great! Fine! Marvelous! They won't like it one bit, but so what?"

I took the phone away from her.

"I've warned them not to go after you and Ronan and Sara Anne. I don't think they've understood my warning. If they try again, you must tell me, understand?"

"We want to keep your family happy, Paddy."

"In the immortal poetry of this land of poets, Frig 'em all!"

"Paddy," Meg marveled, "you've really changed! On the way home they'll say isn't it wonderful the way Cousin Sara Anne has made a man out of you."

"The truth, Megperson, is that her love has called forth my basic humanity."

"That's bitchin'!" she squealed. Then she hugged me and sped back to her room, a woman child whose faith in the basic goodness of reality had been restored.

The family dinner at the Galway Tobins (who had vetoed my idea of dinner at the Great Southern Grill as in violation of all the traditions of Irish hospitality) was a travesty. Dad and Ronan hit it off fine and spent the evening discussing business education in the two countries. Meg and my bride sang songs together, the latter accompanying on her small Irish harp. The hollow men continued to be hollow, laughing on cue. My mother and the two older sisters sniffed, and picked, and raised their eyebrows, and smiled at one another. The attack was directed not at me but at Edna and Sara Anne and the servants who were serving the drinks and the dinner and, as far as I could see, were doing a find job.

The theme of the attack was that the Galway Tobins were uncouth and tasteless and crude. It was hard to respond because they were very good at the game, ridiculing by implication and by words not said—the dinner food was not praised once.

Then they turned on me. The tactic was to tell "funny" stories about how clumsy and inept and absentminded "poor Toby" was.

They laughed at their own stories, as did the hollow men. No one else did.

Alas, most of the stories were true.

"You'll have to learn to be very tolerant, Sara dear."

She listened to three such stories and then drew another line in the sand.

"I wish you'd stop telling those stories," she said softly.

"They're all true," Nicole argued.

"Stop them! I won't permit you to embarrass me man in me own home! I adore him the way he is! Leave him alone!"

"We meant no harm, dear," Mom said, slipping into her hurt-feelings persona, a role at which she was very good. "We were merely trying to entertain you."

My bride had not raised her voice from its original meek postulant level. But her eyes became sapphire-hard, and her jaw was as solid as Connemara marble.

"Ridicule of my man does not entertain me. I will listen to no more of it."

That stopped that.

Dad and Ronan tried to revive the party by talking about college life in the two countries and weaving Meg and Sara Anne into the conversation. It helped a little.

"I wish, Toby dear," Mom said to me as I escorted her to their limousine, "that you would reconsider your choice of Meg as the lady of honor. It really was quite immature of you. After all, she's only a child. Maureen is the oldest in the family and she really deserves it. You've hurt her feelings."

"No."

"But—"

"No!"

They never give up, never.

I expected an unpleasant night. After the conflicts of the day, I thought I'd toss and turn and sleep fitfully. Instead I sank into a deep and peaceful rest. In a dream, Rae (wearing a white medical coat, to which, the Other knows, she is entitled) lectured me with charts and illustrations on the fascinating subjects of the physiological, endocrine, and nervous systems of women and their sexual needs and fantasies. It was, to put the matter mildly, an explicit, detailed, and clinical account of all these subjects. A number of specific tactics were suggested for the various phases of a marriage union. I was shocked and grateful.

On Friday there was another battle.

Meg thundered into my room, where I was trying to write my toast to Sara Anne.

"They're still at it, Paddy. We had a late breakfast with Sara Anne and her mother. You know, let's us girls thrash this all out. It was terrible. They want to change the reception and dinner around completely. No receiving line outside the cathedral, only one toast, from Maureen. The usual stuff. Their big line is, 'Well, *that's* the way we do it in Chicago.' "

I picked up the phone. This time Sara Anne answered.

"Listen carefully, my love. This is your country, your home, and your marriage, and we'll do it your way. Got it?"

"Me ma and I didn't want to have an argument over little things," she said with the patient, long-suffering sigh that the local women so enjoy.

"These are not little things. These are big things. It's your only wedding . . ."

"Isn't that the truth?"

"And we'll do it your way regardless of their feelings. Got it?"

"Sure, Paddy love, aren't you a wonderful man altogether?" I imagined her warm glow charging through the telephone lines.

"This is no time for Irish indirection. Got it?"

She laughed at me.

"Isn't that one thing we can't do my way? But yes, me love, I got it."

I found my mother and my two sisters having a drink before lunch in the lobby of the Skeffington.

"I told you that I did not want you messing with the wedding or reception plans. You did anyway. This is my last warning. Don't do it again. This is her country and her wedding and we'll do it her way whatever we may think about it."

"But, dear, we were only trying to be helpful. Really,

their plans ARE old-fashioned and common. If your little bride is going to live in Chicago, she'll have to adapt to our ways, won't she?"

"No she won't. But apparently you don't understand. I'll repeat myself. We'll do it their way. Got it?"

"Why don't you give us some credit for trying to be helpful?" Nicole complained.

"Leave them alone!"

I turned on my heel and walked out.

They were on their best behavior at the rehearsal dinner. They sat silently, like bumps on a log, through the whole meal while the Burke clan, handsome black Irish lawyers with the sharp wit and the clever tongues that go with the local job description, entertained themselves and us. Peter Burke, the young best man, was particularly funny and patently relished the chance to have Meg as his partner. Dad got along fine with all of them.

There was some worry about Bishop Blackie. The genial Bishop of Galway took the rehearsal because, as he explained, Bishop Ryan would arrive at Galway Airport at half ten. "That'll be plenty of time."

"Do you think the plane will be late?" Sara Anne asked me. "It's supposed to rain."

"Rae won't let him be late."

The Ireland-Mexico match on a TV with a fifty-four-inch screen that Ronan had rented only added to the hilarity of the party. My mother and sisters winced at every cry of anguish or triumph from the Irish fans.

Almost from the beginning of the match it was clear that the Irish were too old and too worn-out by the American heat to fight off the Mexicans. When their legendary goalie, Paddy Bonner, muffed a save, the Galway folks knew it was all over. Yet, unlike Americans whose teams lose, they didn't blame the players.

"Sure, wasn't it frigging grand that they got as far as they did!"

At the end of the evening I kissed my bride good night and described some of the activities I planned for the next night.

She did not listen.

"Don't you think, Paddy, we ought to put this off for a while?"

"No," I said.

"We don't know each other very well, do we?"

"Well enough."

"I'm not sure I want to live in America."

"Like I said, we'll live in both countries."

"I don't think I'd be happy in America or you'd be happy in Ireland."

I realized that this was a serious problem and not a momentary doubt. My damn family had finally got to her.

"I've never been so happy in my life as I have in these last two weeks."

"I know it would break me ma's and me da's heart, but I think we ought to postpone the wedding for a couple of months. Or maybe a year or two. Shouldn't we tell them now?"

"No. We're not going to postpone it."

"I can't promise that I'll be there tomorrow morning."

She sounded so sad, so tired, so discouraged, so unhappy.

"Well, I'll promise that I'll be there."

"Don't make it any harder than it has to be, Paddy. Please."

"And if you're not at the cathedral tomorrow, I'll go across the river to your house and drag you to the wedding."

"I don't want to marry you," she said, tears streaming down her cheeks.

"You're a disgrace to the Claddagh woman," I replied. "I'll not listen to another word."

I turned on my heel and walked out of Ardilawn House, got into one of our limos, and ordered the driver to take me back to the Great Southern. A glum Rae, wearing tight maroon slacks with a thick black belt, a tighter maroon sweater, and a maroon suit jacket, was waiting for me in the easy chair of my suite.

"I thought you said she was cured," I snapped at her.

"She's cured of the violation, but not of ordinary prenuptial fear." She shook her head sadly. "The child has lost her nerve. She's not the first bride to do so. And she has a point; she is young and she hasn't known you long. Not a valid point, but still a point."

"Planted in her head by my mother and sisters."

"Of course. She sees a lifetime of fighting them and doesn't relish the prospect."

"Can you change her mind?" I slumped into my sofa.

"Not without violating our prime directive . . . You did very well tonight, by the way. Not yielding an inch to her fears."

"What's going to happen tomorrow morning?"

"I don't know."

"Odds?"

"Even . . . You meant you'd go over to her house and drag her to the cathedral."

"I did."

She tilted her head and considered me carefully.

"You may have to do it, with all the attendant public, ah, controversy."

Would I do it? It would be totally out of character for

me. A dramatic and romantic scene in which I wouldn't fit.

"Count on it, Rae. I'll do it."

"Just angry enough at the lot of them to make a public scene."

"You bet."

She smiled slightly.

"Let's hope you don't have to."

25

The phone did not wake me in the morning, as it had done on many previous mornings in the Great Southern.

I woke up on my own at nine after an inexcusably peaceful sleep and ordered breakfast from room service.

My possible bride had not called. Could no news be good news?

I ate breakfast and decided that, if I was going to create a scene at the Salmon Weir Bridge, I should know beforehand.

I punched in the Tobin number.

"Tobin House, Megan speaking."

"Your brother, Megperson."

"PADDY!" she shouted.

"Is my bride there?"

"She is, but it's bad luck to talk to her before you see her in church."

"You got the superstitions wrong, Megperson. It's bad luck to see them, not to talk to them. Put her on."

"I'm not sure. I'll ask her."

"You do that."

A moment later she was back on the line.

"Your bride says that this is the last morning in her life that you can't bother her."

"Ah?"

"And she also said to tell you—and I don't know what it means—that she won't disgrace the Claddagh woman."

"Did she now? Well, I guess I'll see you all in church."

"You'd better show up, Paddy Tobin."

"Not a doubt about it."

I called room service for more brown bread and another pot of tea.

The rain didn't come as scheduled, but Bishop Blackie did. Our marriage was elegant and graceful. My bride was certainly not a blushing bride, but a happy, confident, and witty bride. No trace of shame or fear. The Claddagh genes in her had triumphed.

She whispered in my ear as we linked arms and climbed the steps to the altar, "I was a terrible eejit altogether. Lost my nerve. Sorry."

"No problem. I knew you'd get it back."

Which was not the exact truth, but for a wedding day, it would do.

My mother and sisters, in the front two rows, continued to sulk. They shrugged their shoulders, rolled their eyes, arched their eyebrows, and shook their heads in dismay. Mom was furious when the Megperson appeared in the banned best woman's gown. We would have trouble with them afterwards.

The bishop told his famous strawberry wedding story

("The only thing sweeter than the taste of strawberries is the taste of human love!).

"Young woman," he whispered to Sara Anne, just before the exchange of vows, "is my understanding correct that the Kyrie that we have just sung in a multitude of languages is your work?"

" 'Tis, me lord."

"Ah. Should you come to Chicago, I will insist that you accept a commission to produce a Mass for my cathedral. I note that we believe in providing musicians with adequate pay for their work."

"We'll consider it a stipend for today, me lord."

That would have been enough, but not for my Sara Anne.

"Sure," she continued, "if there is Mass for Pope Marcellus, can't there be a Mass for Bishop Blackie?"

Since the whole conversation was transmitted live on the cathedral's public address system, the congregation erupted into noisy Irish laughter.

After we had committed ourselves to one another till death do us part, everyone in the Cathedral of Mary Assumed into Heaven and St. Nicholas rose in a standing ovation.

Everyone but my mother and my sisters, until Dad spoke to them.

Both my bride and I wept for joy. She pulled me to my feet and we turned and raised our arms in a salute of gratitude. They applauded again. For her, I'm sure, not for me.

It was too much altogether.

As we walked arm in arm down the long aisle of the cathedral, I saw Rae and her companion and progeny—on my side of the church. The mists shimmered all around them. There were a bunch of other tall and attractive people with them, the men in morning suits and the women in formal dress. They're all analogues, the whole Seraph crowd. I bowed to them, nudged my wife, who turned and bowed to them too.

They bowed back formally.

The whole solemn effect was spoiled by Rae's outrageous grin.

Outside the wind was blowing softly and the sun was bright and warm—a perfect end for a nuptial Eucharist. Then I noted out of the corner of my eye that my mother and sisters were coming down the stairs towards us, outrage in their eyes. One more battle.

Later my wife would insist that she did not see the beams of angel light. I did, however, three of them.

Clutching their stomachs, Mother, Maureen, and Nicole doubled up in pain, screamed, and fell to the ground on the front steps of the cathedral. One of the Burkes, the family scapegrace because he was a physician and not a lawyer, rushed up to them, diagnosed a severe intestinal disorder, bundled them into one of our limos, and, joined by Dad, rushed them off to the hospital just down the street next to the university. For a few moments the receiving line in front of the cathedral—which my mother and sisters had opposed—halted. What do we do next? everyone seemed to wonder, perhaps feeling that now was the time to call off the rest of the event.

"Sure," Ronan shouted, "the last thing they'd want is to spoil the fun for the rest of us. Jimmy Burke will have them fixed up in an hour or two and they'll be able to join us at Ashford."

He was telling less than the truth. They would very much want to spoil the fun, and no way they would show up for the dinner. Nonetheless, his optimistic words restored the good humor of the crowd, and the reception line pulled itself together.

We were assured by every third person that there was "a lot of that virus stuff going around, but thanks be to God it only lasts an hour or two."

This was not the virus that is always going around, however, this was Seraph virus.

I felt sorry for them. Really I did. Very sorry. They were my family and, however misguided, they wanted only the best for me.

But they would not ruin our wedding celebration.

Like I say, you don't fool around with Seraphs—or make them mad.

❦26❦

The reception at Ashford Castle was super, grand, brilliant—to ascend the ladder of Irish adjectives up to the superlative. Megan was a funny toast person. She insisted that Sara had married me so that she did not have to change the initials on her lingerie or the name on her credit cards. She toasted me as the best brother she ever had, and Sara Anne as the best sister-in-law she would ever have, and, her voice cracking and her eyes watering, she toasted the two of us with the hope that God and His angels who had brought us together would continue to take care of us.

Sara Anne told the story of my proposal and her snatching the engagement ring out of my hand so that I wouldn't have time to change my mind. She toasted me as the best chance for happiness that a woman could ever find.

I admitted that I could not contend with such super,

grand, and brilliant women orators. Then I merely toasted my lovely Sara Anne, my first love, my last love, and all my love, unto death do us part and even beyond.

It must have been pretty good because all the women in the house were dabbing at their eyes.

Dad arrived just as the toasts began.

"Megan is really very good at it," he admitted. "I never would have expected it. My two younger children are filled with surprises, aren't they?"

"I hope so."

"I will see that the proper documents are sent to the lawyer in East Bend, South Dakota, on Tuesday morning. By the way, did you ever resolve the ethical dilemma you saw in that matter?"

"Yeah," I said, and explained my solution.

He rolled his eyes as Rae had and said the same thing that Rae had said about my Jesuit education.

Mom and the girls had recovered from their attack and were resting comfortably in their rooms, though still very weak. Sara Anne and I phoned them. The conversation was pleasant. Perhaps they knew they had lost and were trying to make the best of their defeat.

We danced and we danced and we danced the night away. I danced with Nuala, who wanted to be sure we'd be back in September because, she wasn't promising anything, mind you, but there might just be a wedding then.

I danced with everyone. So did Sara Anne. I think I danced with Rae, but in the mists I couldn't tell whether she was really there. Still she must have been. Otherwise why the mists?

"Don't forget what I taught you in your dream."

Someone surely said that to me, and who else would know about that dream?

Did Sara Anne have a similar dream? Or was that part

of the advice she had received at Kilmacdoagh?

Eventually it was time for us to leave—allegedly to catch the late plane to Manchester where we would stay overnight before leaving for Chicago. We boarded the *Sara Anne* at Oughterard, changed our clothes in the dark amid much giggling, and returned to Ashford Castle under the starlit sky. My wife celebrated my many admirable qualities during the short ride.

We slipped in the back door of the hotel, held for us by a smiling security guard, and tiptoed up to the bridal suite, to which my wife had a set of keys.

One more dragon to slay, I thought uneasily. I don't like this one either. Not at all, at all.

"Too bad about your mother and sisters," she said as she removed her dress and hung it up in a closet.

Even on a wedding night, you have to be neat.

"Herself did it, so they wouldn't ruin the party."

"She didn't!" She was pulling off her panty hose.

"She did. No one was going to ruin her party. Besides, I saw the beams of light. The terrible swift sword."

Her remaining lingerie was only small wisps of white lace.

"She's quite a woman," she said, removing the upper wisp. "Now I'm going to take off your clothes."

She did, not, however, before folding the hose and bra and arraying them neatly on the dresser of our vast suite.

Somewhat later, stark naked, I lay flat on my back as my wife, with the merely symbolic white lace still on her loins, kissed and caressed me and praised the beauty and strength of my body.

I had to stop her before it was too late.

"Sara Anne," I begged, trying gently to slow her down, "there's something we have to talk about first."

"Not tonight."

"Tonight."

I grabbed her lovely shoulders and restrained her.

"Well?"

"Great-Uncle Gerry left me ten million dollars in his will provided I came here and wooed and won you by today."

"Isn't that grand! What a generous man he was! Think of all the good you'll be able to do with it!"

She tried to return to her attack. I held her back.

"You don't understand. If I told you before the marriage, I'd lose the bequest."

"That seems fair enough," she said, puzzled at my concern.

"I want to say that even though I married you for the money, I didn't marry you for the money."

She threw back her head and laughed. Her breasts bobbed above me. I could not hold out much longer. Yet I had to finish my confession.

"I want you to know now before we, ah, consummate our marriage so that if you're offended, it's not too late to be angry at me and cancel the whole matter."

She laughed again and then fell on me.

"You frigging eejit! Wasn't I the one who seduced you? Wasn't I the one who told you that you were in love with me and started the whole thing? You really don't think that in my present condition I'm going to tell you that you're just a frigging opportunist and walk out on you, do you? Besides, didn't your mother and your older sisters, each of them separately, tell me about the will and that you were marrying me only for the money?"

I wanted to be furious. They never gave up, never. However, the pressure of a lovely young body now crushing against my own, breasts both torment and delight, deprived me of my rage.

"What did you say to them?"

"I was me usual charming self. I said, real sweet like, mind you, that I didn't give a good frigging damn if you did marry me just for me money, because I'd still have you anyway."

She began kissing me again. Then she paused and considered.

"Och, sure, am I not a terrible eejit? I understand now, Paddy. You're just being your wonderful, honorable self, glory be to God! Well, I'll say what I should say: I don't care about the money one way or another, Paddy husband, except I'm glad you have it. All I care about is you . . . Now, let's get to the work at hand."

So we did. Our first "ride" (as the Irish like to call it) was not particularly successful, but it was very funny and we laughed happily at ourselves and our clumsiness. Then, a little later, I followed some of Rae's recommendations, which had the promised effect. Then, more confident of my male vigor, I mounted my woman and "rode" her triumphantly as she twisted and squirmed beneath me up the mountain of sexual delight. At the top she cried out sharply in pleasure and I joined her in ecstasy.

"An orgasm on the first night," she said, snuggling into my arms and pressing against me. "Not bad at all, at all. But only because my husband is such a skilled lover."

Then she yawned and went promptly to sleep.

"Well, Paddy Tobin," a familiar voice announced, "you seem very proud of yourself. You have reason to be."

"You were watching?"

"We were NOT."

There were mists in the room, but only her voice, not her analogue, seemed to have materialized. Discretion on the wedding night presumably.

"Listening."

"Not at all, not in the ordinary sense of the word. I just took a quick peek and, judging by the contented glow on herself, figured that it had gone well."

"Second time."

"Not bad at all, at all."

"That's what she said."

"And she responded to your ethical difficulty as I predicted she would."

"She did, very gracefully too, which I should have expected.

"Well, that's that then."

"I saw your beams of light at the cathedral."

"They would have spoiled everything and made you and Sara Anne unhappy and themselves more unhappy too. There was too much bile in them, and that was one way to release it. Ultimately it was their decision. If they had not permitted themselves to become so emotionally upset, the excessive breakfasts they had eaten might not have had such a devastating impact."

"You had something to do with it!"

"I merely accelerated and, ah, focused an effect which would have occurred in any event. Now they've been programmed against a repetition. You may think of inviting your parents to supper at the Four Seasons in Chicago after you've been there for a few days. Despite their lamentable violation of your great-uncle's confidence, the problem will be much less serious in the future."

I didn't know we were staying at the Four Seasons. Presumably my woman did. I was now out of the loop on travel arrangements.

"I hope so."

"Trust me."

"About all this adoration . . ."

"You don't like it?"

"Sure I like it. What man wouldn't? But is it another way to control me?"

"You should be ashamed of yourself, Paddy Tobin. Certainly the young woman is well aware that you dote on her doting on you. But the adoration is all authentic. Trust me."

"I will."

" 'Tis time for me to leave, Paddy Tobin. God bless you both. It's probably time to wake her up again for another ride. We'll see you again soon."

"Again! What do you mean?"

"You don't think that, after all our work, my kind are going to leave you to yourselves, do you? Certainly we'll be around for the rest of your lives. If either of you misbehave, you'll hear about it from us."

"You'll never leave us alone?"

"Certainly not. I told you at the very beginning that our agency never, never loses an account. Good-bye. See you soon."

Well, your Seraph was right about one thing: It was time to wake my glowing wife. If one has come into possession of a Holy Grail, sure, would it not be wrong altogether not to drink from it?

I was not, after all, the worst of lovers.